THE
BRINDAVAN
CHRONICLE

THE
BRINDAVAN
CHRONICLE

Genesis

John Thompson

authorHOUSE®

AuthorHouse™ UK
1663 Liberty Drive
Bloomington, IN 47403 USA
www.authorhouse.co.uk
Phone: 0800.197.4150

Published by AuthorHouse 06/12/2015

ISBN: 978-1-5049-3987-4 (sc)
ISBN: 978-1-5049-3988-1 (e)

Print information available on the last page.

Any people depicted in stock imagery provided by Thinkstock are models, and such images are being used for illustrative purposes only.
Certain stock imagery © Thinkstock.

This book is printed on acid-free paper.

Because of the dynamic nature of the Internet, any web addresses or links contained in this book may have changed since publication and may no longer be valid. The views expressed in this work are solely those of the author and do not necessarily reflect the views of the publisher, and the publisher hereby disclaims any responsibility for them.

To my wife Sarada and my children Ganesh and Gayatri,
without whose continued support and encouragement
this book would not have seen the light of day

ACKNOWLEDGEMENT

With grateful thanks to Hannah Spedding, whose sharp eyes, acute observations and pertinent suggestions made this a better book.

Thanks also go to Andrew Gribble for providing the inspiration for the front cover design.

PROLOGUE

From his position among the conifer trees bordering that side of the field, he heard the funeral procession long before it came into view. At first he was aware only of a low, repetitive, monotonous humming sound, the words themselves lost to him both by the distance and the weather. It was a grey, louring sort of day, with heavy, low clouds that flattened and deadened sound. Although the rain had stopped some time ago, there was a constant *drip, drip, drip* from the branches above, and he shivered now and then as the gusting breeze bit through his damp clothes. Periodically, a drop of water found with unerring accuracy the gap between his coat collar and neck, making him flinch. But otherwise, he remained motionless.

The sound came appreciably nearer, so that he was able to distinguish between the voice of the person leading the chant, and the refrain of the mourners. It was the same four-line chant, repeated over and over, and although he could not as yet make out the words, he knew from the cadence exactly what they were:

Asatho maa, sat gamaye
Tamaso maa, jyotir gamaye
Mrityor maa, amritam gamaye
Aum shanti, shanti, shantihi

Each of the first three lines was chanted by the soloist and repeated by the followers, but all chanted the final line together, stretching each syllable almost beyond endurance, until the final sound seemed to be snatched away by the wind. The meaning of the words had been etched into his memory years before:

Lead me from untruth to truth, From darkness to light
From death to heavenly bliss, Peace, peace, peace

He smiled wryly as he pondered their suitability or otherwise to the occasion, this interment of a man he had once regarded as an infallible teacher, his guru. Across the field, about a hundred yards away, he could see the white-fenced enclosure around what would shortly become the final resting place of that man. In the centre lay a black marble plinth, an engraved headstone already in place at one end, and the slab that would cover the grave resting upon a pallet to one side. He had no doubt that Govinda himself would have planned everything down to the last detail, and that the black gold-veined marble would have been imported from Italy during his lifetime.

The enclosure had been planted with rosebushes, no doubt the heavily scented varieties that Govinda had loved so well. The area within the pale measured about a quarter-acre, he guessed, which hinted that Govinda had planned for future leaders of the community to be buried there also, around the tomb of the founder, their doubtless smaller monuments paying eternal homage to his.

The increased volume of the chanting alerted him to the approach of the cortege, and he stepped back into the shelter of the trees, keeping his eyes fixed on the track that ran away past other fields before disappearing into the scrubby woodland and plunging down the hillside to the valley below. He glimpsed a flash of orange through the trees, and then the head of the procession burst into view. Several paces ahead of the rest was the ochre-robed monk leading the chant: his shaven head looked heaven-wards as he intoned each line, then fell to scan the ground during the repetition. Behind him was a double line of monks in white robes, each carrying a flaming coconut lamp in the right hand, and a sheaf of smouldering incense sticks in the left. Then came the bier, shouldered by four Swamis in orange, the coffin strapped on to prevent any mishap on the arduous journey up the hillside. Two more Swamis shuffled alongside, ready no doubt to relieve anyone should strength fail or grief overwhelm. Behind the bier a small group of nuns in white followed, Magda's being the only face he could identify.

Finally, the throng of lay devotees, mainly Asian but with a sprinkling of white faces, streamed from the trees. At the front of the crowd four white men walked, their arms linked to hold back the press behind, which hustled and jostled as people fought for position: it was a great blessing to attend the funeral of a saint, and best of all to be as near the front as possible so as to witness the actual interment.

As the cortege moved past the fields towards the burial ground, a herd of cows, their innate curiosity aroused by the commotion, lumbered up to the fence to see what all the fuss was about. Those at the front skidded to a halt, while those behind pushed and shoved to catch a glimpse, the heaving mass mirroring the human throng behind the coffin. In the adjoining field three grazing horses looked up briefly, sensed at once that the noise did not herald the arrival of food, and resumed their relentless cropping.

And now the procession was entering the burial ground, and the observer in the trees was able to make out more easily the features of those he knew. As he had expected, and indeed recognised from some way off, Simon was at the head, having it would seem finally assumed the mantle of leadership that he had always coveted. The years had added flesh both to the face and body, but he was still recognisably Simon - or Swami Krishnananda, as Govinda had dubbed him all those years ago. He still bore himself with that same proud aloofness that he had always felt necessary to distinguish himself from the rest, while smugness seemed to have become etched indelibly about his mouth.

Three of the Swamis around the bier were unknown to him: not surprising, given the passage of time. People had always come and gone at Brindavan. He was a little surprised to see the old sceptic Ronan wearing the orange robe; less so that Dennis and Lionel should have attained that rank - they had never shown the slightest inclination to leave the ashram while he was there. He recognised none of the monks in white.

He watched as the monks carried out what was no doubt a well-drilled procedure. Krishnananda mounted the steps of the plinth, walking clockwise around the hole to stand beside the headstone, while the pall-bearers lowered the bier to the ground and stood back. The ropes lashing the coffin to the bier were then removed by three Swamis, while the other three placed planks and ropes across the tomb, and then four of them lifted the coffin by its handles and slowly began to mount the steps of the plinth, with two behind to ensure that the coffin remained on an even keel.

At a nod from Krishnananda, the four each took hold of the ropes and lifted the coffin slightly, enabling the planks to be removed, and the coffin was lowered slowly and carefully into the grave. Krishnananda then began an invocation to Shiva, which was taken up by all present:

> *Aum trayambakum yajamahe*
> *Sugandim pushti vardhanam*
> *Urva rukamiva bhandanan*
> *Mrityor mukshiya mamritat*
> *Aum hrim namah shivaya*

These Sanskrit words too were etched indelibly upon the watcher's memory:

> *We worship the three-eyed Shiva,*
> *who nourishes us, restores our health, and causes us to thrive.*
> *Just as the ripe cucumber falls automatically from the creeper,*
> *may we be liberated from death and attain immortality.*

As the chant died away, the gates to the enclosure, which had been closed after the coffin had passed through, were now opened by the two monks who had remained on guard, to allow the mourners in, and the tomb was soon surrounded, though the people were kept at some distance by the ring of monks in white. All were now quiet and respectful; there was no more pushing and shoving. Krishnananda raised his right hand, and such murmuring as there was ceased at once: the Swami spoke into complete silence. What he said the watcher in the trees could not hear, but he was sure it was a fulsome eulogy.

At the conclusion of his oration, Krishnananda took some flower petals from a shallow basket presented by one of the junior monks, and scattered them into the open grave, murmuring a silent prayer. Each member of the community followed suit in order of seniority, the nuns last of all. Finally, all the Swamis lifted the heavy slab from its pallet with ropes, and struggled up the steps of the tomb with some difficulty; it was then manoeuvred over the opening.

The nuns produced several garlands, which the Swamis placed over the slab and around the headstone, and then Krishnananda walked around the tomb three times, carrying one of the coconut lamps, which he then ceremonially extinguished by dashing it upon the ground. The other Swamis followed suit, then formed a double line behind Krishnananda: the column cut through the crowd like the Israelites passing through the Red Sea, and moved on down the hill. The other monks remained behind to control the people and guard the tomb, while the little group of nuns, after their own homage, followed after the Swamis.

It took a long time for the lay mourners to complete their devotions. Most of them walked slowly around the tomb, hands clasped either at their chest or above their head, their lips moving in silent prayer. Others prostrated at the foot of the tomb before moving away. Some of the older women beat their breasts, tore at their hair, and wailed unceasingly.

Eventually, the last of the devotees straggled away down the hill, and the monks, having performed their own devotions, followed, shutting the gate behind them. As the last one disappeared into the trees, the observer emerged from his place of concealment, stepping over the decaying wire fence, and walked across the damp grass to the burial enclosure. He pushed open the gate, and approached the sepulchre. Suddenly, a weak burst of sunlight pierced a gap in the clouds, lighting up the tomb and the man who stood before it, casting into sharp relief the aquiline nose set in the thin, pale face. Sad brown eyes took in the words engraved in gold upon the gold-veined marble headstone:

HERE REST THE MORTAL REMAINS OF
MAHARAJ SRI GOVINDA KRISHNA SWAMI
HIS SPIRIT LIVES ON IN HIS TEACHINGS

Below these boldly emblazoned words, in much smaller script, were the words of the funeral refrain, firstly in Sanskrit, then in English.

With a shake of his head, the man stooped and laid the single red rose he had held all the while in his right hand on the bottom step of the plinth, then turned sharply on his heel and strode decisively away towards the trees from whence he had come. As he reached the shadows, the sun disappeared.

CHAPTER 1

Easter 1976

'Shit! It's a dead end!' The driver of the old Vauxhall banged his fist in frustration on the steering wheel. 'I told you this was the wrong bloody road!' he growled at his passenger, who had supposedly been navigating.

For the last two miles they had been driving in ever-gathering darkness along a narrow lane that spoke eloquently of local authority neglect by subjecting the car and its occupants to regular bone-jarring and teeth-rattling encounters with potholes that were impossible to spot. The weak headlights of the old car had not helped.

The road was fringed by high, unkempt hedges blocking any view of the surrounding countryside, and apart from a couple of drunken farm signs at the end of lanes even more godforsaken than the one they were on, there had been no sign of human habitation. And finally, the road had simply come to an unheralded end before a bank of dense vegetation.

Sheila sighed. 'According to the map I was given, we're in the right place,' she muttered defensively.

'Yes, it bloody well looks like it!' her companion snorted. 'It doesn't even look as if there's room to turn round.'

He shoved open the door with unnecessary force and got out, standing for a moment and stretching the aches and pains from his back and legs. Sheila got out too, shivering in the cool air. To one side she could see a glimmer of light in the distance. *At least someone lives around here!* she thought. But apart from that, and the mournful lowing of a cow somewhere, there was precious little evidence of human life.

The wind soughed through the trees, and Sheila shuddered: it sounded to her like the sighing of innumerable lost souls wandering in the no-man's-land between life and death, the weeping of suicides and murder victims perhaps, bewailing the fate that had cast them into limbo.

Her morbid reverie was interrupted by a shout from her friend. She looked up, and he beckoned to her; she walked towards him, shadowy and seemingly insubstantial in the pathetic beam of the car lights.

'There is a track here,' he announced, 'but it's very overgrown, so whether it leads anywhere or not, who can say?'

Sheila's eyes were becoming accustomed to the gloom. She could see a narrow, rutted track running away between two high banks: overhanging branches and tall, thick weeds had created an illusion of solidity in the murkiness. She took a couple of paces forward, and her jeans immediately snagged upon a bramble lurking in the grass. Shaking her leg free, she peered down the lane; it looked impenetrably dark and forbidding. Suddenly, she was certain that they were in the right place. 'This is exactly the sort of place Govinda would choose,' she declared. 'Come on, let's go.'

The driver shrugged his shoulders, and followed her back to the car. In first gear, he drove cautiously into the lane. 'If we finish up in a boggy field or a river,' he grumbled, 'just remember it's your fault.'

The track was so overgrown, so pitted and rutted, and so twisty that any speed in excess of five miles an hour would have been foolhardy. In a few seconds, the patch of lighter sky behind them vanished, and they were in an inky blackness that was barely penetrated by the headlights. Overhanging trees blotted out the sky above completely, and their drooping branches seemed to reach out to obstruct the car's progress, twiggy fingers scraping eerily along the roof. All the while, the driver muttered incomprehensibly in his own language.

Suddenly, the trees fell away behind them, and the lane opened up to the evening sky. The banks and hedges here were relatively well manicured, allowing them to see that the land to their right rose up into a hill, and that to their left fell away. The lane rose slightly, and as the car breasted the incline, the engine stalled. In that same moment - magically it seemed to Sheila both then and for years thereafter - a cloud passed on its way over the hills to reveal the rising full moon just beginning to peep over the forested skyline. They sat and watched as, almost imperceptibly, the moon hoisted itself clear of the trees, bathing the scene below them in its soft, silvery light.

The lane ran down into a wide yard, bounded on the left by a tangled hedge, opposite which stood an old house and a cluster of barns and other outbuildings, dark and seemingly abandoned.

'Jesus! It's right out of a Hitchcock film!' whispered the driver.

'It's the right place,' Sheila said. 'I just know it.'

Her companion re-started the engine, and rolled the car into the yard, pulling up just below the house, which stood on a sort of mound. Sheila got out and scanned the surroundings, hugging herself against the increasing chill of the evening. The outbuildings looked decrepit, and the house little better, but the glow of the moonlight transformed them for her into something magical and mysterious. *It's as if we're the first people ever to set foot here, but at the same time I feel as if I've come home.*

The front door opened, casting a beam of light out into the yard. 'I say, who's there?' demanded a plummy voice.

'Jimmy!' Sheila shouted. 'It's me!'

'Sheila? Good heavens, darlin', where've you bin? We expected you hours ago, and I'd jolly well just about given you up! Come on in. Mind the steps, they're a bit crumbly. I'll put the old kettle on.'

2

'At the moment, o' course, there's just me and Govinda here full-time, so to speak,' Jimmy said, pouring himself another mug of tea, 'but some of the others usually manage to get down at the weekends, so we're sortin' out the place gradually. You just would not *believe* the mess here when we arrived. I swear to God the old boy who lived here shared the house with his entire ruddy menagerie! What's now the temple room was literally inches thick with goat droppins, and as for the yard, well, my dears, most of it was knee-deep in cow and pig shit! I haven't plucked up the courage yet to look into some of the outbuildins.'

Jimmy's guffawing laughter boomed around the kitchen, and even Sheila's friend, whom she had introduced simply as "Jazz", and who had glowered throughout the meal Jimmy had whipped up, was forced to smile. Jimmy rocked his chair back against the wall, pulled a packet of cigarettes from his shirt pocket, and lit up. He drew deeply, and exhaled a cloud of smoke with a sigh of deep satisfaction.

'Govinda's dead agin smokin', o' course,' he said conspiratorially, 'but he hasn't got round to bannin' it yet, thank God! If he ever does, I'll probably die of a surfeit of fresh air!' He laughed heartily.

Sheila had a sudden mental image of Jimmy in an earlier incarnation, sitting on the veranda of a colonial bungalow in some corner of the Empire, regaling the company with humorous accounts of his dealings with the natives. He was certainly very nineteenth-century.

'And just who and where is this "Govinda" then?' Jazz asked abruptly. It was the first time he had said anything other than "yes" or "no".

Jimmy regarded him down the full length of his substantial and highly aristocratic nose. '*This Govinda*,' he said, in the icy cutting tone that only a true member of the gentry can muster at will, 'is a realised soul who is presently meditatin' in the temple. He meditates every evenin' between seven and nine, at which time we do the arati.'

'And what's that?' Jazz asked indifferently.

'It is the waving of a light before the deities, accompanied by chanting of the sacred mantras, to bid the Lord goodnight and to ask his protection during the hours of darkness,' said a mellifluous voice.

'Govinda!' Sheila squealed, jumping up and running around the table towards the slight figure in the doorway. She dropped on one knee and touched his feet, while he, his eyes dancing with amusement, placed a hand in blessing upon her head.

'Sheila!' he said softly, 'how nice to see you. Welcome to Brindavan.' As she stood up, her face flushed, he looked directly at her and raised an eyebrow. 'Are you not going to introduce me to your friend?'

She clapped a hand to her mouth. 'Oh, how silly! Sorry!' She drew herself upright. 'Govinda, this is Ijaz Shah, known to his friends as "Jazz". We're at college together.' She turned towards Jazz, eyes pleading for him to be nice. 'Jazz, I'd like you to meet my guru, Govinda.'

'Pleased to meet you.' Jazz stepped forward, proffering his hand.

Govinda appraised him for a moment, then pressed his hands together at his breast, and inclined his head. 'Namaste,' he said coolly, 'greetings. Welcome to Brindavan. Please, do sit down.'

Joining them at the table, he accepted the mug of tea that Jimmy tendered, then turned to Sheila. 'Lord Krishna informed me of your arrival, so I concluded my meditation early in order to greet you.'

Sheila gasped. 'Govinda! You shouldn't ….'

'You are a Muslim, Mr. Shah?' Govinda asked, cutting Sheila off.

'My parents are Muslims, but I have no religious belief.' His tone was defiant.

'It is not good to abandon the religion of your birth. Since it was your karma to be born into Islam, it is your dharma to follow its precepts. If you do not live according to your dharma, how do you expect to evolve?'

'Evolve? Into what?'

'Into the perfect realised being, so that you can then merge back into the infinite oneness of God,' Govinda replied calmly. He did not seem disconcerted by the younger man's challenging, almost contemptuous attitude. He closed his eyes, and a mask of serenity slipped over his face.

'Govinda,' Sheila said anxiously, 'perhaps you could explain karma and dharma to Jazz. He doesn't understand.'

There was no answer. The three of them sat in perfect stillness, hardly daring to breathe, just watching Govinda's blue-black face, shining it seemed with some inner effulgence. Time itself seemed to be suspended.

'What is the point?' the guru said suddenly, his eyes still closed. 'He thinks he is perfect already.' He opened his eyes, stood up, and looked at each of them in turn. 'It is time for arati,' he announced, and walked out.

Sheila glanced at her watch: it was one minute to nine. She grabbed Jazz's hand and dragged him after Jimmy.

3

She lay awake, recollecting the day's events, so different from what she had imagined, and yet so perfectly natural, in particular the awe-inspiring arati that she had attended. The temple, in its bare austerity, had seemed to her totally in keeping with Govinda's teaching of simplicity and freedom from materialism.

'Simplicity is the key to spirituality,' she remembered him saying on one of her visits to his house in Brixton. 'I visited a temple in India,' he had told them, 'where the chief priest boasted of the thickness of the gold on the roof of the shrine. I told him plainly that God was not impressed by ostentatious displays of wealth, and would much prefer the priest to spend the temple income on feeding the beggars at the gates. If you ever catch me involved in such vulgarity, you may sack me on the spot!'

The room set aside for worship had indeed been simple. Three of the white-washed walls were bare of any adornment, and in the centre of the fourth stood a small, plain table serving as an altar. Upon it were three pictures, one of Vishnu, the Preserver of the Universe, one of Shiva, the Power of Destruction, and another of the elephant-headed god, Ganesh. Before them stood a small metal idol of the child Krishna, dancing upon the hood of the seven-headed serpent, Kaliya. Hanging above the altar was a large framed picture of Krishna standing beneath a frangipani tree, his flute to his lips, and an angelic-looking calf at his feet, gazing up in adoration. The only illumination had been provided by two candles on the altar, and an oil lamp in front of Krishna.

Jimmy had motioned them to sit down, indicating a pile of cushions in the corner. Govinda, discernible in the gloom only due to the white dhoti that was his sole apparel, approached the altar holding a sheaf of incense sticks, which he lit from the Krishna lamp and waved before each picture in turn, chanting in a melodious yet powerful voice that sent shivers up Sheila's spine. When he had finished, he sat down to one side of the altar upon a tiger skin, complete with head and vicious-looking fangs.

'We will now meditate for a while upon the infinite glory of Lord Krishna,' he announced.

Sheila had closed her eyes and tried to empty her mind of all mundane thoughts, concentrating her inner gaze upon the centre of her forehead, her "third eye", as Govinda had taught them in London, but it proved impossible: she was far too excited by the idea of being in a real temple with a real guru. Within a short time her legs and buttocks began to ache, despite the cushions propping up her knees, and she began to feel as if she were sitting on a pile of bricks. *I'm too tired to meditate right now*, she convinced herself. *I wonder how long he means by "a while"?*

To distract her mind from her discomfort, she opened her eyes and looked at her companions. Govinda remained sitting in the lotus position, his back straight, his face devoid of all human expression, and yet, Sheila thought, somehow radiant. Jimmy too was sitting motionless, eyes closed. Shooting pains began to run up and down the back of her thighs, and her knees felt so tight that she wondered if she would ever be able to straighten her legs again. She grimaced, and looked over her shoulder towards Jazz, to see how he was coping. He was resting against the back wall, knees drawn up to his chest, a sardonic grin on his face. Their eyes met, and he shook his head, as if to say, "What a load of crap!"

Sheila scowled at him and turned back to face the front, determined to renew her effort, but the silence was suddenly broken by Govinda beginning to chant the Word of Creation.

The two syllables of "Aum" were elongated: a very long "ooooooo", followed by an "mmmmm" that was just a little shorter. As the sound died away hauntingly into the stillness, Sheila watched, mesmerised, the almost imperceptible swelling of Govinda's chest as he inhaled. And then the sound began again, at first very low, but rising to a crescendo that reverberated around the walls, before gradually dying away into its long-drawn-out hum. She was suddenly aware of Jimmy frowning at her, and realised that he too had been chanting, and she ought to have been as well. As Govinda began the final sound, she joined in, her soprano trembling high above the deeper voices of the two men, and then there was complete silence once more.

Govinda rose to his feet in one fluid motion, moved to the altar, and took a brass arati lamp from beneath it; from a small box he shook some camphor tablets into the bowl, igniting them from one of the candles. The fire burned fiercely, sending a plume of oily black smoke upwards and casting a sinister look upon Govinda's face. He waved the lamp before each picture and the idol, chanting once again, and when he had finished brought the lamp firstly to Jimmy, then Sheila, for them to take the divine, cleansing light into their hearts and minds. He cast a brief look at Jazz, lounging insolently against the back wall, then returned to the altar, where he too embraced the light before dousing the flame by placing his palm over it.

'There are only three bedrooms in the house,' he said to Sheila, 'so Mr. Shah will have to sleep in the caravan. Jimmy will show him where to go. If you collect your things, I will show you to your room. Morning arati is at six, so I suggest you both retire now. You have had a long day.'

The couple collected their bags from the car and whispered their goodnights, as Jimmy was standing nearby, torch in hand.

He led Jazz off into the darkness. Back inside, Govinda conducted Sheila upstairs to a small room containing just a single bed, a bedside cabinet, and a cupboard.

'Come downstairs when you have sorted yourself out, and I'll show you the bathroom,' Govinda said, closing the door as he withdrew.

Sheila dumped her bag on the bed and took out her alarm clock. *Wow! Ten already! We were in the temple longer than I thought.* She set the alarm for five-thirty, grabbed her wash-bag and towel, and went downstairs. Govinda was waiting for her, and ushered her through a side door, across a small vestibule, and opened the bathroom door. As she was about to enter, he laid a hand on her arm. 'Sheila, my dear, I know it is none of my business, but are you and your friend sleeping together?'

Taken aback, Sheila blushed fiercely.

'Please don't think that I am prying, or that I am judging you in any way, my dear, but please be careful.'

Returning to the kitchen, Sheila found Jimmy and Govinda sitting at the table with steaming mugs before them, and a third awaiting her. 'Join us for some hot cocoa,' said Govinda. 'It will help you to sleep.'

'Just the ticket!' Jimmy remarked. 'Never miss it, an' always sleep like the proverbial log!'

'A log that is often difficult to wake in the morning!' Govinda exclaimed.

Sheila, still embarrassed by Govinda's directness, was reluctant to sit. 'May I take it up with me?'

'Make sure you drink it all up,' Govinda urged. 'I always put some amrit in our bedtime drink, and it would be a sin to waste it.'

'Amrit?'

'Divine nectar. I obtained some from a very ancient Krishna temple in Maharashtra, where it materialises from the feet of Lord Krishna's moorthy. The container I keep it in never runs out.'

What a day! Sheila thought as she lay in bed. She looked at the mug of cocoa cooling on the cabinet. *Divine nectar! What would Jazz make of that?* But she knew that he would dismiss it as pure nonsense. She picked up the mug and drained it, pulling a face at the sickly sweetness. *How on earth does liquid come out of the feet of a stone idol?* she wondered. But she was asleep almost before the thought had formed.

4

The sun streamed so brightly through the trees that it almost hurt her eyes to look up as she wandered through the forest, the ground beneath her feet carpeted with vivid wild flowers. The mossy grass was cool to the touch of her bare feet, but the air was warm and moist, and she could feel the beads of sweat trickling down her back. *I'm not used to this sort of heat.* The forest throbbed with the songs of innumerable birds, strange trills and calls she had never heard before. She looked down at the faint path trodden through the grass, and became aware that she was wearing a sari. *How come? I don't even know how to put one on!* She followed the path, ignorant of where it would take her, all the time wondering: *What on earth am I doing in India?*

The trees thinned, and she could see a swathe of cleared ground running down to the bank of a broad river, its waters inviting. Although the grass was long and cool, the sun was now beating down upon her, no longer filtered by the trees, and she felt dizzy with the force of it. The river drew her forward, and as she walked across the meadow she heard in the distance the haunting melody of a flute. Downstream, a group of white cows with humped backs stood cooling themselves in the flowing waters. *What a good idea!*

She was not afraid of water, being a strong swimmer, and anyway the ground shelved gently out into a languid current. She could still hear the flute, presumably being played by some cowherd, but he sounded far enough away. Casting aside any doubts, she unwound her sari, discovering that she wore nothing beneath it, and dropped it to the ground, revelling in the touch of the air upon her skin. A slight breeze blew up from the river, caressing her breasts and teasing her nipples into hard little buttons, while the rays of the sun seemed to move up and down her slim legs and lithe torso like the hands of an ardent but gentle lover. She waded out into the stream and slipped beneath the water, its silky coolness bringing her skin out in goose-bumps. Lying afloat on her back, she was only vaguely aware that the music of the flute was now a little closer. She took a deep breath and jack-knifed, plunging down into the green depths until the blood pounded in her ears, forcing her back upwards. Joyfully, she broke the surface, shaking her head and sending flashing beads of water in all directions. Only then did she become aware of him standing on the bank.

Bare-chested, a garland of wild forest flowers around his neck, he wore a golden-coloured dhoti; a long iridescent peacock feather was tucked into a band of cloth around his head that served to restrain his long, wild black hair. His face was as dark as the midnight sky, his teeth gleamed as white as the peaks of the Himalayas, and his eyes shone with the lustre of the full moon; the smile he wore was so captivating that she felt herself trembling at the sight of him. In one hand he held a silver flute, which he twirled between his fingers so that the sunlight flashed off it with shattering brilliance, dazzling her. Then she saw with dismay that in his other hand he trailed her sari, and she was suddenly conscious that she was clothed in nothing but the river. Treading water, she clasped her hands protectively across her breasts, and looked beseechingly at the young musician.

Flashing her another bewitching smile, he flung the sari around his neck, turned on his heel, and danced away across the grass, the ends of the sari trailing behind him. He began to play once more the enchanting melody she had heard earlier.

'Oh no!' she cried in alarm. 'Stop! Please come back!'

Apart from one more backward glance over his shoulder, he paid her no heed, and in a moment more was swallowed up by the trees. The music began to recede, and she realised that she had no choice but to follow if she were ever to recover her clothing. Lunging out of the water, and hoping that no-one else was about, she darted for the forest.

The music tantalised her, now seeming closer, and now further away, but all the time it grew just a little fainter. She ran hither and thither in her desperation, until suddenly the sound had disappeared completely. She was at the edge of a small glade, and could sense from the deepening shadows that the sun was setting fast. Within minutes she would be naked and alone in the darkness, easy prey for any beast that might happen by - animal or man. She clasped her hands to her face and began to sob. 'Oh, God, help me!' she moaned.

'Why do you weep, beloved?' The voice behind her was both gentle and strong, and as melodious as the flute, and she knew at once that it was him, and that he had been playing a game with her all the while, luring her to this clearing, with its soft grass and heavy-scented flowers. She dared not move, afraid to turn her nakedness towards him, yet all the while trembling with anticipation.

At first it was his breath she felt upon the back of her neck, then the soft silkiness of his dhoti brushing against the back of her legs, and at last - at last! - the barely perceptible touch of his fingertips at her waist. Slowly and tenderly he turned her to face him, drawing her body to his own, and placing his lips upon hers. As she melted into the embrace, almost afraid to return his ardour, she felt him draw her down onto the velvet blanket of the grass, and became aware of the fusion of their physical bodies even as her mind floated free in the deep void of infinite space and timelessness.

'Krishna! Krishna!' she murmured, before all consciousness left her.

5

Jazz cursed as a taxi cut him up on the Hammersmith roundabout, shouting an obscenity at the unheeding cabbie. He was in a foul mood. The drive from Devon had been long and tedious, and he regretted now his impetuosity earlier that day in handing Sheila an ultimatum. 'This bloody place gives me the creeps,' he had said. 'I'm going home now, this minute. You can either come back with me or find your own way home.'

Sheila had stared at him in complete astonishment for a second or two, and then her eyes had flashed with a fire he knew only too well, and her face had set into an expression of defiance. 'The trouble with you, Mr. Shah, is that you're so set in your hidebound, Marxist materialistic view of society, that you wouldn't recognise spirituality if it came and kicked you up the arse!'

'Spirituality! I've seen nothing but power and mind games.' He winced even now as he recalled the sneering contempt with which he had laced his retort.

'Well, if you don't like it, you might just as well piss off then!' She had swung round and stalked away.

'I bloody well will!' he had shouted at her retreating back. 'And you can stuff your so-called spirituality up your own backside!'

He had jumped into the car and careered off down the lane at a speed not designed to benefit the suspension. Almost seven hours of driving in heavy Friday afternoon and evening traffic had done little to improve his temper, but as he neared London he began to reflect on a day that had started abysmally and gone steadily downhill thereafter.

Despite the unseasonably warm weather that third week in April, the combination of the clear night sky and the ashram's situation in a secluded valley had transformed the caravan into a refrigerator. Jazz had not thought to bring bedding with him, assuming that he would be accommodated properly, but the two thin blankets he found in the caravan provided little protection against the cold, even though he wore his clothes and overcoat. He had slept but fitfully, and then been wakened by the dawn chorus, which seemed to have organised itself right outside the window. He was just drifting off into a sort of half-sleep when he was jolted awake by a thunderous banging on the door.

'Wakey, wakey! Rise an' shine! Time for pooja!' Jimmy bellowed. 'Comin' in to get you if you ain't out in ten seconds.'

Cursing under his breath, Jazz shouted that he was coming, and stumbled outside. Jimmy had conducted him to an outhouse attached to a barn, where he was confronted by an ancient stone sink and a tap that produced the iciest water Jazz had ever felt. He took his time splashing his face and brushing his teeth in the hope that the others would forget him, but instead, Sheila had come looking for him.

'Jazz! For God's sake get a move on! Govinda's waiting for you!' She grabbed his arm and dragged him into the house. As they crept into the temple, Jazz had not missed the withering look from Govinda as he stood waiting before the altar. *Oh, fuck off!* he thought.

Breakfast consisted of strong black tea - 'Sorry, ran out of milk yesterday!' Jimmy had explained - a thin watery gruel, and a couple of slices of bread smeared with some unidentifiable matter. Govinda was absent, apparently fasting in his room, though Jazz could have sworn he caught a whiff of filtered coffee as Jimmy bustled in and out, upstairs and downstairs.

Sheila had been uncommunicative, seemingly in a world of her own. 'Are you okay?' he had asked.

'Mmm?' she replied dreamily.

'What are you thinking about?'

But she had not heard him, continuing to stare vacantly ahead, elbows planted on the table, her untouched mug of tea in her hands, seemingly oblivious of his presence. She smiled, but clearly not for him.

Irritation rose. 'What's so damned funny?'

Sheila shook her head and looked at him, as if noticing him for the first time. 'Oh, sorry. I was miles away.'

'I could see that. Where exactly?'

'India!'

'India?'

14

'Yes. I had this lovely dream about being in India.'

'Yeah?'

'It was so real! Everything was bright and colourful, and it was so hot, and I was wearing a sari, and there were those funny Indian cows, you know, the ones with the hump, ...' She paused for breath.

'So what were you doing?'

Sheila blushed, but her eyes glittered. 'I met Krishna,' she whispered.

'What? The guy in the picture?'

'Jazz! You can't call Krishna a "guy"!'

'*Sorreey*! So what happened?'

She blushed again. 'I don't really remember,' she mumbled. 'It was all a bit vague really.'

'Dreams don't mean anything,' he remarked dismissively. 'It was just a replay of last night's thing in the temple.'

Sheila glared at him. 'If you say so.' She got up abruptly and went upstairs. A door banged.

Aware that he had upset her, but not sure how, he went to the bottom of the stairs and called her, half-pleading and half-exasperated, but there was no reply. He started upwards, then realised he did not know which room she was in, and the last thing he wanted to do was blunder into Govinda. He retreated, muttering about the unpredictability of women in general and Sheila in particular.

Fifteen minutes later, Jimmy had found him listening to the radio in his car. 'There you are!' he exclaimed. 'Thought I'd jolly well lost you! Care to give me a hand? We've bin clearin' the lane bit by bit, but there's still a long way to go, as you might have noticed on the way in.'

'You want me to help you with some work?'

'We all do our bit, ol' man. Have to earn our keep, eh?'

'Sheila too?'

'Oh yes! I've got lots lined up for her - cleanin', choppin' veggies, and so on. The sort of women's work I generally have to do meself. Though she's in with Govinda at the moment, and I hope he doesn't keep her natterin' too long. Anyway, we can make a start in the meantime.'

They went to the barn, where Jimmy unearthed an ancient sickle, a rusty pair of shears, and a rake, which he dropped into a wheelbarrow that had itself seen better days, and then trundled off down the lane to where the brambles, nettles, bracken and other weeds lay in wait. He handed the sickle to Jazz. 'You chop it down, and I'll rake it up and cart it away. Use the shears on the thicker brambles.'

Jazz began to hack unenthusiastically at the bank, and Jimmy raked up the carnage and scooped it into the barrow with two pieces of plywood. 'I'll go and dump this lot, then see if Sheila's finished with Govinda.' He walked off jauntily, pushing the barrow with its buckled wheel ahead of him.

Time passed, and Jimmy did not return. The sun had risen above the tree-lined hill, and was now beating down warmly, so that Jazz had to remove his windcheater. In no time, his shirt was soaked with sweat, and such little enthusiasm as he had had at the beginning evaporated in the heat. When Jimmy returned with the wonky wheelbarrow two hours later, Jazz was sitting on the bank basking in the sun.

'Takin' a breather?' said Jimmy. 'I've brought you some tea. Sorry to have bin so long, but I had to get Sheila organised, and then the blessed phone wouldn't stop ringin'. I'll take this stuff away - not that you've done much - and then I've got to get on with the lunch.' He loaded the barrow, and left Jazz to it.

Jazz watched him go. Jimmy's off-hand remark had stung him, and he was torn between a desire to show just what he could do, and a wish to go to sleep in the sun and let Govinda and Jimmy rot in hell. He took a drink from the flask Jimmy had given him; the tea was black and not sweet enough, so he tipped it in the hedge. *That should kill a few bloody weeds!* he grinned

He stood up. Pride having got the better of him, he grabbed the sickle and attacked the luxuriant undergrowth with a ferocity that he would have preferred to unleash on Govinda. *Stuck-up fucking prat!* He ignored the stings of the nettles, the rasping scratching of the brambles, and the sweat streaming down his back and chest. By the time Jimmy returned to summon him for lunch, he had cleared a full fifty yards of the lane on both sides.

'Jolly good show!' Jimmy whistled in appreciation. 'That's more like it!' He regarded Jazz's dripping face and sweat-sodden clothes. 'You need a bath, ol' chap.'

'God, yes,' Jazz panted. 'Where's the bathroom?'

Jimmy guffawed. 'It's through the gate in the yard and straight down the field. Just jump right in! Cold as ruddy ice even in this weather, but very, very stimulatin'!'

After collecting a change of clothes and his towel, Jazz found the "bathroom", a deepish pool carved out on a bend of the stream that ran through the valley. He stripped off and leapt in, shrieking involuntarily at the coldness of the water, and rapidly soaped himself before hauling himself out again, teeth chattering. Once he had towelled himself dry, however, he had to admit that Jimmy had been right: the water had been very "stimulatin'".

Upon entering the kitchen, he found the others already eating. 'We decided to bless the food without waiting for you,' Govinda said. 'I do hope you don't mind.'

'I dare say it still tastes the same,' Jazz replied off-handedly. In fact, he felt a little put out that they had not waited, considering that he had been breaking his back all morning on their behalf. 'I'm not much of a one for ceremony anyway.'

'A fact that had not eluded me,' Govinda retorted tartly. 'Indeed, your lack of reverence in the temple makes me wonder why you bothered to come here at all.'

'Sheila needed a lift, that's why.'

'He's bin doin' some sterlin' work on the track, Govinda,' Jimmy intervened, attempting to smooth things over.

'We are, naturally, grateful for your efforts, but you must bear in mind that the principal purpose for which this ashram was established, by the grace of the Lord, is to serve as a place of spiritual retreat, where people can obtain respite from the problems and distractions of the world, and feel closer to God. It is not respectful to mock those who seek spiritual solace.'

'Are you telling me I'm not wanted here?'

'Quite the contrary, Mr. Shah. I want you to stay and realise your divinity, the divinity that is in each and every one of us, whether we choose to acknowledge it or not.' Govinda paused, lips pursed. 'But Brindavan is not Alcatraz. If a person finds it doesn't suit him, he is free to go whenever and wherever he pleases. However, you must first eat, and replenish the vitality you have been so valiantly expending on our behalf. Please help yourself.'

He indicated the pots on the stove in the corner, and Jazz helped himself to a generous portion of rice, dhall, and potato curry. He sat down and began to eat. 'Sheila tells me that you're vegetarian,' he said after a few mouthfuls, his tone markedly more conciliatory.

'The divine resides in all living things, including vegetables, but we regard it as sinful to kill another being simply in order to eat, especially when mankind could eat more cheaply and healthily without having to kill animals.'

'But if God's in vegetables too, isn't it sinful to eat them too?'

'Grains and seeds, fruits and tubers are, of course, life forms, but they are not so much living as containing the potential for life. They are not alive in the same way that a calf or lamb is alive when it is taken to be slaughtered, and so it is less sinful to eat them. When a person attains perfection, it is possible to exist merely by drawing all the energy one needs from the ether. In the Himalayas there are yogis who have lived for centuries in this way.'

'Oh, come off it! How could anyone live without eating? You don't obviously.'

'You may believe it or not as you wish,' Govinda said coldly. 'But let me tell you this: I eat one small meal a day and nothing else. I have been put on this earth to do a job, one which requires the expenditure of a certain amount of bodily energy, and that energy has to be replaced. However, I meditate every day for several hours, and acquire much energy by that means. There seems to me little point in eating a huge meal such as yours to gain energy when so much of that energy will have to be used in digestion. Such a waste of time!' He snapped his fingers contemptuously. 'The great saints and sages who sit in deep meditation for aeons in the holy mountains expend almost no bodily energy, and are therefore able to survive on the prana they take from the air, which is, of course, much purer than the polluted air here in the West.'

'I don't see the point in sitting on your backside doing nothing,' Jazz remarked.

'They are praying for the welfare of the world, that is their job.'

'Not doing too great then, are they, what with all the wars, droughts, famines and so on.'

Govinda stood up abruptly, sending his chair flying. 'You have no concept whatsoever of anything spiritual,' he hissed. 'You are the epitome of modern man, able only to mock and scoff.'

He swept out of the room, bringing lunch to an early and dramatic conclusion.

Jazz tried to speak to Sheila afterwards, but she was hostile, upset that he had offended Govinda.

'I wanted you to like him, but your stupidity and rudeness has ruined everything.'

'Look, I'm sorry, okay? But you know this religious business isn't for me. It didn't interest you either when we first met.'

'Things change, Jazz, and people change too. I've changed, and Govinda is the most important person in my life right now.'

'So where does that leave me?'

'That depends on you. My perceptions have changed, my priorities have changed. You can either live with that, or else do the other thing.' She turned away from him and went upstairs.

Jimmy, who had made himself scarce after Govinda had stormed out, reappeared as Jazz slouched out into the yard. 'The boys'll be coming down this evenin',' he said, 'so you'll have to move out of the caravan. I'll show you where you'll be beddin' down tonight.' He led the way into the barn. 'It can get a bit draughty in here, but there are some mattresses in the corner, and I can rustle up a blanket or two. Just ask. If you can move your stuff out of the caravan pronto, Sheila can give it a bit of a dustin'.'

Jazz looked around the barn. There were no windows, just a number of unglazed slits in the thick stone walls, rather like archers' firing positions in medieval castles. Light filtered through a number of holes in the roof where tiles had slipped, and the scattering of hay and straw on the rough concrete floor looked damp and flea-ridden. He went over to the pile of mattresses: they smelled of mould and mouse droppings. *Well fuck this! I've had enough!*

Returning to the caravan, he packed his things and waited for Sheila to turn up. He had then given her his ultimatum, resulting in his lonely journey back to his digs in London. *I wonder if I'll see her again,* he wondered sadly, sitting on the bed in which they had made love so often.

CHAPTER 2

Sheila had decided to stay for a week; she had brought a couple of text-books with her on the off-chance that she found time to revise, and although that had not proved to be the case over the weekend, with a whole week before her, and just the three of them, she convinced herself that she would find time to read. Already though, she was beginning to wonder whether the hectic life of a solicitor was really what she wanted: life at Brindavan was proving simple, serene and pure. *What more do I really need?* she asked herself. *Why waste energy sorting out the mundane problems of other people's lives, when I could be getting on with my own spiritual life here?*

Jazz's abrupt departure had certainly upset her, and in part she blamed herself for bringing him into an environment for which he was hardly suited, but whenever a thought of him came into her mind, sadness was almost immediately extinguished by recollection of the sweet words of Krishna and his tender embrace.

Govinda's interpretation of her dream had astounded her. 'I do not think this was a mere dream, my dear,' he had told her that Friday, 'but a divine visitation, and if I am right then you have been highly favoured.'

'A visitation! But I was in India, wearing a sari, and everything was so real!'

'Exactly. It is that very quality of reality which convinces me that the Lord himself came to you. In ordinary dreams there is often something that doesn't quite fit in. For example, you may dream that you are back at school with all your old chums, but you are conscious that you are an adult.

'This dream was very different. You did not feel that anything was out of place, but merely marvelled that you were having the experience of being in India, and from what you have told me, it was certainly India that you went to. Moreover, when you awoke you were very aware of the lingering effect of the Lord's presence. And even now, several hours later, how vivid your recollection remains!'

Sheila had blushed then, for she had not confided the most intimate details of the dream to Govinda. 'What I don't understand, though,' she said, 'is if I was in India with Krishna, how could I smell his perfume in my room when I woke up?'

Govinda chuckled. 'You were not in the geographical India of this earth, my dear. You were in the India that exists on the spiritual plane where Krishna resides - or rather, your atma, your spiritual essence, was there sporting with the Lord. Even so, the experience is so real that when you awake, you believe that you can still sense smells, touch and so on.'

'I see,' Sheila murmured, looking at the floor, embarrassed by references to "sporting with" and "touch". 'But why me? What have I done to deserve such an experience?'

'Who can say? Apart from the fact that it is clearly the result of the good karma that you have brought with you from previous births. Let me see what I can discover.'

He closed his eyes, and began to breathe slowly and deeply, the breaths becoming slower and less perceptible. Within two minutes, Sheila had to look very closely to discern any movement of the chest at all. She had never been so close to a yogi before without anyone else being present, and she took the opportunity to examine him closely. The dark face, framed by the lustrous shoulder-length hair, was utterly serene, and she noticed for the first time how long and feminine his eye-lashes were, how full and sensuous the lips.

Embarrassed at such a thought, she closed her eyes too, and sought refuge in meditation. A great peace descended upon her, and she felt herself beginning to drift away from the room. *Where are you going?* asked her mind. *To the forest, to Krishna!* was her answer. Her pulse quickened at the thought of Krishna's embrace, and she felt the heat rising in her body. She was startled back to the present by Govinda's voice.

'There is indeed a strong karmic link between you and Lord Krishna,' he announced. 'In my meditation I went back to his time on earth, and I could feel your presence there. Perhaps like me you were one of his childhood playmates, or one of the gopis perhaps. How he used to tease those young girls! I recall one occasion when several of them decided to take a dip in the Yamuna to cool off, and Krishna stole their clothes so that they could not come out again.'

Sheila covered her confusion with another question. 'You were one of Krishna's friends?'

'It is why I have taken as my own one of his names in every incarnation since - whatever my parents may have chosen to call me! Yes, my dear, I was a friend of the Lord, and I recall it all as if it were yesterday. But,' and he raised a warning finger, 'it is of no purpose to dwell on past lives. If they have been good, that can give rise to pride; and if not, then the spirit can become depressed. Remember, whatever we have done before cannot be changed: the past is beyond recovery. The future, however, is still to come, and what it will bring depends upon what you do now. So make the most of the present, and ensure that you fill your life with good thoughts and deeds.'

She opened her mouth, but he stilled her with a raised hand. 'Enough for now. I'm sure Jimmy has some chores for you. We shall talk again before you go home.'

2

Simon and Anthony had arrived in the evening with Bob, whom she knew only slightly, and Andy, a stranger to her. The first two she had come to know quite well the previous summer, when she had first begun to attend the Sunday prayer meetings at Govinda's house in Brixton. Nevertheless, as the only girl, she felt somewhat isolated, and in truth the boys did not pay her much attention. The conversation at dinner that evening was taken up almost entirely by business, with Jimmy setting out the jobs that needed doing and allotting who should do what. He also went through a list of items that he required for various projects he had in mind. None of them even noticed when Sheila slipped out of the room and went upstairs.

She lay on the bed waiting for the call to evening arati, and inevitably her mind drifted back to the time she had met Govinda the year before. Sheila had shared a flat with four other students, one of whom was a girl called Rosie, and they had become good friends, perhaps because they were different in so many ways. Whereas Sheila was slight of build, almost boyish in appearance with her short, dark curly hair, Rosie was taller than average, of almost statuesque build, with wide hips and a generous bosom. Her large eyes were a deep blue, her lips were full and pouting, and her hair was a tawny halo around her leonine head.

Rosie's boyfriend was an art student who had introduced her to an Indian guru and holy man - "really dishy-looking", she said - and Sheila had allowed herself to be persuaded to accompany Rosie one Sunday afternoon against her own inclinations. They had taken the tube to Brixton, and walked through what had once been a fashionable area of Regency houses, but was now rather run down. The door had been flung open by a debonair chap in his early thirties, clutching a tortoise-shell cigarette holder in one hand.

'Rosie, darlin'!' he gushed. 'Smashin' to see you!' He ushered them in, gave Rosie a prolonged hug and several smacking kisses on each cheek. 'And who's your charmin' little friend?'

Sheila was introduced to Jimmy, who took her proffered hand with exaggerated gallantry, and kissed her fingers several times. 'Delighted!' he crowed. Then he placed a finger to his lips. 'Sshh! Mustn't make any noise! Govinda's leadin' a meditation.'

After indicating where they should leave their shoes, Jimmy led them along a sparely but elegantly furnished hallway to a room at the rear of the building. The door was ajar, but the room was in semi-darkness, heavy drapes drawn across the windows, and the only light provided by two candles on a small table against one wall.

As her eyes adjusted to the gloom, Sheila could see that there were several people in the room, some sitting on chairs at the back, but most upon cushions on the floor. Everyone sat quite still, eyes closed, all facing the table bearing the candles, beside which sat cross-legged on the floor a very dark man, naked from the waist up.

Jimmy motioned the girls towards some spare cushions, and they sat down. Sheila, not having a clue as to what was going on, simply sat and stared at the first "guru" she had ever seen, acknowledging that Rosie had been right: he was rather dreamy. Then he opened his mouth and began to chant the first "aum" that Sheila had heard. Bemused, she had thought at first that he was groaning in pain, but as the others joined in, she realised it was some sort of ritual. As the third "aum" died away, the guru's eyes snapped open, and Sheila had the uncanny feeling that he was looking directly at, if not through, her.

'Divine incarnations, spiritual beings, you must strive to realise the divinity that lies within each and every one of you, buried beneath this coarse layer of flesh and bone and sinew. There is no other purpose to this existence you now lead but to become aware of, and then merge with, that divine essence. Mother and father, brother and sister, spouse and child, friend and foe: all these are illusions that bind you to the maya of the world, compelling you to waste your energies in providing for families, enmeshing you in the snares of the world, causing you to encumber yourselves with mortgages, hire purchase commitments, credit card debts and the like, so that in the hurly-burly of life, the struggle for mere earthly existence, you completely forget the divine inheritance which is yours and so condemn yourselves to the perpetual cycle of birth, death, and re-birth.'

Sheila was so entranced both by the guru's words and his voice, which was soothing, musical and persuasive, that she almost forgot to breathe.

'How then can you escape this vicious cycle? There is only one way: surrender yourselves to God, to Lord Krishna, placing all your trust in him to provide for your wants. Once you begin your spiritual journey in true earnestness, the Lord will take care of all your bodily needs, and then - at the very moment that you think you have achieved detachment from the pleasures of the world - He will shower you with wealth, and the strength of your detachment will then be sorely tested. The higher you fly, the greater the danger of a fall.'

He paused, took a sip of water from a glass beside him, and looked expectantly at his audience. A hand was raised, almost as if prompted. 'Yes, Simon, you have a question?'

'Er, yes,' the young man began haltingly. 'I think I understand what you're saying, but surely it just isn't possible for everyone in the world to lead that sort of life. I mean, there has to be someone to run the buses, grow the food and so on.'

Somewhere in the room there was a half-stifled snort of derision, and a few people giggled. The guru looked sternly around the room, and silence prevailed.

'That presupposes that if the entire world were immersed in God-consciousness, we would still need food and buses,' he said. 'But you are right in one sense. It is not possible for everyone in the world to experience God at this time, for we are all of us at different stages of our spiritual evolution. Some human beings have barely evolved from being animals: the courts and prisons testify to that. People who commit rape and robbery and murder may have to endure many thousands of lifetimes before they even begin to sense their divine nature.

'No, my message is for those who are ready to listen to it. You may think that you are here by chance, because you knew someone who had met somebody else who had been told about me by yet another person, but I tell you this: nothing is by chance, for each and every one of you has been brought here by your karma, due to the accumulation of merit you have acquired by doing good deeds in previous births, and because the time is now right for you to receive this message.'

'But Govinda,' interjected a young man later introduced to Sheila as Rosie's boyfriend, Anthony, 'how can it be fair that some people should be able to spend their time sitting down in prayer and meditation while the rest have to work?'

'Ah, you clearly believe that prayer and meditation are the easy way out. Let me ask you this: for how many seconds can you hold your mind still before it darts away out of control onto some frivolous train of thought? Even when you believe yourself to be concentrating hard upon something - your studies, perhaps - you may suddenly find that the mind has wandered off on a frolic of its own.

'Believe me, my friends, it requires far more discipline to train the mind to obey your will than it does to drive a bus, work on an assembly line, or even to carry out some professional task. It is work of the very highest order, entirely selfless, devoted to the welfare of mankind. Do you think it is merely an odd coincidence that in every civilisation the world has ever known there has been a class of persons whose sole function in society has been to propitiate God - by whatever name they may have called Him - or indeed, Her? Not at all. It is essential that a small percentage of the total population spends its time in perpetual intercession with the Lord on behalf of the rest, seeking His blessing, protection and guidance.'

There were one or two more questions, followed by a meal, and then the gathering was concluded with prayers, singing and chanting, all in a language quite alien to anything Sheila had encountered hitherto. She felt detached from the rest of the group, most of whom were joining in enthusiastically, and this gave her time to consider with greater objectivity what Govinda had said.

Her first year Law exams were only six weeks away, and this so-called guru was telling her that they were of no account, that her plan to become a solicitor was a waste of time, and that what she ought to do was give it all up and become, in effect, a nun. *No way, Jose!* she thought. *"Nul points" for the nun's life!* She had by then been going out with Jazz for a couple of months, and only two weeks before had slept with him for the first time. A couple of years older than her, and more experienced, he had made the experience of losing her virginity less of a ghastly ordeal than she had feared. Having only just discovered what sex, and possibly love, was all about, she was not going to throw it all away on the say-so of a complete stranger, however persuasive and however "dishy".

On her way home with Rosie, Sheila concluded that while it had been an interesting experience, it was not one she wished to repeat, and she resolved not to visit the strange house in Brixton again.

After her exams Sheila had taken a summer job in Selfridges, rather than go home to the dreary little Hampshire town where she had grown up, and to her obsessively proud but suffocating parents and their corner shop. By then she had forgotten all about the Brixton guru. Rosie had gone home to Kent, and though she promised to keep in touch over the vacation, Sheila did not hear from her. She was not bothered, for she and Jazz spent all their free time together.

Although she quite enjoyed her job, which she found rather relaxing after the stress of revising eighteen hours a day for exams, she discovered very quickly its main drawback was that middle-aged men were always trying to pick her up, on the basis, she presumed, that shop-girls were thought "easy".

One afternoon, as she was tidying up her counter, she heard a voice behind her. 'Excuse me, but don't I know you?'

Oh God! What an original chat-up line! she thought, turning round to tell the fellow where to get off. Her mouth open with a ready retort, she just stared in surprise at Rosie's boyfriend. She blushed at the thought of what she had been about to say, and he blushed too. Then she began to speak, at exactly the same time as he did. They both blushed even more fiercely.

'You first,' the boy managed to say.

'I met you at that funny place in Brixton,' Sheila said. 'You're Rosie's boyfriend. I didn't come again because I had exams.' *Why the hell am I making excuses?* she thought, mentally kicking herself.

'Govinda's,' the boy replied. 'Rosie did introduce us, but I can't remember your name.'

'Sheila.'

'And I'm Anthony. Govinda did ask Rosie where her friend was, and she said you'd been working very hard.'

'I was. Eighteen hours a day.'

'And are you working here all summer?'

'Yes. I started a couple of weeks back. It's a doddle compared to Law.'

'I'll bet! We have regular meetings every night now - at Govinda's, I mean - and all day at the weekends. Why don't you come along again?'

'I work all day Saturday, and my free time I spend with my boyfriend.'

'Come on a Sunday then. And bring your boyfriend. I'm sure he'd enjoy it.'

Before leaving, Anthony gave Sheila Rosie's home number and made her promise to call. 'She doesn't come up every weekend, but she'd love to see you, I know.'

That evening on her way home Sheila mused over the chance meeting. She felt a little flattered that Govinda had asked after her. She knew for a certainty that Jazz would definitely not enjoy spending time at the house in Brixton, but as it happened he was flying home to Iran the following Friday, and would not be back until the beginning of term, so she would be free on the Sunday. *Maybe it's Fate! Maybe I should call Rosie.* When she got back to the flat, before Jazz arrived for their regular nightly meal and love-making, she did exactly that, arranging to meet Rosie at Victoria the following Sunday.

Her trips to Brixton became a regular Sunday outing over the remainder of the summer break, and as the weeks passed she felt herself becoming increasingly drawn to Govinda and his teaching. On her first return visit, Anthony had introduced her to the guru himself, who had welcomed her with great warmth, and she gradually got to know most of those who came regularly, but especially Jimmy, Simon and Anthony. By the end of the summer she felt herself to be an integral part of a very special group.

Yet all the time she knew that she was laying up future trouble, for Jazz was a virulent atheist, a fact that he had made known right at the beginning of their relationship. Politically he was a Marxist, and shared Marx's view of religion. Sheila had not been bothered: nominally brought up in the Church of England, she had no strong religious beliefs. Her family attended church solely for the christenings, weddings and funerals of family and friends - and her father avoided as many of those as his wife would let him get away with. 'Circumstances have forced me to go for my own ceremonials on two occasions,' he would protest, and I had no say in the first, and not much in the second. There will without doubt be a third, about which I will also have no power to object. Three times is quite enough, if you ask me.'

With such a background, Sheila had never given religion much thought, and she was somewhat taken aback by Jazz's vitriolic denunciations of religion in general and Islam in particular. She came to understand that his strict upbringing had played a part in forming his views, but as for herself, she did not believe that either Marx or religion had much relevance in twentieth century England.

By the time that Jazz returned from Iran, however, she had experienced a wholly different outlook upon life, which in some way she was unable to define she nonetheless felt was beneficial. Since Jazz immediately resumed his weekend job in a burger bar, she was able to maintain her visits to Brixton without telling him. She knew very well that Jazz's sarcastic iconoclasm was bound to bring about a rupture of her relationship either with him or with Govinda, but she wanted to maintain both. She knew that one day she would have to come clean, but as the implied lie grew bigger, the more difficult it became to own up.

The time-bomb had burst just after Christmas. Govinda announced that he had made an offer to purchase a property in Devon, and that as soon as all the legal formalities had been completed, he and Jimmy would move there to establish a proper ashram. By the end of March they had gone, the Sunday meetings had come to an end, and Govinda's closest followers, such as Anthony and Simon, travelled down to Devon each weekend to help out. An enormous loneliness descended upon Sheila, and no amount of studying could fill the chasm in her life that Govinda's departure had opened up.

It had taken her three weeks to pluck up the nerve to tell Jazz, and, as she had known all along, he exploded. 'You've been seeing this bugger behind my back every Sunday since last summer!' he raged.

'Oh, for Christ's sake, Jazz, you make it sound as if I've been having an affair!'

'In a way this is even worse! You've been hiding something you knew I couldn't possible approve of.'

'I don't need your bloody approval for what I do!' Now she was angry too. 'I'm not some bloody Muslim wife who needs her husband's permission to take a crap! Don't you dare try and tell me what I can and what I can't do!'

The accusation that he was behaving according to his upbringing visibly shocked him, and undermined his belligerence. 'I know that, darling, but we have a good thing going here, don't we? We shouldn't have secrets.'

'I know, but I just couldn't find the right time to tell you. I wanted to; I don't want to have secrets.'

As with all really good quarrels, the two of them ended up in bed, and in the post-coital warmth between them Sheila had persuaded him to drive her down to Devon during the Easter vacation.

And now here she was at Brindavan, and what she had suspected all along would happen, had indeed happened. She stifled the pang of regret with feelings of self-righteousness: Jazz had after all turned out to be the typical Muslim male, expecting his woman to come running when he snapped his fingers. *Bloody good riddance!* she thought, while wondering if she really meant it. *Now I've got the chance to discover who I really am.*

After the evening arati, she sat with Govinda and Jimmy over a mug of cocoa, listening enthusiastically to Govinda outlining his plans for the future. 'This will become one of the most powerful temples in the world!' he had declared.

That night she dreamed of Krishna again.

3

The ensuing week was idyllic, and Sheila's law books remained in her bag. From the Sunday afternoon until the following Friday evening there were just the three of them together, and Govinda encouraged her to spend as much time as possible in the temple. There they meditated together, and he also gave her deeper instruction in the basic concepts of Hinduism, regaled her with stories of the life of Krishna, and spoke to her about the future course of her life.

'Only you can decide what it is that you really want to do. You must look into the innermost depths of your heart to discover what is truly important to you. If it is wealth, position, power and prestige, all those transitory things for which men struggle, and even kill, to acquire, well …' - he snapped his fingers - 'then by all means go and become a lawyer. But if in your heart you discover the true love of God, then you must decide how best you can serve Him.'

'But as a lawyer,' she argued, 'I could really help people with their problems, the poor and helpless who don't have the means, the education or perhaps the wit to stand up to authority.'

'That, of course, is a laudable ambition. Many professional people start out with such ideals, but in time the very nature of their work sucks them into the vortex of materialism. When you live in the world, my dear, you become a prey to the temptations of the world, and it takes someone with great strength of mind and purpose not to succumb. If you really wish to serve the poor, why not go to Africa or India, where there is no system of state benefits to fall back upon. There you would learn the true meaning of poverty.'

Sheila flinched. 'I'm not sure I'm cut out for that sort of work,' she mumbled, troubled by the thought that she had never really given the idea of service to humanity much consideration.

'I do not say that you are. I was speaking generally. But mark my words, Sheila, in the not too distant future there will be much service to be performed here, caring for the refugees from that mad, mad world out there, who will flock here to seek spiritual solace. Brindavan is destined to become a centre of great spiritual energy, to which those who are bound to the trials and tribulations of the world by their karma can nevertheless repair in order to recharge their batteries, and perhaps even to discover their true nature.

'And, my dear, I have a powerful feeling that your destiny is linked to that of Brindavan, that your purpose is to perform some great service to humanity. I do not know as yet what it might be, but these nightly visitations from Lord Krishna tell me that He has some great plan in store for you. In time, we will both know what that is.'

And with those words, his gaze lifted above Sheila's head towards the picture of Krishna and became distant, as if he were seeking to look into the future to see what would come to pass.

One evening, as she sat in the temple after arati, her mind was in a turmoil: all she could think about was Jazz. What was he doing? How was he feeling? Would he contact her on her return? What would happen to their relationship? Was it over?

Suddenly Govinda, who had been filling the oil lamp and replacing the spent candles on the altar, spoke, as if he had been reading her mind. 'There is one important lesson we must all bear in mind, Sheila, and that is to keep company with like-minded people. If we consort with those who have no belief in God, with people of a low spiritual vibration, with those who believe that the petty pleasures of the world are all there is to life, then our own spiritual aura will become tarnished, and our faith weakened. I have been much exercised recently by the fact that since my removal from London, the devotees there no longer come together. There is no reason why you should not all come together, and meet regularly, in each other's houses perhaps. To keep company with like-minded people is of vital importance.'

Is he telling me to dump Jazz? She stared at the floor, not daring to ask him directly in case he confirmed her inference.

'I never interfere in matters of the heart, Sheila. Look into your own heart, and ask Lord Krishna for guidance.'

That night she dreamed that Krishna saved her from a powerful demon.

By the time she returned to London the following Sunday, having been given a lift by Simon and Anthony, she had made up her mind that the relationship with Jazz was over. She threw herself into her studies, and made no attempt to contact him, fortified in her decision by the fact that he had left no message for her. On the Tuesday, however, when she was about to join some other second-year students for lunch in the refectory, Jazz suddenly loomed up before her.

'Where were you all last week?' he asked brusquely.

'Not that it's any of your business,' she replied coldly, 'but I stayed on in Devon and had an enjoyable time with Govinda and Jimmy.'

'What's that supposed to mean?'

'Nothing that's any concern of yours.'

'Where does that leave us then?'

'There is no us. We don't speak the same language any more. Sorry.' She pushed past him and sat down with her classmates.

'Then fuck off!' Jazz hissed, before storming out.

'Bad loser?' asked one of the girls.

'Something like that.'

'Does this mean you're in the market, Sheila?'

'I am most definitely off men at present, Mr. Hargreaves,' Sheila replied in a withering tone, 'but if I really wanted to bugger up my exam chances, you're exactly the sort of bloke I'd choose to go out with!'

4

Jimmy Partington was a man who thrived on company, and he had thoroughly enjoyed the week that Sheila had stayed. Even though she had spent most of her time with Govinda, her very presence had been a breath of fresh air. Once she had gone, the days between Sunday and Friday reverted to their usual barren state, with nothing to relieve the tedium. His relationship with Govinda was an odd one: the two men would often spend the entire week without exchanging a word more than the bare minimum required to maintain a veneer of civilised existence. Some days Govinda would stay in his room, emerging only to perform temple functions, acknowledging Jimmy's presence with a mere nod.

He knew, of course, that Govinda depended upon him financially, for the sale of the family home in Brixton had financed the purchase of Brindavan and put money into the ashram bank account. His natural modesty, and his deference to the guru, had meant that he had never done anything to dispel the notion current among the visitors to Brixton that Govinda had owned the house.

Although he was drawn to spiritual life, he nevertheless liked to think of himself as Brindavan's business manager and financial administrator, with Govinda as the religious head. He did wonder from time to time, however, what Govinda really thought of him, for he had made it clear from the start that while happy to finance the project, he harboured no ambition to become a monk himself. He liked to chant and to meditate, but he also liked his cigarettes and whisky, and although he had heard Govinda discourse a thousand times on the perils of worldly attachments, he was not prepared to forego those two things. He was still unable to tell whether or not this minor show of independence irked Govinda.

As he sat outside on the Tuesday evening after Sheila's departure, he began to question for the first time whether he had done the right thing in abandoning a life-style he had rather enjoyed. As a young man from a nondescript middle-class background, but with a flair for art and design, he had from his college days deliberately cultivated certain affectations, such as the tortoise-shell cigarette holder, the Balkan Sobranie cigarettes, and above all the upper class nasal twang which had in time become second nature to him.

Having done well at art school, he had quickly obtained employment with a well-known but rather staid interior designer. His talent, and his bonhomie, had made him popular with clients, and after a few years he had taken the decision to go it alone. Success had come almost instantly, for he had a remarkable ability not only to create a combination of colour and style that matched his client's premises, but also in some subtle and indefinable way their personality. He was at his very best when given free rein to choose not only the décor but also the furniture, fixtures and fittings, and had been known to gut the comfortable homes of some of his richest clients and then dazzle them with the palaces that he created in their stead. He absolutely adored spending other people's money.

The death of his parents in a car accident had landed him the house in Brixton much sooner than would have been the case, but he did not refurbish his own house the way he did his clients', for he was careful with his own money. Nor did he consider selling it and moving "up market", for he liked the cosmopolitan atmosphere of his neighbourhood. He was an adventurous cook, delighting in the exotic cuisines of other countries, and the area gave him easy access to a wide variety of fruits, vegetables, spices and other culinary essentials. Jimmy's only expensive habits were his clothes, his cigarettes, and his fine wines and whiskies. He did not own a car, never having learned to drive, and travelled everywhere by taxi, billed, of course, to his clients.

In the course of his work, Jimmy naturally mixed with the wealthy, and even the famous, and was occasionally invited to their parties. He never refused an invitation, for he not only adored such gatherings for their own sake, but because they invariably led to at least a couple of new jobs. It was at one such gathering, given by an Indian diplomat for whom he had refurbished a large but neglected apartment in South Kensington, that he had met Govinda.

'Mr. Partington,' beamed his genial host, 'may I introduce you to Manilal Chatterjee, the son of a very old friend of mine. Mani's father and I had the distinction of being locked up together by you British back in the 'forties, when we were enthusiastic members of Gandhiji's Congress movement. He is now a very successful and important lawyer in Calcutta, and Mani is his youngest and most worthless son!' He clapped the young man on the shoulder to indicate that he was joking, and then left them together.

Chatterjee was slightly taller than Jimmy, who was below average height by European standards, but was even slimmer and more elegant. He was dressed in the Indo-European fashion: dark slacks and brogues, a collarless Indian shirt, and a Nehru jacket. His dark face made his teeth and the whites of his eyes almost luminously brilliant, and Jimmy could not guess his age; anywhere between twenty-five and forty could have been correct.

He smiled, switched the glass he was holding to his left hand, and held out his right to Jimmy. 'I am very pleased to make your acquaintance, Mr. Partington.' His voice flowed like a melody.

Jimmy shook the proffered hand vigorously. 'Me too, and please call me Jimmy.'

'Very well ..., Jimmy.' The Indian smiled, perfect teeth shining white.

'So, are you over here studyin' for the legal profession then?'

'Good gracious, no! I have no interest whatsoever in the practice of law.'

'I see. On holiday then?'

'I am here on a mission.'

'Ah, of course, you're another of these government wallahs!'

The Indian chuckled, his laughter like water gently tumbling over rocks. 'Jimmy, my friend,' he said, taking Jimmy by the arm, 'let us leave this so tedious affair and find somewhere quiet to talk, and then I will tell you about my mission.'

'Why not come back to my place then. I can knock up a meal in no time.'

'I am afraid that I do not eat meat.'

'No problem. If I hadn't become the best interior designer in London, I would have been the best chef. Matter of fact, I *am* the best chef!'

They had talked - or rather, Chatterjee had talked - into the early hours of the morning. He had explained how he had tried to conform to his father's ambitions by studying for the law, and then spending a couple of unutterably boring years in the family law firm, before quitting his affluent Calcutta life-style and coming to the West.

'You see, Jimmy, I knew from the age of thirteen that my destiny was to bring the rich heritage of India's spiritual teaching to a spiritually and morally bankrupt Europe, but how does one, at that age, say such things to one's parents?'

He had eventually badgered his father into allowing him to visit the West, with an allowance for two years. 'My father believed that it was simply a case of wanderlust, and that after a couple of years I would have got it out of my system and return home.' He had spent the two years travelling the length and breadth of Europe, visiting as many places as he could fit in, ranging from the Vatican to Auschwitz.

'Ah, Jimmy!' he said sadly, shaking his head. 'Both in Rome and in Poland I could hear the tortured cries of poor souls going to their deaths, the Christians to the lions and the Jews to the gas chambers. The vibrations of such despair and misery sear the very soil of places such as those for thousands of years.'

Jimmy had been spellbound.

Then the day of reckoning had come: his father had demanded his return, and when he refused, cut off his allowance. Chatterjee had come to England, where he had lived upon the charity of his father's contacts until they discovered that his father had cut him off. He had then been compelled to take any kind of menial employment that came his way, while maintaining contact with such of his father's friends as remained amenable.

'As soon as my feet touched the soil of this land,' he declared, 'I knew that this was where the Lord wanted me to begin my spiritual mission, although I fear that the day I will be able to start in earnest is still a long way off. Even with the Lord behind one, it is difficult to establish such a venture from a small bed-sitting room in West Kensington.'

'So what precisely is this mission of yours?' Jimmy asked, intrigued but wary.

'To teach the West that all races are one, that all religions are equal, that God is the same by whatever name different peoples may call Him, and to overcome racial and religious bigotry wherever I find it. There is only one race my friend, and that is the human race; there is only one religion, and that is the religion of love. If mankind could but realise these fundamental truths, conflict and poverty would disappear almost at once.'

'Well, I'll drink to that!' Jimmy raised his glass.

'It would be of the greatest benefit for the young to learn these lessons, for the young people of today are the people who will exercise authority tomorrow, and they will then not repeat the mistakes of their elders, mistakes that have brought about terrible wars, famines and pestilence.'

Jimmy had been genuinely moved. His father had never fully recovered from the wound he had received during the Normandy landings, and his mother had lost two brothers at Dunkirk. 'You know what?' he said earnestly. 'I've got bags o' room here; I'm rattlin' around like a single pea in a big pod. Why don't you move in here and start this mission of yours right away?'

'My dear Jimmy! I am overwhelmed by your generosity! You know, I felt disinclined to attend that boring party, but I could sense the Lord urging me to go - and now I know the reason why!' The Indian jumped up, grasped both Jimmy's hands, and kissed them.

Pulling himself back to the present, Jimmy looked around in the dying light. The yard had been cleared of the piles of rusting junk, and the weeds that had engulfed it had been cut down. Much remained to be done - rotting window frames to be replaced, crumbling brickwork to be re-pointed, and new slates for the roof - but much had been achieved already. He was aware, however, that the cash in the bank was steadily decreasing, and he hoped that his initial enthusiasm did not prove to have been misplaced.

He took a final drag, removed the dog-end from its holder and tossed it away, then went inside to put the kettle on for the evening cocoa.

CHAPTER 3

The last person Jazz expected to see on his doorstep that morning was Sheila. She whirled around as he opened the door, eyes glittering angrily, and slapped his face. 'You stupid bastard! I'm up the duff!'

Jazz stepped back, one hand to his stinging cheek, his mind whirling. 'Are you sure?' he stammered.

'Of course I'm fucking sure, you arsehole! You swore those bloody things were safe, and now I'm in the club, and my future's a mess!' Tears streamed down her face as she began to bang her fists upon his chest. 'You've ruined my life!' she sobbed.

Jazz, uncomfortably aware that his landlady's sitting room door was ajar for eavesdropping purposes, and that a couple passing by on the other side of the road were giving them odd looks, took hold of Sheila's elbow. 'You'd better come in. We obviously need to talk.'

She shook his hand away, but nonetheless followed him upstairs to his room, flinging herself into a battered old armchair and staring moodily at the carpet. Her anger had drained away, leaving only despair in its wake.

Jazz busied himself making tea, the English panacea, glancing at her over his shoulder from time to time. In her anger she had been fiercely beautiful, her eyes flashing with fire and her cheeks hot, but even now, when the fire had died away, there was a haunting beauty about her which he had never seen before - a consequence of the pregnancy perhaps.

He placed a cup of tea on the table beside her, and looked down at her helplessly, not daring to ask the question that had come to his mind. She looked up and saw it written on his face.

'Yes,' she said flatly, 'it's yours. There hasn't been anyone else.'

He let out the breath he had been holding in, almost relieved in a way; glad that she had not been unfaithful to him. 'Well, there's only one thing for it: we'll have to get married. I always hoped we would, eventually.'

For the first time she looked at him with a little tenderness. 'Thanks for that, anyway. I was sure you'd ask me to get rid of it.'

'I don't like the thought of destroying something we've made together,' he said simply. 'I respect a woman's right to decide, of course, but personally I don't like abortion - the one bit of me that's rather old-fashioned, perhaps.'

'How odd that you and Govinda should hold the same view. He's a strong believer in the sanctity of life.'

'You've been back there again, then?'

'I've been there ever since the exams finished. It was only when I missed my second period that I came back to London to see the college doctor. The baby's due in January, so it completely fucks up my final year. There's no point in even starting.' She began to cry again.

'I'm sure we could manage between us,' Jazz said in earnest. 'I've got all the lecture notes, and when the baby comes I can look after it while you study. I can defer my Law Society exams for a year.' He knelt beside her, looking up into her tear-stained face. 'You mustn't give up, Sheila. You had your heart set on a legal career, and your results this year were brilliant. I, um, checked to see how you'd done.'

Sheila was silent for a minute, then she looked him in the eye. 'I'm really grateful for the offer, but I'd more or less made up my mind to chuck it up even before I knew I was pregnant. I'm sorry, Jazz; you haven't wrecked anything. I was just letting off steam.'

'You want to chuck it in? Why, for God's sake?'

She laughed. 'That's it exactly, for God's sake. I've decided to live at the ashram permanently.'

'What!' Jazz jumped to his feet. 'How the hell did that bugger persuade you to do that?'

Sheila bridled. 'He's not a "bugger",' she retorted angrily. 'He's kind and caring, and sort of ... well ... all-knowing really.'

'All-knowing my arse!' He began to pace the room agitatedly. 'You're just on a trip, Sheila, that's all. And it's a trip that's a hell of a lot more dangerous than an acid trip too! You've surrendered yourself body and soul to someone you hardly know, and the fact that you're intelligent makes it all the more bizarre!'

Sheila was on her feet now. 'You've no idea what the fuck you're talking about!'

'And you have no idea what the fuck you're doing!'

'I know exactly what I'm doing! I'm leaving!'

'Wait a minute.' Jazz blocked the door. 'What about the baby?'

'My baby, my problem,' she said scornfully. 'I don't need you, and I certainly wouldn't marry you if you were the last man on earth!' She pushed past him and yanked the door open. 'Oh, and don't worry,' she said over her shoulder, 'I won't come after you for child maintenance.'

Jazz watched her storm down the stairs, heard the front door bang violently. Part of him felt like running after her and begging her to marry him, but the rational part of him knew exactly what her reaction would be. He closed the door, and threw himself upon the bed, his mind a mass of conflicting emotions. Having managed to convince himself that he had overcome her rejection of him, her sudden reappearance, looking more beautiful and desirable than ever, had reawakened all his old feelings.

She's carrying my child! My son, perhaps! he thought. *There's no way she's going to walk out of my life just like that!* He consoled himself with the thought that when Sheila had cooled down, she would realise that the child would need its father. They would work out something between them. He got up, feeling better, and made himself a coffee.

2

Sheila had known she was pregnant when she missed her first period; her monthly cycle was so regular that she could almost set her watch by it. She had half-convinced herself, however, that the stress of working hard for her second year exams had thrown her metabolism out of gear. Immediately after her last exam she had taken the bus down to Plymouth, and then hitch-hiked to Brindavan; in the temple she had prayed that her suspicions might be unfounded. A week passed without any show, and physically she found herself feeling very well, as if her body were telling her that it was happy with its condition.

Mentally, however, she was all over the place. She knew that her parents, already miffed that she had not come home, would have a blue fit when she told them, and insist that she marry the father, but she had no doubt that marriage to Jazz would prove disastrous. She was also exercised about her studies: should she continue or not? She had been inclined to give up the course, but now that an unplanned pregnancy seemed to be pushing her in that direction, the stubborn streak within her felt resentful.

The thought of another summer working as a shop assistant was too much and she decided to stay on at Brindavan if Govinda agreed. She hoped that her period might come - she prayed every day that it would - but if it did not, then perhaps the peaceful atmosphere would help her resolve her dilemma more easily. She spoke to Govinda, who was happy for her to stay. He asked no questions.

As it turned out, the serenity of the ashram gave her far too much time to think. *I'd have been better off with a job!* she sighed. As she sat in the temple day after day trying vainly to calm her mind for meditation, all she could think of was the cataclysmic effect a baby would have upon her future. Not only would she have to give up her studies, but how on earth would she be able to stay at Brindavan with a child?

The date for her period came and went, and she could no longer avoid the certainty that she was pregnant. She decided to return to London and ask the college doctor about the possibility of an abortion, citing her anxiety about her studies, hoping that he would stretch the words of the Abortion Act to cover her situation. She spoke to Govinda, and he promised to speak to Simon about giving her a lift back to London.

The following Sunday, Govinda came and sat down with them all at lunch, not something he did very often. He looked at each of them in turn before beginning to speak. 'We live in an age when no value is placed upon life, when almost no consideration at all is given to the meaning and purpose of life. Two people come together and allow their passions to run way with them, heedless of the possible consequences, and when that most natural of consequences of such behaviour, a pregnancy, occurs, what do they do? Because it will be financially or socially or in some other way inconvenient to them, they decide to destroy that life which they so thoughtlessly created. Quite apart from the mental trauma that the girl may suffer either then, or later in life when the realisation of what she has done perhaps strikes home, there is the issue of the terrible karma that results from taking an innocent life.'

'But if a girl becomes pregnant by accident,' Anthony said, 'it's a bit hard on her to be saddled with a baby, especially if the chap refuses to marry her.'

'There you have it,' replied the guru, shaking his head sadly. 'Young people today have sexual relations without bothering to take precautions, without thinking of the consequences, and then they call it an "accident". Was it an "accident" that they had sex in the first place? Was it an "accident" that they failed to take sufficient precautions to avoid a pregnancy?

'In the golden age, the purpose of sex was procreation, and it took place within the bounds of marriage. Nowadays, you all think that sex is just another bit of fun to be indulged in, like having a drink or smoking a joint. Well, my friends,' and he paused to look at each of them in turn, 'if you indulge in unprotected sex, it is your moral duty to care for the child that you bring into being. All other considerations - *all* other considerations - are of secondary importance.'

'But Govinda,' Anthony persisted, 'some of these people might be too poor, or too young, or unfit in some other way to take proper care of a child. That can't be in its best interests, surely?'

'So it is better to murder it rather than let it live a life that may be less than satisfactory? If we applied that criterion to every pregnancy, there would be very few people on the planet! Many children are born to parents who are unfit to look after them, who neglect them, and even abuse them. Unfortunately, it is the karma of the child to suffer such a life.'

'But might it not be the karma of the child to be aborted?' ventured Simon.

'It may very well be so, just as it may be the karma of a man to be murdered, but that excuses neither the abortionist nor the murderer.'

'But surely the difference is that a foetus only a few weeks old isn't even recognisably human,' Sheila suggested.

Govinda looked at her kindly. 'A doctor would certainly agree with you, Sheila, but spiritually there is no difference between abortion and murder, whatever your law books may tell you. Listen carefully, all of you. There are three things required in order to create a human being: firstly, an egg from the womb, secondly a sperm from the man, but thirdly, and most importantly of all, the divine spark, the atma or soul, that comes from God. The atma becomes infused into the egg at the moment of fertilisation, bringing with it the accumulated karma from previous incarnations. At that very moment, a divine being is brought into existence, and to abort that divinity is to spit in the face of the Lord!'

A deathly silence had followed, and in that silence Sheila understood two things: that she would not abort her baby, and that somehow Govinda had known not only of her condition but also her intention. Her belief in his omniscience was born at that moment.

Back in London, the pregnancy confirmed, Sheila had developed a great anger towards Jazz, who had been careless at best, and possibly deceitful, and she had wanted to hurt him - badly. Now, as she walked away from his digs, she knew that the greatest hurt he could possibly suffer was to be deprived of any part in the upbringing of his child. If Govinda would allow her to bring up the child in Brindavan, that would be twisting the knife in the wound. She telephoned Brindavan that evening, bursting into tears as she told Govinda about the baby.

'My dear Sheila, you must come back here at once and let us look after you. Brindavan is your home, and it will be the home of your child as well.'

Sheila felt great consolation and relief at Govinda's words, even though she doubted that she was cut out for the life of a recluse. *And one with a baby at that!* And as for the boys, if Govinda was not concerned, why should she be? *It might be quite amusing to see how they cope with me waddling about!* she chuckled.

3

Anthony threw himself onto his bunk, bunched up the grimy pillows beneath his neck, and stared at the ceiling, panting heavily. Sweat from his forehead carved tiny gullies in the grime on his face, his sodden shirt stuck to his chest, and his back stuck to his sleeping bag. Even his legs were sweating. He really needed to plunge into the stream, but could not summon up the energy to drag himself down there. Ashram life was not turning out quite as he had imagined it.

When he had first visited the Brixton centre two summers before with Mike Weedon, a dope-smoking friend from art school who had heard about "this amazing Indian guru, man" from some third party, he had had only the haziest notion of Eastern religion, derived mainly from articles in the Sunday press about Maharishi. He had been stunned by the experience, Govinda's discourse making him squirm as he realised how shallow his life so far had been. He went back each of the following three weekends, by which time he had decided that he wanted to give up everything and live the life of a contemplative. He sought a private interview with Govinda, who, to Anthony's great surprise, sought to dissuade him.

'You have a proverb here,' the guru said. 'It says "Look before you leap". This I urge you to do. Although it is meritorious to renounce the world for a life of prayer, and while I am flattered that my simple words should in such a short time have had such a profound effect upon you, you must ask yourself what you really know about me. Before you commit yourself to such a drastic course of action, you must examine and investigate, in order to see whether this sort of life is really what you want, or merely a whim.'

'But I've lost all interest in my course. I just want to be with you all the time, to learn the truth about life, and God.'

'It is far from an easy life, I can assure you. It requires the most intensive training of the mind, a great deal of mental discipline and self-control, in order to overcome the senses. It is beyond even the comprehension of ordinary people. Do you think that you can aspire to that degree of control and discipline?'

'I'd certainly like to give it a try!'

'Keep coming here at the weekends, and see how things appear to you in a few months. It would not be wise to throw up your studies on what may turn out to be nothing but a passing fancy. What is your course of study, by the way?'

'I'm at art school.'

Govinda laughed. 'If life is maya, an illusion, then what does that make art? An illusion of an illusion perhaps. I can understand why you have lost your belief in it.'

'When can I come then?'

'I suggest that you give it until Christmas. By the way, isn't that charming young lady who comes with you your girlfriend?'

'Er, yes.'

'And have you discussed these thoughts and feelings with her? If not, you should.'

During the autumn term Anthony had become increasingly disillusioned with his studies, and looked forward to the day when Govinda said he could quit. At the beginning of December he told the guru that his resolve was undiminished, and it was agreed that he would move into the Brixton house in the new year.

'It will, however, be necessary for you to find some form of employment,' Govinda told him. 'Jimmy is working less and less, and our budget is tight. Have you told your family of your plans?'

'I'm going home for Christmas, so I'll tell them then.'

Christmas had been awful, but no more nor less than Anthony had expected.

'It was bad enough when you decided to go to art school,' his father thundered, 'mixing with all those arty-farty left-wing hippy layabouts! I didn't think things could get any worse! Now you're telling us you're going to join some sort of commune.'

'It's not a commune, Dad! It's a Hindu religious centre.'

'Religious centre my fanny! It's probably just a dressed up opium den!'

'Oh, for God's sake, Dad! Don't be ridiculous!'

'Don't you talk to me like that, you little whipper-snapper! I paid good money for your education, and this is what I get in return? You're just a waste of space, Anthony, a complete waste of space. Just pack your bags and bugger off to your commune and don't bother coming back until you've got all this nonsense out of your system.'

Anthony had not been surprised by his father's reaction. It was exactly what he had expected from a died-in-the-wool Tory civil servant working for the Home Office. He belonged to a generation of dinosaurs which did not understand that their ways were passing, that a new age would begin in the not too distant future, that the ancient wisdom of the East, filtering into the West through teachers like Govinda, would point the way to a new direction that would save mankind from itself. The crass materialism and power politics that had made the twentieth century the age of world wars and genocide would ultimately pass away, and an age of peace and harmony would be ushered in.

Possessed of the unbeatable confidence of the young, Anthony thought it would not be long before he would be able to show his father just how wrong he had been, and to vindicate the path he had chosen. He was also pleased that his father's hostility had allowed him to move into the centre two weeks earlier than planned.

Over the next few months, Anthony held occasional secret phone conversations with his mother - who had made it clear to him (though not to her husband) that she had no intention of severing her ties with him - and with Anna, his sister. The pair had been the best of friends from childhood, always able to talk to each other about anything, happy to confide secrets, doubts and fears with full confidence that understanding, empathy and encouragement would always be at hand.

Anna was an enthusiastic correspondent, and kept Anthony informed of everything going on at home and in her own life in a lengthy, weekly letter. His replies, shorter and less frequent, were sent to her at a friend's home. She also found time to come up from the suburbs at least once a month to meet him for lunch or tea, and although Anthony enjoyed these visits, he was concerned that his attachment to his sister might prove to be an obstacle to his search for spiritual perfection.

Rosie was an altogether different problem. He had met her a few months before his first trip to Brixton, and since he wanted to share everything with her, he had taken her with him on his second visit. It had been almost a surprise to him that Rosie, who numbered rock concerts and horror films among her principal forms of relaxation, had enjoyed herself so much that she had insisted on accompanying him all the time. She had even brought some of her friends on occasion, including Sheila.

Anthony had not managed to pluck up the courage to speak to Rosie about his ambition, deciding to hedge his bets: if things did not work out as he hoped, Rosie would still be there; and if they did, he could always tell her then. But he did not. Instead, he lied to her, telling her that he had moved in with Govinda for financial reasons. Nor did he tell her that he had quit college and taken a job. As a result, life became awkward.

Anthony's bedsit had been the only place available for the pair to make love, since Rosie shared a room with another girl. Even after Anthony had first spoken to Govinda about his spiritual ambitions, the practice of making love two or three times a week in his room continued, for despite his supposed desire to renounce the world, he did not have the will-power to resist when Rosie was in an amorous mood. Moreover, a sudden change of routine would have required an explanation.

That change occurred naturally with the move, much to Rosie's annoyance. 'We don't have any time to ourselves these days,' she complained one evening, 'and we haven't done "it" since before Christmas. Can't we sneak up to your room?'

'We can't do it here, darling!'

'Why ever not?'

'Because it's a religious centre, and if Govinda found out, he'd probably chuck me out.'

Rosie pouted. 'That might not be such a bad idea! Then you'd have to get another bedsit.'

'I don't want to annoy Govinda.'

Rosie was thoughtful for a while. 'Why don't we just find a cheap hotel?'

'I can't afford a hotel!'

'A *cheap* hotel! And I'd go halves.' She snuggled up to him. 'We'd only need to stay a few hours,' she wheedled, stroking his thigh. 'I can feel that you want to!' She took a hand and placed it on her breast.

'Okay! But not here!' Anthony hissed, disengaging himself. 'You find somewhere, and we'll meet up.'

Later that week they went to a seedy hotel in Victoria and spent an entire afternoon making sweaty love. It proved to be the first of several similar rendezvous over the course of the next few months, and Anthony felt increasingly wretched after each session. He felt not only that he was letting himself down, but that he was actively deceiving Govinda. Eventually, the strain forced him to tell Rosie the truth.

'I've got something to tell you, Rosie,' he said, after they had made love.

'Oh no!' she laughed. 'You're pregnant!'

'Be serious for a moment.' He sat up and looked earnestly at her. 'I'm going to become a monk.'

Rosie laughed hysterically. 'That's even funnier than my line!'

'I'm being serious.'

Rosie sat up so suddenly that her breasts jiggled tantalisingly. 'We've been fucking all afternoon and now you tell me you're going to become a monk!'

'Yes. After living with Govinda for all these months, I've decided I'd like to become a proper member of his group.'

'So what becomes of us?'

'Well, of course, if I sort of become a monk, I can't have an ordinary relationship with a woman.'

'Oh, this has all just been an "ordinary relationship" has it? I thought I meant a bit more to you than that!' She began to sob.

'No, Rosie, no! I didn't mean our relationship was ordinary,' Anthony gabbled. 'I just meant that as a monk I'd have to give up the things of the world, you know, like going down the pub with the blokes, that sort of thing.'

'I've given you everything,' she retorted, 'and now I'm just on a par with going down the pub with your mates!'

'You know I didn't mean it like that! You're deliberately taking things the wrong way. I just want to live like Govinda, and the last thing I ever expected was that it would come between us. I can't help myself. Please try to understand.'

She looked dolefully at him through red and puffy eyes. Her mascara had run, her hair was tousled from their exertions, and her breasts heaved. Within seconds she realised that her little-girl-lost look was making no impression. Suddenly, her eyes narrowed. 'That's why you moved in with Govinda!' she exclaimed.

'Er, yes.'

'So in effect you've lied to me for the last eight months!'

'I wouldn't put it like that, Rosie!'

She jumped off the bed and threw her clothes on. At the door, she turned and looked at him. 'You've been a lying bastard all this time, and I was just too stupid to see it!'

Rosie never came to Brixton again, and Anthony was easily able to convince himself that she had found someone else. He knew that she would be a good wife and mother, and would be happier in a new relationship than she would ever have been with him. He persuaded himself that he would have been a lousy father, and that their relationship, founded on naked lust, would eventually have ended. *You've saved her from a lifetime of misery, old chap!* he congratulated himself.

He never guessed the truth: that Rosie had gone home, given her parents many loving hugs and kisses, and gone to bed that night after washing down a large quantity of sleeping tablets with a bottle of wine. She left no note, no explanation; did not point the finger of blame at anybody.

4

Govinda broke the news of Sheila's condition firstly to Jimmy. It was late September, and with her slight frame, the pregnancy was already beginning to show.

'And you're goin' to let her stay until the baby's born?' Jimmy queried, not a little disturbed by the news.

'Jimmy, she has nowhere else to go. Her parents don't want her, and there is no-one else with whom she can stay. What else can we do?'

'I don't want to sound uncharitable or anythin', but an ashram's hardly the right place for a pregnant woman.'

'Why ever not?'

'Well, just lookin' at it from her point of view, we aren't exactly replete with home comforts, are we?'

'In my country, women give birth on a mud floor and bring up children without any of your Western so-called comforts.'

'I know, Govinda, but we don't have the climate for that sort of thing here. And what's goin' to happen once she has the kid?'

'She will continue to live here.'

'But there isn't the space! That room of hers isn't big enough for all the stuff she'll need - and talking of that, who's goin' to pay for cots, prams and all that sort of paraphernalia?'

'Just remember, my friend, that Brindavan is a charitable institution, and it would be against our principles to turn her out. As for space, I thought that you and Sheila could exchange rooms once the child is born, just until we can sort out some other accommodation.'

Jimmy pursed his lips. 'Anythin' you say,' he said stiffly. 'But the boys aren't goin' to like this any better than me.'

'Please, Jimmy! Not "boys", but "brothers". They are monks now, after all. Please address them as such in future.'

'I never expected things to get so formal. I thought we'd knock about pretty much the same as we did in London.'

'You and I can "knock about", as you call it, but Simon and Anthony require discipline. I am no longer their friend but their teacher, their master, and between guru and disciple there has to be some distance, some formality. On their side, they are entitled to be treated with the respect that their decision to renounce the world deserves, and not to be lumped in with any old visitor who drops in for the occasional weekend.'

'Yes, of course.' He rose to leave.

'Oh, Jimmy, one other thing,' Govinda added as Jimmy reached the door. ''Would you please no longer smoke in the house. It not only sets a bad example to the Brothers, but that disgusting, stale smell percolates into the temple and disturbs the vibration there.'

'Oh … alright … sorry about that.'

Jimmy was right: Simon and Anthony were indeed disturbed to learn that Sheila was not only going to be a permanent resident, but that within a few months would have a baby. They decided to speak to Govinda.

'We're a bit concerned that Sheila's going to be living here,' Simon said. 'It was okay over the summer because we expected her to be going back to college, but we don't think it's proper to have a woman living in a monastery.'

'Brother Simon, this is not a monastery but an ashram. In an ashram, renunciates of both sexes live harmoniously together pursuing their spiritual quest.'

'But renunciates don't have babies!'

'And we do think Sheila was a bit underhand getting your permission to stay when she must have known she was pregnant,' Anthony added.

'Sheila was in no way underhand.'

'You mean she told you?' Simon asked, eyebrows raised.

'The Lord told me before she did. The Lord has told me many things, which I cannot yet divulge until the time is right. I will tell you this, however: there is a strong spiritual connection between Sheila's baby and Brindavan. Please treat her with due respect, for she is not only under my protection but that of Lord Krishna himself.'

5

Sheila's life at Brindavan was not all that she had expected. Although she was on the whole happier than she had been for some time, she was unhappy that her dreams of Krishna had ceased. When she had come back after her exams, the dreams had returned on a regular basis with a sexual intensity that made her blush to recall them. She had at first put this down to the fact that she had had no sexual outlet since breaking up with Jazz, but it had been almost shocking to recall the wantonness of her behaviour in her dreams. The Kama Sutra paled by comparison.

She made no mention of the continuing dreams to Govinda; it would have been too embarrassing. Instead, she had sought to sublimate her feelings by spending as much time as possible in prayer and meditation in the temple. It was to no avail: almost every night the dreams returned, each one more sexually explicit than the last.

After her pregnancy had been confirmed, however, the dreams stopped. At first Sheila was relieved, for she wanted her love for Krishna to be spiritual, not sexual. Within a few weeks, however, she began to worry that Krishna had abandoned her because of her impure thoughts and desires; this made her depressed, and she began to doubt Govinda's interpretation of the dreams. *Maybe they were nothing more than dirty thoughts!* Finally, she had to speak to him, for there was no-one else in whom she could confide.

'My dear Sheila, you should have come to me much earlier with these doubts and fears. I could have saved you much worry.'

'I was just too embarrassed! The dreams were so …. well …. you know!'

'I understand. Let me reassure you that I am utterly convinced that your first dream was a divine visitation. At that time the Lord did not reveal to me His purpose, but since then you have become with child, and it seems to me that Lord Krishna has chosen you to be the vessel for a divine incarnation, just as God chose Mary to become the mother of Jesus. I am certain that your child is destined to be a great soul, and a power for good in the world; another Chaitanya perhaps, or another Mirabai.'

'But why did the dreams suddenly stop?'

'I suspect that the Lord saw how embarrassed you were becoming, and therefore decided to give you some peace. Do not fear; He has not abandoned you.'

Two nights later the dreams returned, but in a very different manner. Sheila was no longer the wanton lover of the young cowherd, rutting in the forest, but now the consort of the ruler of Mathura. Arm in arm, she wandered with Krishna through splendid palaces and beautiful gardens, clothed in costly silken robes, respected and adored by the populace.

In the privacy of the royal apartments, Krishna told her of the glorious life that awaited their first-born, all the while stroking her naked body with soft finger-tips, caressing her swelling abdomen, and playfully twining his fingers in the curls of her pubic mound. As he murmured endearments, his lips brushed the hard nipples of her burgeoning breasts, and he made love to her gently, not penetrating her too deeply.

'Although I have taken an earthly form, my love,' he told her, 'yet know that I am in reality none other than Vishnu, the Great Preserver of the Cosmos, and that our child will be both human and divine, destined to be an inspiration to all humanity.'

After two more almost identical dreams, Sheila sought out Govinda and told him what she had experienced.

'It is as I told you, child. I have seen all this in my meditations of the last few days.'

'What I don't understand though, Govinda, is how this could be a divine conception if Jazz is the biological father.' Sheila shrugged her shoulders.

'I cannot say what the biological position is. It may well be that your former friend's sperm began the process that we call conception, but even if that is the case, I can assure you that Lord Krishna himself instilled the spark of divine consciousness in the child at that moment, so that it does not carry the accumulated baggage of karma that ordinary mortals do.'

The dreams continued, occurring two, sometimes three times a week, and Sheila recovered her happiness. She refused to allow the reserve she detected from the men to affect her, and as her abdomen swelled, and the signs of life within her womb became more persistent, she became increasingly radiant. Excused by reason of her condition from almost all chores, she spent a lot of time talking with Govinda, walking in the valley, and meditating in the temple. Relations with Jimmy became strained for a while shortly after Christmas when Govinda decided the exchange of rooms should take place, but as the time for her confinement drew near, all the men-folk became solicitous in the extreme, allowing her to do almost nothing for herself.

Sheila regretted nothing. She did not yearn for her old family or friends, nor for her abandoned studies and forsaken career. Everything she could possibly want lay within the boundaries of Brindavan and the confines of her womb.

CHAPTER 4

When Sheila did not turn up at college for the beginning of her final year, Jazz knew for certain that she had thrown in her lot with the Indian. The temptation to drive down to Devon to see her arose now and then, for she was after all carrying his child, but the thought of Govinda's icy stare and acid tongue was enough to deter him. He absolved himself from a charge of cowardice by persuading himself that his Law studies were more important, for as a solicitor he would be able to earn enough to maintain his child - and perhaps entice Sheila back.

One night all his hopes and fears seem to materialise in a nightmare. He was standing by a potted palm on the terrace of what appeared to be a country house, glass in hand, watching the dancers swirling by inside. Everyone else was in evening dress, but he was wearing ordinary clothes, and feeling somewhat out of place. Suddenly he spied Sheila waltzing by in the arms of her partner, and a warm glow began to spread through him, beginning at his heart and pulsing gradually outwards until every nerve and fibre of his body was tingling with love and energy. He moved towards the French windows to find his love, but Govinda suddenly appeared, blocking his way. He too was in a dinner suit, but on his head he wore a dazzling golden turban, in the centre of which gleamed a huge and blindingly brilliant diamond.

'She is no longer yours,' he said matter-of-factly. 'She now belongs to me.'

Jazz tried to push him aside, but the Indian was as solid as a boulder, his flesh hard and unyielding, as if made of granite or marble, and his feet seemed to be cemented to the floor. As he struggled to push past, he saw the guru reach up for the diamond, which he plucked from the turban, and Jazz saw that the diamond was affixed to a long, shining pin. With a face devoid of any emotion, the Indian held the diamond between his fingers and slowly and deliberately thrust the pin between Jazz's ribs and into his heart. There was an excruciating pain, and his body began to sag at the knees as the darkness of death stole upon him. Jazz woke abruptly, sitting bolt upright, panting for breath and bathed in sweat. For a second he wondered where he was, and then slumped back on the pillow. *He'll kill me if I go there!*

The dream unnerved Jazz for weeks, and robbed him of any will-power to visit Sheila, or even write to her. He did write a note of good wishes in a Christmas card, but she did not reciprocate, and back at college he threw himself into his studies with determined single-mindedness, only to be thrown into utter disarray by the receipt of a short note from Sheila later in January: "I have given birth to a son, whose name is Gopala. I thought it right for you to know, but I don't want to see you. Sheila."

I have a son! I'm a father! The concept of fatherhood both awed and frightened him, and Sheila's terse note confused him. *Why write at all if she doesn't want to see me? Maybe she wrote that because of the guru guy.* He could not decide whether Sheila had written with the guru's knowledge, or whether she had done so behind his back. If the latter, did she still harbour feelings for him, despite her words?

After several days of thinking about the letter and the fact that he was now a father, to the exclusion of everything else, including his studies, he decided that the only way to discover the truth was to go and find out. *And if she tells me to fuck off, at least I'll know where I stand!*

Despite his affected disdain for his Muslim background, Jazz found - somewhat to his surprise - that he was proud that his first-born had been a son: boys carried the family name, and conferred immortality upon a man. He discovered that he desperately wanted to see this son, and determined that no-one would prevent him: *Certainly not some half-baked Indian fakir!* Let him just try, and he would feel the weight of the law; as the father of the child he must have rights, and he would not hesitate to enforce them. Having skipped Family Law, which he had regarded as an area of law best suited to women, he was not sure what the rights of the father of an illegitimate child were, but he would arm himself with the legal situation before going to Devon. For the first time ever, he felt a pang of regret that they were not back in Iran, where the father's rights were sacrosanct.

2

It was a matter of chance that Simon was crossing the yard that afternoon when Jazz drove in. He recognised Sheila's former boyfriend as soon as he got out of the car, and saw from the aggressive jut of his chin and his tight lips that trouble was in store. He quickly crossed to the car, interposing himself between Jazz and the house. 'What do you want here?' he asked, implying with a sneer that he could not possibly have any business at Brindavan.

'I'm here to see my son,' Jazz announced with a grim smile.

Simon mastered his surprise with no little difficulty. 'What on earth do you mean?' he blustered. *The silly bitch must have written to him!*

'Don't give me any of your bullshit!' Jazz glared aggressively at his adversary. 'I know Sheila's had a baby boy. He's my son, and I'm not leaving until I've seen him.'

'You can't!'

'Are you going to stop me?'

'No, what I mean is, that they're not here. The baby was taken ill - jaundice, I think. Babies get it. He's in hospital, and Sheila's with him.'

The two men regarded each other for a few seconds with undisguised hostility; neither flinched. Then Jazz's face softened into concern. 'Where are they?'

'Plymouth General. It's the nearest big hospital. If you leave now, you'll just catch visiting time I expect.'

Jazz regarded Simon for a while, but his bland face revealed nothing. 'I'll be on my way then.'

'Right. Give Sheila our best wishes.' He watched the car until it had disappeared around a bend in the track, then turned on his heel and ran towards the house, his jaws clenched. *I warned*

Govinda against letting that slut stay! He congratulated himself on having been proved right.

Simon had always envisaged himself as a leader of men. His father was a successful financier in a large City firm, and from his teens Simon had seen himself following in papa's footsteps: the idea of moving millions of pounds, billions even, around the world, shaping destinies, making and breaking fortunes, excited him. Regrettably, Simon's ambitions were not matched by a capacity for hard work; he failed to understand that men who acquired positions of power did so not only through aptitude but also through sheer grit and slog. His father had been no exception, spending his early working years in relentless toil to drive himself to the top of the pile. With no time for leisure or pleasure in his twenties and thirties, it was only in his early forties that he found time to marry.

Born into a home where the trappings of success were evident, Simon took them for granted. As an only child, he was doted upon by his mama, who ensured that his every want and whim were satisfied, cementing in the child the belief that he was the most important being in the universe. His father, who still worked hard and accordingly saw little of his son in the most important formative years, took for granted that he had passed on to him the same intelligence and determination that he possessed. He had forgotten that it had been the privations of an underprivileged background and the class snobbery he had experienced at Cambridge, as a mere grammar school boy, which had fashioned his determination to succeed. Grafted onto his native wit, that had given him the fortitude to overcome obstacles that would have daunted lesser men. Thus he made the mistake of many self-made men that his son, starting from a more privileged position than his father, would be in a better position to make a success of life.

Mr. Hill had been brought rudely to earth by Simon's appalling O Level results, which had prevented him from moving into the sixth form at his private school. He had taken firm measures, engaging a set of private tutors to coach Simon at home, and ensuring that he was kept fully informed as to his son's progress. After three years of academic coercion, Simon had acquired decent enough A Levels to obtain a place reading English at a provincial university.

Following three further years of somewhat more relaxed education, but working sufficiently hard to graduate with an average degree - impelled by his father's threats to cut him off if he failed - Simon obtained a job in a well-known publishing house through his father's connections. Although he enjoyed the job at first, he discovered within a year that it was going to take a long time and a lot of hard work to reach the top. He did not want to wait until he was at best middle-aged before he acquired the sort of power and influence his father wielded: he wanted it *now*. He began to grow dissatisfied with his lot in life.

It was at this low point, when Simon was seriously thinking of tendering his resignation, that he met Jimmy Partington at a party given by an author in the publication of whose latest volume he had played a minor role. His greatest quality, one which his employers valued, was an ability to converse with complete strangers in such a way as to make them think they were very important. He had been briefed to attend this particular gathering to approach other authors who would no doubt be there. He met Jimmy at the buffet table.

'I do recommend the canapes,' Jimmy said. 'In fact, I can recommend everythin'. The caterer's a friend of mine, and I got him the job!' He laughed in a horsey sort of way.

Although a little put off by this effete stranger, Simon nonetheless introduced himself. 'I'm Simon Hill, of Hoggarts.' He held out a hand. 'Are you a writer too?'

Jimmy guffawed as he shook hands. 'Great heavens no! I'm Gordon's interior decorator - all this glitz and glamour' - he waved a hand airily about himself - 'is the work of yours truly! In conception only, I hasten to add: I employ other chaps to get their hands dirty.' He laughed again. 'The name's Partin'ton, old boy, Jimmy Partin'ton.'

Simon nodded politely, but said nothing: he did not stand to gain any brownie points from talking to a pansy interior decorator. He began to lade his plate with some of the offerings on display. His new acquaintance laid a hand on his arm.

'Tell me,' he said in a conspiratorial whisper, 'is his writin' any good? Gordon I mean. I never read books meself - life's bad enough as it is, without havin' to read about it, what?' He laughed so enthusiastically that Simon could not help smiling.

'According to some people, it's all pretentious crap, but since it sells, it doesn't really matter,' he replied. 'But don't tell anyone I said so.'

Jimmy roared with laughter. 'Mum's the word!' He mimed zipping his lips. 'Look,' he said, 'why don't we leave these terribly borin' people, and these pifflin' nibbles, and go and have some real food somewhere, what?'

To his own surprise, Simon had agreed. He had momentarily wondered whether he was being picked up, for although his companion was not overtly effeminate, his manner was sufficiently out of line for Simon to question his sexual orientation, but he was undoubtedly amusing, and the party was exceedingly dull. They had taken a taxi to a small but excellent Italian restaurant - 'Not many people know about it,' Jimmy said, 'and I plan to keep it that way!' - and the two men enjoyed a pleasant evening together. This had been largely due to Jimmy's talent for drawing people out, and Simon had found himself talking mainly about his life so far and his disenchantment with his current situation.

As they parted company on the pavement, Jimmy handed Simon a pastel-pink business card, his name, address and number embossed in scarlet. 'I can introduce you to someone who might have a profound effect upon your outlook on life, ol' man,' he said. 'If you think you might be interested, give me a call this weekend.' He patted Simon on the arm, winked, and sauntered off into the night.

3

'Come in, Sheila. Is the baby sleeping?'

'Yes, Govinda. He's as good as gold.' She smiled nervously. Her insides had been churning from the moment Simon informed her with a tight-lipped, self-satisfied smile, that Govinda wished to speak to her. 'Is there a problem?' she asked tremulously, acutely conscious of Simon standing behind her. She could visualise the smug look on his face.

'Simon tells me that your former boyfriend was here this afternoon,' Govinda said, his voice flat. 'The Muslim boy,' he added, waving a hand dismissively.

'Oh. I didn't know.'

'Simon had sufficient wit to send him off on a wild goose chase, but I have no doubt he will be back tomorrow.'

'I see.' Her voice was very small. She knew what was coming.

'But *do* you see, Sheila? Do you really see what trouble this young man could bring upon us?'

'Trouble? I don't understand.'

'He came here to see his son. *His son!*' Govinda rose from his armchair and began to pace the room slowly, like a caged tiger. 'I have to admit that I am not entirely surprised that he came,' he said, addressing the room in general, and not looking at Sheila. 'He is after all a college boy, and presumably has brains enough to calculate the length of a pregnancy. A visit from him has never been entirely out of the question. But,' - and now he ceased pacing, and fixed Sheila with a hard stare - 'I do have to ask myself how he was so positive that the child was a boy.'

'It's all my fault, Govinda,' Sheila whispered, unable to tear her eyes away from his face.

'*Your* fault, Sheila?' he said, placing a hand on his heart. 'How on earth could it be your fault?'

'I wrote to him.'

'I'm sorry, my dear, I didn't catch what you said. Speak up.'

'I wrote to him.'

He looked at her, frowning, as if trying to understand the purport of what she had said. 'Let me get this right,' he said at last, resuming his pacing. 'This person, with whom you have had no dealings since last summer - that is correct, is it not?' He looked at her for confirmation: she nodded. 'Well, let us thank Lord Krishna for small mercies at least. This person, the supposed father of your child, with whom you have had no contact for more than six months, a young man, I have to remind you, who has contempt for everything that Brindavan stands for, you are now telling me that you wrote to him, to this Muslim, and you told him that he is the father of a son!'

His voice, which had gradually risen as he spoke, finished almost on a scream. Sheila shrank back, terrified.

Govinda resumed his seat. 'Tell me, Sheila,' he said quietly, 'when you wrote to him giving him this information, what did you expect him to do?'

'I told him I didn't want to see him,' she wailed.

'I see. After all these months of silence, you thought that the news that he had a son would have no effect upon him because you said you didn't want to see him.' He lay back in the armchair, shaking his head. 'How could you have been so unutterably stupid?' he said wearily.

There was complete silence for several minutes as he sat gazing out of the window, his face as black and bleak as the night outside. 'He will return tomorrow,' he said, almost in a whisper, talking more to himself than the other two. 'He will demand to see his so-called son. He will want to play a role in the child's life, perhaps even try to take him away from us. Yes, yes. He is a Muslim, and he will want his son to be brought up by his own family.'

He looked up at Sheila and Simon then. 'He cannot be allowed to succeed, for he will ruin everything that I and the Lord have planned for Brindavan. Krishna will not allow him to succeed.'

'But he is Gopala's father,' Sheila said. 'He's got a legal right to see his child.'

Govinda leaped from his seat, his face contorted with rage. Both the others flinched backwards. 'No! No! No!' he screamed, clasping his hands to his head and gritting his teeth. 'How many times do I have to tell you before you understand? Before any of you understand? Gopala is *not* this man's child. He is an incarnation of Lord Krishna, and I will not permit this upstart Persian boy to interfere with Gopala's divine mission!'

He strode to the window and stared out into the blackness, his hands clasped behind his back.

'What do we do then?' Simon ventured.

Govinda turned to face them. 'You,' he snapped, finger pointing to Sheila, 'will go to your room and stay there until I decide what must be done. Simon, fetch Anthony and Jimmy. We have to consider how best to circumvent the consequences of this stupid girl's action.'

Sheila began to weep, her slender frame racked with convulsive sobs. 'Govinda,' she whimpered, falling to her knees at his feet, 'I'm so s-s-sorry!'

The guru's manner changed in a moment. He took the sobbing girl by the shoulders and pulled her to her feet, enfolding her in his arms. As she wept into his breast, he patted her shoulder and stroked her hair. 'There, there! Please do not be upset, Sheila. I have allowed my concern for little Gopala's future to spill over into anger, and that was wrong of me.' He held her at the shoulders, and pushed her away to arm's length, smiling his irresistible smile. 'You must forgive me, my dear. We shall just have to make the best of a bad job, eh?' He raised her chin with his forefinger, until their eyes met. 'Am I forgiven?' he asked softly, smiling, almost pleading.

Sheila smiled back feebly. 'I'm the one who needs to be forgiven,' she croaked. 'I don't know what I was thinking of!' Tears began to well up again.

'Enough tears!' Govinda said briskly. 'If you will forgive me, I shall forgive you. Is it a deal?'

She smiled a little more confidently. 'It's a deal.'

'Good. Off you go then.' He ushered her towards the door. 'Simon! I thought I told you to fetch the others.'

4

'I'm not sure I like all this cloak and dagger stuff,' Anthony said the following afternoon, as he lay on his bunk in the caravan idly watching Simon sort out his dirty washing on the floor. 'It doesn't really go with this sort of life, if you know what I mean.'

Simon looked up from his socks and underpants. 'I would have thought you'd find it quite exciting. A darn sight better than having Jimmy on your back all day, surely?'

'There is that, of course,' Anthony replied with feeling. They had spent much of the previous fortnight renovating one of the old byres, since Govinda was determined that Brindavan should have cows. Jimmy had assumed control of operations and been at his brilliant best, directing the two young men in dictatorial style, with the minimum of physical effort on his own part. 'But it's not really spiritual, is it?'

'Nor is rebuilding a cowshed. Anyway, if Govinda and Jimmy had listened to me in the first place, we wouldn't have all this trouble. I didn't want Sheila here from the start: women spell trouble, and pregnant women double trouble.'

'Well, he couldn't really turn her away, could he? It wouldn't have been Christian.'

'He isn't a Christian.'

'You know what I mean. It wouldn't have been charitable, spiritual, to kick her out. She had nowhere else to go - she told me her parents threw a fit when she told them she was pregnant.'

'Just think what they'd say if they saw the baby!' Simon chortled.

'Hmm. He's a lot darker than I would have expected. Her boyfriend was quite fair, though he had black hair.'

'But some of those Middle Eastern types can be quite dark. Maybe his parents were dark-skinned. These things sometimes skip a generation. I remember my mother telling me when I was a kid that I was the spitting image of her grandfather.'

'I suppose. I remember reading once about a girl who gave birth to a black baby, which caused a hell of a fuss, until they found out one of her great-grandparents had been African.'

Simon nodded, then a frown crossed his face. 'What do you make of this incarnation business?' he asked off-handedly, busying himself with his laundry.

'You mean about the baby?'

Simon looked up. 'Yeah. What's your take on it? You're more au fait with Hindu mythology than me.'

Anthony screwed up his face. 'I don't really know,' he admitted. 'I can understand the concept of God taking human form in order to save the world. After all, we've got the same idea in Christianity. But I don't really know how it works, and I don't know what Govinda's said about the baby except what you've told me.'

'That's all I know. He just came out with it when he was screaming at Sheila last night. I suspect he must have talked to her about it before. Maybe you could ask her when you see her next.'

The result of the council of war the previous night had been that Sheila and her baby had been smuggled out of the ashram in the early hours of the morning and installed in a guest house at Torquay, a sufficient distance from Brindavan to make it unlikely that Jazz would discover her. All traces of her presence in the ashram had been removed. Anthony had been given the job of driving Sheila to her temporary accommodation, and by the time that he returned, a furious Jazz had been and gone. Jimmy told him the story over a late lunch.

'Thought the feller was goin' to burst a ruddy blood vessel!' he laughed. 'Flippin' furious, he was! Never seen a chap so irate before. Mind you, havin' bin sent all the way to Plymouth on a wild goose chase, I couldn't really blame him. Really thought he was goin' to thump Simon!'

'What did he say?'

'What didn't he say! Threatened us with legal proceedins, and said he'd come back with the rozzers if we didn't let him see Sheila and the babe pronto.'

'The police! That's all we need.'

'They wouldn't have done anythin', don't worry. Sheila's over the age of consent, and the feller's not a relative or anythin', so they'd have brushed him off. Anyway, gettin' back to the story, I step in at this point and invite him upstairs to speak to Govinda. That takes the wind out of his sails alright. He was probably expectin' the bum's rush again.'

'So what did Govinda tell him?'

'I'm comin' to that! Don't interrupt! The feller looks at me a bit suspicious like, and says, "What can he have to say to me?", as if he isn't quite relishin' the idea of a chat with the boss. So I tell him that Govinda wants to apologise for him havin' bin misinformed the day before, and to tell him what had really happened. He goes a bit pale, and asks if Sheila and the baby are okay. I say as far as I know, and then he follows me upstairs as meek as a lamb.'

'Jimmy! Please get on with it! What exactly did Govinda tell him?'

'Don't rush me!' Jimmy snorted, shaking his head petulantly. 'I don't like to be rushed!' He sat back, arms folded.

'Sorry! I won't butt in again.'

'Well, alright. Govinda, of course, is at his most charmin'. He welcomes the boy in, offers him coffee, breakfast, whatever. The boy says all he wants is the truth. "And the truth is what you shall have!" Govinda says. Then he asks if Sheila had written to him about the baby, and if he's got the letter with him. The boy hands it over, and Govinda looks at the postmark, then says with a dramatic sigh, "Yes, the date ties in." The Persian lad's puzzled: "Ties in with what?" he asks. Then Govinda launches into such a convincing story that I had to pinch meself to make sure I wasn't dreamin'.

'Sheila had run away, he tells the boy, shortly after the date of the letter. Not only that, but she'd run away with one of the young monks - you, by the way - and he had no idea where the pair of you had gone.'

'What?' Anthony exploded, almost choking on a spoonful of dhall and potato. 'He said Sheila had run away with *me*?'

'Yup! Hilarious, ain't it?'

'I don't think it's funny at all! Surely the chap didn't believe it?'

'Swallowed it hook, line and sinker. His shoulders positively sagged. Not long after, he got up and left, lookin' very woebegone. My guess is that he went straight back to London, but nevertheless, Govinda wants Sheila to stay put for a couple more weeks, just in case he's still hangin' around.'

'Why did he have to tell such a lie?' Anthony whispered.

Jimmy looked puzzled for a moment. 'Don't worry about it, ol' man! Sometimes a little white lie's necessary to smooth over a problem.' He patted Anthony's shoulder, and went out.

Anthony sat for a while longer, then got up, shaking his head, and went to the caravan to catch up on his sleep.

5

As it turned out, Sheila stayed at the guesthouse for a further three weeks, and apart from an occasional call from Govinda inquiring after Gopala's health, her only contact with Brindavan was through Anthony, who visited her two or three times a week. He paid the bill, did such shopping as Sheila required - for Govinda had forbidden her from going out and about in Torquay just in case Jazz was still in the area - and drove her out into the countryside to relieve the tedium of her incarceration.

Given the story Govinda had told, Anthony found this a little embarrassing, and suggested that Simon and Jimmy should share the duty. Simon, who thought Anthony's predicament hilarious, refused point blank, and Govinda would not let his cook leave the ashram even for a day.

Anthony had been afraid that being thrown into the presence of an attractive girl outside the confines of Brindavan would test his resolve to become a renunciate to the limit. He need not have worried. Sheila was so preoccupied with her baby that she paid little attention to Anthony most of the time, save to ask how things were at the ashram.

They did discover, however, that they had the same deep interest in meditation, and spent many an hour together on deserted beaches, wrapped in blankets against the cold, with Gopala sleeping in the car, all three oblivious of the eternal sounds of wind, surf and seabirds.

Nonetheless, after three weeks of regular contact, Anthony felt an attachment beginning to develop between them which he found disconcerting, and when Govinda summoned Sheila back to Brindavan, it was with some relief that Anthony made the trip for the last time.

Simon seemed to have become even more disturbed by the situation than Anthony, pointing out the great danger into which Govinda had placed him by allowing him to spend so much time with Sheila unsupervised. 'I know nothing actually happened - and great credit to you for that - but the point is that it might. A man can reach the limit of his powers of endurance, and if a pretty woman's about, heaven help him!'

Anthony, all too conscious of his own repressed feelings, did not gainsay him, and a few weeks later, allowed himself to be led by Simon into a direct confrontation with Govinda.

'Govinda,' Simon began in his most pompous tone of voice, 'we've asked to see you about Sheila. We understand that you're quite happy for her to continue living here, and we have some idea of the importance of Gopala to you, but …'

'Gopala is of no importance to me personally,' Govinda cut in sharply, eyes narrowing. 'His importance is in relation to the future of Brindavan and its message to the world. One day he will be the head of this ashram and a great teacher. Mark my words.'

A profound silence followed, disturbed only by the insistent ticking of the cheap Woolworths alarm clock standing on Govinda's bedside table.

'Yes,' Simon resumed hesitantly, 'we do appreciate that, but for the present, the fact is - how shall I put it? - Anthony and I feel that Sheila's presence is a bit of a … um … distraction, really. We're trying to pursue a monastic life, and we find her presence here is a bit of an impediment.'

'I would have thought,' Govinda said smoothly, a smile playing about his lips, 'that the presence of a rather attractive young lady would be the most suitable means of testing the strength of your determination.'

Behind him, Jimmy snorted into a handkerchief as he tried to stifle his laughter.

'But, Govinda!' Anthony burst out. 'It can be very distracting when she wears revealing clothes, and she's always in our company at meals with the baby. It's a constant reminder of what we're trying to put behind us.' He blushed deeply.

'That is precisely my point. Surely you're not asking me to banish her to some distant corner of the ashram, never to be seen by human eyes again?' Govinda raised a hand to stifle Simon's protest. 'It was not a genuine question, Simon. Seriously, you have to understand that the vows of monasticism mean nothing at all unless they are constantly tested. Let me illustrate my point with a story.

'Many centuries ago there was an ashram in India with a very strict guru, who forbade his brahmacharis, his monks, to have any dealings with women: they were not to speak to them, or even look at them. One day the guru went on a journey, taking a young disciple with him. After some time they came to a river, on the bank of which stood a young, very beautiful, but scantily clad young girl, afraid to venture across because the current was very strong. When she saw the monks, she fell at their feet and begged, most respectfully, for their assistance.

'The young monk cast his eyes to the ground, deeply insulted that this half-naked girl should even have spoken to such holy men. To his astonishment, however, his guru not only spoke to the girl, but even offered to carry her across the river. Scandalised, he watched the old man pick up the maiden in his arms, and carry her to the far bank.

'As the monks continued on their way in silence, as was their rule, the mind of the younger man seethed with indignation. This man is a hypocrite, he thought, a false guru who does not practise what he preaches. He tells us that we must not even look at a woman, yet he carries a half-naked damsel in his arms.

'As dusk began to fall, they made camp in the forest, but the guru could see that his disciple was troubled. "What ails you, my son?" he asked. "Clearly there is something on your mind. You may speak freely." The young monk allowed all his indignation to pour forth. "Reverend sir," he exclaimed, "daily you exhort us to eschew all contact with women, not even to look into their faces in case we are beguiled and forget our vows, but this morning you shocked me to the roots of my being when you carried that half-naked girl across the river in your arms. How could you behave in such a way, contrary to your own instructions?"

'The guru looked kindly at the younger man. "Is that all that troubles you?" he asked. "It is true that I picked up the girl this morning, but once we had crossed the river, I put her down again. You, my son, have been carrying her all day long."

'In the beginning, my dears,' Govinda said quietly, 'it is necessary that strict conditions are observed, but eventually, with the proper practice, such conditions become unnecessary. The guru was detached from the girls' beauty and nakedness, seeing only a fellow human being in need of assistance, but the young monk saw only the girl's beauty and nakedness, even though he never touched her. Similarly, your determination must be tested until such time as you are detached enough to take the vows of poverty, chastity and obedience.

'It is true that at present we operate in a very informal way, which means that Sheila is constantly in your presence, and I understand that you may find that a little disturbing at times. However, I can promise you that before long pilgrims will begin to flock here in great numbers, seeking a haven of peace from the pressures of the mad world outside, and this will necessitate change. We shall need to become more formal in the way we conduct ourselves in order to accommodate the values of the

Asian community. Things will change, quite possibly in ways that you will not understand, or even like.'

He paused, smiling benevolently at them. 'In the meantime, I suggest that you enjoy the present informality, and sharpen your spiritual ambitions in the presence of the lovely Sheila. Before you know it, the time will have come when, even though you may wish to exchange the most innocent of words with her, it will no longer be possible.

CHAPTER 5

Five years later

The sanctuary was illuminated by the flickering light of dozens of oil lamps and candles. There was no natural light, for the two windows that had once looked out onto the yard, now the car park, had been bricked up. A wooden railing, not dissimilar from an altar rail, divided the sanctuary from the public part of the temple; in its centre was a folding double gate, presently closed. Around the walls ran a continuous shelf at about waist height on which rested a variety of pictures and statues of the multitudinous Hindu deities, and above the shelf other pictures hung from the wall.

In the centre of the sanctuary a bronze statue of Krishna, some three feet in height, stood upon an altar, his flute to his lips and a look of bliss upon his face. On either side there were smaller idols: one of the youthful Krishna dancing upon the outspread hood of the serpent, Kaliya; the other of the baby Krishna playing with a ball of ghee. Oil lamps burned before each one, and clusters of incense sticks sent streamers of scent-laden smoke writhing upwards to the low, soot-blackened ceiling.

The public part of the temple occupied about two-thirds of the floor space, but as this amounted to little more than an area measuring about eighteen feet by twelve, into which almost a hundred people were crammed, the air was heavy with the smell of humanity. The congregation had been sitting stoically, and largely silent, for some fifteen minutes since the temple doors had been opened to admit them, under the stern eye of a monk in white robes positioned within the sanctuary, who shushed from time to time any whispering that was on the verge of getting out of hand.

The cramped conditions were rendered less potentially embarrassing by the fact that the sexes were segregated, men on the right and women on the left, with a narrow strip of red carpet running between them as a sort of no-man's-land. Small children used this neutral area to run up and down as they moved from one family member to another, and the sanctuary guardian tolerated this as long as they did not make too much noise. Babies cried from time to time, and were quickly hushed with bottles or other comforters.

The majority of the people were Indian, with no more than a sprinkling of white faces, and the women's side was a riot of colour, with saris, shawls, and shalwar kameezes of every hue of the rainbow, plus a few not found even there. Light glinted from golden and bejewelled ornaments of every description at ear, nose, throat, wrist and ankle. The Indian ladies were definitely on show, and the more sober "Sunday best" of the scattering of European women made them look like intruding jackdaws at a peacocks' party.

The Asian men were almost uniformly attired in dark trousers and white shirts, with a few wearing suits and ties. Only one or two of the older men wore a kurtah, and just a single elderly gentleman had donned a dhoti.

The younger children were dressed almost entirely in Western clothes, the girls mainly in frocks with puffed sleeves and lots of lace and frills. The older girls, those who had reached or were nearing puberty, wore the shalwar kameez, designed to conceal as far as possible the burgeoning womanhood within. One or two of the more "modern" girls were wearing slacks and loose tops, and attracted disdainful looks from most of the older ladies. The boys generally wore shorts or slacks, according to their age, and shirts or t-shirts.

Beyond the double-doored entrance in the rear wall was a large porch area with racks on either side for shoes, and here too stood a crowd of worshippers, either unable or unwilling to cram themselves into the temple proper. Suddenly there was movement behind them, and they were pressed back against the shoe-racks as a procession of monks marched in. At a signal from the sanctuary monk, the congregation scrambled untidily to its feet, and looked around to see what was happening.

At the head of the procession a small boy marched with great solemnity, his hands clasped at his chest in the attitude of prayer, his large brown eyes staring straight ahead. He wore a crisp white kurtah and dhoti, and was every inch an Indian, with golden-brown skin and raven-black hair. When he reached the sanctuary rail, he stepped smartly to one side, taking his place beside the three white-robed women there, while the six monks in white behind him filed into the sanctuary through the opened gates, fanning out to left and right.

An expectant silence followed. Mothers suppressed rebellious infants with fierce whispers and sharp pinches, while craning their necks to catch a glimpse of the Swami they had come to see. Tension mounted. Then a figure in orange robes appeared in the doorway and walked in slow and solemn fashion along the aisle. Those who were there for the first time let out pent-up breath in noisy exhalations of disappointment as they realised he was a white man.

The Swami approached the altar, picked up the arati lamp standing there already charged with camphor tablets, one of which he picked up and lit from the central oil light, dropping it into the bowl of the lamp. The flames from the burning camphor soared up, illuminating his face as he turned towards the assembly.

So preoccupied with him were most of the people that they failed to notice the entry of the dark-faced, golden-robed Swami until he actually passed them in his stately progress down the aisle. Pursued by a growing whisper of excitement, he entered the sanctuary and took the lamp, which he then proceeded to wave before each deity, melodiously chanting the mantras appropriate to each. In his clockwise progress around the sanctuary, he was followed by his aide, ever ready to top up the arati lamp when the flames burned low. Finally, Govinda moved to the central altar, chanting more loudly and at greater length before the image of Krishna, handing the lamp to his assistant at the conclusion, and seating himself on a low stool to the right. The other monks then also sat, followed by the people, who shoved and jostled to reclaim a patch of ground adequate for their posteriors. Gradually, the rustling and whispering died away, leaving complete silence. Only then did the pooja begin.

The orange Swami led the chanting, the others repeating each line after him, with such of the congregation who were familiar with the words joining in. After the chanting, the monks took turns, at a nod from Govinda, to sing a devotional song, or bhajan, to the accompaniment of a harmonium and finger cymbals. Most of the bhajans were well known, and the worshippers joined in lustily, clapping their hands and swaying from side to side.

Finally, the golden-robed Govinda sang to Lord Krishna in his rich and powerful voice, its beauty visibly affecting many of those present: some wept, while others seemed transported, their eyes closed, their faces beaming with ecstasy. When the song concluded, and the last cadence of the harmonium had died away, Govinda stood up, faced his congregation, and bowed to them with palms held respectfully together.

'Divine friends, why are you here? Where are you going? How are you going to get there? These are questions we must all ask ourselves. Why are we here on this earth? What is the purpose of this existence that we have been granted? It is for one thing only: to work out our karma. It is entirely as a result of actions in past lives that we are exactly where we are in this life. If you are successful and happy, this is not due merely to the whim or caprice of fate: it is because you have done good deeds in previous births. But you must not sit back and congratulate yourselves! If you do nothing in this life to help your fellow creatures, but live an entirely selfish existence, you will readily exhaust your credit balance at the Bank of Karma, and the next time around you will find yourself in a less fortunate position.

'So then, where are we going? Are we merely planning to spend our entire existence moving from one life to another with the intention of building up our karmic credit so that each succeeding birth is better than the last? Until perhaps we become a king, or as rich as Rothschild? No, for all earthly life is nothing but maya, complete illusion. Our task is to try and escape from the eternal cycle of birth, death, and re-birth: the goal of our journey is to achieve oneness with the Supreme Being - by whatever name we happen to call Him. Here we happen to worship that greatest of all the incarnations of Lord Vishnu, Krishna, but it is not my aim to persuade or coerce you into adopting our beliefs. Whatever the faith into which you have been born, it is my sincere hope that you will learn to become a better Hindu, a better Christian, a better Sikh, a better Muslim.

'So, how do we attain that goal of oneness? There is in fact only one way, and that is to worship the Lord and remember Him in everything you do. By all means acquire wealth - by honest means! - and give your family a good standard of living, but remember! - everything you possess is held on trust, so use it well and use it wisely. Do not become a captive of the modern consumer society, and a slave to advertising, constantly buying new cars, bigger televisions, the latest gadgets. Where will that get you? You cannot take them with you.

'When you die, and the Lord asks you what you achieved in life, what are you going to say? "Well, Lord, this time I managed to acquire the biggest and best Mercedes that money could buy."

He paused to allow the laughter to die away. 'No, my friends, you must spend time worshipping the Lord, and that is why we are here at Brindavan. We are here to help you in that journey to the Supreme. Come here whenever you can, stay with us for a while, and we will look after you, provide you with spiritual as well as physical sustenance, and recharge your batteries so that you can go back out into the world and face its turmoil and troubles with greater equanimity. And remember, there is no charge at all for any of this. If you wish to make a donation, that is entirely a matter for you. After the closing arati, please join us for lunch in the dining rooms. Jai Hare Krishna!'

2

It was Govinda's habit to walk about the dining rooms during meal-times, bestowing a word here, a gracious smile there. When there were few visitors, he would often sit down and discuss spiritual matters with them, but this was rarely possible at the weekends when the crowds were such that people had to be fed in shifts. Today was no exception, and Govinda merely put his head around the door of the men's dining room and smiled benignly on those present. Before he could retreat, a smartly dressed man of slight build jumped up and spoke to him in Bengali.

'Swamiji, please, I need some advice. It is a personal matter.' His voice quavered slightly, and his spectacles misted up a little.

Govinda glanced at his watch, as if to indicate the preciousness of time, and then smiled. 'Forgive me, but I am afraid I do not know your name,' he replied, also in his native tongue.

'My name is Chaudhury, Swamiji. Dr. Roy Chaudhury.'

'If you go around to the temple door, I will meet you there in two minutes.'

True to his word, Govinda opened the temple door two minutes later, ushered the doctor inside, and re-locked the door. Motioning Dr. Chaudhury to follow, he moved towards the sanctuary and switched on the electric light. 'Now, doctor,' he said, turning to face him, 'you may confide your problem to me here in the presence of the Lord himself. Speak, and He will hear you.'

'Swamiji,' Chaudhury said nervously, wringing his hands, 'I am truly ashamed to be troubling a holy man with such petty worldly problems.'

'My friend, it is my purpose in life to help people towards an understanding of the Divine, but there are many ways of doing that. If I can assist you with a worldly difficulty, and as a result you come closer to God, then I am simply doing my job.' He laid a comforting hand on the doctor's arm. 'Now tell me how I can help you.'

The doctor looked downwards. 'I have two daughters, Swami, and both are causing me problems - mental problems, you understand. My younger daughter, Geeta, is a very dutiful child, married now for nearly three years to a nice boy chosen for her by the family. But after all this time, there is no sign of a child, although she tells her mother that they have been trying for some time.' He stopped, writhing in embarrassment.

'This is not a problem, doctor. One of my specialities is to find babies for young women who are having problems. In nearly every case there is some karmic obstacle that requires removing, which can be done by special prayers and poojas. I will need to meet your daughter in order to discern the precise nature of the obstacle, and then devise the appropriate poojas in order to remove it. This may necessitate her staying here for a day or two. And the other girl?'

Dr. Chaudhury shook his head and sighed. 'Meera is two years older than Geeta, but she has not the slightest interest in getting married and settling down. Whatever boy we find she treats with scorn, and she is breaking her mother's heart. Our fear is that she will soon be too old to attract a good match, and it is a shameful and unlucky thing for a family to have an unmarried daughter.'

'And how old is this recalcitrant young lady?'

'She will be twenty-five very soon, and at that age my wife had already borne two children!'

Govinda smiled. 'I do not think that all is necessarily lost at the age of twenty-five, doctor. Is she here with you today?'

The doctor gave a despairing look. 'No, Swamiji, and that is the other problem. She is not at all religious, and because she has a good job and is financially independent, I have no control over her. She refuses always to go with her mother to any temple.'

'If she has a good job that pays well, she will surely find a husband.'

'That may be so,' Chaudhury replied gloomily, 'but we are anxious that the boy should be suitable, you understand.' He accompanied the wringing of his hands with a nervous shifting of his weight from one foot to the other.

'To put it bluntly, doctor, you are afraid that she might become attracted to a white man.'

'Exactly, Swamiji. I have nothing against the English, you understand. I have many English colleagues and friends. But for the sake of the family honour, I want her to marry a Bengali boy - or at the very least, an Indian of some kind.'

'I understand. Now, Dr. Chaudhury, I want you to send me photographs of your daughters, together with a lock of hair if possible; if not, some other personal item. I will then perform a special pooja on their behalf and seek the Lord's intercession. Once He has told me what must be done, I will contact you - please make sure you write your name, address and telephone number in the visitors' book. It is always best to carry out such poojas on the full moon, so we will arrange a time to suit everybody.'

'Swamiji, a thousand thanks! My mind is already easier, and my wife will be very happy when I tell her.'

'Not at all. It is my duty.' Govinda took the doctor by the elbow and began to steer him to the door. As he unlocked it, the doctor spoke again, waving his hands nervously in the air.

'Swami, I hesitate to mention money in the presence of God, but how much will the pooja cost? Money is not a problem, you understand, but …'

'My dear doctor, at Brindavan we do not charge money for anything. This is not the sort of temple where the priests try to squeeze whatever they can from the people. Charging money for a pooja devalues it. If you feel, as a matter of conscience, that you should make a donation to the temple to enable it to continue its work, that is entirely a matter for you.'

Govinda opened the door. 'Of course, if you decide you would like to make a donation, you could enclose a cheque when you send me the photos.'

'A good idea, Swami. I will do as you suggest.'

'It is not my suggestion, doctor, but your own generous inclination.'

'Ah yes, of course. I understand. It was my idea.'

The door closed on him before he could say anything further.

3

'What are we going to do with all this rice?' asked Simon, now Swami Krishnananda, at one of the regular ashram meetings. 'We've got about seventy large bags of rice already in store, and another fifteen were offered in the temple today. We're running out of room, and it wouldn't surprise me if rodents have got at the bags at the back of the shed. If it carries on like this, we'll be buried in rice by Christmas!'

'Storage is becoming a real problem,' added Brother Ronan, one of whose duties was store manager. 'As well as the rice, we've got bags and bags of lentils, in more varieties than I ever knew existed, sacks of rice flour which no-one knows what to do with, and more sacks of onions and spuds than I can cope with. Even a bog Irishman like me is getting a little tired of potato curry.'

'I can only cook what's there!' said Jimmy, assuming a hurt expression.

'Perhaps we could donate some to hospitals and nursing homes in the area,' suggested Brother Anthony. 'I'm sure they'd be grateful.'

Govinda, who had some time before adopted the formal title of "Swami Sri Krishna Govinda Maharaj", now intervened in the discussion. 'Children, we must remember first and foremost that what the devotees have offered is a gift from the Lord, for which we must always be grateful - even if we are a little tired of potato curry!' He smiled at Ronan, who grinned bashfully. 'Secondly, we must always be mindful of the Lord's bounty, and not let it go to waste, so if mice are a problem, we must build a rodent-proof store. Swami and Brother Ronan should look into this.'

He now turned and looked indulgently at Anthony. 'It is, of course, in Brother Anthony's very nature to think of other people, but I regret to say that in our particular environment, his idea is not very practical. Local people do not eat rice on a daily basis, nor is long grain rice suitable for making milk pudding, while I imagine that most people around here would have little idea of what to do with lentils or rice flour. Onions and potatoes could be given away, of course, but a couple of sacks of potatoes would not go very far in the kitchens of a hospital.

'What I suggest is this: one of our regular devotees runs a wholesale grocery business, and I am sure that he would be happy to sell our surplus provisions for us. The money that brings in could then be used to buy such things as we lack. It is merely an idea which I put before you, and if you do not like it, we can think of some other plan. What do you say?'

He looked from face to face around the table, and no-one objected. 'Good, that's settled then. I'll give Mr. Patel a call tomorrow. Now, about the vegetable garden: I want all shoulders to the wheel this year to expand the area under cultivation, so that Brother Lionel can increase the production of those things which are rarely offered in the temple, such as carrots and green vegetables of all kinds.'

'It might be an idea to put up a notice in the dining rooms with a list of items that we really need,' Simon suggested.

'Ever the practical mind, Swami!' Govinda exclaimed. 'However, we are renunciates, living upon the bounty of the Lord, and it would be quite improper for us to ask the devotees to bring particular kinds of offerings, however much they might be needed. If we did that, we would be no better than ordinary house-holders, and before long we would be asking people to bring cakes and chocolate biscuits!'

He waited for the laughter to stop. 'It sounds funny, I know, but it is not really a laughing matter. Let me tell you a story that illustrates the dangers. There was once a simple hermit who lived in a forest in a hut made of branches. The small amount of food that he required he was able to beg from a nearby village, and his only possessions were a japa mala to chant his mantra and two loincloths. One day he discovered that his spare loincloth had been chewed to tatters by mice, and he went to the village to beg a spare piece of cloth, which the villagers were happy to give, for it is a good thing to help a holy man.

'Naturally, the hermit was a man who eschewed violence, so he took no steps to control the mice, who soon overran his hut and kept chewing up his spare loincloth. So the villagers gave him a cat. This solved the mice problem, but now the villagers found that the hermit begged milk for the cat as well as his own food, so they got him a cow. This meant that he had to clear land to grow fodder for the cow, but all this labour meant he had no time for prayer and meditation, so the village headman, who had an unmarried older daughter he wanted off his hands, suggested that the hermit marry her so that she could do all the chores for him.

'A few years later, the hermit's guru came to pay him a visit, but as he approached he could see no sign of the forest that had once stood there. Instead, there were several fields, some being tilled by workers, and others containing herds of cattle. Where the hermit's hut had once stood there was now a grand mansion. The guru decided to inquire there where his disciple had gone. As he entered the yard, he saw several children running about, and the man of the house sitting on the veranda smoking a hubble-bubble. As he drew nearer, he was astonished to see that the man was none other than his disciple. "My son!" he cried. "What has happened to your vows of renunciation?" "Oh, master," wailed the former hermit, "all I wanted was a spare loincloth!"'

Govinda waited for the laughter to die down. 'It is an amusing story, is it not? But it has a very serious moral: if you grab hold of the things of the world, you will find in time that they have grabbed you and will not let go. There are three keys to a spiritual life: simplicity, simplicity, simplicity.'

4

Sheila tucked the sleeping Gopala into his little bed, lightly kissed his forehead, and drew the curtain which separated the child's bed from the rest of the little hut that had been her living quarters for the past three years. It was one of three, the other two occupied by Sister Fiona, a young girl who had been at Brindavan for only a year, and Sister Magda, a German woman in her late fifties who had turned up as a day visitor almost three years earlier and never left. It had been her arrival that had saved Sheila's sanity, for in the year following Gopala's first birthday, she had felt herself becoming increasingly isolated from the rest of the community.

That first birthday had been celebrated with much gaiety, but only a few days later while she was washing up after lunch, Simon had entered and primly announced the decision that the Brothers had reached at an ashram meeting. 'It's nothing personal, you understand,' he had said, though the look on his face conveyed to Sheila the distinct impression that it was certainly personal for his part, 'but as there are increasing numbers of Asian devotees coming now, it was felt that it would no longer be appropriate for you to live above the temple. The Asians have a much stricter view of morality than we do, you understand …'

'What the hell has morality got to do with it?' Sheila interrupted hotly.

Simon's pomposity was not dented. 'With the Asians, everything must not only be in order, but must also appear to be in order. The simple fact is that you sleep in the room next to Govinda, and share the bathroom with him. People are bound to draw some unsavoury conclusions, however misguided they might be.'

'Well, let them! If they've got such dirty minds, they shouldn't come here in the first place!'

'No, Sheila, we can't afford to take that attitude. It's Govinda's reputation that is the paramount consideration here, and we can't allow his name to be sullied by malicious slanders.' He shifted uneasily for a moment. 'There is also the question of … periods.' He reddened slightly.

'Periods?'

'Asian ladies having their monthly periods are not allowed into temples. It's considered polluting.'

'Polluting!' Sheila shouted. 'How can a natural process be polluting, for God's sake?'

'Please calm down, Sheila. Govinda explained it like this: the womb expels the blood and tissue each month, and they are dead and decaying as they pass out of the body, and you don't bring dead and decaying things into a temple. Therefore, we can't have you living right above it any longer.'

'Govinda's never said anything about this to me.'

'No, but he has come to the conclusion that we should begin to organise the way we do things at Brindavan on a more traditional basis, so that we don't cause offence to Asian devotees. If they believe that we are disregarding Hindu traditions, they'll simply stop coming.'

'I see.' Sheila's words were icy cold, her demeanour grim. 'And has any thought been given to where Gopala and I are to go? Have you all made a decision about that behind my back as well? Am I being asked to leave?'

'My dear Sheila, please don't fly off the handle. We all have the best interests of you and little Gopala at heart, believe me. There's no question of your leaving - unless you wanted to, of course - but Govinda feels we ought to build a little place for the pair of you, somewhere well away from the temple and the Brothers' accommodation - just so that people don't jump to any wrong conclusions.'

Sheila had barely managed to resist the urge to slap the smug look from Simon's face. 'I suppose I have no option,' she said through gritted teeth.

'Not really, I'm afraid,' Simon said brightly, 'but do understand that we're acting solely in the best interests of the good name of the ashram.'

Sheila's smouldering anger was directed as much towards Govinda as at Simon. *Why couldn't he tell me himself, instead of getting this pompous, self-righteous arsehole to do his dirty work?* She turned her back on Simon and resumed the washing-up.

'Oh, there is one other thing,' Simon said as he reached the door. 'Govinda feels - well, we all feel - that it would be more appropriate if you were to wear a white robe for the poojas, and be known as "Sister Sheila". Just as a matter of public image, you understand.'

Sheila whipped round again. 'What? "*Sister* Sheila"!'

'Just for the sake of appearances, Sheila. The Asians will find your presence more acceptable if they think you're a nun. They're less likely to suspect you of being the temple whore.' And he closed the door before she could utter another word.

The next two weeks had been the most miserable of Sheila's time at Brindavan. Govinda had remained elusive, the Brothers exchanged only the barest of civilities with her, and even Jimmy had been uncharacteristically taciturn. Her new quarters had turned out to be nothing more than a large garden shed, albeit well insulated against the biting cold of winter, and brightly painted within. Half the floor space was taken up by the two beds, leaving barely sufficient room for a small wardrobe, a table, and two chairs.

The spot chosen for the new dwelling was about two hundred yards away from the temple, across a field and behind a large, unkempt hedge. There was no separate bathroom facility, so that she had to trek to the car park to use the visitors' toilets in order to wash or relieve herself. The car park 'ladies' had one toilet and a tap, so for bathing purposes Sheila had been instructed to use the bathroom in the house only at certain times, in order to avoid unnecessary contact with the Brothers (and, by implication, Govinda himself). In wet weather, when she could not be bothered to trudge through the muddy field, she would pee outside, and during warmer weather, take a shower *au naturel* in the rain. At such times, her feeling of justifiable rebelliousness softened a little the edges of her sense of isolation.

That sense heightened later in the year when a new women's dining room was built. This had been undertaken partly to spare the feelings of many of the older Indian ladies, who felt uncomfortable sharing a dining room with men, and partly to ease the queues at the weekends. This meant that for most of the week Sheila, as the lone woman, ate in splendid isolation, her food brought to her by a tight-lipped Brother.

The weekends were entirely different, and without them Sheila thought she might have gone mad. As "Sister Sheila", she was nominally in charge, although the women, in typical Indian fashion, refused to sit down and let themselves be served by Sheila, but hustled and bustled about, almost falling over each other in their desire to assist in serving everybody else. It was chaos, and Sheila loved it.

The older women tended to be reserved towards her, though always respectful of someone wearing the white robes of renunciation, but Sheila discovered in time that this was as much due to language difficulties as anything else. The younger women, mostly born and educated in the United Kingdom, were a cheerful, chatty bunch, though careful not to overstep the line between friendliness and familiarity. All the women adored Gopala, and played with him, bouncing him on plump knees until he screeched with laughter, but no-one ever asked Sheila how it had come to pass that she was there as a nun with a baby. That would have been to cross the line.

The abrupt transformation that took place whenever Govinda put in an appearance never ceased to amaze Sheila. The shrill chatter, in a variety of tongues, the sudden outbreaks of belly-laughter, the general clamour that a group of Indian ladies apart from their men-folk were capable of creating, stilled in an instant when the dark Swami entered the room. He generally stayed only long enough to exchange greetings with those he knew, deterring with outstretched hand anyone who showed an inclination to prostrate at his feet, and then he would be gone. The second the door closed, the hubbub resumed.

Occasionally the weekday tedium would be relieved by the sudden appearance of Govinda, flouting his own rule in order to play with Gopala. Sometimes, he would even call the Brothers in, creating an impromptu party during which he would inspire gales of laughter with outrageous jokes and cruel impressions of various members of the Government. Just as suddenly, he would get up, take a courteous leave of "Sister Sheila" (a title he habitually used in the presence of others), ask forgiveness for intruding upon her privacy, and sweep out, leaving his monks scrambling in his wake to avoid being the last to leave. It was unnecessary, for Simon always waited until the undignified retreat was over before sauntering out serenely, giving Sheila a slight nod, the tight smile around his lips seeming to say: "You've had a bit of fun, but now it's back to solitary confinement!" And indeed, these rare occasions only served to magnify the dreariness of the rest of her existence.

One day, she could stand it no longer. She chose her time carefully: Simon was out doing the weekly shop, the others were engaged in the various tasks about the ashram, and Gopala was having his afternoon nap. She marched boldly into the forbidden territory of the men's dining room, passed through and ascended the familiar staircase. She knew that Govinda would be alone, or at least only chatting with Jimmy, and she was certainly not afraid of the latter.

Pausing outside Govinda's door, it seemed an age since she had last stood there, then she rapped boldly. Jimmy opened it, and started when he saw who was there. 'Sheila! Whatever are you doin' here?'

'I need to talk to Govinda!'

'You can't! It ain't allowed.'

'Let her in, Jimmy,' Govinda said, his voice cool and calm. 'Our little business can wait.'

With some reluctance, Jimmy moved to stand aside, but Sheila pushed brusquely past him. Govinda was ensconced in a large, comfortable armchair by the window, his right elbow resting on the arm, his fingers lightly touching his cheek, and a quizzical smile upon his face. He motioned Sheila to a chair by a small round table with his left hand, watched her as she sat down, and then raised an eyebrow. She returned his gaze, but anxiety wreathed her face; her initial boldness had fled. 'Govinda …,' she began nervously.

He stopped her with a raised finger. 'It was agreed at a Brothers' meeting some weeks ago now,' he said slowly and deliberately, 'and I believe that you were informed, that in future I was to be addressed as "Swami". While this is a mere title, which in itself means nothing to me personally, and which I have adopted purely for the sake of formal relations between myself and our Indian devotees, nonetheless, Sister Sheila, it is better that it be used at all times in order to avoid any little slips in public. You do understand?'

'Swami, I'm sorry, but …'

Once again the finger intervened. 'Furthermore, you have entered the Brothers' dining room, which is prohibited to you, and have ascended the stairs to my room, also prohibited to you.'

Each syllable had been enunciated slowly and clearly, and Sheila had readied herself for the impending explosion.

'All this tells me that you must be in some distress.'

The tension drained from Sheila's muscles, leaving her limp and breathless. Before she could even think of how to say what she had come to say, Govinda carried on.

'Sister Sheila, the Lord informs me of all that happens here, and so I know every detail of what troubles you. Don't forget the lesson I have tried to instil in all of you: everything that happens is a test sent by God. We must endure whatever it is that He sends in our direction, otherwise we fail Him. I know that life is difficult for you. Have patience. Things will change. Things will get better. Now you had better go, for if Swami were to return and find you here, we would both be in hot water!'

That weekend, Magda had arrived.

CHAPTER 6

Jimmy was a worried man. With each passing year, his position in the ashram hierarchy seemed to sink lower, and he was beginning to feel that if he did not come to a decision soon, and confront Govinda, his life would soon cease to have any meaning beyond being the ashram chef. At the beginning he had been the unofficial second-in-command by simple virtue of the fact that it was his money that had bought Brindavan. This, together with his greater experience of the world, his more flamboyant personality, and the fact that he had known Govinda the longest, had given him an undoubted superiority over the younger members of the group. But five years on things had changed in ways he had not foreseen, and he now found himself more or less at the bottom of the heap.

The way he saw it, the rot had set in when Simon and Anthony had been induced to take formal vows of renunciation: in some subtle but indefinable way this had elevated them in the hierarchy at his expense. At the time he had seen nothing wrong in it, accepting it somewhat blithely as a natural step on their spiritual path - not one he himself had any intention of taking - and something for which he respected them. Although happy to live at Brindavan and to take part in the temple activities, which he thoroughly enjoyed, he had never felt any inclination to become a monk; poverty and chastity he could endure, but the vow of obedience was one he knew would stick in his throat.

At that time there had still been just the four of them - he did not count Sheila - and in Jimmy's eyes they were still just a bunch of good friends. But as time passed, it became increasingly apparent that Govinda no longer regarded Jimmy as his deputy, and that the baton had passed to Simon. It showed in little ways, such as Govinda taking Simon on the weekly shopping trip instead of Jimmy, and allowing him to conduct the pooja occasionally - but only when there were no visitors. There was also a subtle change in Simon's manner towards Jimmy: while outwardly friendly, there was a superciliousness in his manner that Jimmy found especially galling, since he had been the one to introduce Simon to Govinda in the first place.

As others began to join the ashram, even though their status was that of mere novices, who might or might not make the grade, they nevertheless seemed to assume a natural precedence over Jimmy, which he put down to Simon's influence. Then Govinda had instituted the practice of holding regular Brothers' meetings to discuss ashram affairs, and although Jimmy was not excluded, it quickly became obvious that the views of even the newest monk were accorded greater deference than his own. This had become very apparent at the meeting when it was decided to revamp the temple and adopt more traditional Hindu practices in order to accommodate the feelings of the Asian visitors, who had begun to arrive in increasing numbers.

Jimmy had launched into a vociferous defence of the prevailing order. 'When we set up this place,' he declared, 'Govinda and meself, the intention was to provide a retreat for Westerners lookin' for a new direction in their lives, a haven of peace and tranquillity where they could come to meditate in peace. It was never our aim to create a traditional Hindu temple, and in my view we shouldn't pander to their old-fashioned ideas. A good part of their so-called traditions are based on nothin' more nor less than caste prejudice and sexual discrimination.'

Silence followed. Jimmy looked inquiringly at Govinda, but he seemed intent on examining his cuticles. It was Simon who finally spoke, sounding at his most pompous to Jimmy's ears.

'Well now,' he began, 'with all due respect to Jimmy, and I'm the first to acknowledge everything he's done for the ashram, I'm afraid I take the view that matters which are essentially religious ought to be decided by the monastic community. This is after all an ashram, a monastery, and such matters should be decided by the Brothers - under the guidance of Swami, of course.' He looked complacently towards Govinda, seeking his master's approval.

Govinda looked up from his finger-nails. 'We must never forget that Jimmy and I are the co-founders of Brindavan, or that without his financial assistance it would never have been possible.' He nodded to Jimmy and smiled, but Jimmy noted that the smile did not reach his eyes. 'But having said that, times change, and the Lord pushes us in directions we did not foresee. Although Jimmy has - at present, anyway - no inclination to take vows, it would be churlish for those of us who have to ignore his opinions. Jimmy, I can assure you that Brindavan will always be a haven for those in the West who feel spiritually rootless, but we have to face the fact that orthodox Hindus are beginning to come here in significant numbers, and it would be wrong for us to behave in ways which they might find offensive.

'Whilst it may be true that some old practices are rooted in caste, there are sound spiritual reasons for most of them. As an Indian, I am aware of what is good, and what is not so good, and you must be guided by me as to how we conduct ourselves in the future. None of you has the background, knowledge or experience to make the right decisions about such matters.'

Jimmy had seen the writing on the wall: he would be allowed to express his views, but there would be a united monastic front against him. He would be in a permanent minority of one.

Despite this, Govinda did not in private treat Jimmy any differently from before, and they still took afternoon tea together in Govinda's room and chatted happily about many things, especially politics. It was at one of these sessions that Jimmy, some weeks after that traumatic Brothers' meeting, took the opportunity to raise the question of his future. Replacing his cup in its saucer, he looked Govinda directly in the eye: 'I honestly think it's about time I moved on.'

Govinda looked at him blankly for a second. Then he leaned forward, speaking very earnestly. 'My dear Jimmy, you mustn't let all this nonsense about not being a member of the monastic community upset you. It's necessary for me to establish some sort of hierarchy in order to ensure a smooth future, but as long as I'm in charge there will always be a place for you here.'

He jumped up and began to pace the room restlessly, talking as he went. 'How on earth could we let you go? Who can cook as well as you? And cater for the weekend horde so efficiently? Good heavens! We'd all starve if you were to leave! No, no, no! Let's have no more talk of "moving on"! We need you here, Jimmy! I need you!'

'It's jolly nice of you to say that,' Jimmy said slowly, 'and I do appreciate it. Don't get me wrong, I enjoy cookin' for our little group, though the mass feedin' at the weekends is beginnin' to get me down, I have to admit.'

'Jimmy!' Govinda stopped in his tracks and looked at Jimmy. 'How utterly thoughtless of me! We must put someone in the kitchen with you at weekends to help with the drudgery.'

'That would be a help ....'

'Good! That's settled then.' He dropped back into his armchair, beaming.

'Well, not really.'

Govinda frowned. 'What is it then, Jimmy? What else can I do for you? Speak your mind; we've known each other long enough not to have secrets.'

'I don't feel as if I fit in here any longer,' Jimmy said slowly. 'I don't regret the last five years; it's bin a lot of fun. But things are changin' now, as you said, and I don't feel there's anywhere left for me to go. I feel in need of a new challenge.'

'I can't say that I wouldn't be very disappointed if you were to leave, Jimmy, but - as I've said on more than one occasion - Brindavan is not a prison camp. Everyone is free to come and go, and that applies to you as well as to the others. Naturally, we'd all be sorry to lose you.'

'There is ... um ... another matter.'

'Yes?'

'It's my money. I'll need some capital to get started again in London.'

'Money? There is no money! What wasn't spent on the purchase was used up in renovation and re-building. You know that very well.'

'Well yes, but I thought ....'

'The trouble is Jimmy, you haven't thought properly at all. Brindavan was a partnership between the two of us, and there was never any thought that one of us would pull out after a few years.'

Jimmy opened his mouth to protest, but at that moment the door opened and Simon's head appeared. 'Sorry, am I interrupting something important?' he asked.

'Not at all, Swami. Come in.' And Jimmy knew that the opportunity to reach some sort of financial arrangement had passed.

2

'Come in, Doctor, come in.' Govinda held open the temple door and ushered the Chaudhury family inside.

They entered the darkened temple hesitantly, and in the case of the two daughters, with an obvious reluctance. Govinda led them to the front, stopping and turning so abruptly at the sanctuary gates that the little doctor almost ran into him.

'Please be so kind as to introduce me to your family, Doctor.'

'Swamiji, this is my wife, Gauri,' indicating Mrs. Chaudhury with a little wave of the hand. His wife, though large enough to make two of her husband and with some to spare, was outwardly timid and submissive. She gave a brief look at a point about a foot above the guru's head, clasped her hands together at her ample bosom, and murmured 'Swamiji', before casting her eyes once more to the floor.

'This is my younger daughter, Geeta, and her husband, Mahendran.' Geeta was a slim, graceful and pretty young woman, who also kept her eyes averted from the holy man, but her husband, not much older, taller or broader than his wife, looked the priest directly in the face. They greeted him together: 'Namaste, Swamiji.'

'And these two, are my daughter, Meera, and my son, Narain.' He had all the while been holding the girl by the elbow, and he now pushed her forward. She was perhaps even more attractive than her sister, though it may have been the fire in her eyes that made it seem so. She was clearly a modern Indian woman, her hair cut short and her clothes European, and she carried herself with an air of confidence and self-possession. Her face haughty and defiant, she merely nodded in Govinda's direction.

The son, about fourteen, with a typical moon-round Bengali face, looked earnest and intelligent, his wire-rimmed spectacles giving him the same earnest and intelligent expression as his father. He looked like a nascent university lecturer.

'This daughter is the independent one I told you about, Swami,' Dr. Chaudhury said, still with a tight hold on her arm, as if she might bolt at any second. 'Even to the temple she refused to wear our traditional dress.'

'Appa!' Meera hissed through clenched teeth, then gave a suppressed squeal as her mother gave her a vicious pinch on her buttock. 'Amma!' she growled over her shoulder, eyes smouldering with anger.

'I apologise for my daughter's unseemly attire, Swamiji!' cried the little doctor.

'My dear Doctor,' Govinda replied disarmingly, 'we ask only that devotees dress with decorum in the temple, and in that respect there can be no complaint against your daughter. Indeed, her appearance is very smart.' He smiled at Meera. 'We must remember, now that we are living in the West, that our children will want to wear Western clothes and adopt Western habits. As long as they follow the example of decent people, and do not pick up the vicious habits that so many young people in this country seem to possess, we should not be too severe upon them. After all, "When in Rome ..."'

'But what about her marriage prospects!' Mrs. Chaudhury blurted out, inspiring a daggered look from her daughter.

'Tonight I will conduct a special pooja. The moon is at its fullest just after midnight, so I will start promptly at twelve. You must all attend in order to receive its beneficial effects.'

'Midnight! But we have to leave by this evening at the latest. I have morning surgery, you understand.'

'And I have an important business meeting tomorrow morning,' added Mahendran.

'Can't the pooja be performed earlier?' cried Chaudhury.

'If your daughters are to receive the full benefits of the pooja, it must be performed at the correct time. This is most unfortunate. When we spoke before, I thought I had made it clear that the whole family should be here at the time of the full moon.'

The Chaudhury family was thrown into confusion. Geeta and Mahendran held hands, looking unhappy, while Mrs. Chaudhury whispered furiously in her husband's ear. Only Meera was unaffected, standing apart with folded arms and smiling derisively.

'Would it be possible for your daughters at least to stay?' Govinda asked. 'Since the pooja is essentially for their benefit, it would be a pity to waste the opportunity, especially as all the preparations have been made. We can provide them with comfortable accommodation, and drive them to the railway station tomorrow.'

Geeta looked anxiously at Mahendran, Meera was suddenly on full alert, and Mrs. Chaudhury was once again whispering instructions to her husband.

'I will leave you for a few minutes to discuss the matter in private.' Govinda pulled aside a curtain, and exited through the side door behind it. He returned several minutes later.

'My daughters are willing to stay for the pooja, Swamiji,' Dr. Chaudhury announced, although his words were not entirely supported by the looks of the two girls. Geeta appeared apprehensive, clutching her husband's arm, as if afraid to let him go, while Meera looked sullenly angry. It was clear from Mrs. Chaudhury's fierce expression that all efforts at rebellion had been crushed.

'I am very happy. Now please go round to the dining rooms, and I will personally bring you some food.'

Chaudhury stopped at the door, allowing his family to precede him, and turned to Govinda. 'The cheque, Swami? It was sufficient?' he whispered.

Govinda placed a finger to his lips, and ushered the doctor outside, where his family stood waiting in the watery sunshine, Meera scowling fiercely.

The only persons present at the midnight pooja were the two girls, Govinda and Simon. The latter had collected Geeta and Meera from the dining room, where they had been waiting since the end of the evening pooja, conducting them through the silent dining rooms and into the temple via the side door.

'You may find the pooja a bit long and difficult to follow,' he whispered, indicating that they should sit by the sanctuary rail, 'but just keep an eye on me, and I'll show you what to do and when.'

Rather self-importantly, he then joined Govinda in the sanctuary, the guru no longer wearing the golden robe he wore on public occasions, but a simple white dhoti. His chest was bare save for the sacred thread passing over his left shoulder and beneath his right arm, and a gleaming golden necklace adorned with various precious stones. His eyes were closed, his face a mask.

Before the main altar there stood a black metal tripod from which hung a shallow bowl, and on the floor to either side there were receptacles of various shapes and sizes, each containing a different offering. Govinda sat cross-legged before the apparatus, and the pooja began with him chanting in a low monotone, after which he began placing sticks given to him by Simon into the bowl. Then he poured molten ghee over the sticks, crumbled in some camphor tablets, and lit one tablet from the lamp standing before the image of Krishna. As he dropped the burning tablet into the bowl, flames sprang up; more fuel and ghee were added, and the flames danced higher, sending shadows dancing around the sanctuary, and giving the faces of the two monks an almost devilish appearance. The heat was palpable even at the railing, and Meera could see beads of sweat trickling down the guru's bare back.

Simon then brought a bowl of rice grains to the rail, indicating that the girls should place their hands upon it, so that it became their offering to the deity, handing it afterwards to Govinda, who tipped it into the fire, all the while chanting. Each receptacle, containing pulses of various kinds, herbs, and other fruits of the earth were dealt with in the same fashion, and whenever the flames burned low, more ghee and camphor were added. Finally, a tray bearing small pieces of cloth, some locks of hair, and - to the surprise of both girls - photographs of themselves, was brought to them, and the contents consigned to the flames.

'What is this, some sort of black magic?' Meera hissed, but Geeta nudged her to keep quiet.

At long last, after further chanting, Govinda stood up, lit the arati lamp, which he waved before Krishna before presenting it to the girls. Geeta reverently placed her hands over the flame and pressed her palms to her eyes and breast, while Meera followed suit in rather perfunctory fashion. Govinda then waved his own hand over the flames, and placed it on the head of each girl in blessing, before passing the lamp to Simon.

'It is now very late,' he said, 'and you must be very tired. We have prepared a room for you upstairs, rather than send you to the devotees' chalets at this hour. It is small, but with two beds so that you can be together. But first, I will make you a hot drink to help you sleep soundly. Come.'

They followed him through the door.

3

Anthony was finding it difficult to sleep, partly because his mind was in overdrive, and partly because Brother Ronan, with whom he now shared the old caravan, was a prolific snorer. Simon had moved out of the caravan into the only habitable room in an outbuilding that was gradually being converted into monastic quarters, and Ronan had moved in to ease conditions in the wooden shed next door that the other monks shared. Anthony was in line for the next room to be completed, and it could not come soon enough.

'Ronan!' he shouted. 'You're snoring again!'

Brother Ronan grunted a sleep-befuddled apology and turned over onto his side, but within minutes was snoring again, this time with an even more annoying tone and rhythm. Anthony was not relaxed enough to ignore it; his mind was running over and over the issues that were unsettling him, and both his enthusiasm and his energy had struck a new low.

He secretly shared Jimmy's view of what Brindavan had been meant to be: a small reclusive community geared towards meditation and spiritual development. Although he had seriously underestimated the amount of hard work required to make the place habitable, and although his constant fatigue meant that he fell asleep almost every time that he sat down to meditate, he had always nourished the belief that the end was not far off and everything would eventually settle down into the paradise that he had dreamed of.

After five years of supreme effort, however, it now appeared that everything they did was geared towards catering for the needs of the weekend visitors: more food to be grown, more meals to be provided, more accommodation to be built. Paradise seemed further away than ever.

He was also feeling wretched that he had not had the guts to side with Jimmy on the question of Brindavan's future direction. He had rationalised his silence on two grounds: firstly, that as someone who had merely dipped his little toe into the vast ocean of Hinduism, he was incompetent to take issue with Govinda, who had been born into that ancient religion, so many thousands of years older than Christianity; and secondly, that his vow of obedience to Govinda made it impossible for him to take odds with him. Nevertheless, he felt miserable.

Ronan's snoring had now reached a level that would have made it illegal in a public place, and sleep was clearly not going to come. Anthony slipped out of bed, pulled on his boots and coat, and stepped out into the cold serenity of the night. The sky was clear, and the full moon smiled down upon him, its silvery light sufficient for him to see where he was going without the aid of a torch. He followed the path out into the field adjacent to the temple, hoping that a brisk walk around its perimeter would tire him out sufficiently to overcome Ronan's snoring.

As he walked up the slope towards the top of the field, another disquiet crept to the forefront of his mind: the feeling that Brindavan was gradually becoming corrupted by materialism. It was impossible to ignore the quantities of jewellery that the Indian ladies placed in the offering trays to adorn the image of Lord Krishna. It was never displayed for very long, and Anthony wondered what Govinda did with the gold necklaces and bracelets once they were removed.

Then there had been the donation box that had suddenly appeared some months earlier, without any discussion in a community meeting, cemented into the floor beside the temple doors. Anthony had seen Asian men pull bundles of notes from their pocket, peel off a wad, and stuff it into the box. Brindavan was undoubtedly becoming wealthy, and the fact did not sit easily with Anthony's conscience.

As for Govinda's customary weekend invitation to the Asians to come and stay at Brindavan - "We will feed you and look after you free of charge!": it sat oddly with the fact that the vast majority of the food was brought by the visitors themselves, and that they paid handsomely by donations for such care as they received.

Completing his circuit of the field, and approaching the temple, Anthony's attention was caught by a flickering glare of light from within, brighter than the light cast by the akhand oil lamps, those in front of Krishna left permanently lit, and his first alarmed thought was that fire had broken out. He ran towards the porch, intent on raising the alarm, but as he reached the doors he heard the familiar cadences of Govinda's chanting. For a split second he thought he must have missed some special scheduled pooja. He peered through the doors, his view obscured by the net curtains inside, and dimly made out the dark figure of Govinda sitting before some sort of fire. A flash of orange told him that Simon was also present. Govinda then stood, and Anthony could see that arati was being performed. Only when Govinda turned and brought the flaming lamp to the sanctuary rail was he able to see the two figures sitting on the women's side. *Some sort of private pooja*, he thought. *How much do those cost, I wonder?*

He shook his head to dismiss the unworthy thought, shrugged his shoulders, and decided to do another lap round the field. On his return, the temple was in darkness.

4

It became obvious to Jimmy in the days following his aborted discussion with Govinda that the Brothers had been informed; everyone was noticeably more respectful and considerate towards him, including Simon. *The word's gone out*, he thought. *"Don't upset the cook!"*

He almost laughed the following week when Govinda told him that instead of merely handing Simon a list of what he required in the kitchen, he should actually accompany him to town on the weekly shopping expeditions. The pleasure of getting out and about once again was naturally tempered by the fact that he had to endure Simon's company, but the change of routine was welcome nonetheless. Not that he was deceived by this sudden gesture: he was certain that if he announced a decision to stay on, the old regime would gradually be re-established.

Jimmy knew that he had reached a decisive point: if he did not leave now, it would be too late. Having been away from London for five years, it would be difficult enough to resume old contacts; if he delayed much longer, it would become impossible. The only real impediment was the lack of capital, for he was no longer young enough to meet the challenge of starting at the bottom with nothing but the clothes on his back, as he had all those years before. It had been a long, hard slog when he was young enough to withstand it, and he did not want to have to go through all that again now that he was approaching forty. It was imperative to have a financial cushion to see him through the early years.

Although the financial affairs of the ashram had been taken out of his hands two years earlier, he knew that the community was a lot better off financially than Govinda had made out. Although he realised he was unlikely ever to be repaid the sum that he had sunk into Brindavan, he was reasonably sure that there was enough money in the bank to provide him with the security he required.

He did not, however, want to make undue financial demands upon the ashram, which would always remain his baby. Although - as is so often the case with one's children - it had turned out somewhat differently from what he had envisaged, he still felt affection for it. Although he intended to leave, he planned to visit regularly once he had re-established himself in business.

His decision to broach the subject again was triggered by the sight of a number of cheques a few weeks afterwards. Taking up the tray of afternoon tea and biscuits, he had tapped on the door and entered without waiting for an invitation, finding Govinda at his desk dealing with his correspondence. At Jimmy's approach, he had thrust the letter he had been reading on top of a pile of cheques to one side, but not before Jimmy had seen that the top one had at least four figures in the amount box.

He waited for Govinda to sweep everything into a drawer, then laid down the tray and poured the tea as if he had seen nothing. They sat sipping tea and munching biscuits in companionable silence for several minutes before Jimmy ventured to speak.

''I've bin doin' a lot o' thinkin' since we last talked about my situation here …'

'And you still wish to desert me,' Govinda interjected baldly.

Jimmy looked mortified. 'I think that's puttin' it a bit strong …'

'I was joking, Jimmy.' Govinda smiled.

'Oh … right … good …. um, no, I mean ….,' Jimmy stuttered, nonplussed.

'I have been well aware of the restless state of your mind since our last talk, and I have given the matter much thought, both here in my room and in my meditation in the temple. Perhaps it was selfish of me to put Brindavan first, and not to consider your own needs.'

Jimmy mumbled his dissent from even the possibility of such an idea.

'I realise that if you want to set yourself up in business again, you will need some capital to tide you over until a regular flow of commissions starts to come in.'

Jimmy nodded. 'I'm not underestimatin' the difficulties.'

'I'll be quite frank, Jimmy. We do not have much money in the bank. While it is true that a fair amount of money comes in from week to week, most of it flows out again to meet basic running costs. You know that. You recall how hard it was for the first few years.'

Jimmy nodded again.

'The thought that the Lord put into my head in order to assist you was to raise a small mortgage in order to buy out your interest in Brindavan, and I have already spoken to the bank manager about it. On the basis of last year's income, he would be prepared to advance six or seven thousand pounds, which should be sufficient to keep you going for a reasonable period. Then in the future, as Brindavan grows - and it *will* grow, Jimmy, mark my words - I could advance further sums until the money you invested has been cleared. How does that appeal to you?'

Jimmy smiled ruefully. 'I'd hoped for more, but if I'm careful I suppose I'll get by.'

'I would, of course, be only too happy to give you more, but the bank manager feels that the monthly repayment the ashram will now have to meet is as much as we can afford at present.'

'I understand.'

'There are certain formalities that the bank insists upon. The property is at present in our joint names, but the bank wants you to transfer your interest to me - although I, of course, will merely be a trustee for the ashram. Once that is done, the bank will advance me the money and I can give it to you.'

'Will it take long? The sooner things are sorted the better don't you think?'

'I have the necessary documents here. All it requires is a couple of signatures, and then I need to sign the mortgage documents. It shouldn't take very long. But if you wanted to leave right away, I could give you a thousand pounds tomorrow from the ashram's deposit account, and repay that when the bank advances the loan.'

Jimmy's face brightened. 'Great! I could get goin' at once. Tomorrow even.'

'I think a clean break will be best. Let's seal the bargain over another cup of tea.

CHAPTER 7

Sheila remained in the temple after the evening pooja, which Simon had conducted in Govinda's absence. When he had extinguished those lamps not left permanently lit, he was startled to find Sheila waiting for him by the side door. She handed him a note.

'It's a little late in the day to want to speak to Swamiji, don't you think, Sister?' he remarked, having glanced at the note. 'Couldn't you have asked earlier in the day?'

'I asked Brother Anthony at lunchtime, but I didn't get any reply, and I need to see Swamiji urgently.'

'You *spoke* to Brother Anthony?'

Sheila sighed. 'I handed him a *note*.'

'Well, I'm glad of that at least, but why can't this wait until tomorrow?'

'Swami! I've been trying to see Swamiji for days!' She fought to hold back tears.

'There's no need to get so upset, Sister Sheila. I'll have a word with Swamiji, but I can't make any promises.'

'Of course not, Swami,' she murmured, with a deferential bow of the head. After he had shut the door behind him, she made a face and hissed, 'Pompous arsehole!', before recalling where she was. She turned towards the figure of Krishna. 'Sorry!' she said, her cheeks burning, but Krishna, his head to one side and his flute to his lips, seemed blissfully indifferent to her profanity.

'Sister Sheila, you wished to see me?'

Startled by his sudden appearance, she whirled round and began to babble. 'Swamiji! Sorry about the time! Been trying to see you for days!'

'Calm down, Sister! Now tell me what this urgent business of yours is.'

'It's about Gopala.'

'And what is the problem with our little one?'

'It's not a problem as such. It's just that he's five now, and I was thinking he ought to be going to school, but I don't even know where the nearest school is.'

'I suspected this might be your worry, which is why I came down.' He placed his hands on her shoulders. 'There is nothing to concern yourself about, but let us go upstairs and discuss the matter in comfort.' He ushered her through the door. 'You know the way. Please go up and make yourself comfortable while I fetch Swami Krishna, for it is important that he too hears what I have to say about Gopala.'

Memories of her first few years at Brindavan - good memories - flashed through Sheila's mind as she ascended the stairs. At the top she stood outside Jimmy's room - it had become his again when she had been evicted - and looked across to her old room, where she had first dreamed of Krishna. *No more dreams now!* she sighed. On impulse she stepped to the door and opened it: the room seemed even tinier now than before, perhaps because there were now two beds, with barely space to walk between them. She closed the door softly, and entered Govinda's room, standing diffidently by the door.

Govinda appeared a few moments later, Simon in tow. 'My dear Sheila, why are you standing? I told you to make yourself comfortable. Please, *do* sit down.' He indicated a small armchair, and dropped himself into the grander one opposite.

From the corner of her eye, Sheila took note that Simon had seated himself on a plain chair against the wall; she felt uneasy with him behind her, wary that her back was exposed.

'Swami,' Govinda said, leaning forward in his seat, elbows on the arms, his chin resting on his hands, 'Sheila has quite properly raised the question of Gopala's education. He is now five years old, an age when normal little boys start school. Gopala, however, is not a normal child.'

Sheila sat upright. 'What do you mean? He's perfectly normal!'

'I did not mean that there is anything wrong with him, my dear, merely that he is an extraordinary child; that his conception and birth were very special, as you and I have known all along.

'Swami, what I have to tell you now must not go beyond these four walls. I must have your word on that.'

Not quite sure exactly what Govinda was going to say, Sheila turned to look at Simon, who looked completely perplexed but also somewhat put out. Sheila had to suppress the laughter she felt arising in her stomach as she watched him trying to understand how she could possibly have shared knowledge with Govinda from which he had been excluded.

'Well, Swami?' Govinda asked, his lips twitching as he too tried not to laugh.

'Of course, Swamiji,' Simon stammered.

'Thank you. When Sheila first came to Brindavan, nearly six years ago now, I believe, she had several divine visitations from the Lord. She told me of these dreams, as she thought them to be, and I came to realise their import during my meditation. She did not see fit to tell me every little detail that occurred during these … experiences, perhaps because she was too embarrassed, but subsequently, in my meditation, Lord Krishna revealed to me that it was during these visitations that Gopala was conceived.'

He looked at Sheila, who was blushing furiously at the memory of those wanton dreams, and smiled.

'At the time I thought it very likely that the child would be a divine incarnation, which is why, Sheila, I persuaded you not to name the Muslim boy as the father when you registered Gopala's birth. Since then, however, I have been assured on many occasions that Gopala is indeed an incarnation of Lord Krishna himself.'

Sheila's mouth fell open, and she just stared at Govinda, uncomprehending. Simon almost fell off his chair. 'This is very difficult to take in, Swamiji,' he yammered. 'This sort of thing only happens in fairy tales.'

Govinda eyed him sternly. 'You think all those legends are mere fairy stories, do you? That the story of Krishna's birth in prison, and the guards falling asleep and all the doors opening to allow his father to carry him to Yeshoda's house, is just a bedtime story for children?'

'Well, most of them are, surely? They're too far-fetched to be actually true!'

'Swami, Swami!' sighed Govinda, shaking his head in sorrow. 'Every day in the temple you express a belief in the omnipotence of God, but when you are offered proof of it, you say it defies reason. Of course it defies reason! That is the whole point! God would not *be* omnipotent if He could only do what the rest of us can!'

Simon shrugged his shoulders. 'I just don't get it.'

'Let me ask you something. You have both been brought up in the Christian tradition. Do you accept the story of the virgin birth?' He looked at them in turn, eyes twinkling. 'Swami?'

'Er, well, I suppose so. It's an article of faith.'

'And you, Sheila, do you accept that Mary conceived Jesus by means of a visitation from the Holy Spirit?'

'I guess.'

'But this story happened two thousand years ago! How could you possibly believe it to be true?'

'It was recorded,' Simon said, 'so it's easier to believe.'

'But the acts of Rama and Krishna are documented in the Ramayana and the Mahabharata. Do you dismiss these records simply because they occurred thousands of years before the birth of Christ?'

Neither of his listeners replied.

'You should both read these works,' he said, 'but let us pass on to more practical matters. Sheila has asked about Gopala's education. It is, of course, quite impossible for him to attend an ordinary school. He will learn all he needs to know here, although, as an avatar, all knowledge is within him anyway.'

'Um, Swamiji, I don't quite understand what this has got to do with me,' Simon interposed.

'Of course you don't!' Govinda snapped. 'This is something entirely beyond your experience and understanding. Nevertheless, as the senior monk, it is essential that you have at least an inkling of Gopala's purpose here at Brindavan. In time everyone will know, the whole world will know, but for the present it is only we three. If anything should happen to me - and I do not know what the Lord's plans for me are anymore than anyone else - you must ensure that Gopala's purpose in this incarnation is achieved.'

'And that purpose is?' Simon asked warily.

'Before I tell you, you must both solemnly promise me that you will use your utmost endeavours on Gopala's behalf.' He looked sharply at each in turn.

'I promise,' said Simon, with just the merest hint of reservation in his voice.

'Me too.'

'I have to say, Swami, that I am surprised that you have not already guessed Gopala's future role. Why do you think the child leads the procession every Sunday? Did you think it was just some whim of mine? Something to tickle the fancy of the devotees? I do nothing merely for show; you ought to know that.'

He looked expectantly at them. Sheila was mystified, Simon suspicious; neither said anything. Govinda shook his head sadly. 'He leads because he is destined to become your leader! His divine mission is firstly to become head of this ashram when he is of age, and then to make Brindavan the world centre for the revival of the worship and teachings of Lord Krishna.'

'He's going to become the head of the ashram?' Simon said slowly.

'What? Simon! Did you think that you would be the one to succeed me?' Govinda laughed. 'No, no, it will be Gopala. Why do you think I have spent so much time with him over these past months? Because I enjoy playing with little children? No, not at all. It is because I have already begun to prepare him for his future.'

'But if he's an avatar of Krishna,' Simon said, 'he surely doesn't need any instruction. You said yourself that he already knows everything.'

'As I said before, you have no understanding of these matters. When the Lord takes human form, that naturally imposes certain limitations upon Him. He is born as a weak and helpless infant, dependent entirely upon his mother, and without the sustenance from her breasts would die, like any other baby. That is, the physical form He has taken would die.

'In addition, there is also a mental limitation, precluding the child from being aware of His true nature, for neither the body nor mind of a small child are capable of dealing with such knowledge. So the Lord hides his divinity even from Himself, although it may break through occasionally, as when Krishna's foster-mother, Yeshoda, tried to prise a sweet from the child's mouth, and when he opened it, she saw the entire universe inside!

'The time has to be right, the incarnation ready to begin his mission, and then all is revealed. Christ became aware of his divinity at the age of twelve, when his parents found him disputing with the learned men in the temple. When Gopala will become aware has not yet been revealed to me.

'Now, it is getting very late, and we have to be up for morning pooja in a few hours. We shall talk again tomorrow as how to best educate our young avatar.'

2

The monks filed into the temple through the side door to take their places, some whispering private little conversations. Simon had prepared the temple and gone upstairs to inform Govinda that all was ready, for on the auspicious day of Friday Govinda always conducted the early morning pooja. Anthony, nominally in charge in Simon's absence, delegated Brother Lionel to open the temple doors and let in the Sisters, who were waiting patiently in the porch, but did nothing to check the whispering.

As the nuns took their place by the sanctuary rail, Simon re-entered and strode to the main altar to light the arati lamp, followed very shortly by Govinda. After bowing to the image of

Krishna, he took the lamp from Simon, and then turned towards Anthony.

'I think it would be a good idea if Brother Anthony performed the arati this morning, don't you, Swami?'

It was difficult to detect from their facial expressions whether Simon or Anthony was the more surprised, for Govinda rarely delegated Friday arati at all, and Simon himself had only been given the honour two or three times.

'Take it,' Govinda said softly, proffering the lamp to Anthony.

Although he had performed arati many times before, usually when neither Govinda nor Simon were present, Anthony's hand trembled as he took the lamp, and his mind went blank. *How does the first mantra begin*? he agonised. He walked over to the image of Ganesh and began to wave the lamp in a clockwise direction, his eyes locked on the face of the elephant-headed god. Ganesh seemed to smile benevolently at him, and then the words came effortlessly, and Anthony began to chant, softly at first, and then with increasing intensity as he moved around the sanctuary, his voice soaring upwards as the invocations of power and propitiation flowed from his tongue.

A sense of detachment from what he was doing gradually intensified, until he had the strange feeling that he was watching himself perform this arati from some distant vantage point, a million miles, or perhaps a million years away, while somehow remaining at the centre of what was taking place.

As he stood to complete the arati before Lord Krishna, he became conscious of a trembling in his right arm, as if an energy were being passed from the flame along his nerves and muscles, then passing beyond the arm and engulfing his whole body with a vibrating, quivering energy. He felt heat generating at the base of his spine, then working its way upwards and outwards, until every cell of his body felt incandescently hot.

He was able to note that his hand and arm, as they waved the arati lamp, were quite steady, but within them he could sense such pulsations of energy that he fully expected to see his skin begin to ripple. Now he became conscious that his body was not a solid lump of matter, but composed of billions of sub-atomic particles in perpetual motion, prevented from shooting off into the universe solely by the power of his divine soul.

The arati completed, Anthony held out the lamp for Simon to take, unconsciously replicating the stance and manner of Govinda, then took his place and led the pooja. When the communal chanting concluded, he begin to sing one of the many bhajans to Krishna that he had learned over the previous five years. As his voice soared, he could feel the energy within his body gradually withdrawing and coalescing at the base of his spine, and as the final notes of the song faded away it surged up his spine and into his brain, engulfing him in a burst of radiant white light. That other part of him, the part that watched, likened it to an atomic explosion before it too was overwhelmed by the expanding light, and Anthony became conscious of nothing at all in the world around him.

Govinda took over the conduct of the pooja, bringing it to a swift conclusion, all the while glancing at Anthony, who sat unmoving, his eyes open but focussed upon some other dimension, his face alight with radiant joy, and his cheeks shining as the tears coursed down them.

After the final arati, Govinda shooed everyone from the temple, and himself doused the lamps and candles before resuming his seat and waiting. Anthony continued to sit stock-still, staring into a reality Govinda could not see.

3

Sheila slipped into her cabin, easing the door shut with her finger on the latch to prevent any noise, for Gopala was a light sleeper at the best of times. She stood in the gloom, listening to his light and steady breathing from the other side of the curtain, then cautiously pulled it aside, leaned over the sleeping child, and gently kissed the damp curls.

She slipped off the white habit with a sigh. *Maybe I could snatch a few minutes' sleep before he wakes.* Catching a glimpse of her semi-naked self in the long mirror fixed to the back of the door, she stared at the dim reflection for a minute, then took a candle from the shelf and lit it, placing it so that its soft light would be magnified by its own reflection. She stepped back and coolly appraised herself.

Although now twenty-five, she retained the slight figure of her teenage years, though her body was more mature now, less soft than before, hardened by the labours of the past five years. Her stomach was firm and flat, her legs lean with good muscle tone. *Hmm, quite the athlete!*

On impulse she unfastened her brassiere, and regarded her breasts: they were still small and firm, though a little fuller now, and her nipples seemed more pronounced. *Bully for breast-feeding!* She cupped them in her hands, weighing them, then ran her palms down her torso in a slow caress until her fingertips brushed the top of her panties. She eased them down her legs and stepped out of them, now completely naked, and saw that she was still desirable.

Legs slightly apart, she stroked her thighs, then slowly moved her hands upwards again, the fingers brushing the curly pubic hair, lingering for a moment over her sex, then up her belly to her breasts, grazing the tautened nipples, and on up to her shoulders. Fingertips on her collar bones, elbows pushed outwards, she arched her back and thrust her hips forward, all the while watching herself in the mirror. She felt desire well up within her, and moved one hand between her legs, touching the moistness there. Then she let out her pent-up breath in a loud gasp, and sat down on the end of her bed.

She looked at her hands. *The only hands to touch my body for five years!* A sigh escaped her lips. In all probability, no other hand would ever touch her again. She looked at herself, still so young and desirable, and almost regretted resisting the temptation to masturbate. But she was wedded to Krishna now; marriage and sexual pleasure were denied to her. And after Govinda's revelation, she could see no other path for her to follow.

Shivering in the cool air, she slipped into bed, although there was now no question of sleep. *Wedded to Krishna! What a thought!* Even now she could recall parts of those dream encounters with the God in human form, and her body trembled with the recollection. Desire flooded her mind and body once more, and she moved one hand to her breasts and the other to her crotch, imagining that they belonged to Krishna. *This time I won't stop!* Then Gopala whimpered in his sleep, and her thoughts turned towards him, her darling boy, her little God-child, and all thoughts of sexual pleasure were swept away.

Sheila now began to review the thoughts and opinions that Govinda had shared with her about the little avatar. 'Since he is destined to become the inspiration behind a world-wide religious renaissance,' he had said, 'it is of crucial importance that his mind is not contaminated by the current decadent system of education in the West, which not only fails to instil any sense of morality in children, but even seems to be designed to obliterate any ethical code a child might have been taught by its parents.'

He had decided that Gopala should be taught in the first instance by himself, and later by such suitable persons as he should select.

'But Swamiji,' Sheila had protested, 'surely he needs to mix with other children of his own age.'

'My dear Sheila, have you understood a word I've said? Gopala is not an ordinary child, and has no need to mix with children who are in every way inferior. He needs only to be in the company of spiritual people. What is it that you want him to learn from children of his own age? To smoke behind the bicycle sheds perhaps, or to take drugs? He must be protected from such harmful influences until he is old enough and strong enough to resist them without assistance.'

'But you said that Krishna played with other children!' she had cried.

'That was a far more innocent age than our own, my dear. Children were allowed to remain children in that golden age, and were not subjected to the terrible temptations and the

116

dreadful examples that beset them today: there was no tobacco, no marijuana, no pernicious influence of television. Remember that we live in the Kaliyuga, the age of great evil, the last age before the final battle between the forces of good and evil that will usher in once again a Golden Age. Gopala is one of God's chosen instruments, who will help bring about the final defeat of the demonic forces, and it is our God-given responsibility to ensure that the instrument is not damaged.'

'But what about the authorities?'

'It is not at all uncommon for a child to be educated at home. As long as the child is taught properly, there is no legal requirement to attend school. Gopala is highly intelligent; he will excel.'

Sheila knew this to be true, for she had begun to teach Gopala to read and write when he was barely four, and he had learned quickly. She accepted the possibility that other children might hold him back, as well as teach him things best not known. Even so, her misgivings about bringing up the child in isolation from the rest of the world in the rarefied spiritual atmosphere of Brindavan did not entirely disappear.

Her mind turned to the strange and electrifying experience of that morning's pooja. Preoccupied as she had been with Gopala's future, she had not even noticed that Govinda had delegated the pooja to Anthony, but had merely followed the chants mechanically, her consciousness directed inwards. She had suddenly become conscious that the atmosphere was highly charged, that the hairs on the back of her neck were standing up. She realised firstly that it was Anthony singing, and that his voice had taken on an especially powerful quality. Strange shivers had run through her body, and she felt pervaded by feelings of intense love and joy, sensing too that these feelings were being shared between everyone present, thereby creating a strong bond of spiritual kinship. She looked over towards Anthony, and became aware that he seemed to be in another world entirely, and this had heightened the sense she had that all those present were simply distinguishable units of a great Divine Oneness, as if perhaps they were all tongues of flame belonging to the same Divine Fire.

As she had returned to her hut, she felt an immense love for all creation: for the owl shrieking, for the little animals rustling in the undergrowth, for every tree and plant, every blade of grass, and for every stone beneath her feet.

All this came back to her as she lay there, and suddenly she felt a great unworthiness that she should have doubted her guru. *Where else on earth but Brindavan could I have had such an experience?* she asked herself. *Who else but Govinda can guide me towards ultimate union with the Divine?* She felt a great peace descend upon her, and at that moment Gopala woke.

4

To the disappointment of the rest of the Brothers, who had been eagerly looking forward to a first-hand account of his experience in the temple, Anthony did not appear for breakfast.

'Where can he be?' Brother Douglas wondered, looking expectantly at the door. 'Surely not still in the temple?'

'He's in Swamiji's room,' Simon announced, passing through the dining room on his way upstairs with a fully laden breakfast tray. 'He's not long returned to normal consciousness, and he's resting.'

'Holy Mother!' exclaimed Brother Ronan. 'He must have been in that trance for hours!'

'It was not a trance, Brother Ronan,' Simon scolded, pausing at the door. 'Brother Anthony was in a deeply meditative state, something you might conceivably experience yourself one of these days if you apply yourself to meditation with even half the diligence Brother Anthony does.' He swept out with as much dignity as the tray would allow.

'I don't care what you call it,' Ronan said as soon as the door had closed, 'but Brother Anthony didn't know the time of day in there. In fact, I'd be surprised if he knew what month it was.'

'I just don't know what to make of it!' Douglas declared. 'His eyes were wide open, but he certainly wasn't there with the rest of us.'

'It makes you wonder,' Ronan ventured thoughtfully, raising his eyes in an upward direction, 'why we've never seen anybody else having the same sort of experience.'

'The more spiritually advanced one is, the easier it is to control the divine energy,' explained Brother Dennis, looking up from the book he was reading, 'otherwise one would become immersed in God-consciousness the whole time and nothing would get done.' Brother Dennis was the ashram intellectual.

'Well, you'd know all about that, of course,' Ronan commented.

Brother Dennis gave him a withering look. 'If you ever bothered to listen, Brother Ronan, you would recall that Swamiji himself told us about great sages who have lived in the Himalayas absorbed in meditation for thousands of years.'

'Yes, I remember that!' Douglas enthused.

'Well,' Dennis resumed, glaring at Douglas, 'that sort of thing is all very well for great sages, but it wouldn't help to get things done here at Brindavan if we all started popping off into a trance every five minutes.'

'Don't you mean a "deeply meditative state"?' Ronan sniggered.

'It matters not what you call it, Brother Ronan!' snapped Dennis. 'The simple fact is that you can't do anything if you're in that state. Just look what happened to Brother Anthony: he couldn't even finish the pooja, just tailed off and stopped.'

'What I'd like to know,' Brother Hugh enquired, 'is how anyone can possibly control something like that. I mean, how can a human being master a surge of divine energy?'

'I have no doubt that Swamiji knows the techniques and that he's teaching them to Brother Anthony this very minute.' Brother Dennis was nothing if not sure of himself.

'Well, I was just wondering why we've never seen Swami Krishna in such a state.' Ronan was barely able to disguise the mischief in his voice. 'But perhaps he learnt those techniques you mentioned early, like.'

'What exactly are you insinuating, Brother Ronan?'

'Insinuating, Brother Dennis? Nothing at all. Just making an observation.'

'I've bin listenin' to you old wives gossipin' away,' snorted Jimmy, poking his head through the kitchen hatch, 'and none of you were here in the early days when we had a lot more time for meditation, and I can tell you I've seen both Govinda and Simon sittin' in the temple meditatin' for hours. I've no doubt they do the same now but in the privacy of their rooms, which is what you lot ought to be doin' rather than wastin' your time natterin'!'

He banged the hatch door shut, and the monks looked sheepishly at each other to an angry background of clattering dishes, pots and pans.

Upstairs, Govinda was pouring Anthony more coffee. 'Would you like some more toast and marmalade?'

Anthony shook his head; he had struggled through the first slice. 'Sorry, Swamiji, I'm not really hungry.'

Govinda turned to Simon, hovering behind the guru's chair. 'That's all, Swami. You'd better go and get your own breakfast.'

Simon moved towards the door with evident reluctance, but Govinda waved him away imperiously. Once the door had closed, he turned back to Anthony. 'Now, my dear, if you're ready, I want you to recall in as much detail as possible your experience in the temple. It is important that I know precisely what happened so that I can plan a schedule of spiritual practices best suited to aid your future development. What happened was highly significant, as I'm sure you appreciate.'

'To tell the truth, Swamiji, I think I'm still suffering from shock.'

'That is to be expected, for one's first real spiritual experience can be very traumatic. Just relax, take your time, and tell me what you felt.'

Anthony frowned, and then began to speak slowly, almost haltingly. 'It seemed to happen almost at once. When I began the arati, everything was quite normal, then suddenly I seemed to be standing a long way off. I was aware I was doing the arati, but it was as if I was outside everything that was going on, sort of observing it. Then all I was aware of was Krishna. Everything was dark, and I was looking at Him down a long tunnel, and He was looking back at me. I could still hear my voice chanting, but it didn't seem to be my normal voice - it was somehow deeper and louder, and it reverberated around the walls of the tunnel. And all the time Lord Krishna was smiling at me.'

He broke off, his eyes focussed elsewhere as he re-lived what he was describing. Govinda remained silent, and after several minutes Anthony shook his head and looked about himself, as if surprised to find himself where he was.

'I understand exactly,' Govinda said. 'The first thing that happens is that the senses are dislocated, for it is the senses that bind us to the material world, and they must be shut down in order for you to become fully conscious of the Lord alone.'

'So that's why I wasn't conscious of anyone or anything else?'

'Precisely. What happened next.'

'Anthony's brow furrowed as he tried to recall the pooja. 'As I moved around the temple, I had this strange feeling of slipping in and out of the tunnel. It was really weird. When I came back to Krishna to finish, I seemed to be back in the tunnel and almost at the end, right in His face almost, and my body was humming with energy, as if all its cells were jumping about at atomic speed.'

'That too is quite normal. During arati we are calling to the Lord, asking Him to grace us with His presence, and when He deigns to come, as He did this morning in all His majesty, then everyone present, but especially the poojari, is bathed in His boundless energy.'

'Anthony's eyes widened. 'You mean that Krishna actually came?'

'But of course. I could see Him as clearly as in the days when we used to play together on the banks of the Godaveri river. But enough of that. Please continue.'

Anthony paused for a moment or two, collecting his thoughts. 'When I sat down again to start the pooja, I felt as if I knew, and was aware of, everything in the entire universe. When you first asked me to do the pooja, I was scared I'd muck it up and forget the mantras, or muddle them up, but as soon as I began the arati everything became quite clear. All the mantras seemed to be written on a scroll which just unfurled in my mind in the right order, and I knew then it was impossible to make a mistake. When I sat down, I could see the whole pooja spread out before me, as if somehow it had already happened, and we were merely following it.'

'Were you conscious that your voice had changed, that it had become somewhat higher and more nasal, and that your pronunciation was completely authentic?'

'I couldn't hear my own voice. It was just one of thousands throughout the universe all chanting the same mantras.'

'Ah, your contact with the Divine clearly enabled you to tune in with poojas being conducted elsewhere in the world, and perhaps other worlds too.'

'Then, as I began to sing, I felt a great wave of love sweep over and through me, and although I knew that it had originated outside me, once I was engulfed by it I became part of it too, and I was aware of everything that lived: you and the Brothers, the mice inside the walls, the birds in the trees outside, even the insects.' His voice began to tremble as tears trickled down his cheeks. 'I could feel the vibration of a spider spinning her web up in the roof, and it was working so hard, doing what God had ordained it to do, and I felt the most incredible love for it - even though I normally loathe spiders.

'Then this consciousness spread outside the temple, and I could see in my mind what people were doing for miles around - getting up, going to work, getting breakfast for their kids - and I loved them too, for they were all part of God, and He was within them. And then I became aware of other countries, other continents, and everything was filled with the presence of God, and my heart became so full of love for everyone that I thought it would burst.'

He stopped. Once again his eyes looked elsewhere, as his cheeks ran freely with hot tears and his body trembled. Govinda watched him, silent and unmoving. It seemed an age before Anthony resumed, his voice shaky.

'All of a sudden my entire being became absorbed in a blinding white light, like a nuclear explosion without heat or noise, and I was no longer aware of anything at all that had physical form. All that existed was the light, and although I somehow knew without doubt that the source of the light was a million, million miles away, so far away that it would make a light year seem like a trip to the shops, yet at the same time I was also part of that light, and desperate to lose myself within it for ever.'

His voice trailed away, and his body trembled from head to foot. His face became contorted, as if he were being subjected to some great agony, and he swallowed lungfuls of air convulsively. It was many minutes before he became calm once more.

'And?' Govinda prompted.

Anthony's voice came out in a howl of despair. 'Then I heard the Voice!' He doubled over in his chair, hugging himself tightly. Great sobs racked his body.

Govinda knelt beside him, placing one hand on his head and stroking his back with the other. He remained there until Anthony had wept himself into exhausted tranquillity. 'And what did the Voice say?' he whispered into Anthony's ear.

Anthony looked up, his face mere inches from Govinda's. 'It said, "Wait. Not yet. There are still things to be done." And I was devastated. I felt like a child shown the most desirable toy in the world only to see it snatched away. I felt a huge wail of anger and despair building up inside me, but before I could let it out there was a great blow to my chest, almost like a punch, and the anger and despair were replaced by a feeling of peace, and also a certainty, an absolute certainty that one day the Light would come for me again, and that this time I would merge within it.'

Govinda rose to his feet and walked to the window, standing there deep in thought for several moments. 'Maybe I've been backing the wrong horse,' he murmured to himself. Then he turned to Anthony. 'I think, my dear, that it is time for you to don the robes of a Swami.'

CHAPTER 8

'Now let your breath out slowly through your mouth, using your stomach muscles to expel every last drop of air.' The temple filled with the gentle hiss of expelled air. 'Hold your lungs completely empty for five seconds, and now slowly, very slowly inhale through your nostrils. Push out your stomach and fill every last little space in your lungs until you are comfortably full, and then hold that breath.'

A few seconds later, the instruction to expel was repeated, and so the first official meditation course at Brindavan continued, with Govinda's repeated instructions punctuated regularly by the sounds of inhalation and exhalation from the group sitting towards the back of the temple. Some sat cross-legged upon cushions, some were seated upon low stools, and one or two held the classic lotus position on the floor. All had their eyes closed, their hands either folded in their lap or resting palm uppermost on each knee. There were altogether seventeen meditators, including some of the monks and nuns, and they were all of European extraction.

'With this next inhalation, hold the breath and focus your attention upon your third eye, in the centre of your forehead, and look into infinity. See there what you can!' He paused, watching the still, closed faces in front of him. 'Now breathe out, and repeat the cycle in your own time, remembering always to pause on the in-breath and look into the beyond.'

Govinda had been sitting upon a high-backed chair with barley-twist legs and ornately carved arms and back-rest. Now he rose and began to walk silently between the files of still and silent forms, observing each one closely. Pausing by a woman whose face wore a blandly complacent expression, he placed his left hand upon her head and pressed down slightly. She started in surprise, her eyes flickering briefly open, before her face settled back into a cat-like smile of satisfaction.

The guru moved on to another, older woman, seated upon a stool, her face contorted in grim and furious concentration, as if seeking to compel the attendance of the Divine by mainforce. 'Relax, and look only from here,' Govinda whispered, placing his forefinger at the centre of her brow. The tension in the woman's face, and indeed her entire body, seemed to drain away as she relaxed, the furrows of concentration upon her forehead smoothing out, the grimness of her expression softening.

Govinda moved on to a youngish man wearing a loose white shirt and yachting trousers, sitting ramrod straight upon the floor, his hands resting palm uppermost on his knees, thumbs and forefingers joined in a circle. The teacher took the hands and placed them in the man's lap, right upon left. 'Be comfortable, Charles,' he said softly.

For several more minutes he walked around the group, adjusting a posture here, placing a hand or finger on head or brow there. Finally he returned to his throne-like seat, where he gazed intently at Anthony, sitting directly before him. The young monk's face was absolutely calm, devoid of all expression, Buddha-like in its impassivity. Govinda leaned forward and placed the tip of his forefinger upon the young man's third eye, immediately flinching away as if jolted by an electric shock. He quickly scanned the room, but everyone had their eyes closed.

'Take a final deep breath,' he commanded, 'and then return to normal consciousness in your own time.' He watched as one by one his students began to stir, rubbing their eyes, stretching their muscles, and massaging stiff legs. Only Anthony remained unmoving.

'True meditation is the most difficult thing in the world. Your mind is like a monkey, always dashing from one thought to another, and you must learn how to train it to be still. What a job that is! You sit down, telling your mind to be quiet, and at once it becomes full of thoughts, each one demanding your immediate attention: the book that has to be returned to the library, the lawn you forgot to mow before you came here, the shopping that needs to be done on the way home. Trivial, trivial, trivial thoughts! And then, just as you think that you have put those thoughts away, the mind changes tactics: it tells you that your leg is getting cramp, that your back aches. It will resort to every trick in the book to avoid being subjected to discipline.

'Why does this happen? Let me enlighten you: it is because you have no discipline in your lives. How can your mind be disciplined when your life is not? Why does the mind raise the issue of the letter you meant to write thanking your aunt for the present she sent you? Because you did not have the discipline to write it when you should have done. You shoved that duty aside in order, no doubt, to satisfy some pleasure craving that possessed you; so you watched television, telling yourself you would write the letter tomorrow. But you didn't. Society is like this when it comes to performing a duty: tomorrow will do. You satisfy your desires first, and put your duties second, and so your mind fills up with all sorts of unfinished business and undigested thoughts, which then become the ammunition the mind uses to distract you from meditation. If you dealt with issues when you ought, if you instilled some discipline into your life, instead of indulging yourself in idle pleasures, your mind would automatically become more disciplined too.

'Very few people in the world today can still the mind even for a couple of minutes. I observed each one of you, not merely externally but also internally, and not one person here, apart from Brother Anthony, was able to attain a state of true meditation. Some of you managed to achieve a degree of control over the mind for a little while, and perhaps had some sort of spiritual experience, but this was little more than mere concentration.

'Oh dear! So many downcast faces! Do not be disheartened, my friends. Before a child can walk it must learn to crawl, and then it has to learn how to stand upright in order to toddle. How many tumbles does it take along the way? How many bumped heads and bruised shins? But the child does not give up. You are all now at the tumbling stage of meditation, but with practice and determination you will learn to toddle, and eventually you will be able to walk upright with confidence along the path to liberation.'

Govinda looked at the array of faces that looked up at him; disappointed faces, worried faces, puzzled faces. He smiled indulgently. 'Do not forget that each and every one of us is at a different stage of spiritual evolution, depending upon the accumulated karma that we have brought from past lives. Experiences will therefore be different, and you should not worry that one person may have experienced something that you did not. It may simply be that you are not ready for that, or it may be that you are in fact already beyond it. There is no set of hard and fast rules which says that everyone should have the same experiences in some predetermined order, so attach no importance to the experiences of others. Only your own are important. Yes, Paul?'

The curly-headed young man who had raised his hand frowned. 'So are you saying that it's bad to share your meditation experiences with others, even close friends?'

'If two people are very close, it may not be harmful for them to compare notes, so to speak, but generally it is not a good practice. Some people may recount so-called "experiences" which are actually invented, either because they have vivid imaginations, or perhaps because they are trying to impress others. This is less likely to happen, of course, when you are receiving instruction from an enlightened teacher, or guru, because he will be aware if his students are making things up.'

'So what actually does the word "guru" mean?' asked one of the girls.

'In its most basic interpretation it simply means "teacher", and can therefore be applied to any discipline at all; thus, a music teacher, for example, is, in the Indian way of thinking, his students' guru. In the context of religion, however, it bears a deeper, more subtle connotation, indicating a spiritually enlightened person who takes on the responsibility of revealing to his pupil, or disciple, the way to enlightenment.'

'So does this mean that you're now our guru, Swami?' the fair-haired man at the back asked.

'The guru-disciple relationship is a two-fold commitment, Charles. For the guru to take upon himself the responsibility for the disciple's spiritual welfare, it is essential that the disciple accepts the commitment of absolute obedience to the guru. This is essential, for the guru may have to take extreme measures in order to lead the disciple along the path, and the disciple must realise this at the beginning. So, to answer your question, no; I am not your guru. All of you non-monastics will go home at the end of the week to your families, jobs, studies. The true disciple has no interest in such worldly affairs: he wants only to attain enlightenment.

'As to the members of this community, time will tell whether or not they truly have the necessary degree of commitment; their present enthusiasm for the spiritual life may wane. That is why I allow them plenty of time before they make a permanent commitment by taking vows, for only when a person has one hundred percent determination will I accept them. Let me illustrate the degree of commitment required with a story.

'A man was determined to achieve enlightenment, and resolved to seek out a very holy guru he had heard about who lived high up in the Himalayas. He spent many weeks on his search, oblivious to the freezing cold, and even when his supply of food ran out, he did not despair. Eventually he saw a fire burning very high up a cliff face, and, convinced that he had found his guru, scaled the steep and jagged rocks until he reached the ledge where the guru was sitting with his disciples.

'The man approached the guru very humbly and respectfully, and asked to be accepted as his disciple so that he could attain liberation from the cycle of birth and death. The guru looked him up and down, and then said, "I have no need of another disciple." The seeker was stunned. "But I have travelled hundreds of miles for many months to find you, guruji," he replied. "What am I to do?" "That is not my concern," the guru replied. "You may jump off the cliff for all I care."

'In his heart the aspirant had already accepted the holy man as his guru, and so he obeyed him without a second thought, and fell to his death hundreds of feet below. The guru was impressed by this degree of surrender, and sent the other disciples to retrieve the body, which he then restored to life, and initiated the seeker as a disciple.

'That, my friends, is the degree of commitment that is required.'

For a few moments there was complete silence. Then a middle-aged man with a drooping moustache spoke up. 'That's a very nice story to make a point, Swami, but it *is* just a story. No-one would be crazy enough to jump off a cliff, whoever told them to do it, and even if he did, well, the idea of a battered dead body being brought back to life is absurd, surely.'

'The Bible says that Jesus restored Lazarus to life after he had been dead for three days, Wilf. Three days in a very hot climate. Was that story invented just to illustrate a point, do you think?'

'I don't know,' said Wilf, 'but most of those stories about Jesus weren't written down until a century after his death.'

'So that makes them untrue?'

'Well, it's got to cast a shadow of doubt over their authenticity, hasn't it?'

'Whereas if something is written down at once, that makes it more likely to be true?'

'Not necessarily, I admit.'

'So the time it takes for an event to be recorded in writing is not entirely relevant to its truth or otherwise.'

'I take your point.'

'The problem with the West,' Govinda continued, 'is that unless something can be proved scientifically, no-one believes it, but in fact science has barely begun to scratch the surface of universal truths. Can science explain how a tiny seed can contain the life-force essential to produce a huge oak tree that is capable of living for hundreds of years? Things like this are divine miracles.

'The preoccupation with science is the major cause of the decline of Christianity in the West, because a scientist cannot conceive that divine power of such magnitude can be wielded by a human being that he is able to turn water into wine, or restore the dead to life. So few of you really believe the essential features of the religion in which you were reared that when you are presented with the same features in another faith, you automatically scoff at them too.

'Now, however, I must ask you all to leave quietly, for Brother Anthony is beginning to stir, and he will need all my attention.'

2

'Come in, Jimmy!' Govinda cried cheerfully, as Jimmy put his head round the door. 'Coffee?' Before Jimmy could reply, Govinda poured a cup from the percolator and pushed it across the table. 'Help yourself to cream and sugar.'

'I've good news for you, Jimmy. I saw the bank manager this morning, and all the documents have been signed and are in order. The money should be through in a week or so, once head office has approved everything. In the meantime I took out five hundred just to tide you over, so you're free to go whenever you want. I know I spoke of a thousand, but we're a bit short, so I'll get another five hundred after the weekend crowds have been.' He pushed an envelope across the table.

'Good show,' Jimmy said, with less enthusiasm than might have been expected.

'What is it, Jimmy? Not getting cold feet, are we?'

'It's a big step, you know. It's bin six years since I quit.' He sounded rueful. 'Gettin' started again ain't goin' to be easy.'

Govinda leaned forward and looked Jimmy in the eye. 'It's not too late to change your mind, you know. No-one else knows of your intention, so you could stay on without any feelings of embarrassment. I wish you would, Jimmy.'

After the slightest pause, Jimmy braced himself. 'No, it's no good. I made up my mind, and I won't change it, but ta all the same.' He smiled. 'It's bin a good time, certainly an interestin' time, in so many ways, but deep down I know it's time I moved on.' He drained his cup and replaced it on the saucer; it rattled slightly with the trembling of his hand. He stood up, picked up the envelope and put it in his pocket.

'Not going to count it?' Govinda asked, a wry smile on his face.

'I think I can trust you after all this time.' Jimmy grinned nervously, and shifted from one foot to the other.

'When will you go?'

'At the weekend, I think. Hopefully someone from your meditation group has a spare seat, which'll save the train fare.'

'I'll ask Charles.'

There was an awkward silence. Jimmy edged towards the door. 'Better get on, then,' he said. 'Supper to get ready an' all that.'

Govinda nodded. He stared at the closed door for a while, then shrugged his shoulders, and returned to the newspaper he had been reading beforehand.

3

'Today, I'm afraid, must be our last class,' Govinda announced on the Friday afternoon, to a muted chorus of dismay. 'I know that you are disappointed, but tomorrow is not a good day for a class of any kind. Our weekend trippers will be here to ask God for some favour or other, and we don't want them gawping at us through the doors - or worse still, wanting to join us.'

A ripple of laughter washed around the group, united in its acceptance of the suggestion of spiritual superiority.

'So let us begin. As you breathe in deeply, surround yourself with a feeling of deep love …. and now as you breathe out, slowly, slowly, send that love to all those dear to you. As you inhale again, once more fill yourself with that pure, sweet love, and as you exhale send that love to everyone present. With your third breath, think good thoughts about everyone you know, surrounding yourself with the love they offer you, and on the out-breath send that love to all those you do not like and who don't like you. Finally, draw in a slow, deep breath and cocoon yourself in divine love, so that as you meditate, no evil force can disturb you …. and now carry on in your own time, stilling the mind, and looking through the mind's secret eye into the world beyond.'

As the class sank into a profound silence, punctured only by the faint susurration of breath being drawn in and exhaled, Govinda sat for a while, his hands idly playing with the long necklace of large rudraksha beads that hung from his neck. His eyes played over the still figures of the class, pausing here and there, and then he rose quietly from his chair and moved as silently as a cat into the sanctuary and through the side door, leaving the temple to the unseeing, unmoving forms of his followers.

Twenty minutes later he returned as noiselessly as he had left, and began to move among the class, placing a hand here, a forefinger there, as had been his practice all week, before resuming his seat. 'Gently bring your consciousness back to the here and now,' he instructed soothingly. 'In your own time, without haste, restore yourself to the present.'

In ones and twos the class obeyed, some almost immediately, others more slowly, opening their eyes and blinking as they looked around at their fellows. There was the usual stretching of limbs and chafing of muscles. Once everyone had opened their eyes, Govinda loudly cleared his throat. Everyone fell still and looked to the front.

'You are all here because of the karma that binds you together,' Govinda began. 'I want you to remember that: the karma that binds you all to each other, and also to me. Everyone here is part of the same family, God's family. Every human being in the world, of course, is also a member of that family, but the vast majority not only do not realise that, they do not even wish to know it. All of you, on the other hand, are part of that tiny, tiny percentage which is conscious of the reality of God, and the fact that you made the decision to come her, sacrificing a week of your time, shows that we share a special karmic link.

'Others will have thought about coming, but did not: their determination to know God was not strong enough. Others may have wanted to come, but were prevented by circumstances beyond their control. What really stopped them from attending is that they do not share the karmic link which we share. Every one of you is linked karmically to me, and thereby also to Lord Krishna, and it is as a consequence of your previous good deeds that you have all been here with me at Brindavan this week, seeking a closer union with the Lord. I ask you to remember this when you return to your homes and jobs, and not throw away this great opportunity.

'One of the things I have impressed upon you this week is not to talk about your meditation experiences to others, for this may not only arouse jealousy in the listener but also inflate the ego of the speaker. Today, however, I am going to break that rule. After all, if a rule is to be broken, who better than by the one who made it?' He beamed at the class, and everyone grinned.

'What experiences have you had in your meditation? Has your experience changed in the course of the week? Don't be afraid to speak out, even if you think you have achieved little or nothing. What you may have seen, felt, or even heard during your meditation provides no insight to anyone else, save perhaps myself, as to your particular place on the spiritual path, so there is no need for anyone to feel superior, or inferior, to anyone else. Had there been more time I would have spoken privately to each of you, but that is not possible, so we shall share our experiences. Would anyone like to begin?'

As Govinda cast his eyes over the group, some avoided his gaze and others adopted a blank expression, trying perhaps to signify that they were not yet sufficiently "grounded" to talk. One or two, however, looked eagerly towards the guru, almost shouting "Me, me, me!" with their eyes. One of these was a plump woman of thirty-something, towards whom Govinda had directed a significant amount of attention during the week. Her soulful eyes sat in a round, childlike face, set off by a mass of unnatural chestnut curls tumbling to her shoulders, and she stared at the master intently, hugging herself with quivering anticipation, every fibre of her being radiating the desire to show and tell. Her face fell as Govinda's glance passed over her, but almost at once he looked back.

'Pearl, would you like to go first?'

'Me? Gosh! I'm not sure I can, Swami,' she simpered, hands crossed on her ample bosom. 'How do you put something like that into mere words?'

'Just do your best, my dear.'

'Well, okay then, here goes!' She giggled. 'I have to admit that on the first day I couldn't see anything at all. I tried and tried, but everything was just black.' She looked about the room, seeking confirmation that she had not been alone, and received acquiescent nods from several others. 'But, Swami, the moment you placed your finger on my third eye, everything changed: I could see great swirls of colour, reds and blues and greens, and mixtures of them all.'

'This is a common experience when the third eye begins to open,' Govinda interposed. 'One sees colours, but colours that are so much more vivid than their earthly counterparts, wouldn't you agree, Pearl?'

'Oh yes, Swami! So, so brilliant! Like a thousand rainbows magnified!'

'Just so. And because of that brightness, they often blind the newly opened spiritual eye to anything else. It needs to become accustomed to this brilliance of light and colour before any further progress can be made. This may take some time, or it may happen quite quickly. I believe, Pearl, that you were seeing more than just colours by today.'

'Oh yes, Swami, such beautiful scenes! Great majestic mountains that seemed to soar upwards for ever, and the most beautiful countryside, with fields swimming in gorgeous flowers, and orchards full of luscious fruit. And everything was so much more alive than here on earth.'

'What you saw was the astral plane where the gods reside,' explained Govinda. 'Not where the Lord himself is, but the petty gods and the great saints and sages who have played their part in the evolution of the world. Perhaps you saw some of them, Pearl?'

She hesitated. 'I can't really be sure. Certainly not very clearly, anyway. But I think I caught a glimpse of holy men conducting a ceremony around a fire.'

'Very likely. The saints and sages continue to pray for human salvation even when they leave our humble plane of existence. Well done, Pearl! I knew that you were making rapid progress. On Monday I sensed that Pearl had a great desire for spirituality, and when I placed my hand upon her head, I could feel the thousand-petalled lotus pulsing within her, closed but wanting to open. That is why I opened her third eye for her, with the results that you have heard.

'As you practise more and more, that third eye will open further and further, revealing the divine plane of existence, and once you have experienced that, you will want nothing further to do with television! It has nothing to offer compared to the experience of deep meditation.'

For twenty minutes or so Govinda elicited from each member of the group his or her experience, and to each he offered words of praise and encouragement. The only cloud upon the proceedings was cast by a small, dark-haired woman sitting to one side, who listened to the recitations of her fellows with what appeared to be increasing bewilderment. Govinda finally came to her.

'And what about you, Sarah?'

'I couldn't see anything at all!' she exclaimed. 'When I closed my eyes there was nothing but a thick, black fog, and the harder I looked the thicker and blacker it got!'

Govinda smiled. 'Well, my dear, as I said right at the beginning, we are all at different stages of our spiritual evolution. I wouldn't worry about it.'

The rest of the class grinned.

4

Anthony had not attended any of the meditation sessions after that first day. It had taken him a long time to recover from the effects of his long immersion in meditation, and his duties had had to be carried out by others, causing some resentment. It had taken him an hour after the class's dispersal to "surface", and Govinda and Simon had half-carried, half-dragged him upstairs because his legs refused to function. They had laid him on Govinda's bed, and the guru himself had used a special ayurvedic oil to massage life back into his frozen leg muscles.

'From now on, my boy, you will meditate only with me,' Govinda grunted, his fingers working the oil into Anthony's calves. 'The power within the temple, augmented by the combined efforts of those present, was too strong for you, and because my attention was divided between so many I did not realise until too late how deeply you had become immersed. By then it would have been harmful both physically and mentally to recall you abruptly.

'We will begin with short sessions here in my room. Sitting for such a long time is not good for the legs. Once you have learned to master your bodily functions and can control them at will, there will be no difficulty. Your problem, child, is that your divine consciousness wants to race away into pure bliss, forgetting that it has not yet taught you how to master your body. There! That should do.'

Govinda helped Anthony from the bed and made him sit in his own deep and comfortable armchair, then washed his hands in a small bowl before sitting down opposite. Simon entered with a pot of coffee and three cups on a tray, but to his obvious chagrin was immediately dismissed. Govinda poured coffee into a cup, added plenty of sugar, and pushed it across the table. 'Drink it slowly,' he advised.

He waited until Anthony had drained the cup, then leaned forward, elbows on the table. 'Tell me what happened,' he said, 'and especially whether the experience was different from that in the temple the other week.'

'It was different at first,' Anthony said, his voice slow and deliberate as he tried to remember. 'As I slowed my breathing, I saw these great swirling lights, like comets, the head of each one an unbelievably bright colour - red, green, blue and gold - with the colours fading along their tails. They begin to spin around me, faster and faster, until they merged into one dazzling white light, but in the centre of the light was a black hole, and I felt myself being pulled into it.'

He paused for breath, eyes staring, as if he could still see that black hole. Govinda poured him another coffee, this time adding cream, and Anthony calmed down gradually as he sipped. Govinda did not speak, but when Anthony looked up and caught his eye, he opened his palms, as if to say "What next?"

Anthony put down his cup. 'I seemed to be in a tunnel of some kind. I couldn't see the sides because it was pitch black, but I could feel them around me, pulsing with energy. All the time I was going faster and faster, sweeping around great, wide bends, and always going down, as if I was on some great cosmic helter-skelter.' He paused again, his cheeks flushed and his face animated. 'Suddenly I became aware of a golden light at the end of the tunnel, still a long way off, and I was so desperate to reach it that I felt myself going even faster, until, almost without realising, I was actually in the light, this beautiful golden light all around me, and I was a part of it. A feeling of tremendous peace overwhelmed me, and I felt as if I'd come home after being away for a very, very long time. I was where I wanted to be, had always wanted to be, and I wanted to stay there for ever.'

He stopped, looking completely lost as he remembered that he was no longer in that place. Tears filled his eyes, and he stifled a sob. 'Where was it, that golden place?' he croaked.

'My child, you have been in Vishnu Loka, the abode of Lord Krishna himself. That you were able to go there is the direct result of deep spiritual practice in previous births, the accumulation of much good karma. You have simply taken up where you left off in your last incarnation.'

'But why has it taken until now to happen?'

Govinda laughed. 'Twenty-odd years may seem a long time to you, but to the Lord they don't even amount to the blink of an eye. You must know the hymn that goes, "A thousand ages in Thy sight are like an evening gone". That is exactly right. As for your experience, everyone who takes a human body has to allow time for it to mature physically and mentally before he can resume his spiritual practice. Even in my own case, it was not until I was seven that I became aware of who I was and what my purpose was to be, and even then I had to wait until adulthood before I could begin. Also, many people have to wait until they find a true guru to assist them.'

'Who was your guru, Swamiji?'

'For some of us,' Govinda said with an enigmatic smile, 'a guru is unnecessary. We have already attained enlightenment many incarnations ago, but choose to return to this earthly plane to help others along the path.'

'But even then, you had to wait until you came to this country.'

'The blink of an eye, Anthony. Even Jesus of Nazareth waited until he was thirty before he began his ministry. The simple truth is that we are all blessed and burdened with parents: they nurture us and raise us, always doing what they believe to be for our own good. While we are children, they decide what we can or cannot do, and they have such ambitions for us! Oh, my dear, how my father longed for me to become a lawyer like himself! What a fruitless dream!

'Even Lord Krishna's parents had no idea of his true identity. When Yeshoda forced his mouth open to retrieve a stolen sweet, she saw the whole cosmos inside the little boy's mouth. She had such a fright! But did she understand that her child was the Supreme Being in human form? No. Within seconds she had convinced herself that it had been her imagination.'

'So what do I do now?'

'Come here an hour before dinner every evening, and we will meditate together, so that I can keep a watchful eye on your progress. I will ask Swami to rearrange any duties you have at that time. I will also begin to instruct you as to the role of a Swami, and you can take the vows on Lord Krishna's birthday. Now you had better go and have something to eat.'

When Anthony had gone, Govinda lifted up the tablecloth and switched off the cassette recorder concealed below.

5

It was busier than ever that Sunday in May as Simon stood at the window, already robed for the pooja, and looked down on the colourful chaos outside. The car park was crammed with vehicles of all ages and makes, parked higgledy-piggledy; men staggered from open boots lugging sacks of rice and other goods to the temple porch; women in bright sarees stood gossiping in little knots; and the whole place rang with the joyful shouts and screams of children running everywhere, in imminent danger of losing life or limb from cars still arriving and trying to park.

'We're going to have to put someone on permanent car park duty at the weekends, Swamiji. These people have no idea whatsoever of how to park in an organised fashion.'

Govinda looked up from his coffee. 'Even more important, my dear, is to increase the parking capacity. We will never cope once summer is upon us, especially for the Lord's birthday, with the present facility. Give it some thought, Swami.'

The temple bell began to ring, and the crowd scattered around the building's environs began to move in excited chattering groups towards the temple doors. Among the womenfolk in particular there was a certain amount of undignified haste in order to be as close to the fore as possible.

'It's certainly becoming a problem,' Simon agreed. 'Yesterday lunch-time the cars were backed up down the lane, and when people wanted to leave they couldn't because the driver of one of the last cars had decided to go for a walk. It was utter chaos for a time.'

Govinda joined him at the window. The car park was now empty of people, and they could hear beneath them the murmuring of the devotees thronging into the temple. As they looked, another car came at speed up the lane, bouncing wildly, and screeched to a halt in a shower of gravel. Doors were flung open to disgorge several plump ladies from the back seat, and two men in the front, who all scurried towards the temple.

'Just look at them,' Govinda remarked, shaking his head. 'The stragglers of Bombay!'

After the pooja, most devotees having already left the temple, Govinda emerged and wandered into the public area, nodding to various people and exchanging an occasional word with the more privileged. He espied Dr. and Mrs. Chaudhury at the back, looking hopefully in his direction, and he beckoned them. Oblivious of the jealous looks of some of the others, he drew them into a corner by the sanctuary rail.

'Some news, doctor?'

'We have some wonderful news, Swamiji,' the little doctor said, beaming, 'and some not so good,' his face now clouded with anxiety.

'Let me hear the good news first, and we can deal with the bad news in due course.'

'Our Geeta is pregnant, Swami! We are so grateful!'

Mrs. Chaudhury echoed her husband's joyful tone by almost dancing with glee, her fat, handsome face a picture of delight.

'It is to the Lord you should give thanks, doctor, but I am very happy for the couple. They did not come with you today? No? Then please give them my heartiest congratulations.'

'To God yes,' said the doctor, 'but we also give thanks to the one who interceded on our behalf.' Surreptitiously, he slipped an envelope into Govinda's hand.

'You are too kind. But what of the bad news? This concerns your other daughter, I presume.'

The smiles were wiped instantly from the Chaudhurys' faces. 'Oh, Swamiji!' the doctor exclaimed. 'Almost as soon as the girls returned home after the pooja, Meera packed her bags and moved out. We don't know where she is living, and fear that she might be with an English boy. My wife is grief-stricken at the very thought!'

'Let us hope that things are not as bad as you fear, doctor, though I am bound to say - I would be failing in my duty otherwise - that Meera has far too independent a mind for a young Indian lady. She has been infected with Western ideas about the freedom of women, ideas which are not at all suited to our Indian way of life.'

'It is all my fault!' Chaudhury lamented. 'She was such a bright child that I encouraged her to get a good education, and this is the result!'

'Education can be a dangerous tool in the wrong hands, doctor.' Govinda placed a consoling arm around his shoulder. 'I could feel the rebellious nature of the girl when she was here. Whilst your younger daughter was very attentive during the pooja, Meera's mind was constantly wandering away onto worldly matters, and as a result the effort made on her behalf was entirely fruitless. Not, of course, that I regret having tried, for that is but my duty.'

Both husband and wife were now almost in tears. 'What can we do, Swami?' the doctor wailed. 'If she is living sinfully, her good name is ruined, and our family honour is destroyed!'

'All one can do is pray, doctor. Whatever she has done or said, however much she may have wounded your feelings, it is your parental duty to pray for her and send her your love. The power of prayer and love must never be underestimated. I too will remember her in my prayers and meditation.'

'We will try, Swamiji, but I am not sure that I will ever be able to forgive her for the distress that she has caused her mother.'

Mrs. Chaudhury had not presumed to participate in a conversation between her husband and a priest, but she had followed every word, and now her great bulk began to heave with sobs as she contemplated the shame and disgrace that her first-born child had brought down upon her head.

CHAPTER 9

Jimmy looked around his room somewhat ruefully. It had been termed a flatlet in the newsagent's window, but in reality it was a single large room in an old Victorian house that had been partitioned at one side in order to create a small kitchen and minuscule shower-room. The latter was exactly that: a shower, but no toilet. There were shared toilets on each of the three landings. He sighed. *Bit of a come-down from the old family pile in Brixton!* he thought. Although that had been a smaller house, it had at least all been his. *Still, with a bit of capital behind me, and the old contacts renewed, I'll be able to get me own place in time. Give it three years.*

His first day back in the capital, he had taken a room in a cheap hotel in Victoria, before spending the next couple of days traipsing around the letting agencies and scouring advertisement boards. Brixton had naturally been his first port of call, but he discovered that the character of the place had changed; it was no longer the friendly cosmopolitan neighbourhood that he remembered. The racial tension was almost palpable, and even though one or two of the West Indian shopkeepers recognised him, he was no longer greeted with the overt warmth and friendship that had once been the norm.

It had not taken long to distribute his meagre possessions among the cupboards and drawers, which were more than adequate for his current needs. He could not recall now what had happened to the boxes of books, records, clothes and other personal possessions he had so carefully packed before leaving Brixton. *Probably moulderin' away in the corner of some barn in Brindavan*, he mused. He decided to search them out on his first visit back.

He went into the kitchenette, where there was barely sufficient room to turn round. *No swingin' cats around in here!* He grinned at the thought, then poured a generous measure of

Scotch from the bottle on the chipped formica worktop, filling the glass to the brim with water. 'Your very good health, James!', he said, raising the glass to himself and then taking a good swig. He sighed as the whiskey-warmth spread through his gut, and lit a Sobranie.

His smoking had been well-known to Brindavan's residents, as had Govinda's relentless campaign to drive it outside the building. After the tolerance of the first couple of years, Govinda's ruthlessness in this regard had begun to wear Jimmy down, and had played its part in the waning of Jimmy's enthusiasm for ashram life. A Balkan Sobranie just did not give the same pleasure when it had to be smoked in a hole-in-the-corner fashion in a damp and draughty outbuilding.

One step took Jimmy into the bed-sitting room. He switched on the radio, tuned into a music channel, sank back into an ancient but nonetheless comfortable armchair, and inhaled deeply. He swung his feet onto the cheap Woolworths coffee table, and lay back, alternately sipping the Scotch and drawing on the cigarette. A look of contentment passed across his face, and he raised his glass in another toast. 'You're back, James, me ol' son, and everthins goin' to be just dandy!'

2

It was by pure chance that Anthony happened to be crossing the yard when the mail-van arrived. The postman, a dour local with an inbuilt suspicion of the folks and the goings-on at the ashram that had softened not a whit in five years, thrust the packet of letters out of his window with a non-committal grunt, and drove off. Anthony walked into the outbuilding that was slowly being transformed into a monastic residential block, and into which he had just recently moved, and sauntered down the corridor to Simon's office. One of Simon's responsibilities was to deal with correspondence.

Unable to resist the temptation, Anthony leafed through the bundle of envelopes, though he did not expect there to be a letter for him; even his sister had not written to him for the past three years. As he came to the door of his own room, a pink envelope flicked past his eyes, and he stopped abruptly and removed it. It was addressed to him, in handwriting that was only too familiar, and without thinking of the consequences of his actions, he opened his door and went inside.

He leaned back against the door, his heart beating wildly, for it was a strict rule that all personal letters were vetted by Govinda, ostensibly to ensure that members of the community did not have their peace of mind disturbed by unwonted contact with the outside world. Since having been made a Swami, however, it had been Simon who perused all the mail first, passing on to Govinda that which required his personal attention. Those of the Brothers still in contact with their families resented this, but there was nothing they could do about it. It had not bothered Anthony as he had received no letters for some time before Simon's advancement, but today was a different matter. *I'm damned if Simon's going to read Anna's letter!* He stuffed it under his pillow and took the rest of the bundle to the office.

For the rest of the morning Anthony found himself rushing from pillar to post, worried that the letter, the first in years, contained bad news. When he had handed over the mail, Simon button-holed him for an errand, and then he had become caught up in one job after another, and suddenly it was time to wash up for the midday pooja, and he had no time to read the bad news he was now certain the letter contained; news of illness perhaps, or even death.

The abrupt cessation of Anna's letters had puzzled him, for she had always been a regular correspondent. He had spoken to Govinda about it, and he had shrugged his shoulders and suggested that Anthony's father, so vehemently opposed to Anthony's association with himself, had finally got to her. He had written to Anna a couple of times, but there had been no reply, and he reconciled himself to the idea that Govinda's assessment had been correct.

On returning to his room to wash and change for pooja, he transferred the letter beneath the mattress to be on the safe side, resolving to read it straight after lunch. That did not happen, as all hands were called upon to repair a fence brought down by the escape attempts of a bulling cow. He was not even able to snatch a quick look when he returned to his room to change, for Simon accompanied him and stood in the doorway chatting while he changed into his working clothes.

The next two hours were torture. What with the worry about the letter's contents, coupled with the guilt of having broken the rules, together with the constant and inconsequential chatter of Brothers Ronan and Douglas, and the bang, bang, bang of the mallet on the fence posts, it was no wonder that by four o' clock he had come down with a raging headache. When he vomited his lunch over Ronan's boots, Douglas suggested that he ought to go and lie down.

And after all the worry, the contents of the letter proved entirely innocuous: no one had died or was seriously ill. Anna chided him for his constant failure to answer her letters, while understanding that he wanted to break with his past. Nevertheless, she felt it her duty to let him know how everyone was at home, assuring him that both parents were well, and passing on information about their holiday plans and suchlike. In a postscript she said that she visited Rosie's grave whenever possible, and hoped that he did not blame himself in any way for what had happened.

The headache, pounding viciously against his temples, made it difficult for him to think clearly. What did she mean about not replying to her letters? What had happened to Rosie? He tried to read the words again, but his eyes would not focus, and he slumped back on the bed, the letter fluttering to the floor. The room began to spin, slowly at first, and he closed his eyes, but that only made things worse. He realised that his breathing was rapid and shallow, and tried to calm himself with slow, deep breaths. This only made his head roar, and then he felt the nausea rising again in his gut, and knew that whatever was left of his lunch was about to leave by the way it had come.

Lunging up off the bed, he staggered to the door and threw it open just in time to vomit violently into the passage. The blood rushed through his brain, reinforcing the orchestra of pile-drivers that hammered their insane symphony inside his skull, and he sank to his knees, exhausted and helpless. With great detachment he watched the vomit puddling around his knees, noting some of the still recognisable parts of his lunch, then retched again and again, until his stomach had nothing further to offer. With his head throbbing, his stomach muscles aching, and saliva and vomit trickling down his chin, he stood up and sagged back against the door, which swung gently inwards, and deposited him on the floor of his room, his feet still outside in the mess.

Hearing a noise in the passage, Simon looked outside and saw Anthony's feet protruding from the room, involuntarily crying out in alarm. Tip-toeing as best he could through the sea of vomit, he was relieved to find Anthony was not dead - his first fear - and lugged him up onto the bed before rushing out to fetch Sister Magda. He did not notice the letter on the floor.

3

'He has no temperature to speak of, Swamiji, but he does have a very bad headache. I would guess that he is merely over-tired, not getting enough rest perhaps.'

'There was a hot sun this afternoon too,' Simon observed. 'That may have been a contributory factor.'

'That is quite possible,' Sister Magda agreed.

'But you think it unnecessary to call the doctor, Sister?' Govinda enquired.

'I have given him some aspirin and some water, and he is resting comfortably, so I think it is not necessary to trouble the doctor, but I will observe him tonight and we will see how he is in the morning.' Sister Magda delivered her opinion with

John Thompson

the professional assurance of a woman who had once been a formidable ward sister.

'Thank you, Sister. You have my permission to come and go as you please tonight, and please let me know how he is tomorrow.'

'But of course, Swamiji.' She turned on her heel and left.

When Simon had closed the door, Govinda looked enquiringly at him. 'Is anything troubling Brother Anthony, do you know?'

'Not as far as I'm aware. He certainly hasn't said anything to me - though he probably wouldn't confide in me anyway. He seemed a bit preoccupied at lunch, wasn't very communicative, but that may have been the headache coming on.'

'Perhaps he's just been overdoing things the past few days.'

'It wouldn't have anything to do with these experiences he's been having, would it?'

'Don't be ridiculous! If there were anything wrong due to his meditation, I would know about it.'

'Well then, maybe he was just over-tired, and the hot sun finished him off.'

'That's probably it. By the way, I spoke to Jimmy this afternoon, and I've arranged for us to go up and see him on Friday. We'll have to set off early, so you will need to organise the Brothers so that everyone knows exactly who is doing what. I don't want any slip ups if there happen to be visitors. Brother Anthony will be in charge, of course, but I want it made quite clear that not even he is to take any telephone calls; the answering machine must be left on. We can't risk Ronan answering the phone again like last month; anything could happen.'

'That was just unfortunate. I'd gone to the toilet, and he came looking for me, and at that moment the telephone rang and the idiot answered it.'

'The idiot wouldn't have had the chance if another idiot had remembered to lock the office door! It was pure good fortune that it was merely a clerk in the rating office, and not someone important.'

'It won't happen again.'

'It had better not. Please make sure the answer-phone is on and the door locked before we leave.'

'Right. What time do you want to leave?'

'Jimmy is expecting us for lunch, so we must leave by eight at the very latest, to allow for traffic delays.'

'So you'll want to go to the bank on Thursday.'

'The bank?'

'To collect the draft for Jimmy.'

'Oh, that's already in hand. There's no need for you to worry about it.'

'It's almost nine. I'd better go and light up.'

'You do that. In fact, you take the pooja tonight. I think I'll go and see how Anthony's getting on.'

4

The telephone rang several times before it was picked up. 'Hallo?' The voice was a little tremulous, but it was unmistakeably his mother.

'Mother, it's Anthony.'

'Anthony?' The tone was puzzled for a second, then there was a shriek, followed by a banging noise and scrabbling sounds, before his mother's voice returned, somewhat breathless. 'Anthony? Is it really you?'

'Yes, it's me, mother. What happened?'

'I dropped the phone, dear. You gave me such a shock. Where are you calling from?'

'I'm at the ashram.'

'Oh.' The disappointment was palpable.

'Mother, I have to talk to Anna. Is she there?'

'Of course she's here. Where else would she be?'

'I thought she might be at college, or working.'

'She finished college last year, silly. Don't you read her letters? And why don't you answer them, you wicked boy?'

'It's a long story, mother, and I don't have much time. Can you call her to the phone? It's rather urgent.'

'Very well, dear; hang on.'

Anthony heard her shouting for Anna, her voice muffled. Then she spoke again. 'She's coming; she was in the bathroom. Is everything all right, dear? There's nothing wrong, is there?'

'There's nothing wrong.'

'Are you eating properly?'

'Mother, I'm fine. Where's Anna?'

'She's here now. It's Anthony, darling.'

After speaking to his sister, Anthony checked that the answering machine was on, and left the office, locking the door behind him, before seeking the sanctuary of his room. He did everything automatically, his brain-stem functioning on the mundane level while the cerebral part of his brain tried to cope with what he had just learned.

The postscript to Anna's letter had nagged at him. Obviously Rosie had died, and that was a terrible tragedy, of course, but why on earth did his sister think he might be feeling guilty about it? He had decided he would sneak out late at night and walk to the nearest village to make a call from a phone box, and then Simon had informed him of the Friday trip. Although he knew that the office would be locked, he also knew that Simon kept the key in his room, and it was a simple matter to search for it and open the office to use the phone.

He sat on the bed, his head between his hands. *Suicide! And my fault! Jesus, how can I live with that?* He lay back across the bed, his mind numbed, and his chest tight. He had never felt so unutterably miserable in the whole of his life.

Rosie! He recalled her face without effort, the intervening years falling away. He had so casually dismissed her from his life, with just the odd passing thought since: what was she doing? was she happily married? how many children did she have? But it had not really mattered to him; they were just idle thoughts. He had, of course, thought kindly of her, assuming her to be alive and happy. Taking it for granted that she was. And all the time she had been dead: had gone home after he had broken up with her and killed herself. Just like that. He had assumed that her sudden disappearance from the scene had been her acceptance of his decision to join Govinda, and a desire never to see him again. Obviously she had accepted that he would not change his mind, and her response had been suicide. *Because of me! Because of my decision to abandon her!*

It appeared that Anna had found out about Rosie's death more than a year after the event in a very roundabout way, and had deliberately not told him because of the shock he might suffer. After a couple of years, however, she had decided that he had a right to know, and had broken the news in a long and gentle letter. He had only written once after that, and had not mentioned Rosie, so she never brought the subject up again, even though she wrote to him every couple of months. Only in that last letter had she thought to mention Rosie's name again. *Every couple of months for the last three years! Then where did the fucking letters go?*

But he knew where they had gone. Govinda had confiscated them all without a word, and had then lied to him about Anna's supposed silence. *Why? Why?* He tried to rationalise what had obviously happened, tried to defend Govinda: he had read the letter about Rosie, and decided to protect Anthony from the consequences. Then he had been forced to keep back all the letters, to discourage contact so that he would never discover that terrible truth. *It still doesn't justify it!* He knew now why Govinda had not appeared surprised when Anthony spoke to him about Anna's letters drying up.

Simon! He tried to convince himself that Simon was the villain of the piece, that he had suppressed the letters for his own inscrutable reasons, that Govinda knew nothing about it. But this argument did not wash either. He knew that Simon would not have had the guts to do something as serious as that behind Govinda's back. More to the point, he never did anything without Govinda's express sanction.

How he got through the morning he could not have said. He lurched from one task to another in purely mechanical mode, aware from time to time of the odd looks that some of the others cast in his direction, but quite unable to pull himself together. The lunchtime and evening poojas were conducted without an ounce of spiritual consciousness: his heart, usually so open to bliss, was closed, hard and cold. He led the chanting in a perfunctory, toneless manner, and his singing lacked all devotion.

Throughout the evening service, he had one ear cocked for the crunch of car tyres on gravel, and his one thought was that he had to get out of the temple and into his own room before Govinda and Simon returned. At all costs he had to avoid bumping into him now, when he felt wounded, angry and betrayed, and in sore need of punching someone in the face. But he also felt fear: fear of Govinda's power, fear of his reaction if confronted, and also, undeniably, fear of being rejected. He needed the silence of his room, in the hope that there he would be able to formulate some rational plan of action.

At the same time, he knew that he had to confront his guru some time, for if he did not, if he allowed what had occurred to pass without taking action, he feared that the sense of emptiness and desolation inside him would grow like some unstoppable cancer and consume him, until he was nothing more than an empty, useless husk of a human being. *I must have time to think!* his mind screamed.

He wrapped the pooja up early, pleading another headache, detailed Brother Dennis to see to the sanctuary and Brother Ronan to wait up for Govinda. No-one batted an eyelid, and he fled to the sanctuary of his room.

5

Simon flung his exhausted body onto the bed. The return journey from London had taken two hours longer than anticipated because of the Friday night rush hour in the city and the heavy weekend traffic on the roads to the West country. It had been hot, and the weather forecast for the weekend was for soaring temperatures; people had headed for the coast and the countryside in hordes of Gothic proportions.

He calculated that he had been behind the wheel of the car altogether for over half a day, but despite his bodily fatigue he was unable to sleep; his mind was racing with the events of the day, a day of many surprises. They had arrived at Jimmy's new address shortly before one o'clock, and he had welcomed them on the doorstep in his usual, effervescent, over-the-top manner.

'Govinda! Simon! My dear fellahs! How good to see you. Come in, come in. Perfect timin', everythin's ready to put straight on the table.'

They had followed him up the stairs, and Simon's mouth had begun to water at once as the aroma of exotic cuisine wafted down towards them. Despite Govinda's patient instruction to Brother Dennis, who had drawn the short straw and been drafted as the new ashram cook, the food at Brindavan had taken on an unappetising blandness since Jimmy's departure.

Jimmy had sat them down at the small table in his spartan establishment, then whisked in and out of the tiny kitchen with one dish after another: rice, dhall, vegetable curries both wet and dry, a dish that seemed to Simon to give off a distinct odour of fish, and several kinds of Indian bread. Eventually, he joined them. 'Tuck in, chaps!' he bellowed. 'Must clear everythin'!'

He had been like a cat on hot bricks, constantly jumping up to help one or other of his guests to something, yet still finding time to devour the mound on his own plate, and all the while maintaining an uninterrupted - and uninterruptible - flow of chatter. Simon noticed that the suspect dish had been placed at Govinda's right hand.

'Um … is that a fish curry, Jimmy?' he asked apprehensively.

'Fish curry! Never! Sea vegetables!' He roared with laughter. 'Right, Govinda?'

Govinda laughed. 'In Bengal a lot of fish is eaten,' he explained, 'and consciences are salved by calling them "sea vegetables".'

Simon, already irked by Jimmy's casual use of Govinda's name, was amazed that he had had the temerity to provide non-vegetarian food. 'But, Swamiji, you aren't going to eat it, are you?' he queried.

'Normally I would not eat fish, but Jimmy has prepared this meal with so much love, and I will therefore take a little. The true renunciate will eat whatever is placed before him if it has been cooked with love, for he sees no difference between fish, flesh and vegetable. To him, everything is Brahman.'

'But you insist upon a strict vegetarian diet at Brindavan.'

'That is because the members of the community, even you, Swami Krishnananda, are not perfect renunciates. Meat and fish are full of bad vibrations caused by the manner of their death, and those vibrations are absorbed by those who eat the flesh. A cow, for example, knows that it is going to be killed when it is brought to the abattoir: it is surrounded by the smell of blood and death. It becomes frightened, releasing adrenaline into the bloodstream, and so its fear becomes part of its body at the moment of death. That is why Jews and Muslims drain the blood from the dead animal, but that is not a complete cure for the problem.

'Vegetables, on the other hand, do not contain such harmful vibrations, for they do not have the same consciousness as animals. Accordingly, vegetarian food is purer, and the purity of the aspirant's food assists him in his spiritual quest. Once a person has advanced to a higher level of consciousness, however, nothing he eats can be of harm to him, for he eats with complete detachment, aware that everything is God. The evil uncle of Lord Krishna sought to poison him many times, but the poison had no effect. In fact, it changed into ambrosia.'

As he spoke, Jimmy ladled a generous portion of fish curry onto his plate, which he then proceeded to eat. 'To me,' he said, with an airy wave of the hand, 'there is no difference between this fish curry and that potato curry.'

Jimmy then offered the fish to Simon, who raised his spoon to ward off the approach of the ladle in Jimmy's hand.

'Have some, man!' Govinda snorted. 'One piece of fish isn't going to destroy your spiritual practice.'

Distracted by Govinda's intervention, Simon let his guard drop, and Jimmy deposited the contents of the ladle onto his plate. Simon looked at the pieces of fish in dismay, and tried to eat around them, conscious all the while of the smirking faces opposite. His endeavours were fruitless, for the sauce from the fish had spread to the rice, dhall and potato, and he could not avoid tasting it. Eventually, while Jimmy and Govinda were talking, he slipped a piece of fish onto his spoon and into his mouth. It was the first non-vegetarian food he had eaten for more than six years. It tasted good.

'Nearly forgot,' Jimmy said, jumping up once more and disappearing into the kitchen, where he extricated a bottle of champagne from the refrigerator. 'Thought we'd celebrate my new beginnin' with a drop of bubbly,' he announced, deftly removing the foil and wire.

'Splendid!' cried Govinda. 'Nothing like champagne to liven up a party!' He wagged a finger at Simon. 'Only one glass for you, my lad; you're driving.'

When the food had gone, and the champagne bottle had been emptied, Jimmy produced his cigarette case. 'D'you mind, Govinda?' he asked.

'This is your home, and you are entitled to do as you wish, my dear,' Govinda replied. 'Moreover, I have a little gift to go with it.' He reached under his chair for the little haversack he had brought, and with a conjuror's flourish produced from within it a bottle of single malt whiskey, which he proffered to Jimmy.

Taking the bottle reverently, Jimmy read the label. 'Mm! Twelve years old,' he murmured appreciatively.

'And to go with it, a bottle of pure Brindavan spring water,' Govinda announced, producing a small plastic bottle. 'I collected this myself yesterday.'

'Splendid!' Jimmy enthused. 'You think of everythin', Govinda.' He disappeared into the kitchen, re-emerging with three tumblers.

'Not for Simon, Jimmy. He has a long drive ahead of him. As for myself, I'll take a very small drop neat.'

'This is just great!' Jimmy gushed, pouring a shot for Govinda, half-filling his own tumbler and topping it up with the Brindavan water.

Govinda raised his glass. 'Your very good health, Jimmy!'

'Cheers!' Jimmy responded, beaming as he sipped the malt. 'Ooh! So good!'

'Jimmy,' Govinda said, suddenly serious, 'I'm afraid there's been a slight hitch with the money.'

'Hitch? What sort of hitch?' He was worried.

'It's nothing to worry about. I asked the bank to have the draft ready to collect yesterday, mentioning that I was seeing you today, and the idiots somehow got hold of the idea that you would be collecting it personally today, so it wasn't ready yesterday.'

'Oh, I was sort of relyin' on that.'

'I instructed the bank to draw it up and send it by registered post to this address, so it should be here tomorrow, or by Monday at the latest.'

Jimmy gasped with relief. 'For a moment there I pictured all my dreams comin' crashin' down. Let's have another drink to celebrate.'

Govinda declined, explaining that he wanted to dash about buying up lots of spices and other goods not so easily obtainable in their part of the world. He stood up, shook Jimmy's hand, and embraced him. 'I wish you every success, Jimmy.'

Jimmy poured himself another glass of Scotch, then bustled about retrieving coats and bags. He stood on the top step of the old building, glass in hand, waving a fond farewell and promising to visit Brindavan soon.

'You're very quiet, Swami,' Govinda had said as Simon drove away.

'Just a bit tired.'

Now, as he lay on his bed, he was wondering why Govinda had not mentioned either the gift of whiskey or the problem with the bank on the long drive to London.

6

Edwina Christie was an elderly spinster of genteel background but reduced circumstances who lived in the second floor flat at the rear. Her door was less than a foot from Jimmy's. She did not work any longer, living on a very small private income from a family trust, and her pension, and her meagre income did not allow her to go out very often. She was generally at home in the afternoons and evenings, and was on that particular Friday.

She later told the police that it was just before the six o'clock news on the wireless - she had no television - that she heard a crash from the room next door, the room of Mr. Partington, the new tenant. She was positive about the time because the shipping forecast was being read. The noise had alarmed her, for in the short time that he had been there, Mr. Partington had been a very quiet gentleman. He had, however, had visitors that day, and she had heard sounds of merriment, which made her feel rather pleased for him, as he had seemed a lonely man, much like herself really, though much younger, of course.

She had been deliberating whether to go and knock on his door to see if he was all right when she heard the door wrenched open with some force, for it had banged against the wall. Distinctly worried by now, and indeed a little afraid, she had opened her door a trifle to see what was going on; Mr. Partington was leaning against the wall, sweating, and breathing stertorously. His face was white, his eyes staring.

Opening the door fully, she had asked him if he was ill, which was a silly question when she thought about it later, as he clearly was not well at all. He had not heard her at first, so she asked him, more loudly, if he would like her to call a doctor. He looked at her, blankly at first, and then seemed to recognise her: they had met a few times on the stairs and exchanged greetings.

"Feeling sick," he had said, and then he had lurched forward, presumably trying to get to the toilet on the half-landing. She had stepped forward to offer him her arm, but he had staggered past her and tumbled headlong down the stairs, with an awful crash.

One of the tenants on the first floor had appeared then, and called for an ambulance, but it was obvious that Mr. Partington was dead. His head was at such an unnatural angle. She did not like to speak ill of the dead, but she was positive that his breath had smelled strongly of whiskey, although he had been such a nice man.

CHAPTER 10

Simon had dealt with the unanswered questions relating to the visit to Jimmy by sweeping them to the back of his mind: he certainly had no intention of asking Govinda for answers. They flooded back into the forefront of his mind the following Wednesday, however, following a knock on his office door.

'Come!' he said.

Brother Dennis's head appeared around the door. He was clearly flustered. 'Swami,' he croaked, 'there are two police officers here from London asking to speak to Swamiji.'

Simon leapt up in such surprise that he banged his knee on the underside of his desk. 'Police?' he gasped, gritting his teeth. 'What on earth do they want?'

'They wouldn't say. Just said they wanted to talk to Swamiji. I put them in the ladies' dining room. No-one's likely to come across them there at this time of day.'

'Good thinking, Brother Dennis. I'll take over now, and see what they want.'

Soon after, Simon ushered the police officers into Govinda's room and introduced them. Govinda stood and bowed courteously.

'Please come in, gentlemen, and find yourselves a seat. Swami Krishnananda tells me that you refused to divulge to him the reason for your visit, but have you any objection to his remaining here. He is not only my secretary, but also my deputy.'

The senior detective, Inspector Collins, shook his head. 'I've no objection, sir,' he said, sitting on a dining chair and withdrawing his note-book. Taking his time, he flicked through it until he found the entry he was looking for, while his companion, Detective Sergeant Morrow, took a seat by the door and took out his own note-book and pencil.

'This place is known as "Brindavan", I believe.'

'The emphasis is on the second syllable, Inspector,' Govinda corrected.

'And how would you describe Brindavan?' the inspector asked, without any noticeable change of pronunciation.

'Inspector, if you really wish me to give you a lecture upon the mysteries and complexities of the Hindu religion, I will be only too happy to do so, but I am sure that you came here for some other reason.'

'We're making inquiries into the death of … ', pausing to consult his note-book, 'Mr. James Maurice Partington,' Collins concluded, fixing Govinda with a level gaze.

'Good God!' Govinda cried, starting to his feet. 'Jimmy dead? But how? And when?' He began to pace about the room.

Simon said nothing; just sat in his chair, his mouth hanging open, stupefied.

'Then you knew the deceased, I take it.'

'Knew him?' Govinda stopped his pacing for a moment. 'Of course I knew him. We were old friends, and founded this ashram together. He lived here for six years, and only left recently.'

'And was his departure an amicable one, sir, if you don't mind my asking?'

'Amicable?' Govinda said irritably, pausing again in his perambulations. 'I certainly didn't want him to leave - he was an excellent cook - but we remained good friends. In fact, we had lunch with him in London only last Friday.'

'Would you mind resuming your seat, sir. It's a bit distracting with you walking about.' He waited until Govinda sat down again, either ignoring or failing to notice the glare he received. 'Would you mind telling me the purpose of your visit?'

'I don't mind at all, Inspector. We have no secrets here at Brindavan. Our purpose was to have lunch with an old and valued friend. And now, perhaps, could you tell me what happened. Was there an accident?'

'There was an accident of sorts, sir. Last Friday in the early evening.'

'What do you mean by an accident "of sorts"?'

'It appears that he fell down the stairs while drunk and broke his neck. The remains of a meal for three people were found in the kitchen, together with an empty bottle of champagne, and also a whiskey bottle that was empty as near as dammit, if you'll pardon the expression.'

Govinda sank back into his chair and shook his head sadly. 'I warned him so many times about drinking too much,' he said, looking Collins in the eye. 'I didn't want to say so before, but it was one of the reasons that he had to leave. He just couldn't go more than a day or so without a drink, and I could tolerate alcohol here no longer.' He paused, sighed, and shook his head again. 'But to think of him dying in such a way. Terrible! Just terrible! Did he suffer at all, do you know?'

'The doctor thinks he died instantly. Broken neck, you see.'

'A small mercy!' Govinda muttered.

'I take it, sir, that you were one of the persons who had lunch with the deceased?'

'Yes, indeed. Swami here was the other.'

Collins looked at Simon, whose face had taken on a sickly pallor. 'And how long would you say you were there?' he asked.

'For no more than about two hours, wouldn't you say, Swami?'

Simon nodded.

'And in what state was the deceased when you left?'

'He was very happy. Looking forward to his new business venture.'

'Sorry, sir, I didn't make myself clear. I meant, was he already drunk?'

'Merry, yes, but certainly not drunk.'

'How much had he had to drink, would you say?'

'He had certainly had a few glasses of champagne, that's true. I had a small glass, purely not to offend him, and Swami had none, as he was driving, but I'm pretty sure the bottle was still half full when we left.'

'And what about the whiskey?'

'Ah, the whiskey! Govinda sighed heavily. 'I shall always bear a heavy burden of responsibility for that, Inspector.'

'How so, sir?' Collins asked, frowning.

'Whiskey was Jimmy's favourite tipple, and I bought him a decent bottle as a gesture of friendship. If I'd foreseen that he would drink it all at once, well ....'

'I see. And did he start on your gift before you left?'

'Let me think. I'm pretty certain he opened it, but just to smell the bouquet. He always maintained that you could tell how good a whiskey was from the smell, just like wine. But I don't recall him actually taking a drink from it. What about you, Swami?' he added, looking Simon directly in the eye.

'Er, I don't think so.'

'So you drove all the way to London just for a spot of lunch and to hand over a bottle of Scotch?'

'Not just for that, Inspector. You recall that I mentioned Jimmy was a co-founder of Brindavan, which we established as a refuge for people who wished to escape from the madness of the outside world - madness which you no doubt have to deal with on a daily basis. In the beginning Jimmy was very enthusiastic, and it is a fact that the project would not have got off the ground without him, but as time passed he found that he could not make the commitments that a monastic life demands, mainly due to his addiction to alcohol and tobacco. He had been hovering on the brink of a decision to leave for many months, and it was only his worry that he might not be able to re-establish himself that made him delay so long. He was rather a successful interior decorator at one time, you know.'

'All very interesting, sir, but what I'd like to know is what money you were referring to in this recent letter you wrote to him.' Collins produced a folded sheet of paper from his note-book and passed it over.

'I was coming to that, Inspector. Jimmy and I owned Brindavan jointly, and when he left he signed his interest over to me. He wanted to donate his entire interest to the community, presumably feeling he was letting us down by leaving, but I persuaded him to accept something to keep him going while he sorted himself out. I gave him five hundred pounds in cash when he left, and when we spoke on the telephone he asked if he could have another five hundred. We had been planning to go to London to buy Asian supplies for some time, so I said I would bring the money with me, and Jimmy invited us to have lunch.'

'And you gave the money to him?'

'Yes, while Swami was in the toilet. Jimmy was very embarrassed about asking for the money, and Swami knew nothing about the arrangement. In fact, this is the first time he's heard about it.'

The astonished look on Simon's face confirmed to Collins the truth of that assertion.

'I hope you found the money, Inspector. It was in a white envelope, in twenty-pound notes. Not that I make any claim upon it, of course; it was Jimmy's.'

'We did find the money, yes, under a cushion in the armchair. I thought it an odd place to keep it.'

'I could have sworn he put it in a drawer. Perhaps he took it out to count after we'd left.'

'Unlikely, sir. It hadn't been opened. So you parted on good terms, would you say, last Friday afternoon?'

'Certainly. Jimmy had cooked us an excellent lunch, and we were all in good spirits. His last words were that he would come down here to see us very soon.'

'And he was fit and well, as far as you could judge, when you left?'

'Absolutely. He came down the stairs with us, and saw us off from the front steps, and he was fit and well.'

'And what time did you say you left?'

'I don't believe I did, Inspector. I did say that we were there for about two hours. It may have been a little longer. We arrived not long after one o'clock, and it could not have been much later than three-thirty or thereabouts when we left. We had our shopping to do before the long drive back.'

Collins perused his note-book. 'That seems to tally more or less with what Miss Christie told us.'

'And who is Miss Christie?'

'The elderly lady who lives in the flat next door. She heard visitors arrive, and later heard them leave. It was about six when she heard a noise, and then witnessed the deceased fall to his death.'

'How very unpleasant for her.'

'Did the deceased have any chest problems to your knowledge?'

'He did sometimes complain of breathlessness, and a tight feeling in the chest. I attributed this to his smoking, and frequently implored him to give up the habit.'

'Had he ever seen the doctor for heart problems?'

'Not that I'm aware. Why do you ask?'

'The pathology report states that the heart was in a bad way. It sounds as if he may have been having a heart attack when he fell.'

'His heavy smoking would no doubt have contributed to his heart problem.'

'Very likely, sir.' Collins stood up. 'Thank you for your assistance. If there's anything more we need to know, I suppose we can always find you here?'

'Of course. Swami will give you the telephone number.'

'Already got it, sir.' He waved the letter.

'Ah, yes. Please feel free to come again in happier circumstances, and Swami and I will give you the guided tour.'

'If I'm ever in this neck of the woods again, I might take you up on that.'

Simon came back upstairs after seeing off the detectives, and found Govinda standing at the window deep in thought. He hesitated in the doorway, unsure whether his presence was welcome.

'Come in and sit down, Simon,' Govinda commanded, without turning round.

Simon went to take the chair still warm from the backside of Inspector Collins, thought better of it, and sat down elsewhere.

'You're wondering why I did not tell our friends from London the truth about our agreement with Jimmy.' It was not a question. 'Perhaps it was wrong of me. If so, I shall answer to a higher tribunal. However, I saw little point in telling the police that we had promised several thousand pounds to Jimmy once it was obvious it would be of no benefit to him. Better that we use it here for the benefit of the people than it going to Jimmy's moronic sister.'

'But what was that about five hundred pounds?'

'The bank's head office did not approve the mortgage, and I took the cash to ensure Jimmy did not go short. I couldn't tell him the truth, as he appeared in such good spirits.'

'But how on earth were we to pay Jimmy?'

'I would have found a way - though it hardly matters now.'

'Poor old Jimmy,' Simon mused. 'I can't say I ever really liked him, but ...'

'The feeling was entirely mutual, I can assure you,' Govinda cut in. 'He told me once that he thought you were a ... how did he put it? ... "pompous arsehole" were the words he used, if I remember correctly.'

Simon's face turned bright red. 'Why didn't you tell me about the bank problem beforehand?' he asked belligerently.

'Swami Krishnananda,' Govinda replied icily, 'you are my secretary, not the keeper of my conscience. It is not for you to know everything I think or do, let alone presume to judge me.' He turned away again and looked outside, where one of the monks was raking the gravel smooth. 'On your way out, please tell Brother Hugh to put a little more joy into his efforts; he looks as if he's about to fall down dead with boredom. All work is the Lord's work. And you'd better call a Brothers' meeting for tomorrow morning,' he called after Simon's retreating figure.

2

Anthony went straight from the meeting up into the woods. *I need to think!* There was little possibility of finding peace and quiet down below, given the excitement generated among the monks by Govinda's announcement. The news of Jimmy's death, coming so hard on the heels of his discovery of Govinda's duplicity, had shaken him to the roots. Only he and Simon, and perhaps Sheila, knew that Brindavan had been purchased with the proceeds of sale of Jimmy's house in Brixton, and although he did not know what financial arrangements Govinda had made with Jimmy, he had gleaned from a remark let slip by Simon that Jimmy was to be compensated. He also recalled his last conversation with Jimmy before his return to London, and his confidence in Govinda: 'If push comes to shove, I know he won't let me down,' he had said. Anthony had not attached any importance to what had seemed a throw-away remark, but now he could not help thinking how convenient Jimmy's death must be.

He climbed the hillside slowly, weaving his way between the stunted trees, trees growing too closely together on the poor, thin soil, fighting each other for water, nourishment and light. Many had already lost the battle, standing leafless and forlorn in various stages of decay, the ground at their base littered with mouldering leaves and branches. A thick blanket of composting leaves from the previous autumn still covered the ground, providing nutrients for the hopeful saplings and the perennial weeds.

Anthony kicked savagely at a decayed tree stump, sending a shower of rotting timber, beetles and woodlice, ants and other denizens of decay, in all directions. The act gave him an immense feeling of satisfaction, as if some at least of his doubts and uncertainties had somehow been blown away. He jumped karate-style at another tree trunk, from which all the branches had sheared, causing the upper part to snap off and fall back towards him, breaking on his shoulder. A spray of rotten splinters and insects engulfed him, some going down his neck, but he paid no heed, for he was now seized by a manic determination to destroy whatever lay in his path. He began to run through the trees, targeting all that seemed dead, kicking at them, shoulder-charging them, wrestling them to the ground, screaming and swearing.

Towards the top, the trees began to thin out, and most were alive. At the very edge of the wood one lone trunk stood, denuded of branches, and Anthony made it his final target, putting everything into his charge, as if that one bare trunk represented everything he now felt to be rotten in Brindavan. His shoulder hit the tree with all his weight and velocity behind it; pain lanced down his shoulder and arm as he cannoned off, leaving the trunk quivering but intact. He fell, clutching his shoulder and swearing vociferously. Fire ran up and down his arm, as if a million wicked sprites were sticking hot pins into it, and his shoulder shrieked with pain. *Oh fuck! I've broken my bloody shoulder!*

He rolled gingerly onto his back, holding his right arm steady with his left, panting through the pain like a woman in labour. Tenderly he probed his collar bone, then pressed gently on it; the pain did not increase, so that particular bone did not seem broken. He flexed his fingers, then straightened his arm slowly, but the intensity of the pins and needles did not grow. Cautiously, he moved his arm in its socket: it was painful, but not agonisingly so. *Nothing broken!* He felt oddly cheated: all he would have for his efforts was going to be a huge bruise. He lay back upon the carpet of leaves and began to laugh and cry alternately. *Like some great idiot baby!*

3

Sheila had gathered at breakfast from snatches of overheard conversation between some of the Brothers that a special meeting had been called for that morning, but she did not connect that with the visit of the police the previous day. The fact of the visit was common knowledge, and there had been speculation among the Sisters as to the reason, but no information had been forthcoming to them. Sheila had not really bothered herself about it: her sole concern was the future of her son.

Part of her believed - or wanted to believe - what Govinda had said about Gopala: it was, after all, a nice thought, that one was some latter-day Virgin Mary. But another part of her scoffed at the very idea, the part that remembered only too well the days and nights she had spent rutting with Jazz, and the feeling upon discovering she was pregnant that somehow it had been inevitable.

This part of her saw Gopala as an ordinary child, the child she had carried in her body for nine months, flesh of her flesh, and blood of her blood. This part resented the special teaching Gopala was receiving, the special role for which he was being prepared even at this tender age, and which she knew would ultimately take him away from her. This part of her wanted to snatch Gopala into her arms and run as far away as possible, to some place where Govinda would never be able to find her, and where her son would be hers once more, and hers alone.

She had raised the fear that Gopala was still too young to be moulded into the role of Govinda's successor only a few days earlier, but he had been unrelenting.

'Sheila, my dear, try to understand that Gopala was born into this role, and that there is nothing you, or I, or anybody else, can do about it. Just as Yeshoda had to accept that Krishna was not simply her little boy but God incarnate, just as Mary had to come to terms with the fact that Jesus was more than an ordinary child, so you too must realise that Gopala is your son in name only, that you were merely the chosen vehicle for his birth into human form. That in itself, of course, is a great honour, and that must be your compensation.

'Gopala is not a child save in his physical form. He is already aware of his divine nature, just as Krishna and Jesus were. Do you recall what happened when Mary and Joseph were unable to find Jesus for three days, and eventually discovered him in the temple debating with the elders? When Mary upbraided him, what did he say? "Woman, know ye not that I must be about my

Father's business?" "Woman" he called her! Not "mother", but "woman". How hurt she must have felt! But he did not address her thus in order to hurt her, but because he had become aware of his divinity, and because his mother had become to him no more than any other human being. You too will have to get used to the fact of Gopala's divinity.'

So when Sheila heard about the meeting, she jumped to the conclusion that its purpose was to consider Gopala's future, and, knowing that her own maternal feelings would cut no ice with Govinda, wanted to be as far away from it as possible. Leaving Gopala in the care of Sister Magda, who was always happy to care for the little God-child, she fled up the hillside for peace and solitude, knowing that she would have to face the outcome of the meeting eventually, but unable to sit quietly and wait for the inevitable in her hut.

It was warm, and by the time she reached the top of the hill she was sweating profusely. The long, heavy skirt and thick cotton blouse, buttoned up to the neck, which she was required to wear as "Sister Sheila", clung to her skin, clammy and itchy. She stood for a minute, gazing over the little valley in which Brindavan nestled towards the distant countryside and moorland, then made for her secret place, a hollow just below the crest of the hill with a few trees growing above it. Here she had often come - in breach of the rule that Sisters should not wander about on their own - when she felt sad or depressed, or simply to be alone, away from the ashram, in which, for all its vaunted tranquillity, there always seemed to be someone ready to ask her to carry out another chore.

She threw herself down upon the grass, and rolled onto her back, staring up into the infinite blueness above. Kicking off her shoes, she wiggled her toes in the cool grass, and suddenly felt unbearably hot and sticky. *Fuck the rules!* She sat up and ripped her blouse off over her head with such violence that two buttons shot off into the grass, like two little black bullets. She lay back again, the grass deliciously comforting against her over-heated skin, and the slight breeze playing pleasantly over her face and torso. With another sudden resolution, she unfastened the waist buttons on her skirt and wriggled out of it, like a snake shedding its skin, finally kicking it away. Now more comfortable in only her underwear, she gave herself up to the sensation of the sun and the breeze, caressing her skin with infinite tenderness, and banishing all unpleasant thoughts and fears and worries from her mind. She felt herself drifting like a piece of flotsam on the ocean of timelessness, and was content to drift forever, without the necessity of thought or action, just drifting, drifting unconsciously, obliviously.

It was the shouting that woke her. She sat up in alarm, her arms automatically shielding her breasts; she could not see anyone, but could hear the person who was shouting coming nearer. She glanced at her watch; it was past noon already, so she had slept for at least an hour. She heard a great shout, followed by a cry of pain, and then the sound of hysterical laughter. Quickly pulling on her skirt and blouse, she crawled to the lip of the hollow and peered between the trees. No more than ten feet away, Brother Anthony lay on the ground, apparently laughing and weeping at the same time.

She stood up, uncertain whether to approach him, or to make good her escape. As she dithered, he looked at her, and scrambled to his feet. 'Sheila?' he said, as if unable to believe the evidence of his eyes.

'Brother Anthony, I heard someone shouting. Was it you?'

'Um, yes, I'm afraid it was. I think I went a bit mad for a minute or two.' He rubbed his shoulder, and winced.

'Have you hurt yourself?'

'I fell against a tree. It's only bruised; I can move the arm.' He demonstrated, and winced again.

'Would you like me to have a look at it?'

'No,' he said quickly, stepping backwards.

'Okay. Don't worry, I'm not going to bite you.'

He smiled sheepishly. 'Of course not, it's just ....'

'That we're breaking the rules by being together and talking?'

He laughed. 'I guess.' He paused. 'Look, Sheila ... Sister Sheila, I mean ... I need to talk to someone, and to hell with the rules.'

Sheila regarded him quizzically.

'Can I talk to you?'

The urgency in his voice, and the sorrowful look on his face persuaded her. 'Step into my parlour, sir,' she said, a smile playing about her lips.

'Very cosy,' he remarked, entering the hollow, and sitting down.

'I come up here quite often when I feel the need to be alone, though I know it's against the rules.'

'The dreaded sacrosanct rules!'

'What was it you wanted to talk about?'

Anthony screwed up his face. 'I've been racked by doubts the last few days,' he began.

'About becoming a Swami? After all your experiences, you shouldn't have any doubts about yourself.'

'The doubts aren't about me.'

'About what, then?' Sheila almost hesitated to ask, afraid perhaps of his answer.

She had sat down opposite him, wary of being too close to avoid giving wrong signals, but she now looked into his face and saw the fear and doubt in his eyes, as if they were reflecting her own feelings. Their eyes remained locked together, as if both were aware that they were standing on the brink of a dangerous precipice, and had to decide whether to step off the edge together, or draw back and go their separate ways.

'It's Swamiji,' Anthony said at last.

Sheila's hand went to her mouth, but her eyes did not stray from his face. 'What about him?' she whispered.

Anthony told her about Anna's letter, and his conversation with her, and about Rosie. 'It's obvious that he's been suppressing all her letters for the past three years, and that he lied to me.'

'Perhaps he just wanted to prevent you being hurt by the news about Rosie.'

'I thought that too, but that would mean that he would have had to have read the letters first. How on earth can that be justified? And if he read Anna's letters to me, do you think he doesn't read everyone else's? The whole thing is just completely immoral. And if he can be dishonest about a small matter like letters, it means he can tell lies about other things too.' He looked pointedly at her.

She looked puzzled. 'What do you mean?' Then fear seized her. 'Gopala! It's Gopala isn't it? What have they decided?'

'Decided? What are you on about?'

'The meeting! The Brothers' meeting! Did they decide what's going to happen to Gopala?'

'The meeting had nothing to do with Gopala. It was about Jimmy's death and the funeral arrangements.'

Sheila's mouth fell open. 'Jimmy's death?'

'You didn't know? I thought everyone knew after the police visit yesterday. The Brothers were talking of nothing else.'

'No-one tells the Sisters anything.'

'Maybe not,' Anthony conceded. 'Let me fill you in.' He told her how Jimmy had apparently died, and then voiced his own reservations about how convenient the death was financially for Govinda.

'But he can't have had anything to do with it, surely?'

'The accident - if that's what it was - happened only a few hours after he and Simon left him.'

'But if Jimmy was drunk, it has to have been an accident.'

'It seems so, but it's all just so convenient, and I have a gut feeling that everything's not quite as simple as Swamiji makes out. I probably wouldn't have thought that if I hadn't found out about the letters, so maybe I'm prejudiced.'

Sheila glanced at her watch. 'Jesus! It's almost pooja time! You go first; we mustn't be seen together.'

They scrambled to their feet, and Anthony made to go. Sheila clutched his arm. 'I need to talk about Gopala. I'm really worried. Can we talk again?'

Anthony nodded. 'After tonight's pooja. I'll come to your chalet about an hour afterwards, when everything's quiet.'

4

Simon was looking out of Govinda's window onto the deserted car park, wondering if there would be a late-comer. The Asians had an uncanny knack of turning up at the last minute, and not infrequently the minute after the last minute, when the pooja had finished and the temple was about to be locked. The Brother on duty would then have to wait while they muttered hasty prayers before going for their lunch, making him late for his own. Lunch-time temple duty was not popular for this reason.

Simon glanced towards Govinda, who was sitting at the table reading "The Telegraph", giving no indication that he was ready to go downstairs even though it was past one o'clock. He coughed, but Govinda ignored him. He was about to mention the time when he caught sight of Anthony almost running into the car park, not yet changed for the temple. He chuckled.

'What is so amusing?' Govinda asked, causing Simon to start with surprise.

'Oh nothing really, just Brother Anthony dashing in late. I wonder what he's been up to; I haven't seen him since the meeting.'

'He's probably been meditating. The news of Jimmy's death was a great shock for him - as for us all. I would expect him to seek some peace and quiet in the circumstances.'

'I suppose so.'

'You would find it beneficial if you were to meditate as much as Anthony. Now let us go down. You're making me late with your gossip.'

Simon did not respond to this manifestly unfair remark. As he was about to follow Govinda through the door, a movement outside caught his eye, and he saw Sheila hurrying along from the same direction as Anthony. *Aha! What's been going on there, I wonder? Were they together, or is it just a coincidence?* As he went down to the temple, he decided to keep this particular piece of information to himself: one never knew when it might come in handy.

5

The huts of the three Sisters, and another larger chalet equipped with bunk beds for use by female devotees, were set well away from the main part of the ashram, and males were forbidden to use the path leading to them. The hut occupied by Sister Magda, who had the ears of an owl, was situated by the gate in the hedgerow which divided the Sisters' area from a large field; it was a brave man who risked an encounter with her.

Anthony did not, therefore, take the direct route to Sheila's hut, which was situated between Sister Fiona's and the larger chalet, but approached by means of a flanking movement across the field to the far end and through a gap in the hedge, thereby approaching from the rear. It was later than he had planned, having been button-holed by Simon after the pooja, but it had the advantage that Magda and Fiona would almost certainly be asleep. He hoped that Sheila had not given up on him and turned in herself.

Creeping carefully through the undergrowth, and flicking his torch on at intervals to check for hidden obstacles, he was glad to see a glimmer of light in Sheila's window. He stole to the door and tapped lightly; it opened just wide enough for him to slip through. Sheila had a finger to her lips, indicating with the other hand the curtained-off area at the end. 'He's been restless all evening,' she whispered.

Gopala! How could I have forgotten about Gopala? 'We can't talk if he's likely to wake up,' Anthony said.

'We can go into the women's chalet. I've got a key. And once the light's turned out, Gopala won't wake up.'

They made their way next door, and Anthony flicked on the torch long enough for Sheila to find the keyhole and unlock the door. They quickly went in, and Sheila locked the door after them. 'Just in case.'

Anthony shone his torch briefly around the interior to get his bearings. There were four bunk beds projecting from the wall into the room, and a single bed up against the wall just inside the door, leaving little space for moving around. He gestured to the single bed and switched off the torch. They sat down.

Sheila shivered. The hut was musty and chilly. 'I should have brought my coat,' she muttered through teeth which had begun to chatter, as much from tension as from temperature.

'I saw some blankets on one of the bunks. I'll get one.'

'Get a couple.'

Anthony wrapped one of the blankets around Sheila's shoulders, and spread the other over their laps, and they sat side by side in the dark, not speaking; just listening to each other's breathing. And then Sheila asked the question that had been troubling. 'Do you really think it possible that Swamiji had anything to do with Jimmy's death? I've been worrying about it ever since this morning.'

'I can't say; there's nothing I can put my finger on. I just have a feeling that when things fall neatly into place to someone's particular advantage, it's difficult to resist the thought that maybe the things fell because someone gave them a little push. For example, he didn't want me to write to Anna, and eventually I stopped, but only because he suppressed the letters.'

'And he arranged things after Gopala's birth to stop Jazz from coming back here.'

'He lied to him too, though at the time I thought it was in a good cause, and didn't see it as dishonest.'

'Me neither. In fact, I was glad that Jazz was hurt by not being able to see his son. I hated him so much then; I thought he'd ruined my life.'

They were silent for a while. Then Anthony spoke. 'I rather enjoyed that time when you were away, and I came to see you.'

She could hear the smile in his voice. 'Yes, we had some good times. I was so lonely on the days you didn't come.'

Silence fell again as each thought of that time, a time that now seemed a hundred years ago rather than merely five. It was Sheila who broke it this time. 'Mind you, that loneliness was nothing compared to how life was after all the rules began to come in. I was so isolated that I think I would have killed myself if it hadn't been for Gopala.'

'I'd no idea you felt that way. I always thought it unfair that you were treated like some sort of leper, but I didn't have the guts to speak up.'

'Thankfully Magda turned up, and although she's a crusty old biddy at times, at least I had someone to talk to and share meals with. I began to feel as if I belonged again, and to be fair, Swamiji was very sweet to me most of the time. It was Simon who was such a bastard, always speaking to me as if I were some lower life-form.'

'You do realise, don't you,' Anthony said quietly, 'that he behaves in exactly the way Swamiji taught him? That he does nothing without Govinda's approval?'

'How do you mean?'

'Swamiji tries to control everything and everybody. If Simon was nasty to you, it was because he was put up to it, and then Swamiji could be nice to you, and make you emotionally dependent on him. It's only a variation of the nice cop/nasty cop approach.'

'Oh Jesus! And I fell for it.'

'Everyone falls for it.'

'And I know why!' Sheila cried. 'It's so he can take Gopala away from me.'

'How do you mean?'

'He's always talking about Gopala's divine conception, that he's an avatar of Krishna, and that one day he'll take over the ashram and make Brindavan the centre of the universe.'

'Well yes, but that doesn't mean …'

'Yes it does! He's been comparing me to Mother Mary and Yeshoda, telling me how they had to give up their sons for the greater good of the world, and he wants me to do the same. He's refused to allow Gopala to go to school, and he's already started teaching him himself. God knows what he's putting into the boy's head!'

'But Gopala *is* a special child, isn't he?'

'You see! You've just been telling me what a manipulator he is, and you've swallowed that story yourself. Gopala's just an ordinary kid. He was conceived in the normal way. There was nothing divine about it. Jazz and I used to sleep together, and we slipped up, that's all. I'm not another bloody Virgin Mary!'

'But what about the dream, the visitation?'

'He's told all of you about that, has he? I had a dream, nothing but a dream. It doesn't mean anything. Krishna didn't appear at my bedside and screw me!'

'I see,' Anthony whispered. 'I see it all now. He needs a successor, someone to keep his dream alive, and who better than someone he's trained himself almost from the cradle. With the added gloss of divinity. It's just amazing.'

'And I happened to be at hand, a girl up the spout in the wrong place at the wrong time. It might have been anyone, but it happened to be me. And now he's going to take Gopala away from me.' She began to sob quietly.

'No! We're not going to let that happen!' Anthony's voice was strong, and the arm he placed around Sheila was reliable. She placed her head on his shoulder, trying to stifle her weeping.

'Let it all out!' Anthony said. 'You're not alone anymore.'

She threw her arms around his neck and wept with relief. It was no longer necessary for her to stand alone, to be strong for herself and her child. Tears that had been held back for too long flowed copiously as Anthony held her against him, stroking her hair, and murmuring endearments in her ear. In time the trembling of her body stopped, the tears dried up, and she became still, but he continued to caress her and to whisper words of comfort. She sat up a little, not breaking his embrace. 'Your shirt's sopping wet!'

'No matter.'

'Anthony?'

'Yes?'

'Please hold me tight again.'

He drew her towards him, finding her mouth unerringly in the pitch blackness of the hut, and she responded immediately, her tongue seeking his. Fires which had been suppressed for so many years, now flared up fiercely. His hands roamed her body, seeking zips or buttons, while hers nimbly unfastened the buttons of his shirt. They pulled apart briefly in total understanding of their mutual need, divested themselves of their clothes, until each stood naked before the other, clothed only in the darkness.

CHAPTER 11

Govinda's discourses were usually reserved for the weekends, when the temple was generally full, so it was a surprise to the Brothers and Sisters when, instead of conducting the final arathi that Friday lunchtime, he turned to face the small congregation of one family and a group of students. Simon, who had moved with alacrity to prepare the arathi lamp, crept back to his cushion.

'When you walk hand in hand with the Divine,' Govinda began, 'you never have to worry about anything again, for the Lord provides everything that you need. And I am not talking merely about material needs, such as food, clothing and shelter, although it is a fact that God provides all these things for us here in Brindavan. I am speaking about higher things, such as knowledge and learning. Look at me. I was a hopeless student, far more interested in running about and enjoying myself than reading books. And then one day I realised my true nature, the Divine within me. Since that day it has been quite unnecessary for me to read books or newspapers, for whenever I need to know something, the Lord provides me with the answer. When one of you asks me a question, it is not I who answers you, but the Lord, using me as a mere instrument. Sometimes I am myself surprised to hear the words that pass my lips!'

He smiled, looking around the temple, taking in everyone there: visitors, Sisters, Brothers. 'Without the Lord's guidance, I would not be able to run this ashram. In fact, I would not even be able to run a kindergarten on my own. It is the Lord who tells me what to do, the Lord who tells me what is going on that I need to know, for He is omnipresent. So,' turning to the members of the community and wagging a finger at them in mock solemnity, 'you had all better behave yourselves, for the Lord Himself is my ears and eyes.'

2

Sheila had to stop herself running out of the temple; she could feel her cheeks burning. *He knows!* During Govinda's brief discourse, memories of the previous night with Anthony had risen to the surface of her mind, like bubbles ready to burst in the air and reveal to everyone her guilt. She had not dared look at Govinda in case their eyes had met, for she feared that he would be able to read her mind. Now she hurried round to the ladies' dining room, hoping for a few minutes to compose herself before Sister Magda arrived to take charge.

She sat down on a bench trying vainly to control her thoughts, but all that she could focus on was her coupling with Anthony: the first time fierce and urgent, almost a mutual rape, followed by more gentle love-making, each taking time to explore the other's body, with more thought for each other's enjoyment.

'Are you all right, Mummy?'

Gopala's voice brought her back to the present, and she realised in horror that she had unconsciously lain back upon the bench, mimicking the act of sex, her bosom heaving, her hips thrusting. 'Yes, darling. Mummy was a bit tired, that's all.' *Thank God it wasn't Magda!*

'Did you go for a walk last night?'

'Why do you ask, darling?'

'I woke up feeling thirsty, and you weren't there.'

'That must have been when I got up to go to the toilet. I'm sorry I wasn't there when you woke up.'

'That's okay, I wasn't frightened. Swami Govinda says I don't have to be frightened of anything.'

'He's quite right, darling. You don't.'

'Gopala smiled. 'I've got to go now. Swami Govinda wants me to have lunch with him today.'

'That's nice,' Sheila replied, nervously wondering what Govinda might have to say to the boy. 'Enjoy yourself.'

'I will,' he shouted, already half-way through the door.

Sheila stood looking after him, her heart pounding, and at that moment Magda came in.

'What on earth is the matter, Sister? You look as though you have seen a ghost.'

'It's just that I've suddenly got this awful headache. I think I need to lie down for a while.'

'You are certainly looking a little strained, my dear.' Magda put her hands on Sheila's shoulders and gave her face a searching, professional look. 'Go and rest.' Her voice was softened by her innate kindness, a kindness usually concealed by efficient hustle and bustle. 'Sister Fiona and I can manage easily, and after the visitors have gone, I will bring you some food.'

3

'Did you enjoy your ice-cream, Gopala?'

'Yes thank you, Swami, it was very nice.'

'Now drink up your chocolate, and then you may rest for a little while on my bed. Would you like that?'

'Oh yes. I always have nice dreams when I sleep on your bed.'

'And can you remember them afterwards?'

'Oh yes. I never forget them.'

'Do you remember yesterday's dream?'

'Yes.'

'And did you tell anyone about it?'

'Oh no, Swami. You said not to tell anyone.'

'Not even Mummy Sheila?'

'Not even Mummy Sheila.'

'You're a very good boy, Gopala, and one day you will be a very great man.'

'Uh huh?'

'But don't worry about that now. Tell me about yesterday's dream.'

'It was exciting, but a bit scary too - though I wasn't afraid. The voice told me not to be frightened.'

'That was your inner voice, the voice of the Lord that lives inside everyone. That is a voice you must always listen to, Gopala, because it is never wrong.'

'I know.'

'So what happened in your dream, then?'

'Well, I was bigger than I am now, about ten I think, and I was very strong. I was playing a ball game with some other children; the one with the ball had to try and hit someone else with it. It wasn't a very hard ball, quite soft really, so it didn't hurt when it hit you. You just became "it", and had to pick up the ball and try to hit someone else. One of the girls, a very pretty girl ….'

'Can you remember her name?'

Gopala thought for a second, his forehead furrowed in an effort of concentration. Then he smiled. 'It was Radha. She was my special friend, and when she was "it", she always tried to catch me with the ball.'

'Very good, Gopala. What happened next?'

'Well, this one time she threw the ball and it went over my head and right into the water - I forgot to say there was a big lake there. Radha ran to get the ball before it floated too far out, and suddenly this huge snake came up out of the water, hissing really angrily. It was enormous, and it had seven heads. Radha screamed and fell over because she was so frightened, and everyone else ran away, but I ran up to the snake and jumped up on its hood and grabbed its neck. I shook it really hard, just like Flossie does when she catches a rat, and it roared and hissed at me, but I didn't let go. Then I began to dance upon all its hoods, beating my feet down so hard that I killed it. I jumped off, picked up Radha, and carried her up the bank, and all the others came out from the trees where they'd been hiding and cheered.'

'Very good, Gopala, very good indeed.'

'But what did it mean, Swami?'

'Don't worry about that now. When you are a little older, you will know the meaning. Have you finished your drink? No? Drink it all up, and then rest.'

'The child drained his cup, toddled over to the bed, settled himself in the centre, and yawned. 'I'm beginning to feel sleepy already.'

'Good boy.' Govinda crossed to the door and bolted it, then took a chair and placed it by the bed. 'Close your eyes,' he said softly, 'and I'll tell you a story. Are your eyes feeling heavy? Just go to sleep, and I will tell you the story of how Lord Krishna defeated and killed his wicked uncle, and became king in his place.'

4

'Sheila, it's just another mind game! He wants everyone to think that he knows what they're up to, even what they're thinking, so that no-one ever does anything they know he doesn't like. Can't you see that?'

'But why say that sort of thing just a few hours after we'd …. after last night? I'm sure he knows!'

'It was just a coincidence. How on earth could he know?'

'I don't know. Maybe someone saw you coming back and told him, and he put two and two together. I'm frightened, Anthony. What will he do if he finds out? What if I get pregnant again?'

Sheila had gone to lie down at Magda's direction, but her anxiety had grown to such a pitch that she had been sick. By the time Magda brought her some food, she was looking really ill.

'My dear, you are not well at all. I think perhaps a bug has caught you. Go to bed at once, and I will tell Swami Krishna that you are too ill to carry out your duties.'

Magda had fussed about her until she slipped into bed, but as soon as she was certain Magda had gone, she got up and began to dress. *I have to speak to Anthony!* The thought consumed her; only he could quell her fears. Knowing that he often went out to check the cows after lunch, and that they were grazing just the other side of the hedge, she crept outside and scooted along until she found a partial gap. She squeezed into it, and prayed that Anthony, and not one of the others, would come. Her prayers were answered quickly, and as soon as Anthony was within hearing distance, she called him in a loud stage whisper.

'Are you crazy!' he said, sidling towards the hedge but keeping his back to it. 'Anyone could come along and see us!'

'Then come over here, and we can find somewhere to hide!' she had hissed urgently.

He had ambled along his side of the hedge to the place where he had been able to get through the night before, and Sheila followed on her side. Once through, he had unceremoniously grabbed her hand and led her through some dense undergrowth, and down a steep bank to a small stream, where they found a mossy rock to sit upon. There she had poured out her fears that Govinda was on to them.

'Look, it doesn't really matter anyway,' he said. 'There's no way I can stay here after last night - no way I *want* to stay after last night. I think we should tell him about us and just go.'

Sheila looked at him incredulously, and he felt his certainty slip away. 'I mean,' he said, a note of doubt in his voice, 'I rather took it for granted that we'd leave together. Will you come with me?'

Sheila fell into his embrace. 'Oh yes! Anthony, yes, yes please!'

He held her close, stroking her hair, until she pulled away a little and looked at him. There were tears in her eyes. 'Don't cry,' he whispered.

'It's because I'm happy,' she replied, eyes shining, 'really happy for the first time in I don't know how long.'

He kissed the tears from her cheeks, then from her eyes, and then their lips met urgently, mouths straining together. Sheila suddenly pulled away. 'Gopala!' she exclaimed. 'You'll take Gopala too?'

'Of course we'll take Gopala, silly!' He ruffled her hair and smiled broadly.

'Oh, Anthony, thank you!' She began to unfasten his shirt buttons. He shrugged off the shirt, and she threw herself upon him, knocking him flat on his back, straddling his hips, and began to kiss his chest and nibble at his throat. Then she stopped. 'What if someone comes looking for you?'

'I don't give a shit!'

A few minutes later, the couple's cries and sighs of release mingled with the burbling of the stream over its stony bed and the twittering of the birds in the branches above their heads.

5

The following evening the temple was packed, for it was the day of the new moon, heralding the start of another auspicious cycle that culminated with the full moon; signalling the end of the period of waning, the dark side of the moon, when new ventures were never undertaken if possible, and if unavoidable only after special protective poojas and significant offerings to the gods. Now, however, the moon was at that point of her cycle when she began to wax again, to shed her light upon humankind with gradually increasing benevolence. This was a time for new beginnings, a time to start businesses, to take trips, to conduct marriages, to seek blessings for whatever venture a person had in mind.

And so it was that Dr. Chaudhury and his wife came again to the temple to seek new blessings for their wayward daughter, to offer prayers that she would return to the family and behave like a proper Indian daughter. At the conclusion of the evening devotions, which had involved a special pooja to Lord Ganesh, the elephant-headed god whose titles included the Remover of Obstacles and the Bestower of Success, the little doctor, who had managed with the use of some judicious elbowing to manoeuvre himself to the sanctuary rail, caught Govinda's eye. He motioned for the doctor, who had twisted a handkerchief out of all recognition during the pooja and still played nervously with it, to wait at the railing, and then whispered a word to Swami Krishnananda before leaving the temple.

When the last of the devotees had been ushered outside, and the doors locked behind them, Swami Krishnananda approached the doctor. 'Swamiji will see you upstairs, doctor; please follow me. I will ask one of the Brothers to collect your shoes from the porch and bring them to the dining area.'

'My wife is outside,' Dr. Chaudhury said nervously. 'She will be wondering where I am.'

'I'll see that someone finds her and brings her to the ladies' dining room.'

'You are too kind, Swami. I am very honoured.'

Not bothering to reply, Simon led the way to Govinda's room, knocked on the door, and opening it, stood aside to usher the Bengali doctor through, closing it once more behind him.

'Come in, doctor, come in,' Govinda cried genially, rising from his armchair and indicating that his guest should take its companion. 'I could feel during the pooja that your mind was very troubled, and I spoke to Lord Ganesh about it, asking Him to remove the problems from your life.'

'Swamiji! I am so grateful, so grateful,' cried Chaudhury, his face painted alternately by the conflicting emotions of anguish and relief.

'There are no problems with your daughter's pregnancy, I hope?' He studied the doctor's face. 'I thought not. It is obviously the other one who is still causing you anxiety.' Chaudhury's doleful face and slumped shoulders confirmed the diagnosis. 'It is as the Lord told me' Govinda said. 'Please tell me what I can do to help.'

'She is a disgrace to the family, Swamiji, an absolute disgrace! I do not know where to put my face. If my parents in Calcutta should ever find out about it, they would die of shame and grief!' The doctor was overcome briefly by emotion, and dabbed at his eyes with the remnants of the handkerchief. He sighed deeply before continuing. 'We have discovered for certain that she is living with an English boy. A friend told me in confidence that he had seen her arm in arm with a fellow going into a block of flats in Kensington. One day I followed her from her place of work, and saw her meet a man who matched the description given by my friend. The shame, Swami! That a daughter of mine could live like some English prostitute!

'My wife and I were hoping that you would be able to perform special poojas for her, so that she will give up this fellow and come home. Despite everything, she is still our daughter, you understand.' He brushed tears from his eyes, then withdrew an envelope from his inside jacket pocket and laid it on the table. 'This is just a small token of our respect and esteem for the temple, Swami.'

'My friend,' Govinda said in a low, sincere tone, laying a hand on the doctor's arm, 'I will not only ensure that special poojas for the health of your daughter are done every day until the full moon, but I will conduct them myself. They will, of course, be privately conducted, with no public participation. You are staying overnight, I assume?'

'We have arranged to stay at a bed and breakfast place a few miles away, Swami,' Chaudhury said apologetically. 'My wife is so upset that I want her to be as comfortable as possible, you understand.'

'I quite understand, doctor. Our accommodation is very simple, and at this difficult time it is quite proper of you to put your wife's health and comfort first. When you come tomorrow, we will conduct the first pooja. Come at least one hour before the lunchtime pooja, and ask for Swami Krishnananda.'

'Swamiji, I don't know how to thank you!'

'Give thanks to God, my friend.' Govinda went to the door and called for Simon, who appeared at the bottom of the stairs at once. 'Swami, please show Dr. Chaudhury the way out. And please apologise to your wife, Doctor, that she was excluded from our talk, but for obvious reasons ladies are not allowed into the monks' quarters. Goodnight.'

Govinda shut the door and returned to his chair, picking up the envelope which he had studiously avoided touching during his guest's presence. He took a stiletto-style letter opener from a drawer, slit open the envelope, and removed the cheque inside.

He tossed it casually upon the table, and sat down to wait Simon's return.

A few minutes later there was a tap at the door and Simon entered, clearly disturbed. 'What's all this about special poojas every day for the next fortnight?' he blustered. 'We haven't got the time for things like that!'

'We'll perform one in the morning for the good doctor, and as for the rest, I will speak to the Lord about the girl during my meditation. I think one pooja has to be worth five hundred pounds, don't you?' He picked up the cheque and waved it at his protégé. 'Now be a dear, and go and make my hot chocolate. I'm tired, and I need to sleep.'

6

Brother Ronan was making himself a cup of tea in the Brothers' living quarters, a large chalet situated behind the temple. 'If anyone wants a drink, the kettle's just boiled!' he bellowed.

'Make me a cup, there's a good chap,' Brother Douglas called from his room.

'Make your own bloody tea!' Ronan retorted. 'Is it your servant you think I am or something?'

Douglas came out into the communal area at the end of the chalet. 'Miserable Irish git!' he muttered, dropping a tea bag into a mug.

'We threw off the English yoke sixty years ago, and I didn't come here for you to put it back on again!' Ronan remarked from the comfort of the only armchair.

Douglas threw the hot, squeezed tea bag at him, and scuttled back to his cell before the Irishman could retaliate. The outside door opened, and Dennis came in, looking even gloomier than usual. Never the most exuberant member of the community, any cheerfulness he might have possessed had evaporated entirely since his translation to the kitchen. 'That Indian doctor's been up in Swamiji's room,' he announced. 'I just saw Swami K. taking him out through the dining room.'

'I wonder what's been going on there,' said Ronan.

Brother Lionel stuck his head out of his room; his sharp blue eyes, hooked nose and large ears gave him a distinctly gnomish appearance. 'Whatever it was,' he said sharply, 'you can bet that money changed hands.'

'What do you mean?' asked Ronan.

Lionel emerged from his room, already in his pyjamas. 'These Indians always think they can buy divine assistance,' he said, 'as if God sells favours to the highest bidder! If he's been upstairs, it was to ask a favour, and if he wants a favour, he'll have paid for it. It's the Indian way.'

'Well, I think that's a bit cynical even for you!' Dennis remarked.

'Do you remember that pamphlet someone brought by that Swami who was criticising the Hindu attitude to religion? He was blaming the priests for perpetuating a system whereby devotees paid for divine blessings - so-called!'

'Swami Shantananda,' said Dennis, who had a memory for books and authors.

'Was that the fellow who said that if you made a big enough donation, the priests would arrange for you to shake hands with God Himself?' Ronan asked.

'That's the one,' said Lionel. 'I just hope Swamiji isn't going to allow that sort of attitude to develop here.'

CHAPTER 12

'Well, Simon, do you think the Chaudhurys were happy with their pooja?'

'They seemed to be very happy. It's not everyone who gets a private pooja, and is allowed into the sanctuary as well.'

'True, but do you know what really went down so well with them?'

'What?'

'The fact that they were shown out of the temple in full view of the crowd waiting to come in. If there's anything these Indians enjoy more than being given special treatment, it's having the rest of the world know about it.'

'Is that why you did the pooja at that time?'

'Of course, and also why I asked you to let them out of the main door instead of the side door, and why I put the kumkum tilak on their foreheads. Every person who saw them would have known that something special had been going on.'

'But isn't that likely to create jealousy?'

'Precisely! All of them will be thinking what they have to do to get some special treatment for themselves.'

'But they won't know that Dr. Chaudhury paid the temple money.'

'Simon, Simon! How naïve you are at times! Of course they know he paid, that's the Indian way. What they don't know is how much. You may rest assured that those who want a little bit of special treatment will come forward with their own proposals.'

Simon frowned. 'But what if someone offers only a hundred pounds? You can't refuse on the basis it's not enough; that would look mercenary.'

'Money is never discussed. The devotee will ask for the pooja for whatever reason, and he will make a donation. I cannot levy a scale of fixed charges, for some people are not as well off as others, and it would be wrong. I simply leave it to the Lord to tell the

190

devotee how much to donate, and I will do the pooja, irrespective of the amount given. We must not think of the financial return, for the Lord will provide. However, I will tell you one thing: each person who needs a favour from God will pay as much as, and possibly a little more than, he can afford.

'Now, before the pooja begins, please tell Anthony to come and see me directly after lunch. We must set in motion the training for his becoming a Swami.'

2

'Come in, Brother Anthony! Please sit down. I thought we ought to have a chat about the preparations for your impending elevation.'

'I wanted to talk to you about that myself,' Anthony said dourly, remaining on his feet.

'You have some misgivings? Of course you do! It is only natural to have doubts before taking such a big step, but all these will clear away once we begin the course of instruction and training I have prepared. At the outset, however, let me assure you that I personally have no reservations about your suitability for the role of Swami.'

Anthony remained silent, staring at the floor and shifting his weight from one foot to the other. Govinda's smiling face changed, and he gave Anthony a hard look. 'What is it, man? Spit it out!' he barked.

'I've decided I don't want to become a Swami.'

The words hung in the air between them, but although Govinda's features became rigid, his mouth a grim, taut line, he said nothing. Explanation was clearly required.

'I never said I wanted to become a Swami,' Anthony said at last. 'You told me I should be one, and somehow I just went along with the idea, but I realise now that I don't want to continue as a monk either. I've decided to leave.'

Govinda spoke, his tone calm, his voice icy. 'And what precisely brought about this sudden and unexpected change of heart?' he demanded.

'It's just that I've come to realise I'm not cut out to be a monk.'

Simon had a sudden flash of insight. 'Has this anything to do with Sister Sheila?'

'Sheila! What has Sheila got to do with it?' Govinda asked, looking from one to the other. He saw Anthony's cheeks turn red, and swung towards Simon. 'What did you mean by asking about Sheila?'

'You remember a couple of days ago I mentioned seeing Brother Anthony coming past the temple, obviously late. Just after you'd gone downstairs, I saw Sister Sheila coming along after. I didn't think anything of it at the time, but it suddenly popped into my mind when Brother Anthony said ….'

'And you did not see fit to tell me!' Govinda spat furiously, leaping to his feet. 'You idiot!' He looked at Anthony. 'Well? Is there any truth in this suggestion that Sister Sheila is involved?'

'Sheila's leaving with me,' Anthony said defiantly, his cheeks now white.

'That whore!' Govinda hissed. 'We shall see about that, my friend! Swami, go and find the little tart and fetch her here, by force if necessary. As for you, *Brother* Anthony, sit down there!'

Such was the force of Govinda's fury, that Anthony had obeyed before realising it. Simon exited quickly, and Govinda paced the room angrily, interposing himself between Anthony and the door. He need not have bothered, for Anthony's defiance had been blown away by Govinda's venom, and the thought of escape never entered his head. He sat stock still while Govinda walked up and down behind him, muttering angrily in a mixture of English and Bengali. After ten minutes or so, a period during which Anthony felt he had aged years, the door opened. Anthony looked round in time to see Simon push Sheila into the room. She looked wary, but not frightened. Govinda took two steps towards her. 'You English whore!' he screeched, grabbing her arm and hurling her into the room with such force that she almost fell.

Anthony jumped up and interposed himself between them. 'You touch her again and I'll flatten you, you bastard!'

'How very gallant!' Govinda sneered. 'The errant knight coming to the defence of the whore in distress.'

'And if you call her that once more, I'll smash your fucking face in!' Anthony shouted.

Govinda stepped back a pace, but he was not so easily intimidated by a callow youth. 'And what would you call a girl who gets herself pregnant, comes here and sponges off the ashram for years, and then seduces one of my monks?' he asked.

'I thought you said that Sheila had been impregnated by Lord Krishna in a divine visitation,' Anthony sneered in turn. 'Or was that just as much a load of bollocks as so much else you've told us?'

The rage on Govinda's face evaporated in an instant, and he let forth a great sigh and held up his hands in a gesture of resignation. 'This all goes to show how dangerous human emotions are,' he said sadly. 'We have all been a little hasty perhaps, and even I have allowed the dashing of my hopes to arouse anger and resentment. It appears that you two have let your emotions run away with you, which can sometimes happen in a close-knit community.' He held up a hand as Anthony opened his mouth. 'Please let me finish, Anthony. I don't want to know, now or ever, what has transpired between you, but I would ask you both to go to your rooms and reflect very carefully upon your future, and what you are about to throw away. It is a big decision to join Brindavan, but an even bigger one to leave, and I would not want you to do something which you might come to regret later. "Act in haste, repent at leisure" is the proverb, I believe.'

'I can't speak for Sheila, but I've already made up my mind.'

'Of course you have, Anthony. What I want you to do now is reflect for a while upon whether or not you have made it up correctly. As your Swami and guru, I ask you to do this. I also ask you, as two of my oldest devotees, for the sake of all we have tried to build here from the beginning. And I ask your forgiveness for my inexcusable loss of temper. Will you do this for me?'

The words were reasonable, and spoken sweetly, so that both Anthony and Sheila found themselves nodding, almost hypnotically, their agreement.

'Thank you, my dears. Let us all spend an hour in quiet prayer and contemplation, and then review the situation.'

As the door closed upon the lovers, Govinda rounded upon Simon, who instinctively stepped backwards. 'You have been naïve, you fool, but enough of that for now. Where was Gopala when you fetched Sheila here?'

'She left him with Sister Magda.'

'Go and fetch him here now. Quickly! Before Sheila gets back to him.'

3

Once outside in the fresh air, Sheila and Anthony stood for a moment to gather their wits. Most of the visitors had left already, anxious to get home in reasonable time, but there were still a few cars left.

'What do we do?' Sheila asked breathily.

Anthony remained silent and still, his eyes out of focus.

'Anthony!' He shook his head and looked questioningly at her. 'I said, what do we do?'

'We pack,' he said decisively. 'Go and pack your things, and Gopala's too, of course. With any luck, someone will give us a lift, and if not, we'll walk and try to hitch.'

He stooped and kissed her forehead, then pushed her gently away. 'Go!' he urged. She looked at him, her face tight with anxiety, then squeezed his hand before hurrying away. Anthony went to his room and packed his few personal belongings; there were not many, and it did not take long. After a last look around the room, and a shrug of the shoulders, he went outside, just in time to see Sheila flying across the car park.

'It's Gopala!' she cried. 'I left him with Magda, but Simon came and took him!' She clung to him sobbing, causing an Indian family preparing to leave to stare in disbelief. 'It's the one weapon he can use against me,' she sobbed. 'He'll use Gopala to keep me here.'

'No he won't; he can't. Gopala's your son, and you have the right to take him with you.'

'But I'm sure Govinda's been feeding him all this Krishna reincarnation stuff. If he's told me that Gopala's not really my son, what do you think he's been telling him?'

'He's only a kid, a five-year-old kid. Whatever stories Govinda may have been telling him, to a boy his age they're still just stories. No kid wants to be parted from his mother.'

'Maybe you're right.' She sounded dubious.

'Of course I'm right. We'll go and get your stuff, and put it with mine, then we'll go and find Gopala, even if it means bearding the ogre in his lair. Then we'll go, okay? Dry your eyes, and let's move.'

A few minutes later they were in Anthony's room. 'Wait here,' he said, 'and I'll go and get Gopala.' He kissed her, and they hugged fiercely for a few seconds. 'Lock the door after me, just in case.'

Sheila sat down on the bed and waited. *Always waiting!* she thought. *But at least I'm nearer the gate now!* The thought almost made her laugh. She looked over to the small window in the wall opposite the door, and went over and drew the curtains, shutting out what little light the window had allowed in, but she dared not switch on the light.

Time passed agonisingly slowly. She kept glancing at her watch, but the hands hardly seemed to move. *"They also serve who only stand and wait"*, she thought, but Milton's words held no comfort for her. Twice she almost unlocked the door, but the thought that she might miss Anthony returning with Gopala stayed her hand. After an eternity that had in fact been no more than twenty minutes, she heard the outside door open, and her heart leapt. She stood up, ready to clutch Gopala to her, only to hear Simon's voice.

'Sheila, please open the door. I know you're in there.'

She remained frozen to the spot. *It could be a bluff.* She saw the door handle turn.

'Sheila, there's no need to be afraid. Swamiji wants to sort out the details of your leaving the ashram, if that's what you really want.'

'It is,' she whimpered.

'Then come with me and talk to Swamiji.'

'Where's Anthony? And Gopala?'

'They're waiting for you.'

She went to the door and turned the key. Simon opened it, his eyes unable to conceal his triumph in this little battle of wills.

'Come in and sit down, Sheila.' Govinda's voice was calm and business-like.

Sheila remained standing, and turned on Simon. 'You said Anthony and Gopala were here!'

'Gopala was here, but I asked him to wait in the spare room for a while,' Govinda said. 'There are some things we still have to discuss, and it is better that Gopala does not hear them.'

'What things? And where's Anthony?'

'All in good time, my dear. Let me first tell you what I am prepared to tolerate. I am ready to allow you and Anthony to leave, and I will even pardon you for breaking your vows …'

'I never took any vows!'

'But Anthony did, and you have helped him break them, so you are equally guilty. But as I say, I am prepared to overlook that transgression, and I will even concoct a suitable story to account for your departure which does not reflect badly upon you, or, more importantly, upon Brindavan. The one thing I will not allow, however, is Gopala to leave the ashram.'

'But he's my son!'

'He belongs to Brindavan at present, and eventually to the world. You may have spoilt my plans for Anthony, but I will not permit you to interfere with the divine plan for Gopala. I would be failing in my duty to the Lord if I allowed it.'

'But he's just a little boy! He needs his mother!'

'He's a little boy who is already aware of his divine mission.'

'I don't believe that! You've just filled his head with stories. He loves me, I'm his mother.'

'If you were to be convinced that Gopala really prefers to stay at Brindavan and not come with you, would you be satisfied?'

'Nothing you can possibly say would convince me of that!'

'Not even if he told you so himself?'

'He wouldn't!' But the supremely confident look on Govinda's face made her doubt her words. 'Unless you've brainwashed him!'

'Oh, Sheila, let's not be so melodramatic. Brainwashing! We aren't living behind the Iron Curtain here, you know. Gopala has always appeared happy and normal, has he not?'

She nodded grudgingly.

'He has never said or done anything which could be described as unusual or abnormal?'

'No, but you've tried to separate him from me by saying I'm only his earthly mother.'

'But that is true. His spiritual parentage is greater than you or even I can imagine. However unwilling you may be to face the truth, Gopala is a very special, very spiritual child.'

'But I couldn't bear to be parted from him!'

'Such feelings are only natural, but my concern is for Gopala's welfare not yours - unless, of course, you decided to stay. Gopala would be lost in that awful world the other side of those gates, can't you see that? He would be a prey to influences he is not yet strong enough to resist. He still needs firm spiritual guidance.'

Sheila looked at him, then stared at the floor. She could think of nothing to say that would not sound selfish even to her own ears.

'Of course, if you cannot bear to be parted from him, then you are welcome to stay, and this painful episode will never be spoken of again.'

'No!'

'Then you choose Anthony over Gopala.'

'I want them both!'

'Let me make myself perfectly plain, Sheila.' He came closer, until his face was only a few inches from hers. 'You will not under any circumstances remove Gopala from Brindavan. He does not want to leave, and I will certainly not allow you to take him by force.'

'I don't believe what I'm hearing!' Sheila cried, looking wildly about her. 'I want to see my son!'

'How can you cling to this illusion after all I have told you?'

'His birth certificate says I'm his mother,' she replied doggedly.

'A mere piece of paper!'

'A piece of paper that will stand up in a court of law!'

'Aha, the former law student thinks to use the law against me, does she?' His voice was silky but menacing. 'I would be very careful about showing that certificate to a court, considering it bears a false statement made by you.'

'What are you getting at?'

'The name of the father is false, is it not?'

'You suggested the name, and he pretended to be the father,' Sheila exploded, pointing at Simon.

'Swami! Is it true that you were this woman's accomplice in making a false statement to the registrar?'

'Certainly not, Swamiji.'

'There you are, my dear. If you try to rely upon the birth certificate, you could end up in prison.'

'I want to see my son!'

'But of course. I was about to suggest that Swami should fetch him, now we both know where we stand.'

Simon left the room, returning a minute later with Gopala. Sheila grabbed him and hugged him tight. 'Gopala! I was so worried about you! I didn't know where you were.'

'I was here with Swami Govinda.'

'Sheila, why don't you sit down again, and Gopala can sit here next to you.' Govinda drew a small stool to the side of the armchair. 'Good boy. Now, Gopala, Mummy Sheila has some important news for you, and so Swami and I will leave the two of you to talk. When you have finished, Sheila, we will be downstairs.' Without waiting for an answer, he glided out of the room. Simon shut the door, unable to hide his smirk.

5

As the train snaked into Paddington Station later that same day, lurching and jolting across the points, Sheila remained as numb as she had been the moment she and Anthony had left Brindavan. She had spoken very little since: just a brief account of what had passed with Govinda, and then with Gopala. Anthony had recounted his own tale of enforced incarceration, but she had not responded: nothing was of any importance compared to her own sense of loss. Anthony had made an effort at first to get her to talk, but she had been wrapped in her own misery, like some thick blanket that prevented him from getting close to her. In the end he had given up, and remained in his own corner seat, morosely watching the countryside flash by, unheeding of the places the train stopped.

The denouement of the confrontation with Govinda had been swift. Simon had appeared with a weeping Sheila, releasing Anthony from the outhouse in which he had been locked, and had then driven them to Plymouth, bought them one-way tickets, and waited on the platform until the train pulled out.

Sheila was quite unable to describe her feelings: they were such a tangled skein of grief, desolation, anger, loss and even relief, that she was incapable of unravelling them. Throughout the journey she played and replayed in her mind the events of that dreadful day.

When left alone with Gopala, her first instinct had been to pick up the child and run for it, but she knew that Simon was bound to be on guard at the bottom of the stairs, and she had no idea where Anthony was. Her only hope was to persuade her son to come with her, and then convince Govinda that this was in Gopala's best interests.

'Darling, Anthony and I are leaving Brindavan,' she had begun.

'I know. Swami Govinda told me.'

Sheila was instantly on the alert. 'What else did he say?' she asked, trying to keep her voice calm.

'He said it was up to me. That I had to look inside myself and find the answer.'

Sheila breathed a sigh of relief. *He's left it to Gopala!* Her heart sang for an instant, then her rational mind took over. *He wouldn't leave such a decision to a child. Not unless he knows what the decision is already!* Now her heart thumped wildly. She sensed a trap, something Govinda had told the boy which would deter him from leaving. Looking into Gopala's eyes, she could see herself reflected in the irises. His face remained serene, and he was looking at her quite dispassionately. It made her afraid to ask him what his decision was.

'What is it, mother?' he asked.

'Anthony and I want you to come with us, to make a new life together.'

'To leave Brindavan?' It sounded like an accusation.

'It would be good for you to live in a proper family home, to go to school, and to mix with other children.'

'Why? I'm not like other children, the children I see coming here. If I was like them, I'd come with you, but I'm not. I'm different, and Brindavan is my home.'

'You're just repeating what Govinda's told you to say!' she burst out furiously.

He recoiled a little. A frown crossed his forehead, then passed away, like a ripple on a pond. 'It's not good to get angry,' he said reprovingly. 'Swami Govinda said I should make up my own mind, but here I'll be able to learn the things I need to know for my mission.'

'Mission!' Sheila exploded. 'You're a five-year-old child, you don't have a mission!'

He took another step away from her. 'I think you should go now, mother,' he said quietly.

The door opened. 'Is everything all right?' Govinda asked sweetly.

Sheila whirled round and shook her fist in his face. 'I don't know how you've done it,' she hissed, 'but I know that you've fucking well indoctrinated him, you bastard!' She took a swing at him, but he caught her arm deftly.

'Gopala, my dear, go downstairs and join Swami Krishna.' When the door had closed, he tightened his grip on Sheila's wrist, and for a few seconds they glared at each other. Then he released her, pushing her away a little. 'If you leave now without any more fuss, then I promise you that you can come back to visit the child whenever you want. You only. Anthony broke his vows, and he is therefore banned. If, on the other hand, you make a fuss, then rest assured that I will drag your name through mud so thick that no court in the land will let you within a mile of Gopala. Every monk here will swear that you tried to seduce them, that you drank and took drugs in front of the child ...'

'You bastard!' She took another swing at him, this time successfully, catching him on the ear.

He grabbed both her arms, pinioning them to her sides, and pushed her across the room, his mouth working furiously and his eyes fiery with rage. She tried to resist him, but was shoved back relentlessly until her legs hit the bed and she toppled backwards, with Govinda on top of her.

'You know something, Sheila,' he said through clenched teeth, 'you really are quite beautiful when you're angry.'

She felt his erection pressing into her groin; her eyes widened in shock, and she went completely limp. She saw the leer of triumph on his face replaced by a look of uncertainty, and then he pushed himself upright, panting slightly.

'Get out now! Before I change my mind. Simon will meet you downstairs'.

For a few seconds she could not move, trying to register what had just almost happened. Then she rolled off the bed and ran for the door, stifling a wail of despair in her throat.

She did not tell Anthony about this part of her encounter with Govinda: not then, or ever.

On his return, Simon went straight upstairs, knocked on Govinda's door and entered.

'They've gone?' Govinda enquired languidly, looking up from his newspaper.

'Yes.'

'You saw them onto the train?'

'Yes.'

'And you waited until it left?'

'Yes.'

Govinda stood up and rubbed his hands, smiling. 'Good! Very good! Now we can bring up our little avatar as it suits us.'

CHAPTER 13

The baby was dark, her skin lustrously blue-black, her head covered in a mass of black curls. Her eyes were large and luminously deep brown; her arms and legs were chubby; and her tiny fingers and toes were all present and correct. They called her Sita because of that dark beauty. Her parents were very happy, and the maternal grand-parents ecstatic.

'She is so lovely that I can feel myself spoiling her already!' crowed Dr. Roy Chaudhury. As the father of two daughters himself, he was not surprised that his first grand-child was a girl; nor did he care.

'She is truly a little darling!' gushed Sita's grand-mother.

Geeta lay back in the bed, her daughter in her arms, her lovely, plump brown face glistening with a look of tired triumph. Her husband wiped a stray wisp of damp hair from her forehead, and beamed at his wife and daughter. He was pleased with the reaction of his in-laws, although he knew that his own parents back in India would be chafing for a boy. But there was plenty of time for boys.

'I think perhaps we should allow Geeta to rest,' her father declared authoritatively. 'It has been a long first labour, and she needs to sleep.'

Mrs. Chaudhury kissed her daughter's forehead, then kissed a fingertip and placed it on the baby's forehead. It began to cry at once.

'She probably wants a feed,' Geeta said.

The parents left the private room, allowing Mahendran a few moments with his wife. 'We will come back this evening, darling,' Dr. Chaudhury said from the doorway.

'You must telephone Swamiji straight away,' his wife urged as they strolled down the hospital corridor. 'It is necessary to make arrangements for the child's naming ceremony.'

'The child is only a few hours old, my dear,' the doctor chided, 'and the naming ceremony cannot be performed for at least a month.'

'Telephone anyway,' his wife commanded, with a little shake of her fist.

'Yes, my dear wife,' he said happily.

It was the first time for many months that Dr. Chaudhury had felt really happy, and even now those feelings were tinged with sadness at the thought of that other daughter, now lost to him. Meera had always been a rebel, almost from the cradle, and her strong will and independence of mind were characteristics he had both encouraged and taken pride in. "My little Bengali tigress" he had called her, never dreaming that one day the tigress would turn on him.

The first time that she defied him had come as a great shock, and thereafter she had defied him continually, rejecting not only her native religion, costume and customs, but also all her father's "middle class standards", as she called them. When he had tried to exert his authority, he had found he had none, and resorting to the time-honoured tactic of "Do as I say or get out" had proved disastrous. When he had learned that she had an English lover, his heart had almost broken.

Dr. Chaudhury was a proud man: having issued the ultimatum, he would not back away from it, however much it hurt, and however much his wife nagged at him for his intransigence. Honour and family name were more important than feelings: Meera had chosen her course, and was now dead to him - even though he donated money to the temple for special prayers for her return.

He recalled so often that weekend at Brindavan when he had insisted she accompany the rest of the family, and then had been compelled to beg her to stay overnight. It had been the last time she had done anything he asked, and she had made it quite plain that it was not for him she did it.

'I will stay because Geeta wants to stay,' she had said. 'She still believes all this claptrap, and I will stay with her because I don't want her to be alone in a place like this.'

'What do you mean, girl?' he had replied angrily. 'You are speaking of a temple, an ashram, a holy place!'

He could still see now the look of mingled pity and contempt on her face as she stared haughtily at him. When the girls had returned, she had been sullenly hostile, spending every evening away from home and not speaking a word to him. When he had finally challenged her about her "unseemly behaviour", she had exploded in a vitriolic attack upon the ashram, the Swami and himself, and in his anger he had thrown down the gauntlet of the ultimatum. She had almost joyfully picked it up.

'You are dead to me, do you hear? Dead!' he had shouted as she lugged her suitcase down the path to the waiting taxi, oblivious in his fury to the wife hanging on his arm and trying to pull him indoors, oblivious to the gawping of several English neighbours in their front gardens, and worst of all, from his wife's point of view, oblivious to the twitching curtains of the house directly opposite.

And he had meant it. At the time. She was dead to him. All photographs of her were removed from the house, even her graduation picture, and he had forbidden his wife even to mention her name. The only way to exorcise the shame was to pretend that Meera had never existed.

In his heart, however, he could not pretend: the Bengali tigress was too deeply entrenched.

It was not until several days after Sita's birth that Dr. Chaudhury had any cause for concern. Being a doctor, as well as father and grand-father, he assumed a professional as well as personal interest in the welfare of his daughter and grand-daughter. Glancing at the medical records in the folder at the end of the bed, he noticed that Sita's blood group was designated AB. He knew that Geeta's blood group was A, which meant that

Mahendran had either to be AB or B, but for some reason he had been under the impression that it was O.

He shook his head: either he was wrong, or the record was wrong. The latter was not out of the question: if hospitals could occasionally get the babies mixed up, they could certainly get the records wrong. He decided to have a word with the paediatric consultant's registrar, Dr. Webley, whom he knew quite well, and further decided to say nothing to his family until the error had been cleared up.

Geeta and Mahendran had lived with the Chaudhurys since their marriage three years earlier, an arrangement that suited everyone, but now that Mahendran was beginning to do better at his accountancy firm, having received a recent salary increase, and now that a child had finally appeared, it was time for them to make their own home. Dr. Chaudhury offered to pay the deposit on a house, and they had begun to look for a suitable property that was not too far away. Mrs. Chaudhury, of course, would have preferred something within walking distance.

Dr. Chaudhury became so involved in this project, insisting upon viewing any property that his daughter liked and vetoing anything which he considered unsuitable or in a neighbourhood he thought too low class, that the intention to speak to Dr. Webley went completely out of his mind. Time passed, and eventually a house deemed suitable in every way by Dr. Chaudhury was found. The purchase passed off completely without any hitch in the chain, and the good doctor opened his cheque book once more to assist the young couple to furnish the house, and the young couple had taken possession with great joy. Even Mrs. Chaudhury was satisfied, for the house was only a bus ride away.

Before this momentous event was finalised, the family made the pilgrimage to Brindavan for the naming ceremony. It was their first visit for some months, for although they had made one or two trips early in Geeta's pregnancy, events seemed to have conspired to prevent them since: either the doctor was on call at the weekend, or Mahendran had to work, or Geeta was feeling too unwell to travel. This had not unduly upset Dr. Chaudhury, for the loss of Meera had cast a pall over his relationship with the temple which he had found difficult to shake off.

Mrs. Chaudhury had grumbled at the failure to visit Brindavan, and had had to content herself with visits to a new Durga temple that had opened in a disused church not far from their home, where she was able to do her prayers and poojas for the family - including Meera, despite her husband's attitude.

The arrival of Sita altered everything. Mrs. Chaudhury insisted that the naming ceremony could only be conducted at Brindavan. 'These priests are merely men,' she asserted, 'married like everyone else, and they mumble their mantras so fast that for all I know they could be reciting a shopping list! Only a great soul like the Brindavan Swami can name my first grand-child.'

And Dr. Chaudhury, feeling that in some way Sita made up for the absence of Meera, was only too happy to agree.

2

'So this is the child!' Govinda exclaimed, taking the baby from her mother's arms. 'Look, Gopala,' he said, holding the bundle so that the child could see the baby's face, 'here is a little sister in Krishna for you to cherish and protect as she grows up!'

Gopala looked at the tiny child, in her salmon pink gown trimmed with white, frothy lace, the pink set off by a red silk bolero embroidered with gold thread. She wore a fine gold chain around her neck, and miniature gold bangles on her wrists and ankles. Her eyes fastened upon Gopala with a look of pure intensity, and her forehead creased in a frown, as if to say, "Do I know you?" Then her face lit up in a radiant smile.

'She is smiling at me, Swami!' the boy trilled, extending a forefinger to touch one tiny clenched fist, which instantly opened and then closed upon the offering in a firm grip.

'She knows you from a previous birth, my son,' Govinda pronounced. 'There is a strong karmic connection between these two,' he said to the adults, who glanced anxiously at each other, wondering what significance lay behind the words.

'Come! Let us proceed!' Govinda said. 'On such a special occasion, as parents and grand-parents of a new manifestation of the Divine, Lord Krishna invites you to enter His very sanctuary. Come!'

The little group shuffled into the sanctuary behind the priest, very conscious of the privilege afforded them but in awe of their surroundings. It was one thing to participate in the pooja from the other side of the railing, and quite another to be within touching distance of the holy shrines and images within, conscious of their own unworthiness.

Dr. Chaudhury bowed his head in respect to the large moorthy of Lord Krishna, his family deity, thankful that his forebears had chosen to worship this especially benevolent aspect of the Divine. He was acutely conscious of a large image of Lord Shiva, almost at his elbow, in the form of Natarajah, the Lord of the Dance, surrounded by tongues of fire as he danced his cosmic dance of destruction. Opposite, staring him in the face, it seemed, stood an image of the fierce goddess Durga, sitting astride a rearing lion which was in the act of tearing apart the demon Mahisha. He shuddered. The worship of Durga, and her sister goddess Kali, was strong in his homeland, but they were hard deities to worship, severe and demanding. He had forbidden his wife to have an idol or picture of Durga, her own family deity, in the house, a prohibition that still rankled. He uttered a silent prayer to the wisdom of his ancestors.

In front of the main altar was a small table, on top of which had been placed a large, soft cushion, upon which Govinda now placed the infant. She lay quite silent, mesmerised perhaps by the flickering lights. Swami Krishnananda stepped forward bearing a silver tray on which stood various receptacles, and Govinda took one. 'Some rose water, Swami,' he murmured, taking the bottle proffered to him and adding a few drops to the contents of the pot. He stirred the contents with a tiny spoon, added a few more drops of rose water, and then, satisfied with the consistency, dipped his right fore-finger into the pot.

'And the child's name?' he enquired, looking at Geeta.

She looked anxiously at her husband, who nodded impatiently. 'Sita,' she whispered nervously.

Govinda frowned slightly, then looked at Dr. Chaudhury. 'Sita is a beautiful name, but since this is a Krishna temple, perhaps Radha would be more appropriate. So the Lord tells me.'

There was a moment's silence. Geeta looked again at Mahendran, who hesitated, not knowing what to say: they had used the name Sita for a month, and the name on the birth certificate was "Sita Devi", but to contradict the Swami in his own sanctuary was unthinkable. Dr. Choudhury took the initiative. 'Radha it shall be,' he vowed.

'Perhaps Radha-Sita,' Govinda suggested with a beaming smile. 'Then you can still call her Sita at home.'

'Oh, yes please, Swami,' Geeta whispered. 'Thank you, thank you.'

Govinda placed his vermilion-tipped forefinger in the centre of the child's forehead, holding it there gently as he chanted mantras to Krishna and Radha. He concluded in Bengali as he withdrew the finger, leaving a red blotch of kumkum behind. 'I dedicate this child, Radha-Sita, to the name and service of the Lord.' All the while he looked into the infant's face, and she stared back intently, silent and unmoving.

'The amrit, Swami,' Govinda said, taking the small phial and removing its stopper. He then poured a few drops of viscous liquid into a small spoon. 'This amrit is very special,' he announced, 'and reserved for very special people. It flowed from the feet of the great moorthy of Lord Krishna at Vrindavan when I prayed there many years ago. The priests said it was a great miracle, and collected it into this small bottle, and although I have used it countless times since, it is always full when I open it. Is that not marvellous? It is intensely sweet, the very essence of sweetness, and not for nothing is it called the nectar of the gods!'

He bent over Sita and placed the spoon on her mouth, allowing the liquid to seep in very slowly; the child smacked her lips at the taste, and then licked them. Govinda refilled the spoon, and placed a small drop of amrit into the right palm of each person present. 'This will add years to the lives of each one of you,' he said with a laugh. 'And you,' he said, ruffling Narain's hair, 'will definitely live to be a hundred! But now you must all go and have some lunch before it is finished.'

As they moved towards the door, the doctor hung back, until he was the last to leave. In the doorway he thrust an envelope into Govinda's hand. 'For the temple, Swami,' he murmured.

'Doctor! This is not necessary. We make no charge for our services. But you are most kind and generous.'

3

Simon was counting the money collected from the offering boxes. The largest was affixed to the temple doors, but there were two others, situated outside each dining room, as a reminder to those who might have forgotten to make their donation after the pooja. He had already sorted and counted the notes, mainly fives and tens, but with a respectable smattering of twenties, and a considerable number of rather tatty one pound notes, which people were obviously getting rid of before the new pound coin was issued; he was now laboriously sifting through a pile of coins, sorting out the smaller denominations presumably placed by children. Sweet wrappers and plastic counters were tossed into the waste-paper basket.

'It looks as though we'll break five hundred for the weekend again,' he remarked, glancing across at Govinda, who was stretched out in his armchair reading a "News of the World" left behind in the dining room.

'There's this too,' Govinda said, extracting Dr. Chaudhury's envelope from his pocket and tossing it onto the table.

Simon slit it open and read the cheque. 'Another five hundred! Dr. Chaudhury must have quite a lucrative practice.'

'Not really, he's just an ordinary G.P., but his father's a wealthy businessman in Calcutta, so he's never short of money.' Govinda lowered the newspaper, a thoughtful look on his face. 'Didn't he give us a thousand when I did that pooja for his daughters?'

'Yes, but he gave five hundred after the girl's pregnancy was confirmed.'

'And now five hundred for a simple naming.' Govinda smiled. 'As long as he's keeping up to the mark.'

'I was beginning to wonder if they'd given up on us. It must be months since they came down last.'

'Chaudhury will never stop coming. He owes me too much. He wouldn't be a grand-father if not for me.'

'I suppose not. Do you think she would have conceived eventually if you hadn't done that pooja?'

'Who can tell? Maybe her husband was firing blanks until then. The Lord works in mysterious ways.'

'There was that other woman recently, the fat lady, who asked you to pray for her to have a child. How come you didn't offer her the special pooja?'

'The pooja is not to be performed at the drop of a hat, you know. It is very special, and the circumstances must be right. The Chaudhury girl was desperate for a child, and her sorrow was threatening to mar her beauty. Such beauty! I could sense too that she would make a good mother, whereas this other woman would not.

'Then, of course, there was the pooja for the other Chaudhury girl, a real wildcat that one, a girl who required taming, but perhaps even more beautiful with that haughty, scornful look in her eye. She reminded me very much of how Sita must have looked when defying the blandishments of Ravana.'

There was a tap at the door. 'Come in, Gopala,' cried the guru, thrusting the newspaper behind a cushion.

Gopala entered, but stopped when he saw Simon at the table. 'Am I too early, Swami?' he asked.

'No, child, of course not. Come and sit by me. Swami, go and count your wretched money somewhere else; you attach far too much importance to it.'

Simon cast his mentor a hurt look, but Govinda was already fussing over the child. He began to sweep the uncounted coins into a bag.

'Hurry up, Swami, for Heaven's sake! It's time for Gopala's lesson.'

4

As they prepared for bed that evening, both tired by the long journey, Mrs. Chaudhury recounted the details of the wonderful naming ceremony that had been performed for the sole benefit of her grand-daughter. The fact that her husband had been present to witness each and every detail did not deter her from savouring her recollection, and the doctor knew better than to interrupt her.

'Amrit which flowed from the feet of Lord Krishna's moorthy!' she cooed. 'What a blessing! We are indeed fortunate, husband, to have such a Swami to minister to our spiritual needs. Are you not glad now that I insisted upon going there?'

'Indeed, my dear, though it could also be said that we are simply reaping the benefit of our good karma, and therefore receiving no more and no less than we deserve.'

'That, of course, is very true,' his wife agreed. Settling herself into bed, she gave Dr. Chaudhury an anxious look. 'There was one thing that troubled me.'

'And what was that?' he replied, sitting on the bed to remove his socks.

'What did the Swamiji mean, do you think, by telling that boy he keeps there that our Sita was to be a sister to him?'

'I doubt if he meant anything; it's the sort of thing one says to children. However, we are all brothers and sisters from the spiritual point of view.'

'Perhaps.' Mrs. Chaudhury pursed her lips. 'As long as he has no ideas about that boy and our grand-daughter.'

'What on earth are you implying, woman? He said she was to be a sister, not a wife!'

'I know, but he took great pains to show Sita to the boy, and he did say they were related by karma.'

Dr. Chaudhury thought for a moment, then shook his head. 'I'm sure he meant nothing by it. Anyway, from what I heard, that boy is a half-caste and a bastard as well. No man in his right mind would even consider for a second marrying a pure-born girl like Sita to such a person! Don't worry about it. Now turn out the light, and let us get some sleep!'

5

It was through a chance remark by the health visitor, Maire McDonagh, that Mahendran's suspicions were raised. He was at home with a stomach upset some three months after Sita's naming ceremony on the day that Maire called to carry out a check upon mother and baby. After everything had been satisfactorily concluded, Geeta took the baby back upstairs for her midday nap, while Maire completed her records, and happened to comment upon Sita's blood group.

'AB's quite rare, you know. Perhaps you're one as well, are you?'

'Not me,' Mahendran replied deprecatingly. 'Just a common or garden old O, that's me.'

Maire shook her head emphatically. 'No, that can't be right at all. The little girl's AB, and your dear wife's an A, so it stands to reason you have to be either B or AB yourself.' She packed her bag and looked up with a smile. 'Well, I must be off. Say ta-ta to your wife. Such a pretty wee thing!' And she was gone.

Mahendran's mind raced. He knew for a fact that his blood group was O, for he had become a blood donor while a student. Shouting up the stairs that he was going out for a walk, he made his way to the library and sought out medical books in the reference section. After an hour or so of solid research, he had to conclude that the health visitor had been right: only someone with groups AB or B could have fathered Sita. He made his way home with a hatred and a thirst for vengeance boiling inside him.

His emotions were checked by the presence of his father-in-law's car outside the house. As he walked up the path, the front door opened and Geeta and her parents came out.

'Oh, darling, I'm so glad you're back!' Geeta said. 'Now we can leave Sita with you while we do some shopping.' She thrust the sleeping child into his arms, and followed her mother to the car, the two of them chattering loudly.

The car drove off, the occupants gaily waving to Mahendran as he stood on the front step, his mind blank. Then he pulled himself together and went inside. He dashed up the stairs and thrust the baby into her cot, then stood looking at her, transfixed by two conflicting thoughts: that she was truly beautiful, and that she was not his daughter.

He stood for a long time staring at the still sleeping child, fully aware that no fault attached to her, that the circumstances of her conception were beyond her control, but nonetheless feeling anger building inside him as he thought of the lustful coupling of his wife with someone else that had resulted in her birth. Though innocent, Sita was the evidence of his own shame and betrayal, and all the rage that would otherwise have been directed against Geeta now became focussed upon the child. *I cannot bear her presence in my house a moment longer!*

Trembling with fury he reached for the child, grasping her roughly around the torso and raising her above his head as he turned towards the window. Sita opened her eyes, startled to have been so rudely awoken, and opened her mouth to cry. Then she recognised her captor and chuckled at the game he was playing with her, causing him to look up into her eyes, eyes that gazed back at him with complete trust.

'May God forgive me!' he cried, clutching her to his chest. He lay her gently back in the cot, soothed her until she went back to sleep, then sat down on the floor and began to weep. He was still crying when he heard the front door open. Jumping to his feet, he ran down the stairs, his face contorted with rage. Geeta was in the hallway, carrying two shopping bags, and he leapt down the last few steps and slapped her face as hard as he could. She dropped the shopping and staggered back against the wall.

'Whore!' he screamed, seizing her by the throat. 'Get out of my house and take your bastard with you!'

'What are you doing?' cried Mrs. Chaudhury as she came through the door. 'Are you drunk? Or mad?' She grabbed Mahendran's arm and tried to pull him off her daughter.

Mahendran tried to shrug her off, but she was tenacious, and he let go of Geeta, who sank to the floor, moaning. 'Let me tell you about your daughter!' Mahendran yelled. 'She is a whore! Ask her who the father of her child is, because I'm not, that's for sure.'

Mrs. Chaudhury swung a haymaker and caught Mahendran on the ear. 'How dare you call my daughter such names!' she shouted. 'You are a madman!'

At that point Dr. Chaudhury, who had seen the commotion from his car, came running into the house. 'What is all this shouting and screaming?' he cried.

'Your fucking daughter is a fucking whore!' howled Mahendran. 'Ask her who she's been sleeping with.' He aimed a kick at Geeta, still slumped against the wall, catching her in the ribs.

'Leave my daughter alone, madman!' shrieked Mrs. Chaudhury, hurling her bulk at Mahendran and clawing at his face.

'Get off, you fat cow!' Mahendran snarled, trying rather ineffectually to push her away.

'Stop this madness! For God's sake, stop!' roared Dr. Chaudhury, in a voice he hardly recognised as his own. He pushed himself between his wife and son-in-law. 'Take Geeta upstairs and see to the child,' he commanded his wife, for Sita was by now screaming too, 'and you, Mahendran, will tell me what this is all about.'

It did not take too long to explain, or for Dr. Chaudhury to realise that he had subconsciously buried the idea of speaking to Dr. Webley because he had known all along what the upshot would be.

'Where do we go from here?' he asked, sounding old and defeated.

'They have to go. I won't have them living in my house any longer.'

'It is Geeta's house too.'

'We can sort that out in the divorce. She'll have to admit to adultery.'

'We will need time to find somewhere for her to stay.'

'Why can't she go back to your place?'

'What? Are you crazy? I cannot have her living under my roof with her bastard! The shame of it would kill her mother! What do you imagine people are going to say?'

'But Sita is your grand-daughter. She's your flesh and blood, even if she's not mine.'

'I am sorry for the child, but it is her karma. She was conceived in pollution, and I cannot allow that pollution to taint my home and family.'

Without another word, Dr. Chaudhury went upstairs. Mahendran heard raised voices: his father-in-law shouting at Geeta, and she protesting her innocence. And all the while, Mrs. Chaudhury wailed, and Sita screamed. Then he heard his in-laws come downstairs and leave.

In the relative quiet he could hear Geeta sobbing, with an occasional cry from the baby. He dismissed the thought of going upstairs: he would either beat his wife up, or he would relent and allow her to stay, and each was equally bad. He found a piece of paper and a pen, scrawled a message upon it and left it on the table: "I want you and the child out of here by tomorrow night," it read. "God help us both if you are still here."

CHAPTER 14

Ijaz Shah, Solicitor of the Supreme Court, and very junior dogsbody at Peacock, Peacock and Meridew, Solicitors, of Southampton Row, Holborn, was on the top deck of a number eight bus arrested by traffic lights at Oxford Circus, on his way back to the office after a tedious morning session at Marlborough Street Magistrates' Court of drunks, shop-lifters, prostitutes, hunt-the-lady merchants and unlicensed street vendors. Happening to glance idly down at the crowds milling along the other side of the street, to his amazement he saw Sheila. There was nothing in particular to distinguish her from the rest of the crowd, nothing that made her stand out - no halo around her head, no heavenly arrow pointing at her. It just so happened that among all the faces thronging the street, Jazz's eyes lazily alighted in that particular second upon her face.

Recognition was instantaneous, but he was so stunned at the fact that he had seen her that he was paralysed into inaction for valuable seconds. In that wasted fraction of time the lights changed to green and the bus surged forward towards Tottenham Court Road, widening the distance between himself and his former lover. By the time that he had hurled himself down the stairs and leapt from the moving bus, he was a good hundred yards from where he had spotted her.

Without conscious thought he dashed across the road between moving vehicles, earning well merited oaths from two cabbies, sprinted across Oxford Circus and ran along the gutter anxiously scanning the faces of the shoppers and tourists. Through not looking where he was going, he almost ran into the back of a taxi that pulled in ahead of him to deposit a fare, and narrowly avoided tumbling the elderly lady emerging from its rear seat onto the pavement.

Now on the pavement, Jazz shoved his way through the crowds, drawing ill-favoured looks from those he bumped into, and causing some women to draw back in alarm as he peered into their faces. By the time he reached Bond Street tube station, he knew that he had lost her: she could have turned down a side street, crossed to the other side of the road, or entered any one of a number of shops.

Slowly, sadly, and thoughtfully, he retraced his steps, jostled himself now by those walking more quickly, his eyes darting from side to side in case he should chance upon her again. He did not. He decided to walk back to his office, and it was only when he reached Tottenham Court Road that he realised he had left his briefcase, containing all his legal papers, on the bus.

2

Sheila and Anthony had been back in London for the best part of a year. They had renewed old contacts, found themselves a bedsit, and obtained jobs in a coffee bar-cum-restaurant, Sheila waitressing and Anthony washing up. The hours were long, the money barely sufficient, and their shifts did not always coincide, but for the time being they were satisfied, for everything was purely temporary. Sheila harboured thoughts of returning to college, and Anthony had ambitions that were wholly beyond their present means: he wanted to open a meditation centre, although the practical problems of a suitable location and of finance seemed insurmountable. In the meantime, neither cared what they were doing as long as they had enough to pay the rent and feed themselves. Most of the time, they were too tired to think beyond the basic needs of the human body.

Fatigue was something Sheila welcomed, for it dulled the pain she felt inside at the loss of Gopala. Within days of their return, she had begun to talk about visiting her son, but Anthony had soon sowed doubt in her mind as to the genuineness of Govinda's promise that she could visit whenever she wanted.

'If you turn up unannounced,' he said, 'he'll find a thousand and one excuses why you can't see Gopala and can't stay. Remember what happened when your old boyfriend turned up demanding to see you and the baby? He'd probably do the same sort of thing: whisk Gopala away and lie to your face. And if you contact him to arrange a date, he'll just have more time to invent an excuse.'

Deep inside Sheila knew that Anthony was probably right, but she still felt that Govinda would not prevent Gopala from seeing his mother, whatever he might feel about her and Anthony. After six months she wrote a letter asking Govinda when it would be convenient for her to visit Gopala, and asking if it would be possible for her to take him out for the day. She gave assurances that she would return him to the ashram, and declared herself willing to abide by any conditions Govinda might wish to impose. The reply came almost by return.

She was on late shift that day, and still in bed when she heard the post come through the letter box. Sleepily she got up, pulled on a pair of jeans and a sweater, and went into the hall from the ground-floor front room she and Anthony rented. There was usually a pile of mail, for the house had three storeys plus a basement, and about two dozen people lived there. She picked up the bundle and began to sort it onto the hall table, not really thinking that she would hear from Brindavan so soon.

It was the handwriting that she recognised immediately; that large flourishing script could belong to no-one else. As she held it, she realised that her breathing had become fast and shallow: *Calm down, girl! Take a deep breath!* The fact that Govinda had written himself, instead of letting Simon deal with it, convinced her that the letter contained good news.

She dumped the rest of the mail on the table and slipped back into the room. For a long time she simply sat at the table in the bay window, looking at the envelope, willing it to contain a favourable reply. Eventually, her nerves could stand it no longer, and she ripped open the envelope, withdrew the single sheet of paper inside and unfolded it. It had indeed been written by Govinda himself.

"My dear Sheila," it began, "How very nice to hear from you. I am glad that you and Anthony have found employment and somewhere to live. We would be delighted to welcome you to Brindavan were it not for the fact that within a few days I am departing on a trip to India to visit some of the temples sacred to Lord Krishna. It is a trip I have been planning for some time, and I am taking Swami Krishnananda and two of the brothers with me, as well as Gopala. I plan to be away for about a month, and will write to you again upon our return. You are, of course, welcome to visit the ashram anyway. Yours in Krishna, G."

Anthony was on the early shift, which meant that the two overlapped by a couple of hours in the afternoon. They managed to snatch a quick break together, and Sheila showed him the letter.

'I don't believe a word of it!' he scoffed. 'It's just as I said, a ruse just to stop you turning up. "You're welcome to visit anyway"! What a load of tosh!'

'But he was always talking about going to India,' Sheila argued. 'He even promised to take me when he went.'

'And in the five years we were there, a trip to India never materialised. It was pie in the sky then and it's pie in the sky now.'

'Well I think you're wrong.' Sheila pouted. 'It's a very nice, friendly letter, and if he's taking Gopala to India, I'm really pleased.'

'And how's he going to take Gopala without a passport, do you think?'

Sheila did not know. She had never had the opportunity to go abroad, and so had never applied for a passport, but she thought that Govinda would know how to go about it. When several weeks had passed after she presumed that the India trip was over, and she had not received any further letter from Govinda, Sheila decided to telephone. She recognised Simon's voice at once: 'Brindavan ashram. How may I help you?'

'Simon?' she asked.

'This is Swami Krishnananda speaking,' Simon replied in the pompous tone he used when asserting his authority.

'Oh, yes, sorry Swami. This is Sheila. You're back from India then?'

'Sheila? .... India?'

'Yes, Gov ... um, I mean Swamiji, wrote to me that you were going.'

'Oh, right. Yes, of course we're back. I'd hardly be talking to you if I weren't, would I?'

'No, I suppose not.' She giggled nervously.

'Well, what do you want?'

'Could I speak to Swamiji?'

'He's unavailable at present.'

'I just wondered when it would be convenient for me to come down and see Gopala.'

'You'd better write to Swamiji about that.'

'But I already did, just bef ... '. The burring of the disconnected tone cut her off mid-word.

3

Simon called the meeting to order. All the ordained Brothers of the community and Sister Magda were present: novices and Sisters were generally excluded from community meetings, and Magda's presence signified the serious nature of the agenda. Govinda looked around the table.

'I have called you together to discuss one matter of supreme importance to the future of this ashram. It concerns Gopala. As you all know, when his mother chose to leave Brindavan for the tinsel and trash of the outside world, Gopala preferred to remain here. It is said that the child is father to the man, and in this case a small boy showed infinitely more wisdom than his mother, wisdom which she was unfortunately not able to perceive.

'When she left this place of refuge - for that is what it was to her, having been given shelter here when she was pregnant, rejected by her family, friendless - she promised that she would never attempt to take Gopala away. Now, however, she is having second thoughts. She wrote to me some weeks ago - this is the letter, and you may read it if you wish - asking for permission to take Gopala out of Brindavan on a trip, assuring me that she would return him. I immediately asked myself why a person who had already promised not to remove the child would hasten to reassure me that that was not her intention - unless in fact it was!'

Govinda looked around the table, deliberately catching the eye of each person present. All nodded.

'I am glad that you agree with my analysis, for it is not merely what I have deduced by the power of rational thought. Hah! Rational thought! How many mistakes has mankind made by placing reliance upon so-called rational thought! Knowledge of this witch's true intentions came to me in my meditation, when I placed the issue before the Lord, and Krishna has revealed her innermost heart to me, so that I know her better than she knows herself.

'Now listen carefully. When I received her letter, I was at first unsure what to do. Yes, I admit it; I was uncertain. I am a human being just like the rest of you, and my human thoughts and feelings are as fallible as the next man's. What gives me greater power than the ordinary man is that I have the capacity to put aside these human attributes and communicate directly with the Divine.

'My initial feelings were of charity and generosity. Why should she not come and see the child to whom she gave birth? Why should she not take him out for a treat, like any other child? She is his earthly mother after all, and does she not have rights? These were the questions I asked myself.'

He paused again, and looked around the table to receive the silent plaudits of his disciples for his charitable thoughts and feelings.

'How wrong I was, my friends! How wrong! One must never trust merely human impulses, but always seek the path of the Divine Plan. Once I had sought the guidance of Lord Krishna, He revealed to me her innermost thoughts and feelings. My friends, she hates Brindavan and everyone who resides here; she hates me, and she hates the Lord. Her sole thought is to take Gopala away from Brindavan, by force if necessary, thereby robbing the ashram of its future guide.

'I wrote to her that I would let her know when it was convenient for her to visit, although I had no such intention, hoping that my silence might induce her to give up. But the Powers of Darkness are strong in this Kaliyuga, and she has persisted in her wicked plan. Yesterday she telephoned, and demanded most impertinently to speak directly to me, and I am pleased to say that Swami Krishnananda dealt with her very satisfactorily. However, in my meditation last night, Lord Krishna revealed to me that she will never give up her scheme, and although I have written to her today stating the fact that Gopala does not wish to see her, I know that this will not deflect her from her evil course.

'It is imperative, therefore, that we remain vigilant at all times. I have discussed with Swami certain security measures that will be put into effect. A high fence will be constructed around the temple precincts, with gates at appropriate points, and we will obtain two guard dogs. The gates will be locked after the evening pooja every night, and the dogs will then be let loose. One Brother will be detailed to sleep in the conservatory every night so that he will be more easily alerted by the barking of the dogs should there be an attempted intrusion under the cover of darkness. Sister Magda, since the Sisters' and devotees' accommodation will be outside the perimeter fence, Gopala will henceforth take up residence in my quarters and will be in my direct charge.

'As for the daytime, one Brother each week will be responsible for remaining in the vicinity of the car park to welcome and screen visitors: if she or her paramour arrive, Swami is to be alerted at once. Swami will see to all the details. That is all.'

He rose from his chair, looked sternly around the table, and swept out.

4

Jazz examined at length the feelings that had been aroused by the sight of Sheila's face - always assuming that he had not been mistaken - and that had made him leap off a moving bus and dash up Oxford Street risking life and limb like a madman. He had not seen her for seven years. *Has she been here in London all that time?* he wondered. *And with our son?*

He was fairly certain that his old feelings for Sheila had not been revived, that the sight of her had not rekindled the embers of his love, for those embers had long since turned to mere ash. It was true that after Sheila had gone to live at the ashram he nevertheless harboured a secret thought that she might return to him, but the news that she had simply upped and disappeared from that place, with the child, had destroyed his hopes, and introduced a bleakness into his life from which he had not yet fully recovered.

Shoving the disappointment of a lost lover and son to the back of his mind, he had plunged himself into his studies and his training, and thereafter his work. His emotional life he had placed on hold to avoid any further disappointment. Even when one of the secretaries at his firm, a woman who was married with children, had brazenly offered herself to him at an office party, "no strings attached, darling", he had resisted the temptation. He knew that relationships never came without strings of some kind: it was just that sometimes you never discovered what the strings were until it was too late. And so for sexual relief he resorted to porn magazines and prostitutes: neither carried strings.

Glimpsing Sheila had undoubtedly revived some pleasant memories, but above all had brought to the surface that fact that he had a son, a son who was presumably living with Sheila somewhere in London. He was almost overwhelmed by the feelings this knowledge brought. *My son lives in the same city as me!*

At night he would lie in bed thinking about his son. *Does he look like me? How tall is he now, I wonder? Would I recognise him if I saw him in the street?* He would come out of his reverie and discover that his cheeks were wet with tears. He had to resolve the cause of this misery: he had to find his son.

He put his mind to thinking what Sheila would have been doing in Oxford Street that day. Possibly just shopping, of course, but he recalled that she had not been much of a one for that. It was more likely, therefore, that she was working somewhere in the area. She had no qualifications, and was most likely to be working in a shop, or office or restaurant, and had probably been on her lunch break when he saw her.

At the office, he consulted a large-scale plan of Oxford Street, and listed all the side streets and alleys between Oxford Circus and Bond Street, resolved to visit every shop, restaurant and office building in every street until he found her. Then he went to his supervising partner with a tale of his mother's sudden illness in Iran, and requested two weeks' leave of absence. That granted, he put his plan into operation the next morning.

5

Sheila was working the early shift that week, starting at seven with the breakfast rush and not finishing until after the lunchtime madness. That had now more or less dried up; it was almost three, and Sheila only had half-an-hour to go. The restaurant was now virtually deserted, with just a few late lunchers idling over a final cup of coffee, and Sheila was enjoying a cup of tea at a table in the rear when another customer entered and took a window seat. The other waitress was on her break, so Sheila, cursing under her breath, rose wearily to her feet and went to take the order.

The customer had his back to her, and was staring at the first page of the menu, the breakfast section, which was not served after eleven-thirty. His shoulders were slumped, indicating his fatigue, and Sheila felt an instant empathy with him. 'Excuse me, sir,' she said solicitously, leaning forward, 'but we're on the lunch menu at present. Over the page.'

He turned his head wearily to look at her, their faces no more than a foot apart. 'Sheila!' he exclaimed.

She stared back in amazement. He was no longer the youth she had known, and the long flowing locks had been replaced by a regulation short back and sides, but the face and the voice were unmistakeable. 'Jazz?' she whispered.

They stared at each other, unbelieving, for a full ten seconds, and then burst into laughter. Jazz stood up, and they fell into each other's arms, hugging and dancing on the spot, in the way that friends do who have not seen each other for years, and perhaps never thought to meet again. Two customers a few tables away applauded.

'We haven't seen each other for years!' Sheila explained.

Tony, the owner, emerged from behind the cakes and coffee counter to see what all the fuss was about, and when Sheila explained, he seized Jazz by the shoulders and kissed him on both cheeks. 'Any friend of la bella Sheila is a friend of mine!' he cried with true Latin enthusiasm. 'Sheila, darling, give him anything he wants, on the house!'

When Sheila returned with his order, Jazz laid a restraining hand on her wrist. 'I need to talk to you,' he said urgently. 'I've been looking for you for the past week and a half.'

'I finish in fifteen minutes,' she replied with a smile. 'As soon as my relief arrives, I'll join you.'

It was a bitterly disappointed Jazz who returned to his flat very late that night, having discovered that his son was as far out of his reach as ever. His joy at finding Sheila had been replaced by feelings of incredulity, disgust and anger as she and Anthony recounted what had happened the previous summer in Brindavan. He was angry at all of them for conspiring to deceive him into thinking that Sheila had run away all those years ago, but angry too with himself for having been so easily duped by Govinda.

As for Sheila and Anthony having simply abandoned his son, leaving him in the clutches of that consummate liar and cheat, their story aroused in him feelings of incredulous contempt - feelings which he kept to himself. They had talked and talked, he had questioned and questioned, and as the hours passed Jazz became firmly impressed with the thought that the couple were still afraid of their erstwhile guru.

This revived memories of his first meeting with the man, the personal hostility that he had encountered, but he recalled too his charisma and his charm, which he seemed to be able to turn on or off at will. He had been able to resist the man because he had already rejected all religion as crap, having no belief in a god or an afterlife, seeking no divine explanation for his lot in life. He was a rationalist and a materialist, and believed that life was what you made it. If you were born into poverty and had the brains to get out of it, you could; if you didn't have the brains, too bad. If you had the brains and didn't bother, then don't cry about the bad hand Fate has dealt you.

As the evening progressed, however, Jazz had come to understand that Sheila and Anthony had in effect been brainwashed, though he did not suggest that to their faces. It was clear that the guru had created an aura of divinity around himself, labelling himself as the mouthpiece of God, and that this made it impossible for anyone in the community to question him, let alone oppose him, because everything he said carried the authority of the Divine.

He grudgingly admitted to himself that it had taken guts for Anthony and Sheila to defy Govinda at all, but because they still believed in part at least in the man's supernatural powers, they had accepted his terms on their departure, and abandoned Gopala.

As for the pronouncements about Gopala's divine conception, Jazz dismissed that as manipulative crap, some sort of ploy to attract people to the ashram to see the child wonder, leaving the contents of their wallets behind. The more he heard about him from Anthony and Sheila, the more convinced he became that the man was a dangerous crook.

As he prepared for bed, Jazz resolved that Govinda was going to feel the weight of the law very firmly pressing down upon him. Whatever Sheila's failures might have been, the man had no legal right to keep the boy under his control, and if Sheila was too afraid to start legal proceedings, he was not. Though not named on the birth certificate as the father - Sheila had explained that little fraud - he would be able to demand blood tests in a custody suit which would establish his paternity. Even if he failed to gain custody himself, being a stranger to his son, the proceedings would expose Govinda and force Social Services to step in. They were bound to remove the child, for who in their right mind would allow a small child to be brought up in a religious cult?

I'll start the ball rolling tomorrow! was his last thought before sleep overcame him.

6

'Anthony, I'm determined to go,' Sheila said, as they lay side by side amidst a tangle of sheets and blankets. Their love-making had been fierce and lustful, and to Sheila it had seemed like a failed attempt to drive away the demons that still haunted them both.

Anthony sat up. 'I don't want you to go. It won't do any good. Anyway, the letter he sent said Gopala doesn't want to see you.'

'Wasn't it you who taught me not to believe everything Govinda says?' Sheila could not keep bitterness out of her voice. 'Why are you ready to believe this?'

Anthony flung himself off the bed, dragging half the bedclothes with him. 'He'll just put every possible obstacle in your way to prevent you seeing Gopala,' he said irritably, stomping around the room, 'and it's pointless getting your hopes up, that's all.' He hated arguments after sex, and Sheila always seemed to raise serious issues when he was basking in the afterglow. *Why do women always have a go at their men when they're at their most vulnerable?* He slumped into an armchair, sulking.

'I want to hear Gopala tell me to my face that he doesn't want to see his mother.'

'He'll say exactly what Govinda tells him to say,' Anthony snapped, 'just like last time, if you remember.'

Sheila began to weep softly into her pillow. *Oh, shit!* Anthony sighed. He couldn't bear to hear Sheila cry. He went to the bed, sat down, and placed his hand on her shoulder. She shrugged it off. 'Sheila …. darling ….sweetheart, don't cry, please don't cry.'

'It's all right for you,' she sobbed. 'He's not your child, and you never really wanted him anyway.'

Anthony's shoulders sagged; it was not a new accusation. 'You know that's not true,' he whispered.

She turned to look at him, saw the pain written on his face. 'I'm sorry,' she snuffled, 'I know it's not your fault.' She turned over, and sat up to face him. With the fine bones of her thin shoulders, her small, almost un-ripened breasts, the cropped hair and sad eyes, luminous with tears, she looked like some waif of the streets of a third world city.

Anthony felt fresh desire begin to quicken his veins. He placed his hands on her shoulders, and looked deep into her eyes. 'Why don't we make one of our own?' he whispered.

She did not need to speak; her eyes told him all he needed to know. He kissed her tenderly, moving himself onto the bed and then onto her, while she lay back, pulling him down upon and into her, gasping as he slid inside. As he began to move, she used all the power of her internal muscles to hold him in, and entwined her legs behind his buttocks. As her orgasm began to build, Sheila felt the cry arising deep from within, and at the moment of mutual gratification it burst from her lips in a long, wailing cry.

'Krishnaaa!'

Exhausted by his effort, Anthony collapsed upon her, and the name she had cried in her ecstasy did not register.

CHAPTER 15

'You are all here to attend this Sunday pooja to our Divine Lord Krishna, but for what reasons have you really come?' Govinda's stern gaze swept across the mass of humanity crammed into the temple, and no-one dared to catch his eye. 'You have come here for many reasons. Some of you have come out of habit, for this is what Indians do at the weekend; they go to temple. Others have come simply as a day out for the family, to get away from the city and enjoy a day in the country, with a pooja thrown in as a bonus. Many of you have come to ask the Lord for a favour - to find a husband for your daughter, a wife for your son, success in your business, good grades in your children's examinations.'

Govinda paused, shaking his head slowly from side to side as he surveyed his audience. 'Have any of you come here for the right reason?' He smiled. ''But what is the right reason, I hear you ask? I will tell you: it is purely and simply to become closer to God. It is pointless to come here to pray in this beautiful temple if you forget all about God the moment that you pass through the gates on your way home, if you go away and carry on committing the same old sins as before. You cannot confine God to a Sunday pooja, or keep Him locked up in your altar cupboard, to bring out when you feel like it. He is omnipresent and omniscient.

'I am reminded of the story of the shopkeeper who wanted to make sure that he went to heaven, although his sole interest in life was making money. Having no time for God, how was he to ensure his passage into Vishnu Loka? He decided to name all his children after gods and goddesses, so that when he was on his deathbed, surrounded by his family, he could speak their names and thus die with the name of God on his lips.

'Eventually that great day arrived, and Yama the God of Death came for him. As he lay on his bed, his children all around him, he called their names one by one: "Krishna, Rama, Lakshmi,

Durga, Hari, Saraswathy, you are all here". Then he sat up in great anxiety. "If you are all here, who is minding the shop?" he cried. And with those words he fell back and died. The shop had been his whole life, and accordingly he died with it on his mind.

'Do not be like that shopkeeper, my friends. Do not relegate God to second place in your lives. Keep Him constantly in your hearts and minds. Come here as often as you can to recharge your spiritual batteries, for that is why we are here.'

Govinda turned and beckoned to Gopala, who had been sitting on a footstool beside Govinda's chair, before addressing the congregation once more. 'Today is a doubly auspicious day, my friends, and it is your good karma that has allowed you to be here. Not only is it the day of the new moon, but for the first time I will be assisted in performing arati by our little Gopala, who not only bears the name of Lord Krishna but is a Divine Manifestation of the Lord.'

He turned and approached the grandly decorated central altar, Gopala at his side. The idol of Krishna had been dressed in rich red satin clothes, embroidered with gold thread, and almost smothered in garlands of sweet-smelling flowers. Simon handed the arati lamp to Govinda, and a smaller one to Gopala, and together they began to perform the closing arati, chanting the mantras together, the boy's piping treble rising high above the guru's sonorous tones.

At the conclusion, Govinda ushered the child to the sanctuary gates, where he stood alone to offer the sacred flame to the worshippers waiting in line. Old women knelt and touched his feet, tears running down their cheeks, while others clasped their hands together and bowed reverently before him. All the while, as the devotees came and went, the boy stood straight-backed and solemn, indicating from time to time to the attendant Brother with a glance that more camphor was needed. His face remained throughout a mask of concentration, paying no heed to those who touched his feet or bowed to him. When the last worshipper had taken the flame, he passed the lamp to the Brother, turned on his heel and marched in stately fashion out of the sanctuary to his room upstairs, Govinda and Simon in his wake.

2

'What do you think he meant by "Divine Manifestation"?' Brother William asked Brother Lionel later that afternoon as they toiled in the vegetable garden.

'Exactly that,' grunted his companion. Lionel had been at the ashram for five years, and knew better than to question pronouncements of the kind they had heard that day, whereas William was a relative newcomer, enthusiastic and inquisitive.

'Yes, but what I mean is,' the boy persisted, for he was no more than nineteen, 'if I've understood it right, we're all divine incarnations, aren't we? That's what Swami says in his discourses anyway. So did he mean that Gopala is just another incarnation of God like the rest of us, or did he mean that he's someone special?'

'Of course he's special,' Lionel retorted irritably. 'How many times have we been told he's the future head of the ashram? Now stop gassing and get hoeing!'

'Yes, Brother Lionel,' William said meekly.

In silence they weeded the remaining rows of vegetables, and for several minutes nothing could be heard above the singing of the birds and the rustling of the breeze among the beanpoles but the scratching of the hoes in the dry soil. But Brother William could contain his curiosity only so long.

'But Brother Lionel,' he said eventually, trying to maintain a hushed and respectful tone, 'do you think that Gopala is actually a real incarnation of Krishna, just like Krishna was an incarnation of Vishnu.' He plunged on before Lionel could reply. 'I mean, to have an actual incarnation of God here at Brindavan, walking among us and talking with us, that would really be something, wouldn't it!?'

Lionel straightened his back. 'Brother William,' he said in withering tones, 'let's get this matter cleared up once and for all, shall we? I don't know if Gopala is an avatar of Krishna, and furthermore, I don't care if he's an avatar of Krishna. What I do care about is clearing these weeds before dinner, and I'm not going to get that done if you keep prattling on about divine incarnations. If you really want to know, I suggest you ask Swamiji himself. Now get back to work!'

Lionel attacked the weeds vigorously, but his face softened as the annoyance he had felt was replaced by thoughts of the likely repercussions of Brother William asking Govinda such questions. He kept his back to William to hide his grin. As for Brother William, he too worked vigorously, but his brow was furrowed in thought.

There were only ashram members present that Sunday evening, all the visitors having left in the afternoon. As the pooja drew to a close, the sanctuary door opened to admit Govinda and Simon, to the surprise of all present, for they did not usually attend Sunday evening services, when the singing and chanting was generally rather low-key after the efforts of the midday tamasha.

Brother Lionel was about to perform arati, and was a little self-conscious at standing in what was usually Govinda's place. He looked questioningly at the guru, offering the lamp, but Govinda waved him to continue, which he did, with somewhat more gusto than might have been the case in his superior's absence. When all had been concluded, everyone stood around uncertainly, unsure whether to stay or go, whereas normally there would have been a mad scramble to get to bed. It was disrespectful, however, to depart before the guru, and Govinda showed no inclination to leave. As Brother Lionel doused the arati flame, Govinda bowed to the image of Krishna, then turned and spoke.

'Please sit down, all of you. I shall not detain you long, but this is the first opportunity I have had to speak to you about today's events. Some of you may have been surprised at what happened, and I do not blame you, for I too was taken by surprise. Nothing that I do is planned by me, I assure you; I act only in accordance with what the Lord tells me. I am a very simple man, and without Krishna's constant guidance I could never run an enterprise such as we have built here at Brindavan. No, it is the Lord who pulls the strings, and I am merely His puppet, jerked here and there according to His will.

'The Lord moves in mysterious ways, and it is not for us to question Him. Several years ago He revealed to me that He was to be born again in this age of Kali in order to put the world to rights once more. You will recall his words, spoken thousands of years ago and recorded in the Bhagavad Gita: "For the protection of the virtuous, for the destruction of evil-doers, and for the establishment of righteousness on a firm footing, I incarnate from age to age. Whenever disharmony threatens to overwhelm the world, the Lord will take human form to establish the means of earning peace."

'Well, he has once more taken human form, as our little Gopala. You may ask yourselves, "How can that be? He is the illegitimate son of that woman who abandoned him here all those months past." But history is littered with examples of great saints and sages born in the most humble and obscure circumstances, and in the Christian tradition there is Mary, impregnated by the Holy Spirit and then married off to Joseph.

'And what time of greater need is there than now, in this second half of the twentieth century, when evil still stalks a world ravaged by two great wars and innumerable other conflicts, and genocide has been carried out all over the globe. I must tell you that things will get worse before Gopala comes of age and is able to begin the process of world healing. We have at least another fifteen years of horror and disaster before us.

'Why then did I make this revelation today? My children, it was not my decision. As I addressed the devotees, it was the voice of the Lord that spoke through me, and once again He astonished me at what He made me utter, indeed almost overwhelmed me with His revelation.'

He paused and looked at his disciples. No-one stirred, and several mouths hung open in amazement. The only sound was the sizzling of the oil lamps. 'So there it is, we live here at Brindavan in the presence of a Divine Incarnation, an avatar of Lord Krishna. You may be astounded by this fact, but don't be: it is your good karma that has allowed each one of you to be here at this auspicious moment in the history of the world. I hope that your karma allows you to remain here to witness the ministry of Gopala the man. My own karma has allowed me to be here as Gopala's teacher, just as it permitted me to be a playmate of the child Krishna. I pray daily that I may continue to be worthy of this great duty, and I pray that you too will continue to play your part in the story that will unfold. We are all, remember, capable of succumbing to temptation, all liable to fall from grace. Now finish what you have to do, and go to your beds with my blessing.'

As they left the temple a few minutes later, Brother Lionel did not miss the smug look he received from Brother William, and he decided to allot him the task of turning over the dung heap first thing in the morning.

3

Jazz sat in the solicitors' bench in the Clerkenwell County Court waiting for his possession action to come on; there were seventy-two in the list, and his was number sixty-eight. He was very disgruntled, not only at the slow pace of the proceedings, but also because he had failed to achieve anything in the final two days of freedom from work which he had dishonestly obtained. The clerk in the local registry office had brusquely informed him that since the child had not been born in London, and was not presently living in London, he would have to apply to the registry of the child's residence.

He had telephoned the Plymouth registry only to find that he knew virtually none of the information required. 'Sir, if you don't know where or when the child was born, perhaps you'd better discuss the matter with its mother. I suspect she knows the child's date of birth and where it was born. If she's not willing to amend the birth certificate to name you as the father, then you'll have to take proceedings to prove that you are.' Already wilting under the thinly veiled sarcasm, Jazz had not seen fit to mention that the certificate already contained a name in the "Father" column, albeit a false one.

On the Friday he went to the restaurant to see Sheila, only to discover that she and Anthony had a couple of days off and had gone away for the weekend. Now he was itching to get back to the office to continue his research into what he needed to establish in order to mount a claim for custody of Gopala. *Why the hell didn't I take Family Law!* he fumed.

That evening he telephoned Sheila, to find that she was working lates that week, but was able to tell Anthony what he planned to do.

'I don't think Sheila will like this, you know,' Anthony warned. 'She could get into trouble for not naming you as the father in the first place.'

'I've thought of that. I can say I've only just found out where Gopala's living, and I have no idea where Sheila is.'

'But Govinda could put the police onto us straight away; he knows our address.'

'I don't think he'll make a fuss about it; he won't want any bad publicity - you know, putting pressure on a young girl who's just given birth to give a false name for the father.'

'It's only her word against his, and he's a slippery character. You don't know him as well as I do. He'll deny everything, and drop Sheila in it.'

'I really need to talk to Sheila about this, Anthony. Gopala's her child, and she's the one who should decide.'

'I'll talk to her when she gets back, and you can give her a call in the morning.'

4

Jazz's call unsettled Anthony, and soured the sweet recollection of the past weekend he and Sheila had enjoyed. They had decided to get away and relax completely, forgetting work and the past, to concentrate entirely upon making a baby. They had stayed at a country pub, and when not snatching a quick meal and a pint in the bar, had made love: in the morning, in the afternoon, in the evening, and at night. They had made love passionately and with urgency, and languidly with tenderness; they had made love in their room, and also in the open air on their walks, in fields and woods, and once in an empty and decaying barn. They reasoned that if all this did not produce the desired effect, nothing would.

Now the pall of legal proceedings hung in the air, and Anthony knew for a certainty that whatever Jazz might think, Sheila would inevitably be dragged in, which raised the very real spectre of a prosecution for declaring a false name. Anthony could not think of anything he could do to forestall potential disaster, for Jazz was clearly on a crusade to free his son.

There was also the fear that Jazz's actions might rekindle Sheila's own wish to see Gopala, even perhaps to seek custody herself. He did not see how that could be achieved without a direct confrontation with Govinda, and he could well imagine the slanders that would be aimed in their direction, slanders which would certainly be supported by Simon, and probably others. If Govinda managed to show through lies and trickery that Sheila was an unfit mother, the psychological damage it might cause to her was incalculable.

Worst of all, he realised, was that he was still afraid of Govinda, and the acknowledgment paralysed him, wrapping him in misery and self-pity. He lay on the bed staring at the ceiling, with only one thought in his mind: *What can I do? What can I do?* And at that moment when his mind was almost devoid of thought, the answer came to him: *Find yourself.*

With his body already totally relaxed, it now took just the slightest mental effort for him to let go of everything: his eyelids closed, his lips parted slightly, his leg muscles relaxed, allowing his feet to fall slightly outwards, and as he let his arms go, they turned over, palm uppermost. He slowed his breathing, concentrating his attention on the tip of his nose, where with each indrawn breath he could detect the slight flow of air. While his breathing slowed, it also became fuller, expanding the full capacity of his lungs, thereby allowing his blood vessels to absorb the maximum amount of oxygen.

After a dozen conscious breaths, his mind and body adapted automatically to the breathing pattern, and his mental focus shifted from the tip of his nose to the centre of his forehead, where it remained for a while before soaring off into the Infinite. His breathing now had slowed to such an extent that the movement of his chest was barely perceptible, yet the air continued to flow in and out, gently filling the lungs, replenishing the energy of the body, sustaining its life-force.

He could not recall afterwards exactly what he had experienced once his consciousness left his body. There had been a sudden and exhilarating sense of freedom, an awareness that his essential being, his real Self or Soul, had discarded the clumsy vehicle of the body, which was suitable for moving around on Earth, but not on higher planes of existence. He remembered being surrounded by light of an incredible intensity, a light that suffused his Self, bathing and cleansing it, and he recalled the sense of utter peace that existed in that place, wherever it was.

He had no memories of meeting with gods or goddesses, saints or sages, or with beings of any kind. No-one spoke words of great wisdom or of comfort to him; he received no message for the benefit of mankind. But when he opened his eyes, and became conscious of his earthly surroundings, he knew what had to be done, and he knew that he was no longer afraid.

5

Govinda engaged a firm of security contractors to build the fence around the temple and its immediate precincts. When Simon had protested at the cost, he had been smartly rebuffed. 'We need something that is going to stand up to the wind and weather, Swami Krishnananda, not some haphazard thing built by you and the Brothers that falls over in the first stiff breeze!'

The fence was made of six-feet high steel mesh panels fixed to posts driven deep into the ground. Large wrought iron gates allowed traffic from the lane to pass into the car park, and there were similar, though less ornate gates at the far side of the car park, allowing access into the fields. Smaller gates were erected where pedestrian passage was required, such as to the nuns' and devotees' sleeping quarters. Every gate was supplied with a chain and padlock.

As for dogs, Simon had thought in terms of buying two Alsatian pups which could be trained from infancy, but Govinda had scoffed. 'We need security now, Swami, not in twelve months' time!' So they had scoured the small ads columns in local newspapers, and eventually discovered an adult German Shepherd bitch for sale. Simon telephoned the farmer, who said, rather sadly, that he had been forced to sell the dog because she had become too big and boisterous for his young family, but that she was good-natured and had cost a lot of money.

The truth of the matter was that the dog had turned upon a tormenting child, and had then been given a good thrashing and kept tied up in an outhouse, where she soon became savage. The dog's true nature had been disguised by the farmer by means of a soporific in its morning meal, so that when Simon went to collect her, she appeared very docile, and had almost instantly fallen asleep in the car.

'Her name's Candy, and she seems too sweet to frighten a fly,' Simon remarked when he returned to Brindavan.

'Don't worry,' Govinda reassured him. 'Lock her in one of the outhouses, and don't give her anything to eat. By the time we let her out this evening she'll be starving, and there is nothing quite so alarming to an intruder as a hungry dog.'

In this respect, the guru's words were to a certain extent accurately prophetic. By the late afternoon the sedative had worn off, by which time Candy had smelled out her new home, an old pigsty, and discovered there was no escape. She had been shut into the housing, constructed of stone with a solid door, because part of the outer wall of the enclosure had collapsed.

Although not chained, the dog was to all intents and purposes in the same predicament she had endured for several months past, and whenever she heard anyone in the vicinity, she launched into a sustained bout of savage barking.

'You see, Simon,' Govinda said with a self-satisfied smile. 'That noise is enough to intimidate the Devil himself!'

Brother Wayne had drawn the short straw for the first night's patrol duty. Simon's arrangements had been drawn up as follows: Sisters were to leave the area immediately after the pooja, and Brothers were to be in their quarters by eleven, at which time the duty monk would padlock all the gates, release the dog, and then retire to a truckle bed in the conservatory. Thus it was that Brother Wayne was to be Candy's first, but by no means last victim.

Having locked all the gates, he approached the sty confidently enough. Detecting his approach, Candy began to bark ferociously; she was not only hungry but thirsty, for no-one had thought to replenish her water bowl, which she had emptied hours before. As Brother Wayne placed his hand on the door bolt, the barking ceased, to be replaced by a low, throaty growling, which he did not find especially reassuring. Having no experience of dogs, he felt fearful of what lay on the other side of the door, and the fear transmitted itself to the animal, which began to snarl menacingly.

Wayne thought that perhaps he ought to report to Swami Krishnananda, but the thought of the ridicule that would undoubtedly be heaped upon him by all and sundry should nothing untoward occur deterred him. He therefore made the mistake of opening the door. 'Good dog!' he quavered, as he drew back the bolt. His second mistake was not to put the door between himself and the dog, but to stand in the open.

As the door swung open, Candy saw a figure towering above her, silhouetted against the moonlit sky, and she instinctively went for the throat. Acting also from instinct Brother Wayne threw up his arm by way or protection. Fortunately for him, it was a clear and chilly night, and he had flung on an old donkey jacket for his duty, and this proved sufficient to prevent Candy's teeth doing too much damage to his arm. As he fell backwards under the weight of the dog, he stunned himself against the outer wall, which was also fortunate, for Candy realised in an instant that the inert figure beneath her posed no threat.

Giving the unresisting arm a last shake, Candy looked up: ahead she sensed space and freedom, and the myriad smells of an early summer night. She tensed her muscles and sprang forward, her back legs inflicting upon Brother Wayne's testicles rather more pain than her teeth had managed upon his arm, a pain sufficient to rouse him from his dazed state.

He lay on the ground for a while, moaning and clasping his crotch, then managed to drag himself to his feet. Somewhere in the night he could hear Candy barking, and so he made for the nearest shelter, Swami Krishnananda's quarters. The outside door was locked, and he banged on it with both fists until it opened slightly and the Swami's head appeared.

'What on earth is the matter, Brother Wayne?' he remonstrated.

'It savaged me!' Wayne cried. 'That fucking dog savaged me!'

'Brother Wayne! Language!'

'Sorry, Swami, but that dog's a fucking lunatic!'

6

'And how is Brother Wayne this morning?' inquired Govinda when Simon brought him his morning coffee. He had heard of the incident after the morning pooja, from which Brother Wayne had been absent.

'He was more frightened than anything, though I think his arm might have been a bit of a mess if he hadn't been wearing a coat. He's got a few scratches on the wrist, and his testicles are somewhat swollen.' Simon's mouth twitched.

'What have his testicles got to do with it?'

'The dog apparently trod on them when she jumped on him. She's a heavy dog. With rather large feet.' Simon fought to keep the smile from his lips.

'I see. Poor Brother Wayne. And how did you manage to catch Candy?'

'I decided to let her roam about during the night, let her work off her surplus energy.'

'And no doubt you didn't fancy trying to catch her in the dark.'

'She'd already attacked one person; I didn't want anyone else added to the list.'

'Understandable,' Govinda remarked, nodding sagely. 'So how was she caught, then?'

'It proved quite easy in the end. She was in the middle of the car park fast asleep when we went out before the pooja, though from the state of the flower beds, she'd been pretty busy during the night. As soon as we went near her, though, she woke, and began to growl rather nastily.'

'I do hope you didn't risk your own hide, Swami,' Govinda said, his face a mask of concern.

'I was there, of course,' Simon said frostily, 'but I'm not a dog person as you know. I'd already checked with the Brothers, and it appears that Brother Paul's father used to breed them, so he had some experience of the beasts. I put him in charge of the operation, and he opened a can of dog food, waved it in front of her, and she followed him quite docilely back to her quarters. He also gave her some water. He appears to know what he's doing, and he's not afraid of the animal - he says that helps a lot. Maybe we could appoint him permanent dog-keeper.'

'That sounds reasonable. Has he checked Candy since?'

'He went to see her after breakfast, and though she growled a bit, he gave her a few titbits, and she quietened down. He says she's overweight, and needs a lot of exercise.'

'Let him take her out into one of the fields for a run, but make sure no-one else is about to distract her. She needs to get to know and trust Brother Paul. Until she's settled down, he'll have to be on permanent night duty, so rearrange his duties to allow for that.'

<h1 style="text-align:center">7</h1>

'That's a bloody big dog!' Jazz whistled, passing the binoculars to Anthony. 'I wouldn't want to meet that bugger in the dark!'

Anthony watched the dog being exercised by Brother Paul, and noted that no-one else was in sight. 'Looks as if he's the only one who can handle the dog.' he commented, 'which might mean it's vicious.'

Sheila and Anthony had decided to join forces with Jazz in an attempt to wrest control of Gopala away from Govinda. Sheila had written an account of all that had happened at Brindavan relating to Gopala since his birth, and Jazz's supervising partner, Mr. Willcocks, had undertaken to turn it into an affidavit and then initiate contact with the relevant authorities in Devon. In the meantime, Jazz and Anthony had decided to pay a covert weekend visit to Brindavan to spy out the lie of the land. Sheila had wanted to come too, but both men had refused even to consider her request.

Jazz had discussed the legal situation with Mr. Willcocks, and the plan was firstly to rectify the birth certificate and then confront Govinda to demand that he hand over Gopala. If he refused, as they expected him to, then proceedings for custody would be issued in the local magistrates' court, where applications concerning illegitimate children were heard.

Anthony, however, had suggested making plans for an alternative course of action should the law fail in some unforeseeable way, namely a snatch. 'I doubt if he'd call the police, because of the risk of adverse publicity,' he had said. 'Can you imagine what the Sunday papers would make of a child being kept away from its parents at a religious cult?'

'Blimey!' he muttered. 'Looks as if they've built a security fence right around the temple.' He handed the binoculars to Jazz.

'And I'll bet the dog's let loose at night. The fence is to keep him in as much as to keep anyone out.'

Anthony surveyed the ashram from the scrubby thicket on the hillside where the two of them lay concealed. 'Hang on!' he said. 'The women's quarters are outside the fence, over there.' He pointed to the roofs of a cluster of sheds which could be seen above a thick hedge on the far side of the field adjacent to the temple. 'Gopala stays with the nuns, so we needn't worry about the dog at all! We can just come in and take him from whichever hut he's in.'

'Anthony, think about it!' Jazz said, shaking his head. 'Why would they put up a fence like that? What are they protecting? Not the Crown jewels! From what you and Sheila have told me, the only thing he's afraid of losing is Gopala, which means that the kid now lives inside the fence.'

Anthony grimaced as it struck him that Jazz was right. 'Shit!' he hissed through clenched teeth.

CHAPTER 16

Geeta had maintained a discreet contact with her sister ever since the latter had left the family home, a fact known only to her mother. Mrs. Chaudhury was loyal and obedient to her husband: ordered not to speak to Meera ever again, she would not have dreamed of doing so. If, however, Geeta chose to disobey her father, that was her own affair - she was a married woman after all - and Dr. Chaudhury had not forbidden her to receive news of her elder daughter, or indeed, to pass on news through a third party.

Cast off by her husband, and abandoned in turn by her father, it was only natural for Geeta to turn to Meera for help, and it was just as natural for Meera to offer her sister and her niece shelter, without even bothering to consult the boyfriend in whose flat she lived. Benjamin Samuels had been somewhat bemused to come home from work to find himself suddenly living in the middle of an Indian family, with Meera's sister and her baby ensconced in the second and only other bedroom.

'Um, any idea how long she's likely to be here?' he asked sotto voce as they prepared for bed that evening.

'As long as it takes, Ben. Don't worry, we Indian families are always quarrelling among ourselves. As soon as this tiff has been patched up, she'll go back home.'

'What's it all about anyway?'

Meera sat on the edge of the bed and frowned. 'I don't actually know, she hasn't told me yet. It's probably something really stupid, and Mahendran will be on the phone tomorrow begging her to come back.' Even as she spoke she realised she did not sound terribly convincing.

'Why didn't she go back to your parents?' Ben grumbled. 'They've got more room that we have.'

'I don't know. Pride maybe. Now let's get to sleep, we've both got work tomorrow.'

Ben sat down beside her and began to nuzzle her neck. 'Actually, sleep was the last thing on my mind,' he murmured.

'Ben Samuels, you're a rascal!' She took his face in her hands and kissed him. 'We'll have to be really quiet, these walls are paper thin!'

2

Geeta lay awake listening to the creaking of the bedsprings and the smothered giggles from the next room. *Has my life come to an end?* she wondered. She had not been able to tell Meera what had happened because she herself hardly understood. Both her husband and her father believed that she had been with another man, and this was not true: she had never even thought of another man since her marriage to Mahendran, whom she had loved - and still loved - as an Indian wife should, with her complete being. *What terrible karma has brought this upon me?*

She reflected upon the past. She and Meera were as different as two Indian daughters could be. Meera was rebellious, liberated, independent and Western in her outlook, while she, Geeta, was traditional, obedient and domesticated; she had never disobeyed her parents, and had accepted without demur the husband they had chosen for her, whereas Meera was living with an English boy and clearly, to judge from the noise next door, enjoying her sinful life very much. The great irony of all this was that it had been Meera who had been born in India and lived there during her infancy, whereas Geeta had been born in Bromley.

Geeta had always been a quiet, religious girl, happy to accompany her mother to the temple, punctilious in performing her devotions at home, while Meera had rebelled against religion from her early teens, either refusing to go to the temple or, worse still, wearing Western casual clothes, driving her mother mad with exasperation and embarrassment. *And yet I'm the one who is suffering! I am the one regarded as a whore and adulteress!*

She winced as she recalled her father's words of reproach, and the look of contempt he had given her; he had obviously believed whatever it was Mahendran had told him. Yet neither of them had explained to her what led them to their belief: they had accused, tried, convicted and sentenced her without allowing her to say a word in her defence.

Dear God, why have You allowed this to happen? I have always served You faithfully. I have always obeyed my father and my husband: how could You let them treat me like this? What terrible sin have I committed in a past life which has brought this down upon my head?

Nothing made sense any more. The entire foundation of her existence - belief in God, family and husband - had been shaken to the roots and come tumbling down around her ears. And the only person to whom she had been able to turn for help had been her sister, who was the one actually leading an immoral life.

Although there was silence now from Meera's room, Geeta herself was unable to sleep: her mind whirled around and around the inexplicable disaster that had befallen her, replaying endlessly the cruel words and actions of her husband and her father. She wept endlessly, stifling her sobs so as not to disturb Sita, and finally exhaustion stole upon her and she too slept.

3

Mrs Chaudhury cried every day following her younger daughter's disgrace, although the greater part of her sorrow was for her own situation rather than Geeta's: to have lost one daughter was a terrible blow, but to have lost both was entirely insupportable. She did not display any unseemly or embarrassing emotion when her husband and son were at home, but as Dr. Chaudhury was at the surgery most of the day, and Narain at school, she had sufficient time to vent her grief.

She had been unable to leave the house at all. Having barely recovered from the disgrace and humiliation of Meera leaving home, she knew what lay in store for her beyond her front door, for the jungle telegraph had already begun to transmit the news of Geeta's much worse behaviour. She had already received a telephone call from one of her closest friends purporting to offer sympathy for her predicament.

"I grieve for you, Gauri-bai," the woman had purred. "How can you even bear to live under such disgrace? Were it to happen to me - not that my Savitri would ever behave in such a way, of course - I would feel like slitting my throat! And why your husband did not kill the girl on the spot, I cannot understand. As I said to my own dear husband …."

At that point Mrs. Chaudhury had put down the receiver, and had not answered the telephone for the rest of the week. When Narain came home from school, he answered any calls, and if they were for his mother said that she was not in, as instructed. In the evenings, Dr. Chaudhury dealt with any calls, usually in peremptory fashion.

So when the telephone rang one Saturday morning while her husband was at the surgery, and Narain outside somewhere playing cricket, she let it ring. She carried on kneading her chapatti dough and tried to ignore it, but it continued to ring as if it knew she was there, hiding in the kitchen. Eventually, she wiped her hands on her apron and went into the hall, where she stood watching the telephone as it rang, and rang, and rang. Almost hypnotised by it, she reached out and took up the receiver: 'Hallo?' she quavered.

'Amma, it's me. Please don't hang up!'

Mrs. Chaudhury was stunned. Her mouth opened and closed, but no sound came out. Inside her ample bosom, her heart thumped an uneven tattoo against her rib-cage.

'Amma! Are you there?'

'Meera?' Her voice was ragged with emotion, and tears were already beginning to dribble down her plump cheeks. 'Is it really you?'

'Yes, Amma, it's me. I have to talk to you. About Geeta.'

'Geeta! What is it? What has happened?'

'Nothing, Amma, she's fine, and little Sita. They're staying with me.'

'Oh, thank God she's safe!'

'God has nothing to do with it, Amma. Now listen, I need to know what happened between her and Mahendran. She won't tell me anything, and if I ask her about it, she just bursts into tears.'

Mrs. Chaudhury repeated what her husband had told her. She did not herself understand it, but accepted that he, as a doctor, was right.

'Amma, that's bullshit!' Meera cried angrily.

'Your language has not improved by associating with English boys!' her mother scolded.

'Amma, Geeta isn't the sort of girl to have had an affair! You know that, and father doesn't know her at all if he believes that of her.'

'I know Geeta is not that sort of girl. You perhaps, yes, with your Western habits. But your father says the blood proves it; Mahendran is not the father.'

'Well, I don't believe Geeta's done anything wrong, but at least I can talk to her about it now that I know. Thanks, Amma.'

'Meera! Please keep in touch! Your father is usually at the surgery in the morning.'

'I know, and I will call again, Amma, I promise.'

4

Meera did some hard thinking before she confronted Geeta. Although quite certain that her sister would not have had extramarital sex, it was difficult to believe that her father would have made a mistake about the blood groups. Yet there had to be some rational explanation: adultery was the last thing it was likely to be, in Meera's view.

She recalled only too well Geeta's embarrassment at the mere mention of sex, and how shocked she had been when Meera teased her on her return from her honeymoon. 'No more a virgin, eh?' she had said, giving her sister a dig in the ribs. 'Better than chocolate, eh?'

'Don't talk about such things!' Geeta had said. 'It's not nice.'

'Didn't you enjoy it, then? Or did it hurt too much?'

'Meera! Please! I cannot talk about such things to you. What would my husband say?' She had tossed her head, and tried to look superior. 'Anyway, I am a married woman now, and you are not, so what would you know about it?'

'Hah!' Meera scoffed. 'You think that at my age I am still a virgin?'

Geeta had been deeply shocked. The idea of a well brought up Indian girl having sex outside the confines of the marital bedroom had never occurred to her. Meera thought it unlikely that a girl who had never had a boyfriend at school because it would upset her father had changed her attitude.

Moreover, what opportunity had Geeta had to have a fling? She had eschewed the chance of going to university, staying at home instead with her mother to learn how to run a home, and had then been married off within a year. She had never gone anywhere afterwards without her mother or her husband by her side, had never had the chance to meet another man.

How could two sisters be so different? Meera wondered. At school, she had always had secret boyfriends, although such liaisons had never amounted to more than amateur kissings and fumblings behind the bike sheds or in the park on the way home. Her parents had never allowed her out on her own outside school hours. University had been a liberating experience, and she had spent a wonderful three years working hard for her degree and indulging in safe but indiscriminate sex. A *miracle I never picked up the clap!* she often thought.

The return home after university, to her father's antiquated and unchanging views about the role of women in society, had been depressing in the extreme. She had rejected all attempts to marry her off, to her father's annoyance and her mother's consternation. 'You will become an old maid!' she had scolded constantly. Although Meera had found a job in advertising, and become financially independent of her father, she had remained at home in order to save for a deposit to buy her own place, and avoided her father's complaints and her mother's mournful looks by going out as much as possible.

She had a succession of boyfriends, none of them Indian, and was by no means reluctant to be seen with them in public, to the eternal mortification of her mother, who had to put up with snide remarks from her acquaintances about her daughter's behaviour. By this time Dr. Chaudhury was hardly speaking to her, though he was not averse from making derogatory remarks about her Western morals in her hearing.

Geeta had no such chequered past, no old flame she might have bumped into by chance to re-stoke the flames of a former passion. She had never worked, always been tied more or less to her mother's apron strings. By the time she had her own home, and might have had more freedom, Sita had already been born. *It's a complete bloody mystery!* Meera sighed.

But she could not put off talking to Geeta for ever. One evening, when Ben had gone out to his squash club, she just came out with it. 'I spoke to Amma, and she told me about the problem.'

'So now everybody knows!' Geeta said bitterly. 'Are you going to throw me out too?'

'Oh, Geeta! How could you think that?' She leant across the table and placed a hand on Geeta's arm. 'I'm your sister, after all.'

'My husband and my parents think I am a loose woman! Why shouldn't you?'

'Amma doesn't believe you have been immoral, and as for the other two, they're men! They only think with their balls!'

'Meera! You are too terrible!'

'I know you never slept with another man.'

'Never! Never!' Geeta began to sob into her hands.

'Stop that!' Meera spoke sharply, and pulled Geeta's hands away from her face. 'Crying doesn't solve anything. The only explanation is that somewhere there's been a mistake.'

'But how? My blood is A, and Mahendran's O, and he can't be Sita's father.'

'Then the hospital must have made a mistake about Sita's blood group. Good God! They've been known to give people the wrong babies, so they must have mixed up Sita's blood type with another baby's. Tomorrow we'll go to the doctor and have Sita's blood tested.'

'Oh Meera! That must be it!' Geeta hugged Meera. 'What a relief! But why didn't Appa think of that?'

'Two reasons. He's a doctor, and doctors don't make mistakes. Secondly, he's a man, and his bollocks jumped to the obvious conclusion!'

'Meera!'

5

'Meera! Wake up!'

Ben watched as Meera writhed on the bed, the muscles of her neck taut and straining, beads of sweat running down her face into the pillow. Her eyes were open, but rolled back in their sockets, showing only the whites, as if she were in some kind of trance, and her head thrashed around on the pillow, saliva trickling from her grimacing mouth. All the time she moaned, mumbling half-formed words which Ben could not make out, and she was clearly trying to sit up, but was unable to, as if some force were pressing her down.

'Noooo!' she screamed.

Ben shook by the shoulders, and she woke up, trembling. 'The dream again?' he asked.

Meera nodded, calmer now, her muscles relaxing, her breathing returning to normal. She held out her arms, and Ben held her close.

She had the dream the first time only a few days after moving in with Ben, and he had been terrified, thinking that she was having a fit, or even that she might have been poisoned. He had called the doctor, but by the time he arrived the episode had passed, and Meera had woken up drenched with sweat. She told Ben about the nightmare when the doctor had left.

'I was in some sort of dark place, lit by a few candles, like a cave or something. I couldn't move, as if I was tied up, though

I wasn't, and all I could do was watch as this huge black demon danced around, laughing madly. Then I saw a sort of stone altar, and Geeta, my sister, was lying on it, unconscious and nude, and the demon was leering at her, and making obscene gestures. Then he ripped off his loin cloth, and he had this huge erect cock, which he grabbed with one hand, waving it about, and grinning all the time. He had these sharp fangs, like a wolf, or bear or something, when he opened his mouth. He came over to me, waving his cock about, and the smell was just awful.

'Then he turned away and went to Geeta, and knelt between her legs, all the time making sure I was watching, and licked her. Suddenly he stood up and shoved his cock right into her, and he was sucking and biting her breasts, and then he came, making this horrible howling sound, and collapsed on top of her. All the time, she never moved. After what seemed ages, he got up again, and he still had this huge erection. He looked at me, and said, "Now it's your turn!", in this horrible voice, like something speaking from the grave. He started to move towards me, and then I screamed, and woke up, and you were there!'

As she recounted the dream, her voice had risen, her breathing had become rapid and shallow, and her body had begun to tremble. She had clung to Ben afterwards, and he had soothed her, stroking her hair and back, and taken her back to bed, enfolding her in his arms, and whispering soothing words to her until she had fallen asleep again.

The dream had occurred quite regularly thereafter, and Ben had become increasingly worried, for the dream never varied in any detail. Now he sat down on the side of the bed and handed her a mug of tea. 'We need to sort this out, Meera,' he said.

'I know.'

'Dad has a friend who's a shrink, and goes in for regressions. You know, taking people back into their past to find out what's buried in their memory and causing the problem. I could speak to him, if you like.'

'You think it may be something from my past?' Meera sipped her tea.

'I think it might be. The dream is always exactly the same, and it frightens the shit out of you. Me too, by the way. It might well be some terrible event in the past that your conscious mind is covering up, and if so, then you need to know what it is.'

'If it's from some time in the past, how come I only started having the bloody dream after moving in with you?'

'So it's all down to me, is it? Maybe I'm the demon, and it's just your strait-laced upbringing that's causing all this.'

'My upbringing might have been strait-laced, but I wasn't.' Meera grinned.

'Whatever it is, we ought to try and find out and knock this thing on the head. Agreed?'

'Agreed.'

'Good. I'll try and got hold of him tomorrow.'

6

The telephone rang. 'It's your son, Dr. Chaudhury,' the receptionist said frostily. 'You're through.'

'Appa! Please come home at once …'

'Narain! How many times have I told you …'

'Amma is laying on the floor!' the boy screeched. 'She's unconscious, and I can't move her!'

'Stay with her! Did you call an ambulance?'

'No.'

'I'll see to it. Cover Amma with a blanket to keep her warm, and wait. I'll come home at once.' He disconnected, dialled the emergency services, and gave them the address, grabbed his coat and walked out into reception.

'Dr Chaudhury! Where are you going?' demanded an aggrieved Mrs. Fawcett.

'My wife has had a heart attack,' he shouted over his shoulder. 'The others will have to see to my patients.' And he was gone before Mrs. Fawcett had decided whether to offer sympathy or complain.

His wife's bulk had caused Dr. Chaudhury concern for some years past. He was always telling her to cut down on the use of ghee in her cooking, and not to over-indulge in the sugar-laden Indian sweets of which she was so fond. Now, as he raced homeward, he feared they had finally taken their toll.

He arrived home just as the ambulance crew were placing his wife in the back of the ambulance, and he followed it to the hospital, with Narain beside him. Pacing up and down the corridor of the same hospital in which his grand-daughter had been born not so very long before, he fretted and fumed. *Why was I not more strict with her? Why didn't I just ban all those sweets?*

Eventually he saw the consultant cardiologist approaching. 'It was a severe attack, Dr. Chaudhury,' he said. 'She is carrying far too much weight, as you must be aware.'

'For such a long time I have been telling her to cut down, but you do not know what Indian ladies are like when you start telling them about fat and sugar. Cooking and food are their domain, and they know best. It is like talking to the proverbial wall!'

The cardiologist smiled. 'English wives are not so very different, you know. But from now on, your wife will have to listen more to you. She will need to watch her diet carefully, and she will need to take it easy for a long time; no heavy work until she is quite well again. She is still asleep, and is being moved into the intensive care unit. You can see her shortly.'

'I will ensure that she uses no ghee or sugar from now on,' Dr. Chaudhury vowed. 'And definitely no sweets or cakes!'

'You will need help with the housework. Do you have a daughter who can take over until your wife is fully recovered?'

Chaudhury hesitated for an instant. 'No, doctor, I have no daughters. Just a son.'

'Then you will need to hire a daily.'

'I will do whatever is necessary for her to get well again!' He blinked furiously behind his glasses to keep his tears at bay. 'Perhaps I can see her now.'

Back home, eating the meal which his wife had prepared earlier, Dr. Chaudhury was started out of his thoughts by Narain.

'We must tell my sisters what has happened,' the boy announced.

'You have no sisters,' the doctor replied, repeating his mantra, but with a voice that faltered.

'Appa, you may say that you have no daughters, but I do have two sisters, and you cannot tell me that I don't!' He pushed back his chair and ran upstairs.

Dr. Chaudhury watched him go helplessly. He suddenly felt old and tired and defeated. *What am I to do? I have lost two daughters, and my grand-daughter, and now my beloved wife is seriously ill. Is this all the result of stupid pride?*

He got up and walked slowly upstairs, stopping outside Narain's room; he tapped on the door, and put his head around it. 'May I come in?' he asked.

Narain was too astonished to speak; he nodded.

'You are right, my son,' Dr. Chaudhury said, sitting beside the boy and patting his knee. 'We should contact your sisters. Your mother would wish it. The problem is,' and his voice began to break up, 'that I don't know where they are.' He swallowed, and composed himself. 'Do you have any idea?'

Narain shook his head. 'Perhaps Mahendran knows,' he suggested.

'That is possible. I should call him anyway, to tell him about your mother. He may wish to visit her perhaps.'

Only when Dr. Chaudhury replaced the receiver did he realise he had not mentioned his wife's heart attack, so preoccupied had he been with his daughters. Mahendran did not know where Geeta was, though suspected she might have gone to Meera, but he had no idea where she lived. *Women!* the doctor sighed. *They are a mystery to me! No matter what a man might say, how forcefully he might lay down the law, they just carry on regardless. They are like some secret society, with their own rules and their own agenda, on the surface behaving as their husbands require, but actually doing what they please. What chance does a man have?*

As his mind turned over all the possibilities, he thought that if Geeta had been in touch with Meera, then perhaps his wife had too. He checked the address book on the hall table, then went through his wife's diary, but there was no mention of Meera. *Would she have been clever enough to use a code?* he wondered, and was surprised to realise that he did not know. He rummaged through all the kitchen drawers, and the drawers in his wife's dressing table, in case she had secreted Meera's telephone number in any of them, but he found nothing.

Having given up hope of finding anything, he sat at the kitchen table and buried his head in his hands. For the first time he truly understood the meaning of the assertion that his daughters were lost to him.

CHAPTER 17

Govinda was in the conservatory ministering to his plants. He was very knowledgeable about their care and cultivation: which needed more watering or feeding, than others, which thrived in light and which preferred shade, which required pruning and when, and whether light or hard. It was the one job he never delegated to anyone else, and woe betide anyone who touched his plants without permission.

He had brought a collection of plants with him from Brixton, which he had kept in his room for lack of anywhere else to put them; almost without exception they were tender plants from sunny climes, and not to be entrusted to the English climate, not even in the warmer south-west. For a few weeks in the summer, if the weather was kind, some of them might be permitted outside to benefit from the fresh air, but at the first hint of autumn they would be whipped back inside. The conservatory had been the first addition made to the main building, situated at the opposite end of the house to the temple entrance, facing south and west to catch as much of the sun as possible.

Simon entered from the dining area, and stood and watched while Govinda tended his "children", as he called them; he knew that the guru hated to be disturbed, and his own business could wait. Govinda moved slowly around the many containers, directing his copper watering can where it was required; at times he had to stretch to reach those at the back, so many and varied in size and shape were the pots, troughs and urns.

The largest shrub in the collection grew in a huge terracotta urn placed in the best lit corner, by an open window. It was about four feet tall, with a similar spread, and although its narrow, lanceolate leaves were somewhat dull in appearance, they set off nicely the profuse clusters of pink flowers that bloomed on the end of long stems. Govinda took some secateurs from his apron pocket, and snipped off a few. 'I like to have some of these in my room,' he said over his shoulder, having given no hint previously that he was aware of Simon's presence.

'I've noticed,' his acolyte replied. 'They're very pretty.'

'I acquired this in Italy on my travels,' Govinda said, standing back and regarding the oleander almost with affection, 'and it's been with me ever since. It was a very small plant then, of course, but look how it's grown. No smuggling it through Customs now! It reminds me of India, where they grow wild.'

'So is this the same one you had in your sitting room in Brixton?'

'Yes, it is. You remember it then? It's always been one of my favourites. Some species in India grow to fifteen feet tall, though this variety wouldn't get to more than about six feet, if I let it. The container keeps it to its present size.'

'Even so, it's grown a lot since Brixton.'

'Well, I've re-potted it several times over the years, of course, but it's been in its present pot for about three years. I happened to remark to a devotee then that it needed a larger pot, and he went out and bought this one. I doubt if I'll ever find one bigger than that, so you will have to remain satisfied with your present home, my dear.' He patted one of the branches. 'When you've finished flowering, I'm going to give you a good prune. 'Now, Swami, let us go upstairs and find a vase for these stems, and you can tell me why you came looking for me.'

'Nothing much really.' Simon shrugged his shoulders. 'Brother Hugh seems to have legged it. He wasn't in his room this morning, so he must have slipped off last night before the gates were locked.'

'Good riddance to bad rubbish!' Govinda snapped. 'Any news of importance?'

'No. There was nothing in the post to trouble you with.'

'Good. Fill this can will you.'

'Sure. By the way, what do you call this shrub? I've always wondered, but never remembered to ask.'

'That is because plants don't interest you. But you must remember that plants too are God's creatures, and they all serve their purpose in the scheme of things. It's popular name is the Jericho Rose.'

2

Mr. Willcocks looked over his spectacles at the three young people sitting on the other side of his desk. 'I'm bound to say,' he remarked, 'that if only half what you've told me about this fellow is true, he's one of the most unscrupulous bounders I've ever come across. And I've met a few in my time, believe me!'

'We know that, sir,' replied Anthony, 'and we'd like to try and accomplish everything without going to court, if possible.'

'If it's the expense that's bothering you ...'

'No, sir, it's not that; we know you'd do your best to keep the costs down. It's just that we'd prefer to avoid a direct confrontation in court, because he's bound to bring up stuff and make it sound ten times worse, and that would upset Sheila a lot.' Anthony took Sheila's hand and gave it a squeeze.

'Well, if that's how you believe he'll behave in court, what on earth makes you think he'll just hand over the child without a fight?'

Jazz spoke up. 'If I go to see him not just as the child's father, intending to go to court and have myself proved as such, but also as a solicitor armed with Sheila's affidavit about his conduct over the birth certificate, he might cave in on the basis that he doesn't want that stuff being made public.'

'Well, the hearing would be in private, of course, but I know what you mean. Things do tend to leak out.'

'And he could be charged with inciting Sheila to make a false declaration, which wouldn't do his public image much good.'

'That's true, of course.' Willcocks sat back and pursed his lips. 'So in effect, your plan is to blackmail him into handing over the boy?'

'In effect.' Jazz grinned.

'And what have you got to say about this, young lady?' Willcocks said, giving Sheila a serious look.

'I want my son back, Mr. Willcocks, and if Jazz thinks he can get him back without going to court, then I'm prepared to go along with it.'

'I understand. And when do you propose to go, Mr. Shah, or should I refer to you as "Jazz" from now on? It makes you sound like someone from The Rolling Stones.'

'I think "Shah" will do around the office, sir, if you don't mind. I thought I'd drive down on Friday evening, stay in a hotel overnight, and beard the fellow in his den on Saturday.'

'And you plan to go alone?'

'I wouldn't want Sheila to go, and if Anthony were to put in an appearance, I understand the chap might well go berserk.'

'He doesn't like me much any more,' Anthony confessed. 'Told me never to darken his doorstep again!'

'So be it. And if nothing comes of it, we'll institute proceedings under the 1957 Act on Monday morning. I have agents in Plymouth primed and waiting for the green light.'

3

Joshua Silberstein was a respected member of both the Jewish and the psychiatric communities. He had practised psychiatry for over forty years, in which time he had seen many trends come and go, but had pursued his own course regardless of what the current fashion might be. In his early years he had taught his discipline in the academic atmosphere of the University of London, and he was the author of two text books and several learned articles.

He had always held the view that in the absence of any evidence of organic brain damage, a disturbed mind was the product of individual experience. In many cases the cause was relatively easy to find: if a man had been driving a car and had an accident in which a family member had died, the consequent mental disturbance was invariably due to guilt - whether the patient had been responsible for the accident or not. Diagnosis was in such cases simple, treatment less so, but at least the practitioner knew with what he was dealing.

The most interesting cases, however, were those where the cause of the disturbance lay buried within the patient's subconscious, sometimes at such a depth that it proved almost impossible to excavate. In such cases the patient had usually suffered some acutely traumatic experience, something so awful that the conscious mind would not be able to cope with it, and so the subconscious mind had spared its twin the horror by burying the memory. The dividing line between the two parts of the mind, however, was permeable, and bits of the buried memory could filter through in dreams and nightmares.

For some years past Dr. Silberstein had adopted the practice of seeking to recover buried memories by means of hypnosis, regressing his patient back to the time of the trauma. He did not, however, believe that current psychological problems might result from experiences in "past lives", and regarded those who purported to take people back to a previous life as circus acts at best and charlatans at worst.

But he did not plunge into hypnosis immediately, for the patient himself might be able to provide valuable clues to diagnosis. 'Sit down and make yourself comfortable,' he told Meera, 'and tell me about this nightmare of yours.' He switched on his recorder. When she had finished, moderating her language appropriately, he sat back and sucked his lower lip for a while.

'The demon is masculine,' he said at last, 'and undoubtedly represents some male figure who has played a significant part not only in your own life but your sister's too.' He paused. 'How is your relationship with your father?'

Meera laughed. 'At the moment, non-existent.' She explained what had happened. 'But if you think all this might have been caused by my father molesting us when we were kids, you're barking up the wrong tree. He loved us to bits when we were young, and it's only the grown-up daughters he can't stand!'

'I see. Any other significant male figure in your lives?'

'Not really.'

'Well, let us see whether hypnosis can uncover anything. Lie back on the couch and make yourself as relaxed as possible. The process may uncover an event, or events, which you will find difficult to cope with, and your relationship with whoever this person is that your mind has demonised will almost certainly be damaged beyond repair - depending upon what precisely the nature of the trauma is. It is not going to be easy for you to cope with, so if you feel that you would rather not know, and just live with the nightmares, now is the time to tell me.'

'No, Dr. Silberstein, I want to get to the bottom of this, and to hell with the consequences!'

'Very well.' Silberstein took out a small soft leather pouch, from which he extracted a crystal on a length of thread. He began to swing the crystal from side to side before Meera's face. 'I want you to watch the crystal, and to empty your mind of everything. Put all your concerns to one side for the time being, and just watch the crystal, nothing but the crystal. Now you are beginning to feel a little tired, a little sleepy. It's fine to go to sleep. Your eyelids are heavy, so close your eyes. At the count of three you will be asleep: one, two, three.'

He wrapped the crystal in its cloth, tucked it into its pouch, and put the pouch in his top pocket. Then he switched on the recorder. 'Meera, can you hear my voice?'

4

'I have called this Brothers' meeting to discuss one or two matters which need to be dealt with, but principally to consider the reallocation of Brother Hugh's duties. As you all know, Brother Hugh - and I call him that quite deliberately, for he took monastic vows from which he has not been released - Brother Hugh, I say, left Brindavan two days ago like a thief in the night. He did not have the courage to come to me and tell me what was troubling him, so that I could help him.

'Had he done so, I would most certainly have helped him, and had it proved to be the case that it was better for him to go than to stay, I would have released him from his vows and sent him on his way with a cheery goodbye and money in his pocket. It has never been my wish to detain anyone here against their will!'

Govinda sat back in his chair, resting his hands on its arms, and surveyed the room. 'Does anyone else want to pack his bags and leave?' he asked silkily. Then he leant forward, darting fierce looks at all present. 'You are free to go! Every last one of you! I do not need anyone!' He relaxed again into his chair and closed his eyes.

There was an awkward clearing of throats, shuffling of feet, and shifting of backsides on seats in the silence that followed. Govinda opened his eyes. 'You are all still here, I see! I hope that this means we shall have no more desertions under cover of darkness.' He smiled suddenly, and the hard, contemptuous look passed from his eyes.

'It is very important that everything in life is done properly. Just consider what bad karma Brother Hugh will now create for himself. Firstly, he took a vow of chastity, but will no doubt soon find a girlfriend, maybe several. Then he also took a vow of poverty, but will now find himself a job and start spending money on himself. Finally, he took a vow of obedience, which he has already broken by leaving without my permission, and which he will continue to break every day for the rest of his life, because he will go back to eating meat, drinking alcohol, smoking, and indulging in other dirty habits which are forbidden here. It's fine to live that sort of life if that's what a person wants; that's his problem. But not when you have taken monastic vows. I would not want to be in Brother Hugh's position for anything.'

He stood up. 'Swami will deal with the administrative details. Good morning!' And he swept out.

There was a deathly silence for a moment, then Simon spoke. 'Brother Hugh's main responsibility was maintenance, since he'd worked in the building trade. Does anyone here have a working knowledge of electrics, plumbing, that sort of thing?'

When the duty roster had been adjusted to Simon's satisfaction, and matters relating to punctuality and demeanour in the temple had been dealt with, Simon dismissed the Brothers, but before anyone could move, Brother William put his hand up.

'Yes, Brother William,' Simon said wearily.

'It's this business of vows and karma that Swamiji mentioned.'

'What about it?' Simon was already tapping his fingers on the table.

'Well, since I haven't taken my vows yet, does that mean that if I left I wouldn't be creating all that bad karma that Swamiji talked about.'

'Thinking of doing your own moonlit flit, are you, Brother William?'

'Not at all, Swami. I just wondered what the karmic situation would be, that's all.'

'I'll speak to Swamiji and let you know, Brother William. Now, we've all got work to do, so let's jump to it.' He stood and went upstairs.

'It's just that someone of us have got more work to do than others,' Brother William muttered to his neighbour as they left, in no particular hurry.

5

Geeta had wanted to speak to her mother ever since Meera had told her about her own call, but she had prevaricated because she did not know what to say, how to explain. And now, when all her hopes had been dashed, she was even more lost for words. The blood test had merely confirmed the situation: there had been no administrative error at the hospital, and she now knew for certain that Mahendran was not Sita's father.

How can this be? she tormented herself. *Am I going mad?* Perhaps she was already mad, she thought, one of those people with two distinct personalities, a dutiful Indian wife on the one hand, and a sex-mad tart on the other. Had she become pregnant while fornicating with someone in that other personality, and now, in her demure personality, had no recollection of it? *But I'm not that sort of person!* she howled inwardly. *I'm normal and boring!*

I never wanted anything else but a husband and children. How can this be happening to me?

Finally, she decided to call her mother. Just to hear her voice again would be so reassuring; even to be scolded by her would lend an air of normality to her life. She looked at the clock: three-forty. Her father would have gone to surgery, and Narain would not be home from school; she dialled the number. At the other end of the line, the telephone rang and rang, but no-one answered. *Amma would not be out at this time of day.* She let it ring a little longer, in case her mother was in the garden, but finally gave up.

It is a sign! Her husband and father had cast her out, her sister's optimism had proved ill-founded, and now her mother was refusing to answer the phone. *God has abandoned me! I have nothing left! Even to my darling Sita I will be a millstone around her neck!*

She went into the kitchen and wrote a note for Meera on the back of an envelope, then went into the bathroom and began to fill the bath. Returning to the bedroom, she took off her blouse and sari, then opened a suitcase and took out her wedding finery. *It is fitting for an Indian woman to die wearing her wedding sari.* Carefully avoiding to look at Sita, asleep in her carry-cot, in case her will should weaken, she returned to the bathroom and turned off the tap. In the bathroom cabinet she found an unopened packet of Ben's razor blades, and sighed with relief; she did not want to use a dirty one, for everything about this final act should be clean.

She donned her wedding blouse, then wrapped herself carefully in the heavy scarlet and gold brocade sari in which she had been married, and climbed into the bath. The hot water soaked into the sari. *It will cling to me, but I will be beyond caring!* She lay back in the bath and began to unwrap a blade.

It was Meera who found her. Already traumatised by what she had learned from Nathan Silberstein, she had heard Sita bawling as she climbed the stairs to the flat, and wondered why

Geeta was not attending to her. She had gone straight to the bedroom, picked up the howling baby and tried to soothe it, then, calling her sister's name softly and lovingly, had pushed open the bathroom door. Geeta lay beneath the crimson water, her dark hair spread out around her still and peaceful face, beyond any further reproach.

It was Ben, returning from parking the car, who found them all: Geeta silent, Sita crying, and Meera screaming her sister's name over and over. From somewhere he found the strength to cope.

6

Brother Damien was on gate duty that Saturday morning; he had been at the ashram for almost three years and was preparing for his final vows. Although he had known Anthony and Sheila, he had never met Jazz, and so welcomed him warmly and directed him to a parking space.

Jazz stepped out of his car and took in the surroundings. *A lot of changes since I was here last!* he mused, noting the large porch at one end of the house, presumably the new entrance to the temple, and a spacious conservatory at the other. Anthony had briefed him, and he knew that it was likely that at this time of day the obnoxious fellow called Simon would be in his office. He crossed the car park and saw the door into the converted cowshed which was Simon's sole domain, and took a quick look about him; there was no-one else about, and he was out of sight of the fellow at the gate. Ignoring the "PRIVATE: NO ENTRY sign on the door, he pushed it open and went inside; he walked down the corridor to the door at the end, which Anthony had told him was Simon's office, and knocked on the door.

'Come!' The voice sounded imperious.

He opened the door, and went inside, and was amused by the startled look on Simon's face.

'Excuse me,' he said, standing up, 'but this area is private. Didn't you see the notice on the door?'

'Yes, I did, but I wanted to speak to you.'

Simon's eyes narrowed, and he looked intently at Jazz. 'Do I know you?' he asked, suspiciously.

'We met a long time ago. I'm Gopala's father.'

Simon's face was a picture of confusion and alarm. 'What are you doing here?' he demanded.

'I've come to speak to your boss.'

'Impossible! He wouldn't agree to see you.'

'I think he might if you give him this,' Jazz replied grimly, handing over a long brown envelope that he withdrew from his briefcase.

Simon hesitated for a second, then took the envelope. 'Come with me,' he said primly.

Jazz followed him out into the yard, and around the back of the building into a single-storey extension that bore the sign "Dining Rooms". They went through the door marked "Men", where Simon instructed him to wait, and himself passed through a door at the far end bearing another "PRIVATE: NO ENTRY" sign. Jazz guessed this led into the room where he had first encountered Govinda what seemed like a lifetime ago.

After several minutes, the door opened. 'He'll see you now,' Simon said. He stood aside to let Jazz pass. 'Through that door and up the stairs. It's the door at the far end.'

'You're not staying?'

'I've things to do.' He sounded huffy.

Jazz went up the stairs slowly, remembering how all those years ago he had baulked at following Sheila in case he met Govinda: now he was here to see the man himself. He walked across the landing, and knocked on the door. It opened almost at once, and there was Govinda before him, looking exactly as he remembered.

'Mr. Shah, it has been a long time!' Govinda said. 'And you have changed.'

'Whereas you haven't changed a bit,' Jazz replied.

'For a Saturday morning, you look extremely formal.'

Jazz had come dressed to impress: dark pin-striped suit, gleaming white shirt, dark blue silk tie, and gleaming black shoes. 'I'm here on formal business.'

'So I gather from your documents. Please come in and sit down, so that we can discuss matters in a civilised fashion. I have asked Swami Krishnananda to arrange for coffee to be brought up.' He ushered Jazz into the room, shut the door, and seated himself in his armchair.

Jazz took a seat at the table, where the copy documents he had brought were scattered. 'You've read Sheila's affidavit?'

'Naturally.'

'You see that she states that you induced her to make a false declaration about Gopal's parentage, naming Simon Hill as the father.'

'Not worth the paper it's written on!' Govinda murmured.

'I beg your pardon?'

'It's a tissue of lies. Swami and I had nothing to do with it. The woman is a consummate liar.'

'That's easy to say!'

'You believe her to be a truthful woman, I suppose?'

'Naturally.'

'Let me put you in the picture, Mr. Shah. She no doubt told you some harrowing story about being forced to leave her child here against her will, and because Gopala is in fact here, you no doubt believe her. If she had told you that she left Gopala here because he was an obstacle to her plans for a new life with her lover - have you met her lover, by the way, the monk Brother Anthony? - if she had told you that, do you think you would be here now?'

There was a knock at the door, and Brother Dennis poked his head around it. 'Are you ready for coffee, Swamiji?'

'Please leave the tray on the table, Brother Dennis.'

When the door had closed, Govinda poured coffee into two cups. 'Milk and sugar, Mr. Shah?' he asked sweetly.

'Just milk,' Jazz growled.

'Now, where were we?' Govinda sipped his coffee. 'Ah, yes, Sheila's lies.'

'Why should I believe anything you say? You lied to me before when I came looking for her.'

'That was for her own protection. She didn't want to see you because she had confessed to me that she wasn't sure that you were Gopala's father. She had apparently been with several other men.'

'She told me he was my son!'

'She may well have done, but that doesn't mean it was true. Let me tell you Sheila's story as I know it. She came here seeking refuge when pregnant, as you know, telling me that she had been rejected by her family and by you.'

'That's not true!' Jazz cried. 'I offered to marry her!'

'That may be so, but I am telling you what she told me. Since she had no-one to turn to, I offered her sanctuary here, against my better judgement I might add. After Gopala was born, she told me that although you might be the father, it might also have been one of a number of other young men with whom she had had sexual relations.'

'But why did she write to me telling me that I had a son? I don't understand.'

'She was sorry about that. When I questioned her about it, she confessed that she had wanted to hurt you, knowing how important a son is to a Muslim: taunting you, in effect.'

'Whatever the truth of the matter, blood tests can prove paternity one way or the other, and whether I'm Gopala's father or not, the fact is that Sheila is his mother, and she wants him back.'

'Just wait a moment, Mr. Shah, and let me fetch Gopala. He can tell you what happened, and what his wishes are.' As he was speaking, Govinda crossed the room and opened the door. 'Gopala! Are you there?'

Jazz heard a door open, and then a child's piping voice. 'Yes, Swami, I'm here. Is it time for my lesson?'

'Soon, Gopala. I want you to come and meet a very important man from London, a lawyer, who wants to speak to you.'

Jazz's eyes were locked on the door to catch sight of his son for the first time. Govinda ushered the child in, and Jazz's heart skipped a beat. *My son!* He had no doubts: the child had a Mediterranean cast to his skin, his hair was dark, and his eyes deep brown. *He's beautiful!*

'Come and sit down here,' Govinda said, indicating a chair on the opposite side of the table to Jazz. 'This is Mr. Shah, and he wants to know some things about your mother.'

The boy's face clouded instantly. 'Why?' he asked.

'He wants to know what happened when your mother left Brindavan. Do you remember that?'

'Yes. She ran away with Brother Anthony.'

'And why didn't you go with them?' Jazz asked.

'They didn't want me. Anthony didn't like me much. I heard them talking, and he said I'd be a cumbrance, or something.'

'They'd both like you to go and live with them now,' Jazz said softly. 'Would you like that?'

Gopala frowned. 'No. This is my home. I've always lived here, and I don't want to live anywhere else. They left me, and I don't like them anymore.'

Govinda stood up. 'That's all for now, Gopala. Go and play.'

Gopala's face lit up, and he skipped to the door.

'Don't forget to say goodbye to Mr. Shah.'

The child stopped and turned, smiled. 'Goodbye, Mr. Shah,' he said. 'It was nice meeting you.'

'You see, Mr. Shah,' Govinda said once the door had closed. 'He doesn't want to go.'

'I hardly think a six-year-old child is to be left to determine his own future. The court will decide where it's best for him to live - with his mother, or in this place.'

'I can guarantee that no court in the land would allow him to live with his mother, Mr. Shah. She is not fit to look after a child. Not only did she seduce Brother Anthony, one of my staunchest monks, and a young man with genuine spiritual gifts, here in this holy ashram, but afterwards I discovered that he had not been the first. She seduced a number of others too, each one believing in his shame that he was the only one until she fled with Brother Anthony. It has had a dreadful effect upon morale. One of them, Brother Hugh, never really recovered, and I had to persuade him to leave this very week. All these young men will testify as to her wanton behaviour.'

Jazz was stupefied. 'I can't believe this,' he muttered, shaking his head.

'Confront her with it, Mr. Shah, and watch her reaction closely. Then see if she wishes to persist with her application for custody.'

Jazz stood up. 'I have to go now,' he said. 'I need time and space to think.'

'Why don't you stay a little longer, and join us for lunch. Please be my guest: we eat a little better up here than downstairs.'

'No thanks, I have to get back.'

'Then I'll have some sandwiches made up for you. Sit down while I see to it.' He left the room before Jazz could protest, returning a few minutes later. 'Brother Dennis is making some cheese sandwiches. We can collect them on our way out. I'm sorry we don't have any meat here for you.'

'Cheese is fine.'

'And you will need something to drink!' Govinda said. 'I always keep several bottles of our spring water chilling in my little refrigerator. Would you like it plain, or shall I add some squash?'

'Plain's fine.' Jazz was anxious to get out. He took the proffered bottle, and placed it in his briefcase.

They collected the sandwiches on their way out, and Govinda accompanied Jazz into the car park. Several more cars had arrived, and a number of people were standing around. They gawped as they saw Govinda walk this smart young man to his car, chatting amiably.

'A rather more up-market vehicle than the one you used to drive,' the guru remarked.

Jazz nodded, unlocked the door, and got in, tossing his briefcase onto the passenger seat.

'Have a safe journey, Mr. Shah, and drive carefully. May God go with you!'

Jazz almost snarled as he heard the final words, and drove off almost as fast as the first time he had been there, watching the diminishing figure of Govinda in his rear-view mirror until he turned a bend in the lane.

CHAPTER 18

Dr. Chaudhury had taken leave of absence from the surgery. Worry about his wife's condition, coupled with his despair at not being able to trace his daughters, had rendered him quite unfit for work. He had telephoned the Swami at Brindavan for support and guidance, only to be told that personal calls could no longer be entertained, and that he should write a letter stating the nature of the problem. He had tried to write, but it had proved impossible: the act of putting down his dilemma on paper brought out his grief in full force - his hand had shaken uncontrollably, and he had been almost unable to see the writing pad for the tears in his eyes. He threw his pen down in disgust.

What is the use of asking someone else to pray for me? he castigated himself. *Am I not capable of praying myself?* And it was a fact that he prayed every night: prayed for the life of his beloved Gauri; prayed for the restoration of his daughters. But God had not answered him, and he felt that he was being justly punished for the sin of intransigent pride.

When the telephone rang that Saturday morning, he felt disinclined to answer it. It would just be another of Gauri's so-called friends pretending to express concern over his situation: "And how are you managing, Doctor-sahib, with your wife in hospital and your daughters gone?" It was as much as he could do not to curse them, and he was not as a rule a man who allowed coarse words to pass his lips.

The insistence of the telephone eventually dragged him into the hall. *It could be Narain after all.* 'Hallo?' he croaked. There was silence. 'Who is that? he demanded, before the connection was cut.

2

From the time that she had left Dr. Silberstein's surgery in Harley Street on Friday afternoon, Meera had been dreading further conversation with her mother, unsure whether she ought to tell her, or indeed anyone, what she had discovered. There was no acceptable way that one could reveal such horror, and she knew that even if her mother were inclined to accept it, her father would not, and would almost certainly accuse Meera of making malicious and slanderous accusations. By the time they arrived home, she had decided to leave it to Geeta: if she did not want their parents to know, then Meera would keep her lips sealed. Then she had walked in to find Geeta dead, and the issue had at once been pushed to the back of her mind.

Ben had found the note on the kitchen table: "Please bring Sita up as your own. She will have a better chance of a happy life in the society you have adopted." He had not shown it to her until the doctor, the police, and the undertaker had all gone, and she was sitting on the bed dry-eyed with grief cradling Sita in her arms. She had fed the child on automatic pilot in the midst of the hullabaloo, and Sita now slept peacefully, oblivious that her world had just turned upside down. Sitting beside her, Ben put an arm around Meera's shoulders, and showed her the note.

'Oh, Ben,' she sighed, resting her head against him, 'what are we going to do with a baby?'

'Well, I suppose the first thing we ought to do is get married, so she has some proper parents.'

Meera sat up and looked at him in utter amazement. Then tears began to flow. 'Ben Samuels,' she said, half-crying, half-laughing, 'I love you so much!'

'My mother, of course, will throw a fit,' Ben said mournfully.

They both laughed, and then Sita awoke and looked up them, gurgling in response, and in the midst of the darkest despair they found a mite of personal happiness.

But the tragedy did not go away, and Meera now had perhaps even more terrible news for her mother. The shock of hearing her father's voice made her freeze for an instant before she replaced the receiver. Her heart was thumping madly. *God! I wasn't prepared for that! What's the old bugger doing home at this time of day?'*

She made herself a coffee and sat down at the kitchen table to think. Her father's voice had sounded old and tired. Perhaps he was not well. She tried to persuade herself that she should call again, that he had a right to know about Geeta, but it was easier to convince herself that she should wait until she knew her mother would be home. *But why wasn't she?* she wondered.

Instead of calling her father again, she called Mahendran. 'It's me, Meera,' she said.

'What do you want?' he asked curtly.

'I need to talk to you urgently. Can I come and see you?'

'If it's about Geeta, don't bother. I won't take her back!'

'No, it's about something else.'

'Alright,' he said with evident reluctance, 'but don't bring Geeta or the kid with you, or I won't open the door.'

'Don't worry, Mahendran,' Meera replied sadly, 'I won't be bringing Geeta.'

She was surprised when he broke down. She moved to the sofa to sit beside him. 'I really loved her, you know,' he sobbed, 'I really loved her. I didn't expect to when I first met her, but I did. And then she did that to me! It's nearly killed me, I tell you. A day doesn't pass that I don't think of topping myself.'

'Oh, Mahendran!' Meera murmured, stroking his hair. 'One suicide in the family's enough!'

'Why did she do that to me?' he moaned.

Meera pulled his head round to face her. 'Listen to me!' she said fiercely. 'Geeta did nothing wrong! Do you hear me? Nothing wrong! She was raped while she was unconscious, drugged probably, and she never knew.'

Mahendran pulled away, his face a pattern of conflicting emotions: surprise, relief, mistrust, anger. 'How could you know that? You're making it up to protect her reputation!'

'No, I'm not,' Meera said quietly. 'It's a long story, and I found out almost by chance. I can't tell you how, it's confidential. Maybe one day. But you must believe that she wasn't to blame.'

He regarded her for a while, convinced by her simplicity. 'Who was it?' he asked with quiet menace. 'I tell you, I will kill the bastard!'

'I can't, Mahendran. I'm still not absolutely sure myself.'

He took her hand. 'When you know, promise me you'll tell me!'

She nodded. Then she asked him to take the terrible news to her parents. 'I can't just tell them something like this over the phone.'

Mahendran threw back his shoulders. 'I am her husband. It is my duty.'

3

Sheila fretted all Saturday evening and Sunday morning, waiting for Jazz's call, and phoned his flat several times. By Sunday evening she was really worried, and Anthony tried to calm her nerves.

'You know what a tricky devil Govinda is. He probably avoided Jazz yesterday just to make him come back, and for all we know he may have refused point blank to see him.'

'Then why hasn't Jazz called to tell us?'

'Why bother calling to say nothing's happened? He'll call us when he gets back.'

But he did not, and further calls to his flat were fruitless. On Monday morning, on her way to work, Sheila called his office. A secretary told her that he had not been in, but that according to his diary he was due in court that morning, and would probably not be back much before lunch.

Everything seemed to be quite normal on the surface, but Sheila had a nagging feeling that all was not right, and this feeling refused to go away. At work she was distracted, not able to concentrate on what she was supposed to be doing. Before the onslaught of the lunchtime crowd, Tony called her into his tiny office.

'Sheila, my darling, I love you very much, but this morning you ain't doing the job proper. You kept three customers waiting to order already, and you got two orders wrong. This ain't like you, and this I don't need. You got something on your mind maybe, but that's not my problem; you don' let it affect your work. If you wanna talk later, I'm all ears, but lunch crowd is coming soon, and you make one more mistake, I look for another waitress, okay?'

Sheila managed to pull herself together, and the midday rush was such that she had no time to think. Only when she sat down for her own lunch around two-thirty did she remember her intention to call Jazz's office. The news was not encouraging: Jazz had not attended court, or contacted the office, and Mr. Willcocks had set inquiries in motion. Sheila asked if Mr. Willcocks could call her later at home with any news.

She pushed her lunch away, afraid that she might bring it straight back up. The lurking fear at the back of her mind strengthened, and she needed to talk to Anthony. He was due to start work at three-thirty; Tony seemed to be keeping them in different shifts deliberately. It had been sweet of Tony to offer to listen to her problem, but he would not understand. They had not even told Mr. Willcocks the full story, for Anthony had never voiced his concerns about Jimmy's sudden death. *Oh God!* she thought. *We let Jazz go there without telling him about Jimmy!*

By now she was almost sick with worry. When Anthony arrived, she quickly told him what she had learned.

'Look, I'm certain there's a rational explanation. Everything'll be okay, you just see.' He gave her a quick hug and kiss, and a reassuring smile, but Sheila saw the concern in his eyes.

At five o'clock Sheila could wait no longer. From the moment that she had arrived home she had been unable to settle to anything. She had paced the room, wringing her hands and grinding her teeth, working herself into a state of nervous exhaustion. The sweet tea she made to accompany the aspirins she took for the headache that had started to pound her temples had been vomited into the sink within minutes. She looked continually at her watch, the hands of which seemed to dawdle at a snail's pace, and her stomach knotted at the slightest sound from outside. She felt like screaming.

Finally, she went to the payphone in the hall and dialled Jazz's office, only to hear a recorded message to the effect that the office had closed for the day and would be open again at nine in the morning. She felt like crying, and her hand trembled so violently that she could hardly place the receiver back in its cradle. She stood and stared at it, willing it to ring, willing it to be Willcocks, hugging herself in her misery.

The doorbell made her jump, and she almost screamed. She turned to look, and could see a shadowy figure through the frosted glass. *How long have I been standing here?* she wondered. The bell rang again, more insistently, and she realised that the sound came from her own flat. Slowly, she walked to the door and opened it, to reveal Mr. Willcocks on the step, looking very serious.

And she knew at once why he was there.

4

Dr. Chaudhury had still not informed Mahendran about his wife's heart attack. Although he knew that he ought, as a matter of duty, to tell his son-in-law, he found himself reluctant to talk to him again. He did not blame Mahendran for what had happened, for that had been understandable - unavoidable in fact: he would have done exactly the same in the boy's position. Now however, with the benefit of hindsight, and with the gravest suspicion that Geeta's expulsion from the family had at the very least contributed to his Gauri's heart attack, he wished that he at least had acted differently, if only for the sake of the blameless Sita. To speak to Mahendran would be to pour salt into the wound of his guilt; the guilt he felt because he had acted out of pride and vanity, putting aside feelings of decency and humanity. *Such behaviour would be intolerable with respect to a stranger!* he chastised himself. *What sort of human being am I to have done that to my own daughter and grand-daughter?*

Gauri was slowly recovering her strength, and he would visit her that afternoon. The previous day she had been able to converse with him quite comfortably, without over-tiring herself, but he had deduced from what she had not said that she was pining for her daughters, and he desperately wanted to make her happy.

He thought back to their wedding day, the first time he had ever met her, and he could see little enough of her behind the wedding veil. *Oh God,* he had thought, *let my parents not have married me off to an ugly girl!* And then the time had come for him to lift the veil, and his prayer had been answered: Gauri's face was round and pretty, with large dark eyes her most attractive feature, although in those days she kept them cast to the ground save when they were alone. It was not seemly for a woman to look a man in the face then, not even her husband when others were present.

She had proved a good, loyal and dutiful wife, and he had never had any regrets. Although she had rather let her figure go after Narain's birth, becoming increasingly overweight with each passing year - whereas he had maintained his spare frame without effort - they had become good companions in the middle years of their lives, and he did not know how he would live without her if she were to die. He would have done anything at all to preserve her life, but the one thing he knew would revitalise her he was unable to do.

And on that Sunday afternoon, all his suspicions and fears materialised when his wife laid a plump but feeble hand on his arm as he took his leave, and looked pleadingly into his eyes. 'Husband, please bring our daughters to see me,' she whispered.

Mahendran had been unable to contact his in-laws on the Sunday, his thoughts and feelings still too raw, but on the Monday morning he called his office, explained that his wife had died suddenly, and was excused work for as long as he needed. Then he plucked up his nerve, and drove to the Chaudhury residence. He was as surprised when Dr. Chaudhury opened the door as that gentleman was to see his son-in-law on the step.

'Mahendran!' the doctor stammered. 'What are you doing here?'

'Sir,' Mahendran began, a sob rising in his throat. 'I have bad news! Very bad news!'

It would have been difficult to say which of the two men was more devastated by the exchange of news. Dr. Chaudhury, who had already begun to age in the week following his wife's illness, felt as if karma had struck him a double hammer blow. The news of Geeta's death added considerably to the burden of guilt he already felt, and he knew that this fact was more likely to kill his wife should she learn of it than anything else. She could not be told, of course, not until she was much stronger, but would the continued absence of her daughter not in itself rob her of the will to live? And if he brought Meera and Sita to visit her, that would immediately make her question where Geeta was. He did not know what to do.

As for Mahendran, while still trying to come to terms with his feelings of responsibility for his wife's death, he now feared that he might have his mother-in-law's death on his conscience too.

And so the two men sat opposite each other in the living room, each wrapped in his own thoughts, each overshadowed by clouds of guilt and remorse, and neither knowing what to do next. The minutes ticked away relentlessly, and still they sat, each incapable of reaching out to the other and offering comfort.

5

Sheila had at last slipped into a sedated sleep, while Anthony and Mr. Willcocks sat opposite each other at the cheap vinyl-covered table, drinking their umpteenth cup of coffee. Mr. Willcocks had proved a tower of strength, with a degree of sensitivity that Anthony would not have attributed to the average solicitor. Knowing that the news he had would be extremely upsetting to Sheila, he had eschewed the easy option of a telephone call and made the trek into south London to break the sad tidings in person. As soon as Sheila had opened the door, he had perceived that she recognised his presence as the harbinger of ill news, and he had moved swiftly to place a supporting arm around her slight frame, guide her into the room, and settle her in the one armchair.

She had looked at him, her face as bleak as the mountains of the moon, her eyes asking the question, and he had nodded in grim confirmation. She had turned away from him then, burying her face in her arms, though to his surprise she did not cry. It was in fact the absence of weeping that worried him, and so he telephoned Tony's restaurant, identified himself, and demanded to speak to Anthony. He had obtained the name of their doctor, and then instructed Anthony to return home at once.

The doctor arrived promptly, carried out a thorough examination of his unresisting and listless patient, and given her a sedative. 'She's in deep shock,' he explained. 'If she's not fast asleep within the hour, call me again.'

They had moved Sheila to the bed, where she lay fully clothed beneath a light quilt staring blankly at the ceiling for fully forty-five minutes before her eyes finally closed. In the meanwhile, an extremely anxious Anthony had arrived home by taxi courtesy of Tony, and though he sat on the bed holding her hand and whispering her name, Sheila had not looked at him. Eventually he had given up and joined Mr. Willcocks at the table.

Only when Sheila's breathing took on the regular sound of a person fast asleep did Anthony relax, the tension visibly draining from his neck and shoulders. 'What happened?' he asked the solicitor.

'As far as the police can ascertain, Ijaz was on his way back to London on Saturday afternoon when he apparently lost control, swerved into the fast lane and collided with another vehicle. A heavy goods lorry then ploughed into both cars, and they burst into flames.' He paused, grimaced, and swallowed. 'The body was very badly burned, quite unrecognisable - though I hasten to add that I did not tell Sheila that particular fact.

'The police traced him through the car registration plate, and by chance the local officer sent round to the address happened to arrive at the same time as the office boy I'd sent to see if Ijaz was ill.'

'Do they have any idea why he lost control?'

'Not at present. There will be an autopsy, but in view of the state of the remains, that may not reveal very much, depending upon whether any of the vital organs are intact. I'll let you know if I discover anything.'

The solicitor rose to leave, and Anthony took his hand, shaking it fervently. 'I'm more grateful than you can ever know,' he said, glancing towards the bed. 'She means the world to me.'

Mr. Willcocks gave a tired smile. 'She's a lovely girl, who's had more to contend with in the past year than many people have in a lifetime.' He sighed. 'I wouldn't tell her about the grisly details. If she asks, just say he died instantly, which is probably the case anyway. And when things have settled down a bit, let me know what you want me to do about those proceedings; in the meantime, I'll keep everything on hold. And now I'd better get home; my wife will be wondering where on earth I've got to.'

Afterwards, Anthony moved the armchair so that he could keep watch over the sleeping figure on the bed. He turned off the lights, save for one small table lamp, and settled himself into the chair. Eventually, he too slept.

6

Mrs. Chaudhury was awake when her husband came to visit her on that Tuesday afternoon, and was disturbed to see how much he had aged: hair greyer, face more creased, and frail in appearance. *He looks so old!* she thought. *But fifty-two is not old. I must get better!* She smiled as he sat down and took her hand, pressing it gently: she accepted it as an act of intimacy, for kissing in public for couples of their generation was out of the question. In the whole of their married life they had never exchanged an intimacy in the presence of another, not even their children. His touch now meant more to her than all the kisses that other spouses exchanged at visiting times. She made a firm resolve to get better quickly before this man whom she had come to love - despite his austere and unbending pride in family name and honour, his belief in decorum and right behaviour at all times and under all circumstances, and his insistence upon standards that were difficult for the rest of them to achieve - before he wasted away for lack of care.

'I am feeling *so* much stronger,' she declared. 'I will soon be home again to look after you.'

'No, Gauri, it is I who will take care of you,' he insisted. 'You will need to take it easy for many weeks before you are anywhere near fully fit.'

She stared at him in surprise: he never as a rule spoke her name in public, for it was not polite. *He has changed somehow!* She wondered what had been the cause. 'But who will do the cooking and cleaning, husband?' she asked. 'You?'

'It is being taken care of, wife,' he replied, adopting her formal mode of address. He patted her hand. 'Now, there are visitors if you feel well enough to see them.'

'Not that old gossip Mrs. Rana Bannerjee, I hope!' she exclaimed. 'I cannot bear the thought of her crowing over me in this condition with her false expressions of concern!'

'It is not her. It is our daughter Meera.'

'Meera!' she cried. 'Our daughter, Meera?' She had not missed his deliberate choice of words, words that spoke volumes to her - of forgiveness, of reconciliation, of healing.

Her husband nodded, grinning broadly.

'Then bring her in at once, you old fool!' she scolded. 'As if I'm not well enough to see my own daughter, the idea!'

'I truly believe that you are indeed getting better, wife,' her husband replied on his way out.

Mahendran had called Meera to tell her that he was going to the Chaudhury home with the news, and she had decided to phone so that she and her mother could sob together. The call interrupted the long silence between the two men, and Mahendran had answered in case it was some busybody friend of his mother-in-law's. He returned from the hall after a minute or two. 'It's Meera,' he announced. 'She wants to talk to you. I haven't told her about her mother.'

Dr. Chaudhury went rapidly into the hall and picked up the receiver. 'Meera, my daughter, please come, your mother is very ill.' He gave her the details, and she promised to come at once.

She was there within the hour. Mahendran answered the door, indicated the living room, and disappeared into the kitchen. Meera stood in the doorway, and regarded her father: always so strong and decided, he had looked lost and helpless. He returned her gaze, the anxiety in his eyes unmistakeable, and she had realised with shock that he was half-expecting a verbal tirade. In that moment she understood him better than she had ever done: a conservative man from a foreign culture, afraid of the rapidly changing alien society in which he found himself. And also, perhaps because she represented best of all the threat of that society to his values and beliefs, afraid of her.

She had gone to his chair, knelt beside it, and thrown her arms around his neck. 'Oh, Appa, how I've missed you!' He responded, hugging her to him, an act of intimacy he had discouraged since the onset of puberty, and in the warmth of that embrace, without the necessity for words, they had asked for and given each other absolution.

When tears had been dried, and voices were able to speak again, throats having been oiled with tea made by Mahendran, they had held a council of war. Since they could do nothing about the dead, their task had to be to preserve the living: the news of Geeta's death would be suppressed as long as possible, until it was thought Mrs. Chaudhury well enough to withstand the shock without risk of a further attack. They would have to play their parts with fortitude, but their new-found family unity would give them strength. They decided that Meera should visit her mother the next day.

And so Meera approached Mrs. Chaudhury's bed, her arm within her father's to demonstrate with all possible clarity that fences had been mended. Meera bent over to embrace her mother, and their tears mingled on the pillow. 'I brought Sita with me,' she announced. 'She is outside with Uncle Narain!'

'But where is Geeta?' her mother asked anxiously.

'She is not well, Amma,' Meera exclaimed calmly. 'She has been staying with me, but Mahendran is with her now.'

'Mahendran is with her!' Mrs Chaudhury was both astonished and delighted.

'Yes, Amma. He has forgiven her, and she is now back home.'

All this was literally true. Geeta's body had been taken to the marital home, where it lay in its coffin prior to the cremation that had been arranged for the Friday, and Mahendran was maintaining a vigil by her side.

'Now,' Meera said brightly, 'would you like to see your grand-daughter?

CHAPTER 19

There were seven people present at Jazz's funeral service: Sheila and Anthony, Mr. Willcocks and his secretary, two of Jazz's old college friends, and his sister, Nasreen, who had been contacted by Mr. Willcocks and collected by him only that morning at Heathrow. Although cremation was not part of Muslim custom, it had been decided that in the circumstances it would be more appropriate. The conflagration on the motorway had been so fierce that there was little left to bury, and nothing to establish a cause of death. The police had concluded that he must have fallen asleep.

It had also been agreed that in view of Jazz's virulent atheism, a purely religious ceremony would be inappropriate. Mr. Willcocks himself presided over the brief ceremony, which consisted mainly of tributes from those present, and a reading from the Koran (in English) as a gesture to the deceased's sister.

Outside, Mr. Willcocks introduced Nasreen to Sheila. 'You are the mother of my brother's son?' Nasreen asked in perfect, though slightly accented English.

'Yes.'

'I would have liked to see him, but Mr. Willcocks explained that he is away at the boarding school. When I come again to England, perhaps I may see him then, yes?'

Darting a quick glance at the solicitor, Sheila nodded. 'I hope so.'

Anthony shook hands with the dignified, almost regal Iranian girl, and followed Sheila out into the sunlight. They looked at the small array of wreaths and flowers, then stood around aimlessly, wondering whether to wait for Mr. Willcocks or go, and as they hesitated, the hearse for the next funeral drove into the grounds, followed by one mourners' car.

'Looks like another big funeral!' remarked Anthony.

The limousine contained only five people: Dr. Chaudhury, Meera and Narain, Mahendran, and the Hindu priest who was to conduct the ritual. Meera had left Sita with a child-minder. At the entrance to the crematorium building, the priest and Meera got out first, leaving Mahendran and Narain to help Dr. Chaudhury, who was almost in a state of collapse.

The undertakers had removed the coffin from the hearse and placed it on a trolley. The priest sprinkled holy ash and water on the coffin, chanting in solemn, nasal tones. Meera watched him for a minute, then noticed two people standing to her right, presumably mourners from the previous funeral. They looked familiar. *Where have I seen them before?* she wondered.

As the undertakers began to push the trolley towards the crematorium doors, Meera met the eyes of the woman, and they half-acknowledged each other with a little start of surprise, as people sometimes do when not sure whether they know each other or not. The exchange lasted no more than a few seconds, and then Meera had followed the coffin and her family through the doors.

'I'm sure I know that woman!' Sheila exclaimed.

'She did look vaguely familiar,' agreed Anthony, 'but we used to see so many Indian women at Brindavan that I couldn't swear I could tell them apart.'

'You men are so useless at this sort of thing!' Sheila snorted. 'Anyway, not too many of them used to wear Western clothes. But you may be right; perhaps I did see her at the ashram. I think she recognised me too.'

'Or maybe she came into the restaurant for a coffee.'

Sheila shrugged. 'Maybe.'

Mr. Willcocks emerged from the building with Jazz's sister. 'I'm taking Miss Shah to her hotel. Maybe you two could join us for lunch.'

Knowing full well that the solicitor would insist on paying the bill, they agreed.

2

Dr. Chaudhury had agonised over telling his wife about Geeta's death. There was first and foremost her health to consider, and the effect the shock would have, but in his heart he felt that it would be wrong not to tell her before the funeral. 'How much greater might the shock be,' he said to his family, 'if she learns not only that Geeta is dead but has also been disposed of without her being told?' They had agreed.

He had thought first to ask Meera to break the news, for she was a strong, sensible girl, but finally he had decided that it was his duty, and one he could not shirk. It might have been true, as his wife had noted, that he was beginning to unbend a little in the wake of the family's misfortunes, but his sense of duty remained strong.

The rest of the family had accompanied him for moral support, although he had stipulated that he should go in alone to tell his wife of the latest disaster. He took a few steps away from the group, then turned and came back. 'Meera, my daughter,' he said, 'I want you to know that this is as difficult for me to do as it was to tell you to leave our home. Whatever you may think of me, that was not an easy thing to do. I know now that I was wrong, but even then I felt as if I were cutting off my right arm!'

Meera squeezed her father's arm. 'Don't worry, Appa. Your right arm is back where it belongs!'

'That is true, but now I have to tell your mother that *her* right arm has been cut off, for ever!' He kissed his daughter on the cheek. 'Don't look so concerned! I may be a thin and dry old stick, but I'm still up to the job.' And he turned away once more and went into the ward.

Mrs. Chaudhury was sitting by her bed in an armchair, and she gave him such a beaming smile that Dr. Chaudhury almost reneged on his decision then and there. He took a chair and sat down beside her, not quite sure how to begin.

'There is a sadness in your eyes, husband,' his wife said. 'It was there yesterday, and it has not gone away. Meera too was sad.'

'Naturally,' he replied. 'I have been very concerned about you.'

'No, it is not that. Your are not anxious, but sad, very sad.'

'Oh, Gauri,' he said, trying to control his voice, 'I have bad news.'

'Is it about Geeta?'

He stared at her, his mouth open. 'How did you know?' he asked at last, his voice hoarse with suppressed emotion.

'I was worried about her, especially when you said she was not well, and I could not get her out of my mind.' She sniffed, and blew her nose. 'Last night she came to me in a dream. I was in the garden, cutting some flowers for the pooja, and she appeared in the garden, looking very happy. I asked her what she was doing there. "I have come to say goodbye, Amma," she said. "I am free now." And then she flew away, like a big, beautiful bird.' She dabbed at her cheeks, where the tears were running fast now. 'I knew than that she was no more, and I knew then why the sadness was in your eyes. It is true, is it not? Our Geeta is dead.'

'It is true, Gauri.' He wiped away his own tears, then took her hand. 'God moves in mysterious ways. He knew that this task was almost too much for me, and so He took on the burden of telling you Himself.'

'I knew it was true, and I have wept much for her this morning. It will be a grief to me until my last breath that we parted on bad terms, and that I never saw her again.'

'And to me!' cried Chaudhury. 'And to me! My stupid pride was to blame. Can you ever forgive me?'

'The good Lord balances things out,' his wife replied gravely. 'He has taken one daughter, but in so doing has restored the other. We must accept His judgment, taking both what is hard to bear and what is good. What profit is there for us to cast blame at each other and sour our remaining years together?' She looked at him tenderly. 'You are my life, husband, and have been ever since we walked around the wedding fire together.'

'I do not deserve you.'

Meera told her father about Geeta's note when they returned from the crematorium, and of her decision to accept the duty her sister had laid upon her. 'Mahendran is agreeable, for Sita is not his child, but she is of our blood.'

'In all the worry about your mother, I am ashamed to say that I had given little thought to Sita,' he confessed, 'but you realise that your mother, when fit again, will insist on bringing up the child herself.'

'You two are the grand-parents. It is not your responsibility to bring her up, just to spoil her when she visits.'

'But, Meera, how can you bring up the child on your own? You have a job, after all.'

'That's what I wanted to speak to you about. I'm afraid you are in for another shock.' When she had told him about her relationship with Ben and his proposal, she sat back and awaited his reaction, her muscles tense with apprehension.

Dr. Chaudhury sighed deeply. 'You have always been a rebel, and when you were a child, it was a quality in you that I prized. I used to call you my "little Bengali tigress".'

'I remember.'

'And then when you grew up, that very quality I had so admired became irksome to me because you would not follow blindly our customs and traditions. What a fuss you made when your mother decided it was time for you to wear your first traditional dress.'

'I was such a brat!'

'I will tell you why I was so upset at your nonconformity. When you were born we were still living in India, and I went to a very famous astrologer in Calcutta, a man who had calculated the horoscopes of kings and princes, and important men from all walks of life, even from the West. I was very upset when he told me what was in your character and your future: "She will be a headstrong and unruly girl," he said, "and she will marry a foreigner and bring up the bastard child of another man." Well! Can you imagine how angry I was? When I was younger, I had a very fiery temper; you have only seen the moderated version of what I was then!

'I told that famous man where to get off, believe me. "You talk rubbish!" I said. "No daughter of mine will have a bastard child or marry a foreigner! You are a fraud and a charlatan, preying upon the weak and helpless!" I tore up his calculations before his eyes and flung the pieces in his face - I feel shame even now at my behaviour.

'And do you know what, Meera? He didn't even flinch. He sat there on the floor - he was a very simple man despite his great fame - and he said, "I have seen what I have seen, and all the anger in the world will not change it."

'So now you know why I used to become so angry with you - because I was afraid. All my married life I have been afraid of the possible shame and dishonour that you might bring upon the family name. And now, after all these years, that simple man has been proved right: you will marry a foreigner and bring up …. well, let us not cast names upon a poor, defenceless child. However, you will bring up the child of another man, even though she is not yours. Had the astrologer been able to tell me that, I might have felt a little less apprehensive.'

'And what about Geeta? Did you have her horoscope cast?'

'No. We were in England by then, and I had rejected astrology.' He sighed. 'And thank God for that! Had I known what lay in store for my poor girl, I would probably have been driven to an early grave!'

'Maybe it's a good thing not to know what the future holds.'

'I think you are right, although there is no harm in speculating about what the future may hold for you and Ben. He is Jewish, you say? The Jews are also a very traditional people, like us in many ways.'

'That's what Ben's afraid of!' Meera laughed. 'He hasn't told his mother yet!'

Chaudhury laughed too. 'At last!' he chortled. 'The boot is on the other foot!'

3

The week after the funeral Sheila and Anthony told Mr. Willcocks of their decision not to pursue legal proceedings.

'I can understand how you feel,' he said, 'but I think you're wrong to let this man get away with it. What sort of life is that child going to have?'

'You can't possibly understand how I feel, Mr. Willcocks,' Sheila said, fighting back her tears.

'We never told you about our worst suspicions,' Anthony said. He recounted the story of Jimmy's departure from Brindavan, and his sudden death after a visit from Govinda. 'Jazz's "accident" has reinforced our fears,' he concluded.

Mr. Willcocks looked unconvinced. 'This is very difficult to believe. Surely Mr. Partington's death was properly investigated?'

'The police did come and speak to Govinda, but nothing happened as a result.'

'Then they must have been satisfied that the fall was an accident.'

'A very timely one,' Anthony commented.

'That may be so, but you can't go bandying accusations of such a nature without evidence.'

'That's why we've said nothing before,' Sheila replied, 'but we wish now that we'd told Jazz, so that he could have been on his guard.'

Mr. Willcocks shook his head, frowning. 'I don't know what to make of all this. A second fortuitous accident ....'

'Just after seeing Govinda!' Anthony interjected.

'Precisely so. It does look somewhat out of the ordinary, but ..... but there's no evidence,' he concluded weakly.

'He's a very clever man,' Anthony said, 'and we suspect he's very dangerous too, which is why we don't want to take any more chances, especially now.'

'Now?'

'I'm pregnant! And we're going to get married.'

'Well, well, well! I'm very pleased to hear it. I hope you'll be very happy, and I'm sure you will be!' He jumped up as he spoke, came around his enormous desk, kissed Sheila on both cheeks, and shook Anthony's hand enthusiastically. Then he reined himself in, looking faintly embarrassed, and retreated back behind his desk.

'There is one other thing,' Anthony said.

Willcocks resumed his business manner. 'And what's that?'

'We'd like you to come to the wedding.'

'And to be the baby's godfather,' added Sheila.

'I would be delighted to accept on both counts. Just let me know the date - *both* dates!'

After he had seen them out, Mr. Willcocks returned to his desk and perused the notes he had made semi-automatically as Anthony had spoken. He shook his head. *How on earth did I become involved in all this?* he mused. Then he made a mental note to initiate some discreet inquiries.

4

Dora Samuels almost had a seizure when she opened the door to her son and his fiancee and saw the dark-skinned baby nestling in the girl's arms, for Ben had omitted to mention Sita's existence when extolling the merits of his chosen bride to his parents. She looked at the baby with barely concealed incredulity: *That child is never my son's!* was her primary thought.

Nevertheless, with commendable poise she invited them in, and for many years afterwards, when regaling her friends with her account of that first meeting with Meera, she congratulated herself for not having thrown a fit then and there on the doorstep.

The pall of aloofness which Sita's presence had cast over the proceedings was dispelled as soon as Meera, noticing her future in-laws' bemused expressions, explained the situation. She gave Ben a resigned look. 'You didn't tell your parents about Sita.'

'I forgot.' he said lamely.

'Oh, my dear, how terribly tragic!' Dora cried. 'And how noble of you both to take on such a responsibility, though I have to say that is just so typical of Benjamin.' She went to Meera and held out her arms for the baby, who went to her without a murmur. 'What a darling!' she cooed. 'You will tell her when she's older that you aren't her real parents?' she asked, just a little anxiously.

'Of course,' Meera assured her. 'When she's old enough, we'll tell her my sister was her real mother.'

'We'll probably tell her that her mummy went to heaven, and then try to explain it properly when she's old enough to understand,' Ben added.

'I assume that you plan to adopt her, to make everything legal,' Ben's father said. Mordecai Samuels was a leading Q.C., who still harboured a faint regret that his only son had not followed in his footsteps but had chosen the world of advertising, an indication he thought of the turn for the worse life had taken, when advertisers and newspaper hacks played such an influential role in people's lives. His distaste did not, however, prevent him from accepting briefs on behalf of newspapers in libel cases.

'Don't worry, Dad. The legal ball's already been set in motion.'

'Glad to hear it,' his father replied drily.

'That's one reason we want to get married quickly,' Ben explained, 'so that we're legal for the adoption proceedings.'

'That's my son for you!' exclaimed Dora. 'He keeps us waiting for ten years, then insists on getting married in ten minutes!'

'Momma, you're dramatising as usual.'

'Well, I hope you're not planning to have some hole-in-the-corner wedding in one of those ghastly registry places!' Dora retorted.

'Don't worry. I convinced Meera that if you weren't allowed to have your own way, and allowed to organise a grand wedding spectacle, you'd never speak to us again.'

'And she agreed? My dear, you're an angel! Come and help me in the kitchen, and we can start making plans right away.

295

We'll leave the men to talk about whatever men do talk about when deprived of a civilising influence!' She marched out of the room, still carrying her future adoptive grand-daughter.

'Now you'll have to move out of that poky flat you insisted on buying,' Mordecai remarked once the ladies had gone.

'We'll start looking for a little semi somewhere in the suburbs. Meera's already given up her job, so we'll only have my salary to live on - though, I have to assure you, I'm earning well enough to support a family.'

'Not as well as if you'd followed me into the Law,' his father growled.

'That's as may be, Dad, but I preferred to make my own way rather than make a living by clutching onto your coat tails.'

'Maybe so. But enough of this nonsense about a semi in the suburbs! I'll buy you a decent place around here as a wedding present.'

'Dad, we couldn't possibly accept!'

'You don't accept, and I don't come to the wedding! How do you think your mother will like that, eh?'

'Dad, you're impossible! How can we ever repay you?'

'It's a gift. You don't have to repay it. You're the son of a lawyer, and you don't know that much!'

5

After leaving Brindavan Anthony and Sheila had contacted their respective families, and had paid occasional visits, but not together. Only now, with the pregnancy confirmed and the decision to marry made, had it become necessary to bring everyone together. Anthony's fear that his mother and sister might not like Sheila proved completely unfounded, and Sheila got on better with them than with her own parents. Indeed, her relationship with her father had hardly improved at all.

He had been especially proud of his only child when she, a mere shopkeeper's daughter, gained a place to read Law, and had been correspondingly disappointed when she became pregnant, dropped out of university, and went to live in a religious cult, as he saw it. The depth of his bitterness had hardly been lifted by more recent events: while glad that she had left the cult, her attachment to another drop-out with no apparent prospects and the fact that she was pregnant again, was an improvement he regarded as marginal at best. She had wasted her talents and thrown away the best years of her life; all his hopes for her had been dashed.

Her mother was genuinely glad to have recovered her daughter from the weird cult that had ensnared her, but she found it impossible to understand how any mother could abandon her child. Sheila had tried to explain, but the whole thing had been beyond her mother's powers of comprehension: she had never, in her limited suburban existence, met anyone as compelling, as devious, and as manipulative as Govinda, and was never likely to. *And thank God for that!* Sheila had thought.

Anthony and Sheila had decided not to mention the existence of Gopala to his parents, and hers were quite willing to go along with the concealment of a bastard grand-son they had never met and never would. All that needed to be said was that they had met at Brindavan, fallen in love, and decided to leave: it was the truth, if not the whole truth.

Mr. Makin's hostile reaction to Anthony joining the ashram had been matched with equal delight at the news he had left. A firm believer in "getting things out of the system", he believed that his son had put all the Hindu mumbo-jumbo behind him and would now sort himself out: get some qualifications, followed by a decent job. He had been dismayed, however, to hear that Anthony had saddled himself with a potential family: that ought to have come later, much later.

Anthony's mother, on the other hand, was happy for him, and took the view that the obligations of a wife and child would settle him down as a matter of necessity more quickly than anything else. Best of all, the commitment would ensure that he never returned to "that place", as she called it. She had been made privy to Govinda's duplicity with Anna's letters, and her views about "that man" - for she would not utter Govinda's name - were "quite unprintable". Suffice it to say that she classed him with all those other religious cults that sought to divide families, a practice she regarded as abhorrent.

As for Sheila, 'I think she's a very nice girl, dear,' she told Anthony. Had she known about the past she would have been horrified, and have regarded Sheila as a most unsuitable bride for her son. But she did not, and accordingly judged her on the qualities she was able to see for herself, and was content with her son's choice of partner. She would have preferred the pregnancy to have come after the wedding rather than the other way around, for people were bound to do the maths, but she was wise enough in the ways of the world to accept that Anthony was at least equally to blame.

Only Anna knew from the start that the pregnancy was not an accident, and in due course she confided this to her mother. 'Oh dear,' Mrs. Makin sighed. 'Why do young people these days always seem to put carts before horses? Don't tell your father, dear; he'd prefer to think it was just a slip-up.'

And so it was that both sets of parents accepted the match while not being overly enthusiastic about it, and were content that it should be solemnised at a registry office. Sheila's mother was a little upset that her daughter would not have a white wedding. but she did think that a church wedding would have been a little hypocritical, taking everything, both past and present, into account. Mrs. Makin did not mind at all: she had her own daughter's wedding to look forward to in due course.

The wedding party was kept deliberately small, and the reception was naturally held in Tony's restaurant, the catering (including champagne) provided free as his wedding gift to the happy couple. And if it was not the grandest wedding in the metropolis that July Saturday, and if the respective sets of parents came away thinking that they would have as little to do with their new in-laws as common decency would permit, at least Anthony and Sheila were happy, and that was really all that mattered.

6

'Mazeltov!' yelled the guests, to the sound of breaking glass, at a very different wedding a week later. A civil ceremony had been performed on the Friday afternoon, and now on the ensuing Sunday a traditional Jewish wedding had taken place in the garden of the Samuels residence. There was a marquee for the reception, with seating for over five hundred, almost all on the groom's side, with an adjoining circular tent for dancing, complete with wooden dance floor, where a sixteen-piece orchestra was to play, hired at a special rate because its owner and conductor was related to Dora Samuels. The driveway and front lawns (upon which special matting had been laid), and the road outside, were all filled with prestige cars nose to tail, including several Rolls Royces and Bentleys, and innumerable Jaguars and Mercedes; BMWs were two-a-penny.

Dr. and Mrs. Chaudhury, who had been extremely impressed on their first visit to the house a week before, were almost overwhelmed by the magnificence of the occasion. Leading figures from the legal world, including two Lords of Appeal in Ordinary, mingled with Harley Street specialists (including, to Meera's dismay and embarrassment, Joshua Silberstein), rubbed shoulders with television producers and film directors, discussed books with well known authors, and condescended to exchange pleasantries with important men of business, including a few baronets and life peers.

Mrs. Chaudhury surveyed the glittering scene with an air of not inconsiderable satisfaction. 'Our Meera has done well for herself, husband,' she murmured. Her close brush with death had made her more aware of the importance of those things which made those she loved happy, and more tolerant of matters which she would once have regarded as upsetting. She had accepted Meera's match with even more equilibrium than her husband, although his own acceptance without demur no doubt made it easier.

'A good, traditional Jewish husband is likely to be a better husband and more faithful partner than some of our own young men with their tendency to adopt Western habits,' he had said to her. She had raised an eyebrow, but wisely said nothing.

'I never dreamed of the sort of circles in which she would move, I must confess,' he said now. 'And how absolutely beautiful she looks!'

In contradiction to previous behaviour, and to the surprise of her parents, Meera had decided to wear traditional Indian wedding attire, and did indeed look stunning in the deep red and gold sari she had selected, after much searching, with the joyous assistance of her mother. Her hair too she wore in a traditional bun, with flowers and jewels set in it, with the pleasing effect of drawing attention to her elegant neck and fine facial bones. With a gold choker around her throat, contrasting wonderfully with her dark skin, she was every inch the Indian bride.

At the conclusion of the wedding feast, a sumptuous repast by any standard, and after the traditionally amusing speech by the best man, Mordecai Samuels rose to speak. 'I do not intend to detain you long, my friends, and I say to those members of the judiciary here this afternoon who may groan upon hearing those words, this time I mean it!'

There was a round of applause, heaviest from those tables at which members of the legal profession were clustered, together with a few cheers.

'Today we celebrate the marriage of my only child, Benjamin, and his beautiful bride, Meera. Children are important, my friends. They are the life-blood of our nation. It has always been a matter of regret to my wonderful wife, Dora, and myself that God never blessed us with more than one, but that fact, of course, makes our son even more precious to us, and this solemn but happy day more important than ever, for we shall celebrate the weddings of no other children.'

As he paused to take a sip of water, the silence was absolute: no restlessness, no shifting in seats, no clearing of throats, nothing. Everyone hung upon his words.

'On a day such as today, I have to be honest about my feelings. When Benjamin informed us of his intention to marry outside race and religion, Dora and I, like all Jews who face this issue I dare say, lamented. What had we done wrong? we wondered. We had brought up our son, to the best of our ability, to be a member of the Jewish community, to be aware of his roots and his history, and here he was telling us that he intended to marry a girl from a different religion and race. Not even a mere Christian, but a Hindu no less! Someone from a religion of which we knew nothing - less than nothing.

'Well, my friends, I have to tell you this, for I have after all promised to be honest. My son's chosen bride is not only, as all can see for themselves, a most beautiful young woman, but she is possessed of the highest human qualities that any parent could wish for in a daughter-in-law. I will not embarrass her by listing them now, for I promised not to detain you long. Let me just say that I wish the young couple health and happiness, long and fruitful lives, and many children! I ask you all to stand and raise your glasses: to Benjamin and Meera!'

'Benjamin and Meera!' resounded around the marquee.

'I must also say this,' Mordecai resumed, as everyone sat down again, to loud groans from the legal profession. 'I had never met an Indian family before. Dr. and Mrs. Chaudhury were people I would have passed in the street without a second glance, noticing them perhaps as just another family of immigrants. We have so much more in common than we realise. So many of our finest Jewish families today were immigrants to this country once upon a time, whether in the nineteenth century or more recently. Also, our Asian friends have fine and time-honoured traditions which are no less meritorious for being different from our own. My new relatives are people I am proud to know. We have much to learn from each other.'

Prolonged applause followed.

'Finally - and this time, my lords, it is - contrary to all tradition, and at the risk of estranging my son permanently, I claim the first dance with my enchanting daughter-in-law!'

Two hours later, Meera stood at a bedroom window looking down upon the continuing festivities in the garden. She now wore sensible travelling clothes, her wedding sari having been carefully folded and wrapped in tissue paper by her mother. She had said goodbye to her parents and brother shortly before: her mother was over-tired and over-excited, and Dr. Chaudhury had decreed an early departure.

Meera held the sleeping Sita close to her heart. She had insisted on taking the baby, despite the offers from both her mother and Dora to look after her while they were away, and Ben had supported her.

'We're starting out with a ready-made family,' he had declared, 'so let's not break it up right at the outset.'

Sita stirred, whimpering in her sleep, and Meera rocked her gently in her arms. The baby would be a constant reminder of a dark and sorrowful secret that would always cast its shadow over her life. 'Until your mother is avenged, my darling,' she whispered. 'However long it takes!'

An extract from

THE BRINDAVAN CHRONICLE

2. NEMISIS

In one corner, waiting for the mass of humanity to disperse, sat two Asian women who were clearly mother and daughter. The older had a fashionably short hairstyle, and wore a dark blue patterned sari with a gold border. She was slightly above average height for an Indian lady, of medium dark complexion, with a neat and tidy figure, and could have passed for thirty-five, though in fact nearly ten years older.

The daughter appeared more traditional, her long hair tied in a plait that reached all the way down her back. Her face was the blue-black hue of the rain cloud; her large brown eyes reflected the myriad lights of the temple; her cheeks were soft and downy, and her lips full and promising. The clinging folds of her pale yellow sari concealed, yet at the same time provocatively hinted at, the round contours of a fully grown woman, although the simple innocence of her wondering expression made her seem younger than her eighteen years.

One of the ushers approached and informed them somewhat condescendingly that it was time to leave, that the temple would soon be locked. The mother flashed him a look of disdain.

'Young man,' Meera Samuels said in perfect, accent-less English, while casting a haughty glance at the heaving mass in the temple porch as people pushed and shoved each other in their efforts to find shoes, coats, handbags and small children, 'if you think I'm going to crush this expensive sari in that madhouse, you are mistaken. My daughter and I will get up and leave when it is possible to do so without risking life or limb.'

Meera had told him about Geeta a few weeks later. When she had finished, he had sat in stunned silence, his mouth slightly open, his lower lip trembling. She had expected denials and remonstrations, but he had clearly believed every word. 'Are you alright, Appa?'

'No,' he said weakly, 'I am not alright. I have always known that evil is manifest in the world, but that it should destroy my own family! And in such a manner! What had we done to deserve that? Was my karma so bad?'

'I'm sorry, Appa, but I thought you ought to know. I couldn't say anything while Amma was still alive; it would have killed her.'

'Perhaps it would have been better for her to die sooner than for us to have lived a lie for so long!' he replied bitterly.

'There's one more thing you should know.' She paused, and her father looked up enquiringly. 'I vowed to avenge Geeta, and I intend to keep that vow.'

Fear had sprung into the old man's eyes. 'Your face is as hard as rock,' he whispered, 'and your eyes are as cold as the snows of Mount Kailash!'